Rachael Johns

Just One Wish

FICTION
HQ

First Published 2019
Second Australian Paperback Edition 2020
ISBN 9781867207955

JUST ONE WISH
© 2019 by Rachael Johns
Australian Copyright 2019
New Zealand Copyright 2019

Published by
HQ Fiction
An imprint of Harlequin Enterprises (Australia) Pty Limited (ABN 47 001 180 918), a subsidiary of HarperCollins Publishers Australia Pty Limited (ABN 36 009 913 517)
Level 13, 201 Elizabeth St
SYDNEY NSW 2000
AUSTRALIA

® and TM (apart from those relating to FSC®) are trademarks of Harlequin Enterprises (Australia) Pty Limited or its corporate affiliates. Trademarks indicated with ® are registered in Australia, New Zealand and in other countries.

A catalogue record for this book is available from the National Library of Australia
www.librariesaustralia.nla.gov.au

Printed and bound in Australia by McPherson's Printing Group

Praise for Rachael Johns

'If you like your chick-lit with a dash of intelligent social commentary, *Just One Wish* is the perfect summer read. Rachael Johns's latest novel is sparklingly funny, quirky and totally of this moment.'

—*Herald Sun*

'Johns knows how to weave the experiences of different generations of women together, with nuance and sensitivity, understanding how competing contexts shape women's choices ... Johns has a unmistakable talent for storytelling, while throwing a compelling romance in to hook us even further. Exploring themes like motherhood, the roles of women, and lost love, *Just One Wish* will make you look at the women in your own life and wonder what stories they haven't told.'

—*Mamamia*

'Johns draws readers in with her richly complex characters.'

—*The Daily Telegraph*

'Polished writing, and great dialogue drive this story forward. The perfectly structured plot holds plenty of surprises, but it's the beautifully crafted characters that are the glue in this wonderful novel. I adored all three women, but especially Alice. There are also a whole cast of colourful, glorious minor characters, and an unusual family structure that is a delight to read ... Utterly delightful ... and predictably great.'

—Better Reading

'*Just One Wish* is a passionate and powerful family saga. It is a book that is going to have its readers talking about it... Whether you are a fan of Rachael's or a debut reader of hers then you are going to enjoy this book.'

—Book in One Hand Coffee in the Other

'Rachael Johns once again provides her readers with a fabulous contemporary family drama through the life experiences and choices of three generations of women. ... *Just One Wish* is most certainly a realistic portrayal of the complexity of modern day families that is sure to resonate with many readers.'

—Great Reads and Tea Leaves

'*Just One Wish* is a fabulous novel of family love, sorrow, secrets, betrayal and heartbreak.'

—Beauty and Lace

'The themes of infertility and pregnancy loss are movingly interwoven into a multifaceted story ... [Rachael Johns] writes wisely and naively, hopefully and cynically, and there's a character for everyone to identify with in *Lost Without You*. A gorgeously moving read.'

—Mamamia

'Heart-warming and compassionate ... Any book lover interested in life's emotional complexities and in the events that define and alter us, will be engrossed in *Lost Without You.*'

—Better Reading

'A delightful glimpse into the life of families and friends who come together in the most unexpected ways.'

—Starts at 60 on *Lost Without You*

'Full of heartache and joy with a twist that keeps the pages turning ... *The Greatest Gift* will appeal to fans of Jojo Moyes and Monica McInerney.'

—Australian Books + Publishing

'I really have no idea where to start because this book was an amazing gift ... Once again Johns has written a story that will appeal to different types of readers and it is clear that her talent is becoming more finely honed with every release.'

—Beauty and Lace on *The Greatest Gift*

'Heartbreaking and heartwarming in equal parts, Rachael Johns' *The Greatest Gift* takes readers on a rollercoaster ride of emotions. My advice? Make sure you have tissues handy!'

—Lisa Ireland, author of *The Shape Of Us*

'Rachael Johns has done it again, writing a book that you want to devour in one sitting, and then turn back to the first page to savour it all over again. I loved the characters of Harper and Jasper; their stories made me laugh and cry, and ache and cheer and ultimately reflect on all the many facets of that extraordinary journey called motherhood.'

—Natasha Lester, author of *A Kiss From Mr Fitzgerald,* on *The Greatest Gift*

'A beautiful story of love and loss, heartbreak and hope—this is Rachael Johns at her very finest. With achingly endearing characters and a storyline that packs a punch, *The Greatest Gift* will make your heart swell as you reach for the tissues and leave you smiling when you turn the final pages. Told with warmth, empathy and wisdom, it's a book that will appeal to everyone who has laid plans for their life and discovered that life is something that can't be controlled and that even if you think you have it all worked out, you never know what's around the corner. My favourite Rachael Johns by a country mile.'

—Tess Woods, author of *Love At First Flight*

'The bond between Flick, Neve, and Emma blossomed as their sons grew up, but even best friends keep secrets from one another ... Fans of emotional, issue driven women's fiction will welcome Johns' US women's fiction debut.'

—*Booklist* on *The Art of Keeping Secrets*

'... a compelling and poignant story of dark secrets and turbulent relationships ... I fell completely in love with the well-drawn characters of Flick, Emma and Neve. They were funny and flawed and filled with the kind of raw vulnerability that makes your heart ache for them.'

—Nicola Moriarty, bestselling author of
The Fifth Letter, on *The Art of Keeping Secrets*

'Written with compassion and real insight, *The Art Of Keeping Secrets* peeks inside the lives of three ordinary women and the surprising secrets they live with. Utterly absorbing and wonderfully written, Johns explores what secrets can do to a relationship, and pulls apart the notion that some secrets are best kept. It is that gripping novel that, once started, will not allow you to do anything else until the final secret has been revealed.'

—Sally Hepworth, bestselling author of
The Secrets Of Midwives

'A fascinating and deeply moving tale of friendship, family and of course—secrets. These characters will latch onto your heart and refuse to let it go.'

—*USA Today* bestselling author Kelly Rimmer on
The Art of Keeping Secrets

'Rachael Johns writes with warmth and heart, her easy, fluent style revealing an emotional intelligence and firm embrace of the things in life that matter, like female friendship.'

—*The Age* on *Lost Without You*

Rachael Johns, an English teacher by trade and a mum 24/7, is the bestselling, ABIA-winning author of *The Patterson Girls* and a number of other romance and women's fiction books including *The Art of Keeping Secrets*, *The Greatest Gift* and *Lost Without You*. She is currently Australia's leading writer of contemporary relationship stories around women's issues, a genre she has coined 'life-lit'. Rachael lives in the Perth hills with her hyperactive husband, three mostly gorgeous heroes-in-training and a very badly behaved dog. She rarely sleeps and never irons.

Also by Rachael Johns

The Patterson Girls
The Art of Keeping Secrets
The Greatest Gift
Lost Without You

The Rose Hill novels
Talk of The Town
Something to Talk About

The Hope Junction novels
Jilted
The Road to Hope

The Bunyip Bay novels
Outback Dreams
Outback Blaze
Outback Ghost
Outback Sisters

Man Drought

The Kissing Season (e-novella)
The Next Season (e-novella)

Secret Confessions Down and Dusty: Casey (e-novella)

This book is dedicated to author and friend Beck Nicholas, who holds my hand through the writing of every book and is always available to talk me through a plot problem; to my mum, Barbara Denton, who is both a practical support and an emotional one and who believes in me more than anyone; and finally to my publisher, Sue Brockhoff, who is always championing me and my career, but most of all, pushing me to write the best book I can.

Prologue

1964

'Alice Louise Abbott, you are the girl of my dreams, the love of my life, you light up my heart like the sun lights the sky. Please, will you do me the greatest honour of becoming my wife?'

Oh God. Alice's heart shook as she stared down into the dark eyes of the gorgeous Henry French. Any other girl would be jumping at the chance to marry him. Henry, who'd been courting her for almost twelve months, was without a doubt the best person on the planet. She loved everything about him—from his cheeky smile to his warm heart, not to mention the way he looked when he got all dolled up in his swish grey suit. Within moments of making Henry's acquaintance at the birthday party of her best friend's brother, Alice had fallen head over heels.

But Alice wasn't the marrying kind. The way she saw it, marriage benefited men way more than it did women and, for this reason, she didn't think she'd ever enter into such a contract. And she'd thought Henry knew this about her. She'd thought he understood and respected her stance.

1

So why the *hell* was he down on bended knee at the end of St Kilda Pier on this beautiful summer's night that had been perfect in practically every way? They'd had a delicious dinner at Leo's Spaghetti Bar and were enjoying a lovely stroll before heading back to his place for a 'nightcap'. Or so she'd thought.

She laughed as if she thought he were joking, when in her heart of hearts she knew he was not. 'Henry! Get up. You'll ruin your trousers and people are looking at us.'

Henry didn't make a move to stand. Instead, he reached into his jacket pocket and pulled out a small, black velvet box. 'I don't care who looks at us—I only care about you and me. I've been offered a big promotion at work and the new role is in Geelong.'

'Geelong?' she whispered, feeling as if she'd been punched in the gut.

Still smiling, he nodded. 'And I want you to come with me. I want you to come as my wife. So ... will you marry me?'

He opened the box and a stunning square-cut diamond glistened up at her, almost winking in the moonlight. Alice couldn't deny its beauty, and for a moment she tried to imagine what being married to Henry French would be like, but all she felt was dread.

Maybe in a couple of years or if his proposal involved staying in Melbourne, she might have relented, but right now she needed to establish her career. And while she was happy for Henry's promotion, he didn't seem to have considered her work at all. Geelong might only be a few hours away but it felt like the ends of the earth. No way would she be able to commute there on a daily basis. She'd finally secured a role in the labs at the university, but she had ambitions far bigger than that.

A voice from deep inside told her that if she said 'no' she could kiss Henry French goodbye. That thought was almost too awful to bear, but even worse would be giving up her dreams for a man.

'You know I can't,' she whispered as Henry gazed up at her.

His face fell.

Had he really expected any different ending to this uninvited, unanticipated, *undesired* proposal?

Still, her heart squeezed and twisted at the tortured look on her beloved's face.

'I'm sorry, Henry.' Alice's own voice choked. 'You know I love you, I'll always love you, but I can't marry you. Congratulations on the promotion. I'll support you, and come visit as much as I can. I'd move in with you in a second if you were staying in Melbourne, but I can't move to Geelong. My work is here.'

But Henry didn't hear anything about her work. 'Move *in* with me?' he scoffed as he jumped to his feet, his cheeks turning crimson as he snapped the box shut and shoved it back in his pocket. 'Your head is stuck in the clouds if you think that would be possible. I don't know what fantasy world you're living in, but if I want to be a respectable businessman, I need a wife, not a floozy!'

'F-f-floozy?' Alice spluttered, unable to believe the words coming out of his mouth. How *dare* he!

'I'm sorry, Alice. I didn't mean ...' His face a picture of distress, he reached out to grab her, but she stepped back.

The damage was done. She'd seen the real Henry—a Henry she'd dared to believe didn't exist. But he was just like every other man. Just like her father. The fact he genuinely thought she'd be overjoyed by such a romantic proposal only showed how little he really knew her. And she him. She held up her hand and shook her head, unable to speak. Tears threatened at the back of her throat.

'I didn't mean that. You're not a floozy,' he said, his tone desperate, pleading. 'But can't you see that you're being unfair? I love you and I want to be with you, but the bank doesn't take kindly to unmarried couples living together, and long-distance relationships never work.'

Alice raised her eyebrows, unable to believe her ears. She didn't give a damn about the opinion of a bunch of stuffy bankers.

'And what about children?' he went on. 'You can't believe it's okay to bring them into the world out of wedlock?'

To be honest, she hadn't given much thought to children—possibly she didn't want them, definitely she didn't want them in the near future. There were other things more pressing, more important for her to dedicate her time and energy to. As much as she loved Henry, accepting his proposal, becoming his wife, would mean turning her back on everything she believed important.

'I'm sorry, Henry,' she said, gulping back her tears, 'but I just can't.'

And that was the last time Alice Abbott saw Henry French for over fifty years.

1

Now

'Carly and I are thinking about getting back together.'

What? Christos could not be serious! I almost gagged on my prosecco as I yanked the sheets over my bare chest and searched his flushed face. Was this some kind of sick joke? After almost a year together, I was comfortable, confident, in our relationship. But my boyfriend didn't look like he was joking. Although his eyes refused to meet mine, the serious expression on his face turned my insides to ice.

But hang on, he'd only said 'think'.

'What do you mean you *think* you're getting back together? Are you? Or are you not?'

He slowly raised his head and when his gaze met mine his eyes were watery. *No.* Dread poured into my stomach and slithered up my chest like a snake working its way up my oesophagus.

'I'm so sorry, Ged. I love you, but first and foremost I'm a dad, and things haven't been that great for the kids lately. They're really struggling with our living situation and Carly and I have been wondering if the best thing for them is if we try to make a go of things again.'

Make a go of things? Again?

He made it sound so casual, so easy, but they were divorced, which I'd thought was final. I couldn't believe my ears. Surely in a second he'd pull me back into his arms and tell me he was pulling my leg.

But there was no laughter. Only a man who thirty seconds ago I thought I knew better than anyone else in the world. A man who, despite his complicated living situation, I believed only had eyes for me.

'Oh my God. You're serious?'

'Nothing's set in stone yet—we're just considering our options. But I didn't want to keep you in the dark. I'm sorry.'

'Sorry?' I'd left work early for *this*!

It was Christos's week with his kids, so we'd arranged a Thursday afternoon rendezvous at a fancy city hotel around the corner from our office and I'd been looking forward to it all day.

But suddenly I felt sick, dirty, like some kind of harlot.

'Does this mean we're breaking up?' I hated the way my voice cracked. 'You're choosing your kids and your ex-wife over me?'

'Ged, please. It's not like that.'

'But you are considering getting back together with Carly?'

He confirmed my worst fear with another slow nod.

'I can't believe you still came here, that you let us …' I couldn't bring myself to say the words as I tried to swallow away the pain that suddenly burned in my chest. 'Why couldn't you have told me in a text message like a normal bloody person? Or at least in a cafe where I could have thrown a hot drink over you?'

We both eyed the half-flute of prosecco still in my hand but no matter how mortifying the situation, no way was I wasting good alcohol on Christos. I poured it down my throat instead, threw back the sheet and leapt from the bed.

I snatched up my tangled black lace knickers and tailored navy pants and yanked them apart. I couldn't put them on fast enough. My top had landed on the plush velvet armchair and my heels were near the door but where the hell was my bra?

'Ged. Baby. *Please*. Don't be like this.'

Holding my silk blouse against my bare breasts, I glared at him. 'How the hell do you expect me to be?'

Oh Lord, my eyeballs prickled painfully but I refused to cry in front of Christos. To hell with the bra. It had been a gift from *him* anyway.

I tugged the blouse over my head, grabbed my handbag and raced out the door. Half-walking, half-running and occasionally hopping, my hands shook as I tried shoving my feet into my shoes without stopping. God, how far was the lift? The long corridor stretched out in front of me in a tear-blurred tunnel and I hauled in a noisy, snot-filled breath. A guy from housekeeping glanced up, presumably to smile, but took one look at me and retreated into the room he was attending to.

At the elevator, I stabbed my finger so hard at the down button that it hurt. I winced but the pain had nothing on the ache in my heart. How could Christos do this? He didn't love Carly—not in the way he loved me.

I glanced over my shoulder, half-expecting to see him running after me, ready to tell me he'd made a mistake. But all I saw was the cleaning man venturing back into the corridor.

Maybe I should go back and talk to him? Make him see sense.

My grandmother's voice rang out loud and clear in my head. *You do not need a man to give you value. Certainly not one who could treat you with such disrespect.*

And, no matter how much I loved Christos, what he'd just done hadn't made me feel respected in the slightest. I wasn't about to beg. I was furious at him for making me even consider it.

The lift pinged and the doors opened to reveal it was empty. I rushed inside and scrutinised my reflection in the mirrored walls. Mascara streaked down my bright red cheeks like some ghastly painting; my hair had taken the term 'bird's nest' to a whole other level and my nipples were clearly visible through my crumpled blouse. No chance I could slink back to the office looking like this.

I emerged into the hotel lobby, feeling as if everyone's eyes were on me, and rushed out onto Little Collins Street, where I dug my phone out of my handbag. I couldn't call Darren, my boss, because I wasn't sure I could talk without crying, and overwrought female wasn't the persona I wanted to give off in the office—especially not when I was vying for a promotion against two other capable colleagues.

I started tapping out a message instead: *Sorry. Something's come up. Family emergency. I need to take the rest of the day off. Will explain la*

In the nick of time I realised the error of my ways: *Won't be back in the office today as I just had a lead on a story*—but I was interrupted by the buzzing of my phone.

I grimaced as the word 'Mum' flashed up at me. I didn't feel like talking to anyone right now, least of all my mother, who would immediately pick something off in my voice and start an interrogation. I pressed the little icon that would autoreply that I was in a meeting (which she'd believe as she was always berating me for working too hard) and then finished texting my boss.

I'd barely pressed send when a message from Mum popped up—since when had she got so speedy at thumb typing? Only two years ago she didn't even have a mobile and now, not only did she have a smartphone, but also an Instagram account, Snapchat *and* a YouTube channel, but that's a whole other story. And possibly my fault, since I was the one who'd dragged her into the modern age and got her on Facebook so she could see all the photos my sister-in-law posted of her grandbabies.

Don't forget, you're picking Gralice up for her birthday dinner tonight. And wear something nice—I'm filming the whole thing. She ended with a little emoji of a movie camera.

My heart slammed to a halt. Could this day *get* any worse?

I adored Gralice—my Grandma Alice—and wanted to celebrate her eightieth birthday, just not tonight. Not when all my family would be there and I'd have to pretend everything was okay, or admit it wasn't and subject myself to their sympathy. I wanted to be strong, but one kind word and I was likely to fall apart. An image of me sobbing on the sofa between Granddad Philip and Granddad Craig landed in my head. That probably wasn't something Mum wanted on her YouTube channel.

And wear something nice?

The audacity! I'd once worked in fashion mags for goodness' sake.

I stared at the screen as I headed towards my tram stop, trying to work out how to respond to my mother, when suddenly I was falling. My hands shot out to break my fall and my phone catapulted out of my grip even before I worked out what had happened. Two seconds later I heard the crunch of whatever iPhones are made of against the bitumen as a car drove over it.

No. My whole life was in that device—my emails, my appointments, my banking, all my photos of Christos. My heart squeezed. And hang on, was that blood I could taste on my lip? Dirt in my mouth? Pain throbbing in my ankle?

Apparently, this day *could* get worse.

'Are you okay?' sounded an elderly male voice.

I raised my head enough to see not only was there indeed an elderly gentleman peering down at me, but a small crowd had gathered around us.

'Shall I call an ambulance?' someone asked.

'I've got a first aid kit in my bag,' announced another.

'No. No. I'm fine.' I felt as if I'd been hit by a freight train as I tried to heave myself to my feet, but I did not want attention drawn to me this close to the hotel or the office. A couple of people reached out to help and within seconds I was upright, however, it immediately became clear that standing on two feet was going to be a challenge. My ankle hurt so badly I had to lift it off the ground and hover on one leg.

'I think this is yours.' A twenty-something with a grotty cap on backwards and a skateboard under one arm held out the remnants of my phone. The sight brought tears to my eyes all over again.

'Thank you.' I took the pieces and shoved them into my bag.

'Looks like you've done a right number on your foot,' said the old man. 'Can we call someone to help you?'

My mind went to Christos and immediately rejected that thought. 'No, thank you. I was heading to the tram. I'll be fine once I get home.'

'Let me call you a cab.' The concerned gentleman was already leaning into the road, his hand outstretched.

Almost immediately a taxi slowed to a stop by the curb—at least one thing was working in my favour. The gentleman held the door open for me and I crawled into the back seat, eager to escape this mortification. My rescue crew on the pavement waved me off like I was on a royal tour and I forced myself to wave back when all I wanted to do was bury my head in my hands and bawl.

'Where you headed?' The driver had a strong British accent, Geordie I thought, although it had been over ten years since my gap year backpacking around the UK.

I told him my address in Carlton, was thankful when he didn't complain about the short trip, and even more so when he didn't try and engage me in conversation. Was there anything worse than beauticians and taxi drivers who wanted to know your whole damn life story?

As he parked on the street outside my apartment block, I dug my purse out of my bag.

'It's all paid for. Your granddad gave me a fifty when you got in. Said I could keep the change.'

Ah, so that accounted for why he hadn't grumbled about the distance. After Christos's behaviour I'd been beginning to lose hope in humankind but the stranger's actions helped remind me the world wasn't all bad. I would get over this—it would likely just take a little time and an ocean of alcohol.

I thanked the driver and limped into the building, grateful not only that my apartment was on the ground floor but also that I didn't run into any of my neighbours in the lobby. If I hadn't already looked a sight with my tear-stained make-up and messy hair, the grazes I could feel burning on my face had sealed the deal. Pity it wasn't Halloween—I wouldn't even have to hire a costume!

My five-year-old groodle greeted me as I pushed open the door. I sank to the floor and buried my face in her soft fur. 'Oh, Coco. You won't believe my day.'

If she had any idea what had happened, she'd be as distraught as I was. She adored Christos. Let's face it, everyone did. All my friends—especially the coupled ones—were hugely jealous of our relationship.

Dating a divorced father of three had never been a walk in the park, especially because he and his ex were involved in the new custody trend of nest parenting where their three kids stayed in their marital home and Christos and Carly took turns living there, one week on, one week off. They'd rented a two-bedroom apartment to use on their weeks 'off'—they had a bedroom each and strict rules about keeping the communal areas clean—but recently it had become more Carly's place as Christos had all but moved in with me on his non-kid weeks.

In theory having a week-on-week-off partner was pretty much the perfect arrangement. I had plenty of evenings where I didn't have to share Netflix with anyone and I always knew that sex and companionship were just around the corner. But oh, how I missed him on those long weeks between. A fresh wave of pain washed over me as I realised not only would there be no more lunchtime rendezvous, but that I wouldn't be coming home to Christos ever again.

I looked around my apartment; it suddenly felt cold and empty.

Coco whined, and for a moment I thought she was commiserating with me, until she put her paw against the door. I hauled myself to my feet, grabbed a tissue and my keys and took her out into the communal garden at the back of the building.

Each step felt like torture. I wondered if I'd broken my ankle. Perhaps I should get an X-ray, but the thought of going to the hospital or even to a doctor … it was too much right now.

After Coco had relieved herself we went back inside and I hobbled to the freezer. Wasn't ice supposed to fix everything?

I popped a couple of Panadol and then, with my foot dressed in the finest of frozen veggies and elevated on the sofa, I opened my laptop and logged into Messenger.

Happy birthday, Gralice. Hope you're having a great day. Really sorry but I can't drive you tonight. I tripped this afternoon and sprained my ankle. It's pretty bad. Also broke my phone—so if you need to contact me for the next couple of days it'll have to be via email or here. And I'm not feeling so great so think I'll have to give tonight a miss. I'll drop round tomorrow after work and give you your present. xo

I felt awful bailing on Gralice's big birthday bash, but she'd have the rest of our family to celebrate and this felt more like Mum's party than hers anyway.

I decided not to break the news to my mother for a few more hours in order to delay the lecture that would inevitably come— at least she couldn't call me—and, in an effort to try and distract myself from the train wreck that was my heart, turned my attentions to the next issue. Buying a new phone.

In this day and age, but in my line of business especially, a mobile was something I couldn't live without.

I woke a few hours later to the buzzing of my intercom and Coco barking up at it as if she'd never heard the sound before. I tried to get up but groaned when pain shot through my ankle, bringing back all the horrid events of the day.

Christos had ended our relationship.

Could it be him at the door?

My heart tingled. Maybe he'd called and, unable to get through, had hurried over to beg me to take him back. *Well, stuff him!* It would take a lot of grovelling to put the pieces of my heart back together. Let him feel a little of the anguish I had.

It was only when the buzzing continued—no pauses at all, as if a little child had their finger jammed on the button and was refusing to let go—that I realised Christos still had a key and wasn't the type to be kept waiting. If he wanted to talk he'd already be here, standing in my small apartment, saying his piece. Disappointment filled me as the pain in my ankle travelled through my body and settled back in my chest, making it difficult to breathe.

I couldn't remember ever experiencing such heartache over a guy before, but I'd honestly thought Christos was it, *the one* I'd spend the rest of my earthly days with. I'd dated heaps of men on and off throughout my twenties, but, far more focused on my career, I hadn't been serious about anyone.

Then I hit thirty, met Christos at work and 'serious' suddenly became my middle name. My feelings for him had blindsided me. I didn't care that I might never have sex with anyone else in my life, I only wanted him. He was the perfect guy for me—we were both in newspapers so understood the pressures that came with the job and, as he already had children, he didn't want things from me I didn't think I wanted to give.

We'd been together for almost a year now and had been planning an overseas holiday to spend Christmas and New Year in New York. I'd thought he might propose while we were there. Christos came from a family as Greek as his name and was very traditional about stuff like that. I didn't really see the point of marriage, but I must admit I'd already had the odd schoolgirl fantasy about becoming the next Mrs Panagopoulos. Not that I'd take his surname, I couldn't understand why any woman would, so there'd be no double-barrelled surnames either. Can you imagine Mrs Geraldine Johnston-Panagopoulos? *No, thank you.*

But, I loved him and was quite prepared to compromise if he thought the piece of paper important.

I hadn't actually given much thought to how such a marriage would co-exist with Christos's current arrangement with Carly, but I guess I never thought the nest-parenting thing would be permanent. Everything I'd read about it indicated it was a temporary situation while the kids got used to their parents being apart, and also while finances and permanent custody arrangements were finalised. That's certainly the way Christos sold it to me. His and Carly's divorce had just come through, so I'd assumed it wouldn't be long before he moved in permanently with me or we got our own house so his children could stay with us every second weekend. I might have already been perusing real-estate-dot-com in my spare time. Even with Christos's child support obligations, we might have been able to afford to buy something nice if we went a little further out of the city or if I got the promotion I was working my arse off towards.

But it looked like my fantasy was about as unlikely to come true as it was for me to find a baby unicorn at the local pet shop. At least I still had my job.

The buzzing continued to echo loudly through my apartment and I was this close to screaming and giving it a run for its money. Who on earth could it be? I still hadn't got around to messaging my mother and letting her know I wasn't coming, so it couldn't be her come to drag me to their place by my hair. *Could it?* I might be thirty years of age, but the way Mum sometimes acted you'd think the three and zero were the other way around.

Whoever it was, if they didn't stop pressing that buzzer soon, I was going to set my dog on them.

One look at Coco jumping up against the door like a crazed chipmunk and I realised the idea that she would ever hurt anyone was also a fantasy and I was going to have to give the intruder what for myself.

It hurt to stand and hurt even more to shuffle across the room to the intercom, which only exasperated my shitty mood.

'Who IS it?' I yelled into the speaker on the wall.

2

'It's your grandmother,' Gralice's voice shot back, 'and you should be ashamed of yourself leaving a little old lady outside in the cold for so long.'

Little old lady, my arse.

I pressed the button to let her in to the building and opened my door.

She appeared moments later and I opened my mouth to say 'Happy birthday' but the words died on my tongue as she took one look at me. 'What the fuck have you done with yourself?'

'Didn't you get my message? What are you doing here?'

'You didn't think I was going to let you off the hook? If I have to suffer through one of Sappho's family dinners on camera, then you're sure as hell coming as well.'

You might have guessed that Sappho is my mother, named by Gralice after the Greek poet and more commonly known by her middle name, Marie, after the French-Polish physicist and chemist,

Marie Curie. Gralice is the only one who ever calls her by her first name—no one else would dare. Personally, I think Sappho a far more sophisticated name than Marie and much nicer than Geraldine. If my name were Sappho I'd never let anyone call me anything else, but my mother has never liked being different; hence the unoriginal and boring names she'd bestowed upon me and my older brother.

'I can't come. I can barely walk.' I gestured to my bulbous ankle; the peas had barely made a difference.

Gralice glanced down and frowned. 'What happened?'

'I tripped,' I said, deciding not to tell her I did so while running from Christos. She wasn't the type to commiserate over a broken heart. Gralice didn't believe women should waste time pining over any man and, although there'd been lovers over the years, she would never have considered herself attached to any of them and thus had been happily single all her life.

But I wasn't ready to give up wallowing yet. It had only been a few hours, and right now I wished for the kind of grandma who knitted and baked and would feed me chocolate cake as I blubbered my little heart out.

'You *do* look terrible,' she conceded, 'but we'll be sitting down most of the night anyway. You can use this as a walking stick if need be.' She held up her umbrella and little droplets of water splashed onto the floor. It had been sunny out when I got home, but this was Melbourne—all four seasons in a matter of hours.

'Geez. Thanks.'

'Now, get in the bathroom and make yourself presentable. Sappho will have a fit if you turn up looking like that and Tony will be here in fifteen minutes to pick us up.'

Tony (my father) who, since being retrenched from his job at the Holden engine production factory two years ago when the car industry in Australia took its final breath, also happened to be an Uber driver. And a lollipop man, but he only did that twice a day for a short forty minutes at a time.

'But, I ...' I didn't know why she was so adamant about my attendance, but if she'd made up her mind I was going there was no point wasting my breath trying to fight.

'Good.' Gralice smiled, punctuating the expression with a nod as I limped into my ensuite to start the process of making myself presentable.

I turned on the shower, and as I started to remove my clothes, my gaze landed on Christos's toothbrush. I reached out to steady myself against the wall as a fresh wave of pain washed over me. Leaving such an item in my bathroom, along with the spare jocks and few work shirts he kept in my wardrobe, had seemed such a significant decision. But would he even bother retrieving them now? They were just things and if he could treat me with such disregard, he likely wouldn't even pay a thought to his stuff.

I wanted to be angry, raging that he'd done this to me, made me such a fool. I wanted to toss his toothbrush in the garbage and take to his clothes with scissors—but all I felt was utter devastation and instead I crumbled to the floor.

'Ten minutes,' called Gralice, appearing moments later in the open doorway. 'Have you picked an out—' Her question died on her tongue as she took one look at me and frowned. 'What on earth is the matter?'

'Christos and I are over.' I didn't even bother to try and halt my tears. 'He's getting back together with his ex.'

'What? Oh, honey.' Then, very un-Gralice-like, she stepped into the room, dropped to her knees (which were still surprisingly good for an old chook) and pulled me close.

'I don't understand. I thought we were happy.' A thought struck that made me freeze. 'Maybe he and Carly aren't getting back together? Maybe he needed an excuse to break up with me. I should have asked him exactly what was going through his head.'

Gralice tsked. 'Who ever knows what's going through a man's head.'

Surely now she would call my father and tell him that neither of us were coming to dinner. We could order our favourite Thai takeaway, not that I had much of an appetite for anything. Except wine.

'I know you're upset,' she said instead, 'but a woman doesn't turn eighty every day and I want my only granddaughter there to celebrate. So get in that shower. The heat will make you feel better, and I'll choose your outfit.'

The fact Gralice thought hot water could even begin to heal my broken heart showed how little she knew about love—at least the romantic variety—but she was right. Eighty was a milestone to make a fuss over, and not going would mean Christos had ruined not only my day but Gralice's also.

'Okay.' I sniffed as I pushed myself off the floor—*ouch!*—and started to strip for the shower.

Less than ten minutes later I was dressed, no longer looked like an assault victim and, with the help of Gralice and her umbrella, was making my way outside to meet my father who had parked his Holden Commodore (still his pride and joy) on the street.

'You look swish tonight, Dad,' I said trying to sound chirpy as he pulled away from the kerb. He was wearing an honest-to-God suit, making him look like a fancy chauffeur. The last time I'd seen him wear it was to his mother's funeral two years ago. Or was it Will's wedding? They were around the same time.

'I think I look like a right tosspot. Who wears a suit to have dinner in their own house?' he said. 'How's your foot?'

'Sore. Thanks for coming and getting us.'

'It's my pleasure—gave me an excuse to get away.'

'Oh Dad, is it that bad?'

'It's getting worse by the second. It used to be I couldn't eat my dinner before she took a photo for that Insta-thing, but now I have to dress like I'm dining with the Queen for a meal in my own house.' He scratched his near-white, receding hairline. 'I don't know how much more of this I can take.'

'You could always learn to cook yourself, then you can eat whenever the hell you like,' Gralice suggested.

Dad chuckled as if such a thing was as unlikely as humans establishing a settlement on Mars.

Now's probably a good time to mention that my mother is what can only be described as an Instagram and YouTube sensation. You may have heard of her. Her handle is @TheHappyHappyHousewife, and no one is more surprised than me by the fact she has over a hundred thousand followers on all her social media platforms and her YouTube channel (yes, she has her *own*) has been trending for months. She's an advocate for the social movement 'new domesticity'—a crusade that promotes the revival of the lost domestic arts of cooking, cleaning and taking care of one's husband and children at the expense of all else.

If you ask her, it's all about being proud to be a homemaker, not needing, wanting or looking for satisfaction and self-fulfilment outside the home. If you ask Gralice, it's a terrifying step back in time, a slap in the face to all the hardworking women like herself who fought for gender equality and women's liberation in terms of their bodies, children, work and relationships. Gralice does not approve of Mum's new 'hobby' any more than my mother approves of Gralice's lifelong activism.

'Have you told Mum how you're feeling?'

'I've tried, but she tells me to stop being a grumpy old man.'

'Well, you can't have your cake and eat it too, Tony,' Gralice said. 'It's all the things you've enjoyed all your married life that she's now promoting to the masses. Why should you be the only man to benefit from her archaic ideas?'

Dad didn't appear to know how to respond to that, so I jumped in. 'Have you got any new Uber stories?' He often met the most fascinating people in his job and I loved hearing about them, but right now I also thought it would be good for all of us if we thought about something other than Mum and Christos.

'I did meet this rather interesting fellow this morning,' he began and entertained us the rest of the way as we navigated the rush-hour traffic, telling us about the American magician he'd collected from the airport. 'He's in Australia for a few weeks and gave me two free tickets for next weekend, but I doubt I'll be able to convince your mother to go with me. She's too busy with Rosa these days.'

'Who's Rosa?' Gralice asked the question before I could.

Dad snorted. 'You'll find out in a moment,' he said as he slowed the car in front of their house.

My parents live in Port Melbourne. They bought their quaint, red-brick, two-storey semi-detached house a few years after they got married, long before the suburb became gentrified and trendy. There were already two other cars parked outside—one I recognised as belonging to my brother, and I wondered if the third belonged to this Rosa person, as I knew my grandfathers would have caught an Uber.

Dad and Gralice argued over who was going to help me.

'I'm fine.' I swung my legs to the ground and immediately winced as I tried to put pressure on my sore foot.

'Here.' Gralice thrust her umbrella at me and I used it to limp to the house.

Mum met us at the door wearing an apron over a pink dress I'd never seen before. She glanced down with clear disapproval at Gralice's outfit as they exchanged an awkward hug and Gralice said, 'Happy birthday.'

'Hi, Mum.' I leaned forward to give her a kiss, expecting her to mention my foot, ask what I'd done and offer some sympathy, but she looked right past me.

'Where's Christos?'

I knew I shouldn't have come.

'It's his week with the kids,' I said, gulping. She'd always been able to tell when I was lying, and while I wasn't technically telling an untruth, it felt like now would be a good time to confess we'd broken up. But I didn't want to. It was a stab to my heart just thinking about it. Speaking it out loud might make it more real and I couldn't bear Mum's disappointment—she'd probably be almost as heartbroken as me. She'd seen in Christos the possibility of me finally settling down.

'Yes, I know. But it's Gralice's eightieth birthday. This is important. I thought he was going to get a babysitter.'

And, *oh my God*, she was right. In the shock of this afternoon's events, I'd totally forgotten that Christos was supposed to be coming tonight. He said he'd booked a babysitter—had that been a lie? How long had he and Carly been contemplating this decision? Maybe he'd already moved back in with her and was just letting me down gently. This week, when he was supposed to be at their house alone with the kids, had he been there with *her*? I felt ill.

'He couldn't make it,' I said, my tone not inviting further discussion. 'By the way, have you had Botox?' I was mostly trying to deflect attention from me, but her face did look suspiciously fresh and her crow's feet were almost unnoticeable.

Gralice frowned as she scrutinised my mother—she believed in growing old *dis*-gracefully.

Mum lifted a hand to her brow. 'So what if I have? Everyone's having it these days and I have a public image to uphold.'

'It's cool, Mum. You look good.' It appeared she'd also had her hair done. Her often limp, blonde, shoulder-length hair had been cut and blow-dried into a layered bob and she'd definitely had highlights, making her look younger than her fifty-four years.

She beamed. 'Thank you, darling. A good housewife always tries to look her best. Now about—'

I cut her off. 'Do you mind if we head inside? I can't stand on this foot for much longer.'

And I needed a drink. One good thing about not driving was that I didn't have to worry about my blood-alcohol level. Wine would be my friend until I could no longer remember Christos's name.

'Oh,' she said, finally peering down at my ankle. 'Is that why you're only wearing one shoe?' She tried to frown, but only half her face cooperated. 'I guess we can make sure we don't get your feet in the video.'

'I'm *not* going in your video,' I told her. My appearance might have slightly improved since my run in with the pavement, but I probably still had puffy eyes and blotchy cheeks from all the crying. Plus, I'd recently discovered people from work, many of whom usually only watched the ABC, were subscribed to Mum's YouTube channel. They found her hilarious. Thus she would have to pay me—big bucks—to appear on it.

'Okay, I'll tell Rosa.' I'd expected an objection but guessed she didn't want my unsightly appearance to ruin the aesthetics of her latest vlog.

'Who *is* Rosa?'

Mum's eyes sparkled. 'Ooh, Rosa is my new assistant. You're going to fall in love with her.'

'Your *assistant*?' Gralice and I spoke at once, our eyebrows creeping skyward.

'She's fabulous,' Mum said, oblivious to our shock. 'Come on through and I'll introduce you.'

I don't know what I was expecting, but Rosa was not it. The word 'assistant' evoked images of a person barely out of their teens, wearing the kind of suit you got from Portmans and speaking one hundred words a minute. At least that's the type of assistants I was used to at the newspaper. Rosa was not any of these things. At a guess, she was mid-to-late forties; she had long, dark, wavy hair, lovely brown skin, smile lines around her sparkling chocolate-coloured eyes, and was wearing a brightly coloured kaftan kind of thing. My entire family were cramped around the dining table— mismatched chairs brought in from all over the house—as she sat at the head, her hands flying all over the place as she spoke. Whatever she was saying, they were all hanging off her every word, no one noticing Gralice's and my arrival until Rosa herself announced us.

'Oh,' she exclaimed loudly, jumping from her seat so the chair legs scraped on the vinyl. I waited for Mum to tell her off like she would us, but she didn't so much as give this woman a disapproving glance. 'You must be Ged and Alice. Aren't you both divine? I'm Rosalicia, but who on God's earth has time for that kind of mouthful, so everyone just calls me Rosa.'

I smiled as this animated woman threw her arms around us each in turn, then looked down with concern at my foot. 'And what, my dear, have you done to yourself?'

'I tripped and sprained it this arvo.'

'That's terrible.' Her perfectly shaped near-black eyebrows drew together. 'Does it hurt much?'

I nodded. The painkillers I'd swallowed a few hours ago had well and truly worn off.

'You must sit.' Rosa wrapped an arm around me and helped me over to a chair, while the rest of my family rushed to give Gralice birthday hugs.

I had to say, they were all looking rather swanky—Mum had obviously also been in their ears about looking nice. Like Dad, my brother Will and our two grandfathers, Phil and Craig, were wearing dinner suits. My sister-in-law Sophie, in a long navy dress, had also made an effort, and my niece and nephew, who looked adorable no matter what they wore, were in their Sunday best. Six-month-old Oliver was wearing an outfit almost identical to his dad's—I didn't know they even made suits that tiny—and three-year-old Charlotte wore a cute floral number.

Gralice, of course, had ignored Mum's wishes and was in her usual uniform of black leather pants, a T-shirt proclaiming 'Girls just wanna have fun-damental rights', silver Doc Marten boots and a brown felt coat. She was the hippest eighty-year-old I knew and looked about as grandma-like as Miley Cyrus. And, since she'd been the one to choose my outfit, I probably fell short of my mother's expectations too.

'You look fabulous, darling, not a day over seventy-nine,' Philip exclaimed as he handed Gralice a massive bouquet of pink-and-white variegated chrysanthemums. He and Craig, although in theory retired, still owned a very successful flower shop in St Kilda. I'd spent many hours in their shop as a child, playing among the buckets of blooms, so now one of my party tricks was being able to recognise and name more flowers than anyone in my social circle.

'Oh stop,' Gralice said, air-kissing both his cheeks.

Now might be a good idea to explain the whole two grandfathers situation. Philip is Gralice's long-*long*-time friend. She'd boasted a gay best friend way before chick-lit and rom coms made it fashionable. In 1964, she decided she wanted to have a baby, and there was no such thing as sperm banks so she propositioned him. I can only imagine the scandal her pregnancy would have inspired, but she wasn't in much contact with her family by then anyway.

And, actually, I didn't *need* to imagine anything, because my mother had made it very clear my whole life how much she disapproved of her parents' behaviour. I thought the sixties was supposed to be an era of free love and everything goes, but apparently growing up she was the brunt of all kinds of jokes and some rather nasty bullying thanks to her very un-conservative family situation. She wanted nothing more than to be part of a 'normal' family, which perhaps had something to do with her getting married when she was barely out of her teens.

Anyway, I digress. Craig is Phil's 'new' husband, although they've been partners for longer than I've been alive, longer even than my parents have been married. Not long after the marriage laws changed in Australia, Philip and Craig, eighty-two and seventy-five respectively, tied the knot in the most beautiful ceremony in the cutest little chapel at the foothills of the Dandenong Ranges. There was standing room only, guests spilling out into the garden, and not a dry eye in the church—everyone so happy that after many, many years of not being free to display or acknowledge their love in public, they were finally able to shout it from the rooftops. Gralice and another one of their friends were witnesses and although the average age at the reception was over seventy, we partied at a nearby hotel until the early hours of the morning. I smile every time I think about that day and how lucky I am to have Craig as well as Phil in my life.

And, for all my mother objected about her childhood, she adored her father and her stepfather as much as the rest of us—

her relationship with them had always been closer than hers with Gralice.

'Are we doing presents now?' asked Sophie, interrupting my reverie.

Dammit, in my haste to get ready, I'd left my gift at home.

'No!' Mum's one word made everyone startle. 'Presents will be opened on camera. In fact, now that we're all here, let me explain to you tonight's schedule.'

Gralice and I exchanged glances across the table. So much for this being *her* birthday dinner.

'We've already filmed me getting ready for tonight—cooking and decorating the table—and I'll do a little tribute to Gralice myself, talking about what she means to me ...'

I try not to smirk. *That* should be interesting.

'But what I want to show is my family benefiting from my care and attention to domestic duties. This vlog will be titled "How to host a special family dinner", so, Rosa is going to film us eating and having fun together and opening the presents—but I want you all to pretend she's not even there. Later, Rosa will edit the actual footage down to about two or three minutes max. Everyone got that?'

My family nodded and I wondered if Mum had put some kind of spell over them that made them agree to this exploitation, or if they were all secretly looking forward to their moment of fame. I could believe that of Will at a stretch, maybe even Sophie, and Phil and Craig doted on Mum so would do anything she asked, but Gralice? Something was not quite right with her tonight.

'Don't forget I better not be in any of the footage,' I warned.

Rosa started a very expensive-looking camera rolling, and Mum, with Sophie's help, started bringing out all the dishes, explaining in detail what each one was. Thankfully, she also conjured wine, acting like Martha Stewart or someone as she filled everyone's glasses with over-the-top flair. I drank half of mine in one gulp.

'Is there anything else I can get for anyone?' she asked.

When we all said we were fine, she plopped a kiss on the heads of both of her grandchildren and sat at the head of the table. I couldn't help noticing my dad, at the other end, looked miserable.

At first we were all terribly conscious of the camera in the corner recording every moment of our conversation. Everyone was being exceedingly polite, and Sophie looked like she might have a coronary when Charlotte scooped up some mashed potato in her fingers and spread it over her baby brother's head.

'It's fine.' Mum smiled adoringly at her granddaughter. 'The potatoes are organic,' she said towards the camera, 'and I used milk and butter, fresh from a local dairy. It'll probably do his cradle-cap good, but I'll go get a lovely warm flannel to clean him up.'

I wanted to ask what dairy farm was local to Port Melbourne but bit my tongue. Stilted conversation went on for another five minutes before everyone forgot Rosa was there. For someone who was clearly a very charismatic person, she also knew how to blend into the background when required.

I had to admit the evening was going well. Dinner was delicious, but Mum *had* spent over thirty years perfecting the art of cooking— she could give all those contestants on *MasterChef* a run for their money. And it was good to sit back and relax with my family. I only thought of Christos maybe once or twice. After the main meal, we had an intermission so Mum could clean up a little and Will could go settle Charlotte in the spare room.

My mother made a comment—which sounded more disapproving than admiring—about how hands-on fathers were these days and then, *thank God*, it was time for the cake. My mouth watered as she carried out her marvellous creation, a two-tiered chocolate and vanilla marble cake with gold icing and chocolate numbers—eight and zero—seemingly erupting from the top. It almost looked too good to eat but, after an out of key, very loud rendition of 'Happy Birthday', we devoured it.

There were tears in Gralice's eyes and she sounded rather choked up as she thanked Mum for dinner and everyone for coming. I frowned, trying to recall another time my grandmother had been so emotional. Perhaps turning eighty did that to a woman. I reached across the table and squeezed her hand.

Sophie looked to my mother. '*Now* is it time for presents?'

'Yes. But I get to go first.' Mum clicked her fingers and Rosa stepped away from the camera long enough to retrieve an artistically wrapped box from the side table.

Gralice took the gift and tugged at the ribbon. 'A candle,' she exclaimed a few moments later as we all stared at the purple candle, its wax speckled with what looked to be hundreds and thousands.

'Not just *any* candle,' Mum said, again speaking to the camera rather than her own mother. 'I made it myself. The container is an old recycled jam jar, and anyone who wants to make one themselves can check out my latest vlog. Candles do really add so much to a home and the scents can also be very useful alternative therapies.'

'Thank you, I'm sure,' Gralice said and I had to smother a laugh. She wasn't one for smelly things—didn't see the point—and the fact that Mum either didn't know, understand or care only highlighted their differences.

Will and Sophie gave her a framed photograph of Charlotte and Oliver and, although Gralice had also never been the sentimental type and had very few photos on display in her little terraced cottage in Fitzroy, she exclaimed in genuine delight as she hugged it against her chest. Phil and Craig gifted her some expensive whiskey glasses in addition to the flowers they'd already given her. These were perfect, as a tipple (or two) of an evening *was* something Gralice enjoyed.

'I'm sorry,' I said with an annoyed-at-myself sigh. 'I did get you something'—I'd found a signed first edition of *A Brief History of Time* online—'but left it at home.'

'Don't worry.' Gralice sniffed and wiped her eyes with the back of her hand. 'Now, it's my turn.'

Her turn? We all frowned as she bent to retrieve something from her handbag. 'I also have a little gift for myself,' she announced, holding up three white envelopes.

3

An Elvis tribute cruise?

In each of Gralice's envelopes was a ticket to a four-day, three-night cruise, leaving tomorrow morning. She had one for me and one for Mum—the third was, apparently, for herself.

'Have you lost your mind? Since when have you liked Elvis Presley?' my mother asked, uttering my exact thoughts. While Mum had always been an Elvis tragic, Gralice had never shown *any* interest in his music. 'Or cruises for that matter. I'm sure I remember you mocking me when I suggested Tony and I go on one for our thirtieth anniversary.'

I remembered this also. And although Gralice and Dad didn't agree on many things, they did on this, so my parents had gone out to the theatre to celebrate instead.

'I don't *mind* Elvis.' Gralice shrugged and I couldn't help raising my eyebrows. 'I just never loved him as much as *you* did. And anyway, I'm eighty years old, I don't need to justify my likes and dislikes to you. Isn't it a woman's prerogative to change her mind?

I thought this would be a good way to continue my birthday festivities and celebrate my imminent retirement.'

'Retirement?' All of us spoke at once. Gralice was a sessional tutor in physics at Melbourne University where she'd spent much of her working life. She'd stepped down from her position as professor a decade ago but hadn't been ready to give up work entirely.

'Oh, haven't I mentioned that?' she asked as if she'd forgotten to tell us she was dropping round for dinner. 'I finish up in a couple of weeks. I thought it was finally time.'

'Wow.' Gralice's scientific work, along with her trailblazing role in Australian women's rights, had always defined her. 'What on earth are you going to do with all your free time?'

'Well, I'm starting with a cruise—maybe I'll get hooked.'

The idea sounded very unlikely to me. I may have tripped and hurt my foot but I suddenly wondered if Gralice had had a similar fall and banged her head.

'And you want *us* to go with you?' Mum stared at the ticket like it was a two-headed baby elephant.

Gralice scowled. 'You could say "thank you"! I thought it would be nice for the three of us to spend some quality time together.'

'I'm sorry.' Mum blinked. 'It's just a … surprise. But a lovely one,' she added quickly.

'I like a bit of Elvis,' Rosa said, and then broke out into a few lines of 'Hound Dog'. We all stared at her in amazement—she should have been on the stage. 'Besides, think of all the Instagram opportunities.'

My mother's eyes lit up and she looked to my father. 'There are some frozen meals in the freezer. Will you be okay on your own for a few days?'

He opened his mouth—probably to object—but Gralice jumped in before he had the chance. 'We can board the ship any time after eight in the morning, so we should get there about ten to avoid the rush of eager beavers. It doesn't *depart* until four, which will give us plenty of time to settle into our cabins and have some lunch. Tony, you can drive us to the dock after you've done your morning lollipop duties.'

Dad nodded begrudgingly.

'Why didn't you buy tickets for us, Gralice?' Will looked hurt. 'It could have been a whole family thing and Sophie and I need a holiday way more than Ged does.'

He had no idea how much I needed a holiday right now—or at least an escape.

'This is a girls' trip, Will. I want to spend some quality time with your mother and I didn't think Elvis was really your thing. But let's talk about sending you and Sophie off somewhere when Oliver is a little bit older.'

This seemed to appease my brother and so Gralice looked to me. 'What do you say?'

'This is very generous ...' I glanced down at the ticket still in my hand. 'But now's not a good time to get time off work at such short notice—and I can't leave Coco alone for four days.'

'I've already cleared it with your boss.'

Of course she had. Gralice never did anything by halves.

'And,' she winked, 'I told him you might even get some ideas for articles on board, so he's completely okay with it. And Tony can look after Coco. She can keep him company.'

'It would be my pleasure,' Dad said, and took a long gulp of his beer. As if he had any choice!

'Ooh, there'll be plenty of fodder on the ship,' Rosa exclaimed. 'You could write about the number of deaths and disappearances that happen on cruises—the statistics blow my mind. Or about the pirates!'

'Pirates?' My father raised an eyebrow. 'Off the south coast of Australia?'

'Well,' Rosa conceded, 'maybe not on this particular cruise, but I once went on a cruise in the Indian Ocean near Somalia and we were attacked.'

I had to say, this did sound fascinating, and a few days away from the office, away from Christos, was very appealing. Right now all I wanted to do was curl up in a ball and hibernate from the world with my broken heart. 'But what about my foot? I can't even walk properly.'

'We'll hire you a wheelchair if need be, and there are lifts on ships.' Gralice smiled a sweet old-lady smile that did not match her personality. 'It'll do you good to come away for the weekend and take your mind off the Greek. Who knows? You might even find someone on board to help ease your pain. The best way to get over one man is to get some from another.'

My father almost choked on his beer.

'Gralice!' Will was horrified. It's an unwritten rule that women in their later years, grandmothers especially, are not supposed to make these kind of suggestions—but Sophie seemed to find the whole thing amusing.

'Hang on!' My mother held up her hand, silencing everyone. 'Why do you need to take your mind off Christos? Have you broken up?'

All eyes around the table stared at me in expectation.

I gave Gralice a look—*thanks a lot!* She shrugged, totally unapologetic.

I nodded, willing the lump in my throat not to explode. 'He's decided to get back together with his ex-wife. They're doing it for the kids, *apparently*.'

My cheeks burned as I admitted this and I couldn't keep the bitterness out of my voice. Who goes to the effort of getting divorced and then back together for the children? You'd think if they were so worried about the wellbeing of their three little cherubs they'd have worked harder to make a go of it the first time.

'Oh, sis, I'm so sorry,' Will said. 'I really liked him.'

Everyone else made mutterings of agreement.

I swallowed. 'Me too. But, anyway.'

'Didn't his divorce only just finalise?' Mum asked. 'What a waste of money.'

That was some consolation.

'Do you want us to go *visit* him?'

I couldn't help but chuckle at the sinister tone Craig used for the word 'visit'.

'Thanks, Granddad, but I'll be fine. I just need a little time.' And more wine. Why on earth was no one filling up my glass?

'It is a shame,' Mum said, 'but you've got to give him credit, thinking of his kids before himself. And perhaps it's a blessing in disguise?'

'What?' I shook my head in annoyance. 'How do you figure that?'

'Well, he already has children, and didn't you say he didn't want any more? So it was never going to be a long-term thing. Now you can find someone with less baggage.'

The irony was that Christos's 'baggage' had only made me like him more—his love and dedication to his kids had been very appealing. Yet now conflicting thoughts swirled in my head—if he loved me as well, couldn't he find a way to do right by all of us? And what kind of man slept with someone right before breaking up with them?

'You're not getting any younger, you know.'

'I'm very well aware of my age, thank you very much, Mother.'

I could say a lot more, but swallowed it all. Mum could never understand that I was pretty certain I didn't want children. Babies were cute, sure. I liked cuddling my niece and nephew, but I liked giving them back equally as much. I was thirty years old and so far hadn't even *heard* the ticking of my biological clock but had been more than willing to be a doting stepmother to Christos's offspring—I'd even read a couple of books on the topic. Gralice had annoyed Mum for years, urging her to pursue a career in addition to her homemaker duties, and she'd stayed true to herself. Why couldn't she accept my wishes and let me do the same?

I waited for Gralice to stick up for me, but she remained uncharacteristically quiet on the matter.

Rosa piped up instead. 'She doesn't need a man to have a baby.'

'Thank you.' I smiled, liking this woman more and more. 'But I don't need a baby either.'

'I can set you up with a friend of ours?' Will offered, looking to Sophie. 'Blaze?'

'Ooh, yes.' She nodded approvingly. 'He's very nice. Funny. And smart. Not bad-looking either, if you can get past his red hair.'

I wanted to scream! *Blaze?* He sounded like an American cowboy. I hadn't even been single five minutes and already my family were plotting my next move.

Finally, Gralice spoke, and what came out of her mouth was better than any defence I could have hoped for. 'Boyfriends aside, Ged, I've been thinking … Maybe it's finally time for me to let you write that book you've been badgering me about for years. You could start interviewing me for it while we're on the ship.'

It took a moment for me to realise what she'd actually said. Putting down my empty glass, my heart shaking a little, I said, 'Really?'

She nodded. 'If you seriously think anyone would be interested in reading about an old chook like me. I don't think anyone cares much about second-wave feminists these days—it's all about intersectional feminism.'

'Enough of the old chook, Gralice. Everyone will want a piece of this book.'

I sprung from my seat, rushed around the table and threw my arms around her. It felt like someone was shooting tiny arrows into my ankle, but I didn't care. My excitement and surprise overruled the physical pain, and maybe even eased a little bit of my agony over Christos. At least I'd have something else to focus on now.

She laughed and hugged me tightly. 'I guess that means you're coming?'

'Hell, yeah.'

Since I was fifteen I'd wanted to be a writer—not a novelist, although I do love a good whodunnit and have been known to sneak-read some of my mother's Mills & Boons, but please, do not mention the latter to Gralice. She thinks romance novels portray women as *needing* a man and are the work of the devil. When I was a teenager, Gralice fed me biographies and non-fiction articles of courageous women throughout history and, much to my mother's chagrin, I devoured them. My copies of *The Feminist Mystique*, *The Second Sex* and *A Room of One's Own* still have pride of place on my bookshelf, along with many other tattered classics.

I'd always dreamed of one day having a book of my own sitting on that shelf and I knew without a doubt what, or rather who, I wanted to write about.

You might be wondering what makes my grandmother a worthy subject for a book. Well, even if you haven't heard of my mother, you've probably heard of Gralice—or Alice Abbott, as those outside our family call her. But, for anyone living in a cave for the past fifty years, here's a quick rundown.

I'm not going to say too much or you might not read the biography, but after studying physics at university, Alice Abbott became a single mother and continued on to achieve not one, but two PhDs. All her adult life she's been a voice for woman, championing for equal rights and opportunities, especially for single mums. She also still has a long-running column in our national newspaper, in which she explains in layman's terms the physics of everyday items such as toasters, hotel room keycards and mobile telephones. Gralice is a bit of an academic celebrity and even these days is a sought-after speaker at conferences, but whenever I'd pestered her about writing her biography she'd always baulked.

Honestly, I could barely contain my excitement. Now I was looking forward to the weekend, rather than dreading it.

4

My foot still hurt the next morning, but thankfully not quite as badly. Some of the swelling had gone down overnight and, miraculously, my first thought was of the cruise and Gralice's biography, rather than Christos and his reckless treatment of my heart. I climbed out of bed, fed Coco, scoffed a bowl of muesli, showered and dressed. I'd packed a small suitcase last night and also gathered Coco's food and leash into a bag, so that by the time Dad arrived to collect us, we were waiting by the side of the road.

'Morning.' I leaned forward to kiss his cheek as he took my suitcase.

'Hullo, sweetheart.'

My dog and I climbed into the back seat so Gralice could take the front. Station Pier, the Melbourne cruise ship terminal, was at Waterfront Place, only a stone's throw from my parents' house, so once we'd collected Gralice from Fitzroy, Dad delivered us to the dock before going back to deposit Coco and collect Mum and her luggage.

'How much does she need for a three-night cruise?' Gralice tsked as we dragged our cases towards the terminal.

'Remember, she has a public appearance to uphold.'

We both laughed.

'How are you feeling this morning?'

'Well, I can walk, so that's a start. And I'm super excited about getting stuck in to our project.'

Gralice smiled distractedly and glanced at her watch.

The security terminal was already swimming with people, some of whom were dressed in Elvis and Priscilla costumes. Gralice looked around as if searching for someone, or maybe the costumes were giving her second thoughts.

'Mum won't be here yet.'

'What?' She shook her head as if confused. 'Oh yes, I know.'

I glanced through the terminal windows to the ship. 'I wonder which are our rooms,' I said, pointing out at the rows and rows of tiny portholes in an attempt to distract my grandmother from her impatience and irritation at my mother. She'd booked one room for each of us, probably because she and Mum were liable to kill each other if they were unable to escape occasionally.

'Could be any one of them. I got us balcony rooms, so we can look out to sea.'

'You've really splurged, haven't you?'

'Well, you can't take your money to heaven—not that I'm likely going there—so I thought we may as well enjoy it while I'm still here.'

'I'm sure you'll be here for many, many years yet,' I told her sternly. Aside from a little arthritis in her hands, she'd had no health problems to speak of and my guess was she'd live long enough to get her letter from the Queen (unless the Queen went first, which was highly likely considering she was over a decade older). 'But, since you're shouting the cruise, the coffees are on me.'

'Okay.' Gralice pointed to a few rows of plastic pews. 'I'll sit over there and mind the luggage while you get them.'

'Good idea.' I ordered three takeaways from a little coffee cart inside the terminal and was heading back to my grandmother when someone called my name. I turned to see Mum and her assistant hurrying towards me, dragging suitcases behind them.

'Hello, sweetheart.' Mum pulled me into a quick hug. 'Where's Gralice?'

'Over there.' I nodded to the waiting lounge, wondering what Rosa was doing here. She was wearing another fabulously bright kaftan and I didn't know how she wasn't freezing. Not only was it a nippy cold May morning, but the terminal's temperature felt arctic.

'It's lovely to see you again.' Rosa's smile filled her whole face. 'I hope you and Alice don't mind me crashing your little trip, but—'

'Rosa and I have a lot coming up in the next few months,' my mother interrupted, 'and I couldn't afford to lose four days' work, so I went online yesterday and booked another cabin before the bookings closed. I got a great last-minute price too.'

'I'm sorry, I would have got you a coffee if I'd known.'

'Don't be silly. I'll get a cocktail once we're on the boat.'

I grinned, liking her more and more. And, Rosa's presence could be beneficial as it meant Gralice and I might have more time alone to get stuck in to her biography.

We went over to my grandmother and I filled her in about Rosa's presence, trying not to smirk when I mentioned all the 'work' Mum couldn't afford to miss. Did she know how ironic that sounded coming from someone who professed to be a happy *housewife*?

'Well,' Gralice pushed herself to her feet, 'the more the merrier I guess,' but her tone and the expression on her face didn't quite match her words.

Coffees in hand, we joined the line of what seemed like thousands waiting to check in.

'You mentioned you'd been on a cruise before?' Gralice said to Rosa as we waited our turn.

'This will be my tenth, or is it eleventh? I can't get enough of them.'

'Who do you normally go with?' I asked.

'My ex-partner got me into them originally—we went on a few together—but when we broke up, I started cruising with friends.'

'Are you with anyone now?' I hoped I didn't sound rude; sometimes I had a habit of overstepping the line in conversation, forgetting I wasn't meant to be interviewing the person.

'Nope. Not at the moment, but I'm happy with my own company.'

Finally, we got to the front and a young, dark-haired guy gave us all plastic tags on lanyards. 'Wear these whenever you're out of your cabin.' He explained it was not only our room key but could also be used to charge any drinks or other purchases to our total bill. 'You're all set. Have fun.'

We progressed to security and deposited our handbags in little tubs so they could go through the screening machine. I put my laptop in a separate one.

One of the officers chuckled. 'Don't think you'll have much time for work this weekend.'

I smiled politely, planning to get plenty of work done over the next few days. It wasn't like I was interested in any of the themed parties I'd heard some people in the line raving about. No amount of fancy cocktails would be enough to get me singing Elvis karaoke.

Escaping security, we stepped out into the open air with the ship looming in front of us. Gazing up at its majestic size, I felt very, very small. Noting the many lifeboats suspended from the decks, an image of *Titanic* landed in my head, but knowing a little (thanks to my grandmother) about the physics of cruise ships, I quickly discarded it. Gralice led the way, striding onto the bridge—according to Rosa the correct term was 'gantry'—that led from the dock to the ship.

'Stop!' Mum yelled when we were halfway across. 'We need a photo for Instagram before we go any further.'

Somehow, I managed not to roll my eyes as she forced Gralice and me to 'cosy up' so Rosa could take the shot.

'We're holding up the traffic,' Gralice growled a few minutes later when a couple in their mid-thirties appeared at the edge of the gantry.

'Oh my God,' squealed the woman, rushing forward. 'Are you the Happy Happy Housewife? Can I get a selfie, please?'

I will never get used to people recognising my mother, never mind them fawning over her like she's some kind of pop star.

'Of course.' Mum beamed, almost shoving Gralice and me aside. 'What's your name, love?'

'Jayne, with a Y,' the woman added, as if that extra letter made all the difference. 'And this is my husband, Trent.'

'Pleased to meet you.' Trent blushed as he offered his hand.

'I just love what you do,' Jayne gushed. 'In fact, we owe you for saving our marriage. Things were pretty bad, but then, after watching some of your videos, I quit my job and am now loving life as a full-time homemaker. Trent, myself and our two little girls are so much happier for it.'

'That's wonderful.' Mum pressed a hand against her heart and looked as if she were about to cry.

Gralice coughed—obviously trying to cover a snort. I linked my elbow through hers and we continued up the gangplank, or whatever it was called.

I looked back in bemusement and clutched my grandmother's arm. 'Oh my God. Is she signing that woman's handbag?'

While I found this highly amusing, Gralice cursed and shook her head as if she had grave concerns for the state of the world. Thankfully, a few moments later, Mum and her groupies were forced to move along.

'Welcome, welcome aboard,' sang a man at the entrance to the ship.

'This is the atrium,' Rosa said as we emerged into an area that looked very similar to the grand lobby of the hotel where Christos and I had our last tryst. I'd thought he might seek me out at work yesterday, but he hadn't.

My heart twinged and, as I fought the lump of emotion that rose in my throat, I vowed to exorcise him from my mind; I would *not* let that bastard ruin this adventure.

Mum let out a whistle as she gazed around. 'This is impressive. Doesn't even feel like we're on a ship.'

The atrium stretched up four or five levels and everything was so damn shiny—it must have been someone's full-time job simply to keep all the golden balustrades gleaming. Already Elvis's voice drifted from hidden speakers, where I guessed all of his songs would be on repeat. Surely they couldn't play *only* Elvis?

Could I survive four days and three nights of the King?

Mum had played him on repeat on the stereo while I was growing up and you know what the best thing about moving out of home was? Leaving her Elvis obsession behind.

'Let's go find our cabins,' Gralice suggested, fingering her lanyard as she glanced down at the number on her plastic card.

Rosa led the way towards the elevators and we took one up a few levels, emerging into a much smaller foyer. Still ornately decorated with gold and polished wooden panelling, this area led off into two long corridors of cabins on either side. Ours were on the starboard side of the ship.

As we arrived, a steward introduced herself as Raquel. She had a lovely Spanish accent and told us she and her colleague Felix would be looking after us and our rooms for the duration of the cruise.

'Just find me if there's anything you need. Nothing will be too much trouble,' she finished with a swish of her long, dark ponytail.

Gralice thanked Raquel and then, her hand poised to insert her key card into the lock, said, 'Let's all settle in our rooms and meet for lunch in about an hour.'

My cabin was far lovelier than I'd imagined. There was a queen-sized bed, a TV, tea and coffee making facilities, and a bathroom with the tiniest shower I'd ever seen. I checked out the mini-bar (which, devoid of anything, was a bit of a let-down) and crossed to the glass doors that led out onto my own private balcony.

Cool air gushed at me as I stepped outside, so after a quick glance down at the people still boarding the ship, I retreated inside and began to unpack. I didn't bother with my clothes—I could happily live out of a suitcase for three nights—but took great care in unloading my laptop, notebooks and pens, and setting them up on the tiny desk. I imagined Gralice and I would do most of our interviews at various bars throughout the ship, but this was such a monumental project we were about to embark on, I wanted to be as professional and organised about it as I was about my day job.

Once the desk was to my liking, I went to grab my mobile from my handbag so I could take a photo for Instagram. Unlike Mum, I had only a small number of followers, but one of them was Christos and it would do him good to know I wasn't home alone pining after him.

That's if my phone wasn't currently back at my apartment, smashed into a thousand tiny pieces. *Bugger*. I'd ordered a new one online before I left and it should be waiting for me when I got back on Monday. Although I wasn't exactly happy about this forced digital detox, apparently we'd lose coverage out at sea anyway. And perhaps it was a good thing; at least I wouldn't be able to embarrass myself by sending drunken texts to my ex.

I picked up the TV remote and aimlessly scrolled through the channels, my mind boggling when I found two solely devoted to Elvis—one for his movies and one for his music. Mum would be in heaven, but finding nothing of interest to me and not wanting to be alone with my thoughts in my cabin, I decided on a walk around the ship instead.

I took the elevator down a couple of levels to Deck 5 where people were still boarding and slowly progressed upwards, checking out the restaurants, the many bars, boutiques, food courts, theatres, and even a casino on the middle levels.

'The pokies don't open until the ship sets sail,' said a stout man wearing a Hawaiian shirt and leaning against the wall next to the entrance as if he were counting down the hours.

'Good to know,' I replied and kept walking. One of the bars boasted not only incredible spirits but also special gin-making classes. Now perhaps *that* was something Gralice and I could do on a break between interviews.

By the time I neared the top of the ship, my ankle was making known its disgust at the exertion and I drifted towards the bow, where on Deck 12 there was apparently a day spa. Maybe I'd treat my poor foot to a long overdue pedicure. I passed the pool and made my way into the area that housed the beauty salon and day spa. Finding a queue at the reception desk I went a little further, peering into the fitness centre.

The ship hadn't even left port but there was one lone guy in there sweating it out on an exercise bike as if he hoped pedalling hard enough might take him someplace else.

With his buzz-cut ginger hair, stern expression, broad shoulders and larger than average biceps (not at all hidden by his tight white tee), he didn't look like anyone else I'd seen on board so far. I tried to imagine this guy in an Elvis costume and instead found myself thinking about what Sophie had said about redheads. Maybe she'd rethink her position if she saw this one. He wasn't good-looking in the tall, dark, handsome way Christos was, but he had a hard, kind of dangerous edge that appealed to something carnal inside of me.

The man cleared his throat and I realised he'd caught me gawking. He yanked one earbud out. 'Can I help you?'

'I was … I was …' Never usually lost for words. 'Just trying to work out what kind of person comes on holiday and heads straight for the gym?'

'Maybe the kind of person who didn't want to come on holiday,' he shot back without a moment's hesitation. 'Now, if you don't mind.' He nodded towards the door, shoved the bud back in his ear and resumed pedalling.

I was tempted to stand there and watch just to annoy him, or maybe to progress further into the gym and take to one of the machines myself. My foot injury aside, I might have done so if I didn't have a lunch date to get to. Without another word, I turned and walked away, keeping my head high.

The others had already found a table and by the time I arrived, Mum and Rosa were sipping cocktails.

'They look good,' I said as I took the seat beside my grandmother.

My mother giggled. 'They taste even better.'

'Do you want me to get you one?' asked Rosa.

I looked to Gralice. 'Are you having one?'

She shook her head. 'Too early for me, but you go ahead if you want.'

'I might hold off a little longer.' I wanted to have my wits about me when we started the interview. 'But I will get something to eat. You coming?'

Gralice nodded and pushed to a stand.

The food hall boasted an array of choice and we did the full circle of the perimeter before Gralice chose an Indian dish and I had good old-fashioned fish and chips. Their cocktails near empty, Mum and Rosa took their turn and returned a few minutes later with fresh cocktails and their meals.

'Do you all like your cabins?' Gralice asked as she picked at her lunch.

'I love mine,' I said. 'Everything is so compact. Have you seen the shower?'

'I know.' She chuckled. 'Lucky I'm shrinking in my old age.'

I bristled. What was with her sudden obsession with age?

'What does everyone want to do this afternoon?' Rosa asked, picking up a serviette and wiping a little hot sauce off her chin.

'There seems to be so much on offer I don't know where to start.' Mum glanced down at the information sheet on the table: today's ship news sheet, which informed about all the various shows, movies, tribute singers and other activities on board. 'So many parties, and what's the muster drill?'

'That's a safety briefing before the ship leaves port,' Rosa explained. 'There'll be an announcement over the loudspeaker and we'll need to fetch our life jackets and meet on the deck nearest to our cabins.'

'Does that mean you won't be with us?' Mum looked a little put out at the prospect of having to part ways with her assistant. Did she expect Rosa to carry her life jacket or ward off possible fans in want of selfies?

'It won't be for long,' Rosa reassured her. 'Afterwards we can grab another drink and sit out on one of the decks to watch as the ship leaves port.'

'Sounds lovely.' Mum leaned back in her seat and smiled like the cat that had the mouse between its teeth.

'Is that what most people do?' Gralice asked.

Rosa shrugged. 'Everyone's different. I suspect a lot of this crowd,' she gestured around us, 'will be hitting the pokies the moment they can.'

I thought of my guy in the Hawaiian shirt downstairs, wondered if he was still there waiting, and smiled. A quick look around showed that he wasn't the only one sporting a loud shirt. I guessed they were a tribute to Elvis's many beach movies. I was glad to see that the vast majority of people were plain-clothed like us, but there were a few others already getting in the tribute mood. Some of the women were wearing beautiful 1950s dresses.

'Elvis wasn't in *Grease*, was he?' At Gralice's question, I followed her gaze to see a group of women at another table dressed as the Pink Ladies from the iconic high school classic.

'No, but the girls in the movie were fans, remember?' I quietly broke out into 'Look at Me, I'm Sandra Dee'.

Gralice laughed. 'Good God, girl, don't quit your day job.'

'Not planning on it any time soon, unless I get a six-figure advance for your bio.' I winked, knowing this was unlikely and knowing that even if I was a billionaire, I'd still work. I loved everything about my job—interviewing people and investigating nitty-gritty topics sent my blood racing more than an upside down rollercoaster ever could. My job opened me up to new things and helped me make sense of the world. Writing my grandmother's biography would simply be an extension of this.

'Speaking of which,' I said, pushing my now empty plate aside. 'Did you want to get started on the interviews this afternoon? We could find a quiet place to get a drink and—'

'Let's see how I'm feeling after this muster thing,' Gralice interrupted. 'I might need a little nap. It's been quite a day.'

'Okay.' I tried not to frown. Did she look older all of a sudden? Sure, she'd just turned eighty, but I'd never known Gralice to take a siesta in her life. 'Are you okay?'

'What? Yes,' she said tersely. 'Why wouldn't I be? I'm allowed to have a rest if I want, aren't I?'

'Of course. You tell me when you're ready.' I turned to Rosa, not wanting to push things with Gralice. 'So how did you and Mum meet?'

'I was presenting an Instagram course and Marie was one of the attendees. She was so eager to learn and we hit it off instantly.'

'Have you been working in social media long?' This from Gralice.

Rosa rubbed her lips together as if in thought. 'About five years. As well as teaching the odd course, I'm a virtual assistant and have my own business helping people with their newsletters, websites, social media posts, that sort of thing.'

'So, Mum's not your only client?'

'Oh no,' Mum exclaimed, looking up from where she'd been tapping madly away on her phone while we still had good coverage. 'Rosa has a very full stable of clients. I'm lucky she squeezed me in.'

'I do have plenty of people on my books, but Marie is my most successful. In fact if her career kicks off the way it looks like it will, I might have to hire another employee and hand some of my other jobs onto my staff.'

Mum beamed. 'Rosa thinks we should launch a *Happy Happy Housewife* line of merchandise—tea towels, aprons, maybe even some T-shirts—to sell on my website.'

'Since when do you have a website?' I couldn't hold back my surprise.

'Since last week. Rosa helped me set it up.'

'That's wonderful,' Gralice said and asked them about statistics—downloads, page views, that kind of thing. Did she *know* what Mum's website was about?

Not long after, we were interrupted by a short siren, immediately followed by a request boomed from above that everyone report to muster.

As we scrambled up and joined the hordes of people heading to their cabins to collect their life jackets, a buzz of excitement shot through me. Soon the ship would set sail. I could leave all my man troubles behind as we cruised out to sea, and focus on Gralice's biography instead.

5

Following the muster, which had made me feel like a sardine squashed in a tin with a bunch of over-excited strangers, Gralice went off for her nap and Mum was eager to locate Rosa ASAP.

'We need to film a quick vlog before the ship heads out to sea and we lose coverage. Do you want to join us?' she asked me. 'My fans love when I have guest appearances. And afterwards we could go grab a cocktail.'

While the cocktail appealed, making a cameo on *The Happy Happy Housewife* did not. 'Thanks, but I think I'll go back to my room and work for a bit. Catch up later?'

'Sure, but ...' Mum cocked her head to one side. 'All work and no play makes Jill a very dull girl.'

'Lucky my name's not Jill then. And what exactly do you call what you're planning to do?'

She looked perplexed as if she'd forgotten her vlog was 'work', but then almost puffed up her chest and nodded. 'Touché. Come and find us for pre-dinner drinks later.'

I kissed her goodbye and hobbled back to my cabin. Putting my feet up for an hour or so was probably a good idea, but I found my room painfully quiet and cold. I turned on the in-room heater and picked up the remote, trying to find some sort of music channel that wasn't playing Elvis and would give me a little background noise. Stopping on some classical music station—hey, it was better than 'Jitterbug' and 'Blue Suede Shoes'—I made myself a coffee and sat down on the bed with my laptop and notebook.

The coffee was lovely and warming to my bones, and the small room filled with heat in a matter of moments. Snuggled under the blankets, I started to jot down questions for Gralice. I hadn't worked out yet whether the biography should be in chronological order, starting with her early years in the Melbourne suburb of Malvern, or whether I should begin with something monumental, like the protest where she was arrested or her decision to become a single working mum. There was so much I adored and admired about my grandmother, but there were also many years I knew little about. She rarely spoke about her childhood, and when she'd attended her brother's funeral when I was little, I remember being so surprised she had one.

I felt a little kick of excitement inside me at the thought that I might finally get some answers to the many questions that filled my head: *What were your parents like? Were you ever close to your brother? Was he your only sibling? Why did you leave home so young? What was it like being one of very few women studying science? Were there any significant romances?*

This last question made my heart ache as I thought of my significant romance. It still didn't feel real that Christos and I were actually over.

It wasn't until a tear dropped onto my notebook that I realised I was crying. *No!* I threw back the covers, climbed out of bed and snatched up a tissue from the box on the desk. I refused to waste any more tears on a mere man.

Wondering if Gralice would be awake yet, I shoved the notebook and my laptop into my bag, ventured out into the corridor and limped the few steps to her door, hoping my knocking wouldn't jolt her from slumber.

'Are you looking for Ms Abbott?' Raquel asked. 'She left about half an hour ago.'

I blinked. *Half an hour ago?* So much for taking a nap. 'I don't suppose she mentioned where she was going?'

'No, I'm sorry, but I can leave a note in her room for you for when she gets back if you like?

'Thanks, but I'll go look for her,' I said and started towards the elevators. How hard could it be to find someone on a ship?

Forty-five minutes later, my foot feeling as if it might fall off my leg at any moment, I had my answer. I'd been in every bar and eatery, every boutique, scanned the cinema, which was showing *Kissin' Cousins,* and even walked through a room containing an Elvis memorabilia collection. Mum would be in heaven—she had a much smaller shrine to the King at home—but neither she, Rosa nor Gralice were in sight.

Grumpy and frustrated, I found myself on the pool level. There were a bunch of tipsy adults in the spa but the actual pool was empty. Although a few of the many loungers surrounding it were occupied, everyone looked engrossed in books and I felt confident I could stake my claim on one, have a much-needed drink and maybe continue my notes without too much distraction.

I grabbed a glass of wine from the bar and took it to a lounger as far away from anyone as possible.

Perhaps ten minutes later, a shadow walked past me and I looked up from my laptop to see the guy from the gym dropping a towel on the lounger beside me. I sucked in a breath as he proceeded to rip his shirt over his head. Was he for real? I didn't know if the water was heated but the temperature surrounding it was certainly not. He couldn't seriously be going *swimming*. And why did he insist on dumping his things right next to me when there were at least twenty other vacant loungers?

Once again, he caught me gawking. 'We meet again.'

'Don't tell me you're going swimming.'

'That's usually what one does in a pool,' he said as if I was the crazy one for asking such a question.

Before I could think of a sarcastic response, he turned and swooped into the pool, droplets of water exploding out of it and all over me. My crankiness escalated to a whole other level as I wiped water off my keyboard.

Oblivious, he started churning through the water as if he was in training for the Olympics or something. The pool wasn't very long, so he only managed a few strokes with his longer-than-normal arms, before doing one of those fancy underwater summersault things and turning back the other way. I might not be an expert in all things swimming, but he was pretty good. Maybe he *was* in training for the Olympics.

Aside from watching the odd game of the Australian Open, I didn't pay much attention to the sports news. He could be a record holder, a gold medallist or number one in the world and I wouldn't recognise him. Christos would. Did I mention he's the editor for the sports pages?

Not that I wanted to think about him.

Shaking my head, I was about to down the last of my wine and leave when I decided that would mean the exercise junkie had got the better of me, so I turned my attention back to my notes.

After a while, I stumbled over to the bar for another glass of wine and then returned to the lounger. I raised my knees and rested the laptop on them so when appearing to glance at the screen, my eyes were also on the pool. I wasn't sure if it was the wine or the view, but I felt my grouchiness lessening with each lap he swam. When he eventually pushed his arms against the edge of the pool to heave himself out, I had to bite my lip to stifle my groan of disappointment. Saying that, the actual act of him climbing out was something to appreciate in itself.

Those arms! Those thighs! He almost made me want to buy some pencils and take up life drawing.

As he stood our eyes met and he swaggered over to me. He scooped up his towel and, despite the voices in my head telling me to look away, I couldn't.

'What kind of person works on a holiday?' he asked as he ran the towel over his head.

I gave him a dirty look—did he think he was funny?—and racked my brain for a witty answer. Too much time passed. His thick ginger eyebrows raised in anticipation. Ginger eyebrows should *not* be attractive, but somehow his defied the laws of nature. 'Who said I was working? Maybe I'm writing a holiday journal?'

'On a laptop?' He moved the towel lower, rubbing it quickly over his chest before wrapping it around his waist and plonking himself down on the lounger beside me.

'Yes, is there some law against that?'

'So what have you written so far? We've only been on board a few hours.'

It would really be much better if he were mute.

'I'm not telling you.' I snapped my laptop shut. 'It's private.'

'Fair enough.' He leaned back into the lounger and linked his hands behind his head as if settling in for the long haul.

'Aren't you cold?'

'Nope.'

I took another sip of my wine. 'Aren't you supposed to put a tracksuit or something on after exercise?'

He chuckled. 'You got a problem with my bare skin?'

I almost choked on my wine. 'No. Be cold if you want.'

'I'm not.'

Silence lingered between us a few long moments. I thought about getting up and leaving but again, I didn't want him to think he'd won. For some reason, it felt like we were in a competition.

'So ... what's a pretty girl like you doing all alone on a cruise ship?' he asked eventually.

Was he *hitting* on me? 'What makes you think I'm alone?'

'Because I've seen you twice today and both times you haven't been with anyone. You also seem on edge, kinda depressed. I haven't seen you smile once.'

Now that was the pot calling the kettle black. 'Do you always say exactly what's on your mind?'

'Yep. I wasn't put on this earth to pretty up the truth for others.'

'Really?' I couldn't help but smirk. 'So what exactly were you put on this earth for? To irritate people like me?'

I think he almost smiled. 'No. That's just an added bonus. What's your name anyway?'

I contemplated not telling him but decided I was too old to be petty. 'Geraldine.' Only friends and family had the privilege of calling me Ged. 'You?'

'Jay.'

'Short and sweet,' I said, thinking the name did not at all matcheth the man.

'So if you're not alone, who are you with?'

'My grandmother, my mother and her assistant, to celebrate my grandmother's eightieth birthday.'

'So why aren't you?'

'Why aren't I what?' It was very distracting maintaining a conversation while he was half-naked beside me.

'Celebrating?' He nodded towards my now empty wineglass. 'Unless your family has a weird tradition of drinking alone for special birthdays.'

'Ha ha. You must be one of the ship's resident comedians. I was supposed to meet them for a drink, but I can't find them. They're probably somewhere listening to some guy masquerading as Elvis.'

His lips twisted upwards—definitely a smile this time—and he was even more attractive when they did. 'You're not a fan?'

'Not really. You?'

He laughed as if this were the funniest thing he'd ever heard. It looked like I may have found the only other non-Elvis fan on the whole ship aside from Gralice.

'I guess not then,' I said. 'So what brings you onto an Elvis Tribute cruise *alone*?'

'What makes you think *I'm* alone?'

It was my turn to laugh. This conversation was like déjà vu. 'Let's see. I've seen you twice today and both times you haven't been with anyone.'

'I happen to be on board with my grandparents as well. And my whole damn family. Granddad's a super Elvis fan and so he shouted the whole family to a cruise to celebrate their fifty-fifth wedding anniversary.'

'Wow—fifty-five years. Impressive.'

'They're going to renew their vows on Sunday.'

'Aw, that's so sweet.' Christos and I hadn't even made it to our first anniversary.

Jay snorted.

'You don't think it's sweet?'

'I think it shows stamina or stubbornness or stupidity. Why anyone would stay with one person for that long is beyond me.'

'Maybe because of love?'

He snorted again as if he didn't believe in the concept.

'Aren't you a bundle of joy?'

'Nope. I'm just a realist. Relationships fuck you up. Ones that last are few and far between, and half of those are between unhappy people who are too scared or lazy to break up.'

I wanted to object but in my current emotional state I had to concede that maybe he was right. Maybe aspiring to Happily Ever After was akin to chasing the pot of gold at the end of the rainbow.

'If you're so scathing of their marriage, why come on the cruise?'

'Because they wanted me to,' he said simply, nodding towards my empty glass. 'Can I buy you another drink?'

Despite his cynical attitude, I was enjoying his company and since we'd been talking I'd only thought of Christos once. But I was already two rather large glasses of wine down—another one and who knew what I'd think was a good idea. Besides, I hadn't come on this cruise to get drunk with some stranger, no matter how attractive said stranger might be.

'Thanks, but I think I'd better go find my mum and grandmother.'

'No worries.' Jay shrugged, then picked up his things. 'I might see you round.'

And, as he swaggered off, I wasn't sure whether I hoped he would or not.

6

I didn't find the others until just before dinner, or rather Gralice found me. A knock sounded on my door and I stumbled from the bed where I'd been watching *GI Blues* (don't judge me, it wasn't as bad as I thought) to answer it.

My grandmother stood there, wearing her faithful leather pants, a crimson silk shirt and a smart black blazer.

'Where the hell have you been?'

'And it's lovely to see you too,' she said, pecking me on the cheek. 'I had my nap, then went and watched your mother do a video.' Her lips curved into a bit of a smirk. 'We came looking for you but you weren't here, so we checked out the Elvis display, before parking ourselves in a bar. Your mother and Rosa are still there.'

'I looked all over the place.'

'Well, you can't have looked everywhere. Anyway, I've found you now and I'm famished. Are you ready?'

'Should I get changed?' I was still wearing my skinny jeans and oversized jumper.

Gralice looked me up and down. 'Maybe put something fresh on up top.' She stepped inside, closed the door and sat on the bed. 'So what did you get up to this arvo?' she asked as I scavenged in my suitcase.

'I spent some time by the pool, writing down some questions for our interviews.'

'Don't work too hard. This is supposed to be a holiday, remember?'

Unbidden, an image of Jay landed in my head.

'Writing your biography won't feel like work-work, but I do need to finish an article for Darren too. It was good of him to give me the time off at such short notice and I can't afford to rest on my laurels if I want that promotion.'

'If?' Gralice raised an eyebrow.

I smiled. 'You're right, there's no *if* about it.'

'That's my girl. Now,' she nodded towards my suitcase, 'what are you going to wear?'

I tugged my jumper over my head and replaced it with a black, slightly see-through blouse.

'You look lovely,' Gralice said as I upgraded my make-up from day to night, finishing with a bright orange lipstick that matched the flowers on my blouse.

'Where are we having dinner?' I asked, grabbing my faithful denim jacket as we headed for the elevators.

'We're meeting the others at the waterfront restaurant. They have table service, which will be easier on your foot.'

As we navigated around the other guests also making their way to various dinner spots, Gralice warned, 'Rosa has been plying your mother with alcohol all afternoon and they're both quite sloshed.'

'Really?' I couldn't recall Mum ever being drunk before, only slightly tipsy after a glass of champagne at Christmas. Usually she was too busy cooking, cleaning and taking care of everyone to drink.

'Yes, I'm not sure whether Rosa is a good influence or a bad one, but it's nice to see your mother loosening up a little.'

Mum was so loose that the moment we entered the restaurant she stood up and started frantically waving us over to their table by the window. 'Yoo-hoo!' It was dark now and the coastline was no longer in sight, but there was a small strip of choppy ocean surrounding us that was visible due to the ship's lights.

'Shed, *darling*!' Mum threw her arms around me. 'You must try one of these de-lush-us cocks.'

I raised an eyebrow as I extricated myself and glanced down at her fluoro blue drink. 'Maybe *you* should have something to eat,' I said, and nodded hello at Rosa as I slipped into one of the vacant chairs.

She gave me a sheepish grin. 'Evening, Ged.'

Both Rosa and Mum were a sight to behold wearing matching mini-dresses, gold sparkly jackets, fishnet stockings and dark, gold-rimmed sunglasses perched atop their heads. The phrase 'mutton dressed as lamb' popped into my head but I chastised myself for it. Who was I to make judgements on what women could wear at certain ages?

'Where'd you get the costumes?' I asked with a smile.

'Don't we look gor-jus?' Mum ran her hand over the shimmery black fabric and wiggled her eyebrows at me.

'We bought them in the boutique,' offered Rosa. 'We thought we'd hit the *Viva Las Vegas* party later.'

'Yes.' Mum glared at Gralice. 'They were expen— expen—' She couldn't seem to recall the full word. 'Pricey. We could have organised cheaper ones if you'd given us more warning about coming.'

'Mum! It wouldn't have been such a lovely surprise if she'd given you warning.'

'I told you I was happy to pay for your costumes and anything else you want to buy on the ship,' Gralice said.

'Yes, that was very generous of you.' Rosa smiled at my grandmother and then looked to me. 'Anyway, Ged, did you have a nice afternoon?'

I was grateful to her for trying to smooth things over—usually it was down to me to calm the storms between Mum and Gralice. 'It wasn't too bad.'

Before I could elaborate, a friendly waiter—who introduced himself as 'Oleg' and had a strong Russian accent—arrived and asked if he could tempt Gralice or me with a drink. We ordered a glass of pinot gris each and Oleg ran through the evening specials before giving us time to peruse the rest of the menu.

'Is anyone having an entree?' I asked.

'I don't think so, I'm not that hungry,' Gralice replied.

I frowned. Only fifteen minutes ago, she'd told me she was starving.

'Why don't we skip the entrée and go straight to mains, that way we'll have room for dessert?' Rosa suggested.

Mum nodded, her lips wrapped around the straw of her drink.

'I like your thinking,' I said. 'I'm torn between the soy and sugar glazed trout and the three cheese ravioli.'

Gralice looked to me. 'Why don't you get the ravioli and I'll get the fish and you can try a bit of both?'

'Good plan,' I said, laying my menu on the table.

Oleg reappeared with our glasses of wine. 'Are you lovely ladies ready to order?'

'Yes, please.'

We gave him our choices and he nodded his approval.

'So, Alice, Ged,' Rosa said as Oleg disappeared once again, 'I'm so excited for this opportunity to get to know you both. I want to know everything about you. Leave no stone unturned.'

Gralice and I exchanged a bemused look.

'You're a journalist, aren't you, Ged?'

'Yes, I work in features for the weekend lift-out magazine and I love it. My boss is retiring soon and I'm hoping I'm in with a chance of being promoted to editor.'

'Marie said you were a hard worker. She's very proud of you.'

'Really?' I looked at Mum, unable to keep the surprise out of my voice. She rarely paid any interest in what I was writing because she was usually harping on at me about settling down.

'Well, of course I am,' Mum said, picking up a slice of sourdough bread.

'Did you always want to be a journalist?'

I nodded. 'I've always loved words.'

'That's true,' Mum agreed. 'She always had her head in a book as a child—even preferred books to TV.'

'And I also like people. They fascinate me, in the way the world and how it works fascinated Gralice.'

While my grandmother smiled, Mum snorted. 'Poor Alice, she desperately wanted someone to follow in her scientific footsteps, but Geraldine chose words instead, Will became a sports teacher, and I may have studied science but it wasn't the type you wanted, was it, Mum?'

Gralice twisted her wineglass between her fingers. 'None of you are a disappointment. I only ever wanted you to be happy, to do something you're passionate about. I'm proud of how Ged's progressed in her career.'

'Yet, you were never proud of me? Were you?'

Oh boy. This conversation was rapidly disintegrating into an episode of *Jerry Springer*.

I took a big gulp of my drink but thankfully Oleg chose that moment to return with our meals and a basket of warm bread.

'Aren't you clever being able to carry all that.' Rosa grinned up at Oleg, and I wasn't sure if she was as impressed as she sounded or just overjoyed to have a distraction.

He beamed. 'Why, thank you. I hope you all enjoy your meals.'

Immediately, I picked up my fork and popped a piece of ravioli in my mouth. 'Ooh, wow, this is delicious.'

The others took my lead and dug in, while I racked my brain for something banal to talk about. When Mum and Gralice were together there wasn't any topic that couldn't turn bitter in an instant.

'How's the trout?' I asked Gralice, but my words were lost as a child's ear-piercing scream stole my and everyone else's attention.

Our eyes snapped to the source, which appeared to be a small boy being dragged by his arm by a woman—who I hoped was his mother—to the corner of the restaurant where a massive group were being seated.

'I wanna stay in the kids club,' the boy wailed, but I barely heard him as I noticed one head that stood taller than everyone else in the party. My insides squeezed as just at that moment Jay surveyed the restaurant and our eyes met. He hit me with a lazy smile as he lifted a hand and waved.

Mum caught me staring. 'Do you know someone over there?'

I gulped and turned my attention back to my dinner companions. 'Not really. I met the tall guy by the pool this afternoon. We chatted briefly.'

They all stared mortifyingly in Jay's direction.

Rosa winked at me. 'He's quite dishy, if you like that kind of thing.'

Not quite the word I'd have used, but still.

'Really? I hadn't noticed.' I feigned nonchalance, all the while feeling my cheeks heat, calling me out as a liar.

'Did you talk for long?' Mum interrogated. 'What does he do? Who's he on board with?'

I could see where she was going with this. 'He's here with his family, celebrating a wedding anniversary.'

She sighed. 'Never mind, plenty more fish in the sea, or rather on board.'

Annoyed, I looked to Gralice to roll my eyes but she didn't see. She was still fixated on the corner where Jay and his family were now sitting.

'Earth to Gralice.' I waved my hand in front of her eyes and she blinked out of her trance.

'What is it?'

'Do *you* know someone over there?' I asked, following her gaze to where Jay and his family were sitting.

Of course he chose that moment to look up again and catch me in the act.

'No. I thought I recognised someone, but ...' Gralice shook her head but sank a little lower in her seat. 'When you get to my age, everyone starts to look familiar.'

'Would you stop going on about how old you are?'

'I'm eighty, Ged, there's no point pretending I'm a spring chicken.'

'Fine.' I didn't want to start an argument. 'What were we talking about again?'

'About how disappointed your grandmother is in her daughter,' Mum said, downing the last of her drink and stabbing her fork into her pork.

Oh, that's right. I turned to Rosa, thinking it would be much safer to talk more about her. 'Do you have any children?'

She shook her head as she finished her mouthful. 'No. Thought about going it alone a couple of times but never got further than the thinking stage.' She looked to Gralice. 'It must have been a very brave decision to have a child by yourself in the sixties.'

'But Gralice wasn't alone,' I said, smiling. 'She had Phil.'

Rosa nodded. 'True. Some would say that was an even bolder move. Was your family supportive?'

'I didn't really care what my family thought by that stage.'

'Mum's never cared what anyone thought about anything,' said my mother.

Gralice ignored that. 'I'd already been living away from them for many years but our relationship was strained to say the least. I caught up with my mother every couple of months but barely spoke to my father. Me having a child out of wedlock was the last straw. They both washed their hands of me, embarrassed by how my bastard child would make them look.'

Mum visibly flinched, and I made a mental note to get Gralice to talk more about this in our interviews.

Rosa noticed and smiled. 'You were obviously a very wanted child.'

'Maybe ... or maybe Mum simply liked the shock value of having a baby with a gay man.'

'I assure you, Sappho,' Gralice said, her tone controlled, 'that *wasn't* the reason.'

'What was the reason then? Because you seemed way more interested in your work and fighting for all your causes than you ever were in me.'

'That's not true. Once you came along, everything I did was because of you. I worked to support us—to keep a roof over our heads, to put food in your mouth, and to show you what women can achieve if they put their minds to it. But you also taught me so much and opened my eyes up to other problems with society. If it wasn't for you, sure, I'd still have pushed for less discrimination and better rights for women at work, but I might never have seen the desperate need for things like federally funded daycare for working mothers or the single mother's benefit.'

'But you had Dad helping you financially,' Mum said. 'So it wasn't like *you* really needed those things.'

Gralice hesitated a moment. 'Yes, Phil, and later Craig, were both very generous when it came to looking after your needs, but we were in the minority. Most single mums at the time had it much tougher and I couldn't stand by and do nothing. I'm proud of the part I played in these milestones for women and I'm also proud of everything I've achieved in my career. I'm sorry if you felt neglected because of these things but none of them were ever as important as you.'

My heart squeezed at her words, but Mum didn't appear to be affected. In fact she was wearing the glazed expression she adopted whenever Gralice's achievements came up.

I opened my mouth to give her what for, but my grandmother caught my eye and almost invisibly shook her head, so I focused back on my ravioli.

Once again Rosa attempted conversation, but this time steered clear of all things personal by instead starting a game of people watching. She'd pick a person, couple or group at one of the tables surrounding us and ask us what we thought their story was. It was just my kind of game, and also managed to succeed in dissipating the tension—even Mum and Gralice were laughing at each other's suggestions.

'I reckon those two are on a dirty weekend away from the kids,' Rosa whispered as a couple in their late thirties or early forties walked past our table. His cheek was smeared with pink lipstick and he had his arm wrapped so tightly around her it was hard to tell where he ended and she began.

'What about them?' I pointed discreetly to a table a few feet away that held about ten women, all dressed as Vegas showgirls.

Gralice made a clicking noise with her tongue. 'Mothers' group. Kids all teenagers now though and they're letting their hair down.'

Somehow as we chatted, I managed to devour my pasta and half of Gralice's trout. For someone who'd proclaimed to be starving, she'd barely eaten three mouthfuls.

'Are you not feeling well?' I asked during a lull in the game.

She grimaced and put a hand on her stomach. 'I think I might be a little seasick.'

'Me too,' Mum announced, and she did look a little green.

Rosa and I both reached for her glass of water but Gralice got there first. 'Drink this.'

'Thanks, Mum.' My mother actually smiled at her as she took the glass.

Oleg arrived not long after to tempt us with dessert but we all agreed we were stuffed and a change of scenery would be a better idea.

'As you know we're off to the *Viva Las Vegas* party later, but I'd like to watch the Elvis show in the theatre first,' Mum said as we left the restaurant. 'Do you two want to join us?'

I looked to Gralice. 'Maybe we should find a quiet spot and get started on your interview?'

'I'm too tired for that tonight.' She smiled apologetically. 'And we probably should see at least some of the shows.'

My heart sank, but it was clear Gralice had made up her mind. I thought I'd better go along just in case World War Three kicked off between her and Mum again.

'My shout. What's everyone drinking?' Gralice asked when we'd found red velvet seats in the dimly lit theatre.

I decided to take a leaf out of Mum and Rosa's book. 'I'll have the first cocktail on the menu, please.'

As Rosa went to help Gralice with the drinks, Mum lowered herself into the chair opposite, tugging on the hem of her dress so as not to flash her knickers. Dad would have a stroke if he saw her dressed like that; she was probably showing more skin than he'd seen in years.

'What's so funny?'

'Nothing.' I shook my head, contemplated talking to her about what Gralice had said earlier but then decided to leave it for now. 'So how are you enjoying yourself so far?'

'Ooh, it's fantastic. We've met so many interesting people. And when a fan spotted me in the bar this afternoon, someone from the ship overheard, and now I'm going to participate in the Elvis cooking show tomorrow afternoon.'

'The Elvis cooking show?' Now I'd heard it all. 'When did the King have time to cook?'

The others returned with our drinks before she could reply. I popped the hot-pink straw between my lips and sucked up a few mouthfuls of the lime-green drink Gralice had given me. If I could slurp these while some Elvis tribute singer did his thing, perhaps I'd even enjoy it.

Before long, the lights dimmed even more, the show began and it was as torturous as I'd imagined. As I sipped my cocktail, my mind drifted. Christos landed in my head and his absence evoked a painful pang in my heart. I thought about what we'd be doing if we were on this cruise together. Yes, there might be a few cocktails, and maybe we'd even attend the odd tribute show for a bit of a laugh, but we'd also spend a lot of time in our cabin.

Together less than a year, we were (or had been) still at that can't-get-enough-of-each-other stage. I wasn't naïve enough to think that would last forever, instead I'd actually been looking forward to the next stage of our relationship—where the sex might not have been as frequent but we'd be comfortable and happy hanging out, talking, even doing the mundane tasks of everyday life like washing up and arguing whose turn it was to put the bin out.

It might seem weird to be fantasising about such things but I was ready to be irritated by the things that I had, in the beginning, found endearing.

'Are you okay?' Rosa whispered.

I realised a tear had snuck down my cheek. 'Yes. Just got something in my eye.' I swiped at the tear, embarrassed Mum's assistant had caught me so maudlin and vowing not to let my thoughts wander to my ex-boyfriend again.

A little while later, there was an interval and everyone took the chance to grab more drinks. Mum and I were returning to our table when my gaze caught on something, or rather someone.

Jay was talking to a woman with hair almost as red as his. I recognised her as the woman with the child earlier. I looked away quickly and tried to concentrate on the conversation between the others.

Only after the lights had dimmed once more and the performer was enthusiastically belting out 'Suspicious Minds' did I allow myself to sneak another glance his way.

This time I found him already looking at me. He made a face that told me exactly what he thought. I grinned and turned back to watch. When after another five minutes or so some of the people around us started to join in with the tunes, I looked over again. He mimed holding a gun to his head and I spat out the mouthful I'd just taken, which made him laugh and Mum give me a stern look across the table.

'Sorry,' I mouthed, reaching for a serviette to soak up my mess.

The next time I looked (which I'll be honest was only mere moments later), Jay wrapped his hand around an imaginary glass and lifted it to his lips, then nodded towards the exit.

I leaned in and whispered to Gralice. 'I think I'm gonna call it a night. I'm stuffed.' I added a yawn for good measure, blew kisses to Mum and Rosa, and made my escape.

7

'Any longer in there and I was gonna throw myself off the edge of the ship,' Jay said as I met him outside the entrance of the theatre.

I snorted despite myself but I could so relate. 'Tell me about it. What kind of fresh hell is this?'

'Anyway, you want to get that drink now?'

'Yes, will we be able to find an Elvis-free zone?'

'Did you bring your bathers?'

I wasn't sure I still owned bathers—my body hadn't seen a beach or a pool for a very long time. 'No. And you're not suggesting we—'

'What does your underwear look like?'

'*Excuse* me?' I swear I turned from pale to hot pink in a matter of seconds.

He grinned wickedly. 'Relax, I wasn't suggesting anything untoward, but there's an adults-only spa and bar at the top of the ship and I'm pretty sure there's no Elvis tribute singer up there. If you don't have bathers, you might be able to get away with wearing your underwear.'

This discussion of my underwear with a man I'd met mere hours ago was both uncomfortable and electrifying. But even if the water was heated, and even if I did have matching bra and knickers, I wasn't about to unclothe in front of Jay.

'Look,' I said, recovering, 'who cares about Elvis? Let's find the nearest bar and get pissed.'

'I like your style.' He turned and started off towards midship. After about twenty seconds it became clear I couldn't keep up with his giant strides. 'What d'you do to your foot?'

I contemplated telling him I'd hurt it while playing some kind of sport—this seemed far less mortifying than the truth—but I'd never been much of a liar. 'I fell after fleeing a hotel room where my boyfriend told me he was getting back together with his ex-wife.'

Jay's lovely sea-green eyes widened and he winced. 'Youch.'

I nodded. 'Not the best day of my life.'

'Sounds like you need this drink. What do you reckon about this place?' He slowed his steps and nodded to the entrance of the bar where I'd found Mum and Rosa earlier that day.

'Perfect.'

We found a comfy sofa by one of the windows.

'You sit, first round's on me,' Jay said. 'What do you want?'

'Second cocktail on the menu, please.'

As he went off to the bar, I rested my foot on the little table in front and prayed our easy banter would continue. To be honest, I wasn't sure what this was, but I knew that right now I wanted to be with him more than I wanted to be sitting in an Elvis show.

He returned with a bright pink cocktail with a yellow umbrella for me and a glass tumbler of something dark for himself.

'Cheers.' He handed me my drink and lowered himself onto the sofa beside me. I couldn't help but notice his hands were so different to Christos's. His were the smooth, unmarked hands of someone who works indoors, whereas Jay's were tanned and weathered as if they were worked hard on a regular basis.

I went to take a sip of my cocktail and realised there was no straw.

'What's wrong?' he said, noticing my frown.

'They didn't give me a straw.'

'I told them not to. They only had plastic ones, which I'm sure you'll agree are a luxury we should all do without.'

His tone dared me to object and, if it wouldn't have made me sound like a bimbo who didn't care about the environment, I would have. I did care about the environment—I always remembered my reusable bags when I went shopping—but I also liked sipping cocktails through a straw and I didn't like being told what to do by a guy. Slightly peeved, I lifted my glass to my mouth and drank.

'So, Geraldine,' Jay said, after taking a mouthful of his own drink, 'when you're not cruising the seas in honour of Elvis, what do you do?'

'I'm a senior features writer—most of my stories appear in the weekend magazine.'

'A journalist?' Jay's expression was slightly scathing.

'Why? What do you do?' I asked, accusation in my tone.

'I'm a cop.'

Ah, that explained it. Cops and journos were rarely BFFs.

I didn't know any policemen, although I'd dealt with a few in my job and most of them seemed to be one of two types—the kind who cared about people and wanted to make the world a safer place, or those who thought they were better than everyone else and liked the way control and power made them feel.

Something told me maybe Jay was the latter.

'What kind of cop?'

'The kind that keeps the bad guys off the street.'

In other words, either a run-of-the-mill constable or someone who worked for some special agency where he wasn't supposed to talk about what he did. I didn't do well with secrets, but I also didn't like his tone, which seemed to imply what he did was more important than what I did.

'Don't forget that often you crime fighters need us newshounds in order to nab a final clue or vital piece of information. You're always so quick to say a bad word about us but who do you call on when you need to get word out to the masses?'

Jay held up his hands. 'Hey. Point taken. Let's not get into an argument this early in our relationship.'

'I didn't think you did relationships.'

'I don't. It was a figure of speech.' He stretched his arm along the back of the couch and hit me with a slow smile. 'So, Geraldine, tell me something interesting about yourself?'

I blinked. Usually I was the one asking such direct questions. 'Well ...' I stared into my drink, unable to think of one single thing that didn't involve Christos or work. Then it suddenly hit me. 'My grandmother was appointed an Order of Australia a couple of years ago. You may have heard of her—Alice Abbott?'

Recognition dawned in his eyes. 'The feminist?' he said as if there was only one. 'Wasn't she the one that set up camp in the male bathrooms and chained herself to the urinal at Melbourne University when she was passed over for a job or something?'

'That's the one.'

Gralice's protest led to the male applicant—who had much less experience than her—being stood down and her being appointed associate professor in her early thirties. But it also made her women's lib royalty, along with the likes of Merle Thornton and Rosalie Bogner, who had chained themselves to the bar of the Regatta Hotel in Brisbane. I was impressed Jay actually knew about this and, unlike my mother, super proud of everything my grandmother had achieved for women.

'She's a lot more than just a feminist. The Order of Australia was for her work in science, all she's done in making physics accessible to everyday folk. I'm actually about to start writing her biography.'

'Was that what you were doing by the pool this arvo then?'

'Yes, I was brainstorming questions to ask her. We're starting the interview process this weekend.'

'I'm sure she's a fascinating woman ...' Jay looked right into my eyes as he spoke. 'But I asked you to tell me something about *you*.'

The intensity of his gaze made me feel like I was the only person in the room. Thoughts of my cyber-famous mother, my two gay grandfathers, my adorable niece and nephew came into my head, but I didn't think he'd rate them either. Why hadn't I ever taken up some kind of hobby? Stamp-collecting? Crochet? Sky-diving ... I shuddered at the thought.

'I have a dog,' I blurted. 'Coco, after Coco Chanel. She's a groodle and so adorable. I love taking her for long walks.'

'Who's looking after Coco this weekend?'

'My dad. Although I think it's probably more a case of her taking care of him. Do you have a pet?'

'Nope. Don't see the point.'

'The *point*?' I wasn't sure whether to laugh or feel sorry for him. 'Well, quite aside from the companionship, science has proven that having a pet is good for your health.'

He raised one eyebrow and downed the rest of his drink.

'A study in the US ...' Damn, I wished I could remember the name of the university; I'd written a whole article about this in my women's magazine days. 'It found that people who lived with at least one animal experienced less stress than those without. They had lower blood pressure, they were better able to cope with grief, the researchers even found pets could prevent strokes and lower cholesterol.'

'Okay, okay.' He was smiling now. 'But they're so tying. What if you want to travel? And they're expensive. My sister's cat has to have dialysis and it's nearly sending her broke.'

'Maybe your sister knows there are more important things in life than money.'

'Maybe.' His tone was both aggravating and strangely alluring. 'Anyway, do you want another drink?' He nodded towards my glass, which was almost empty. These cocktails went down far too easily.

'It's my shout,' I said, removing my foot from the table ready to stand. It would be good to put some distance between us for a few minutes. 'What are you having?'

'Bourbon on the rocks. Do you want me to get them cos of your foot?'

I thought a moment ... Did I trust him with my room card?

My ankle throbbed in response, so I ripped my lanyard over my head and flopped back down as I handed it to him. I watched as he sauntered to the bar and engaged in a brief conversation with the barman, which gave me the perfect view of his behind. He was wearing faded jeans that fit like a second skin and I couldn't help but feel a little affected by the sight. The more time I spent with him, the more he reminded me of someone—looks, not personality—but I couldn't put a finger on who.

To be honest, I wasn't sure whether I liked him or not. I liked the fact he was keeping my mind off other things and we'd bonded over our shared aversion to the King, but I was beginning to wonder if this was the only thing we had in common.

'I've got it,' I cried as he sat down and handed me another cocktail—this time a sunny yellow one with a large piece of pineapple perched on the rim of the glass. It tasted so good I no longer cared about the straw, or lack thereof.

'Got what?'

'You look like Michael Fassbender!' I felt smug I'd finally worked it out.

'Who?'

I rolled my eyes, men were always hopeless with celebrities—with the exception of Jennifer Aniston (what was it they saw in her?) and Angelina Jolie, thanks to *Tomb Raider*. 'He's an actor.'

'Right.' Jay downed half his drink in one gulp. 'Is that a compliment? Do you think this Michael dude is hot?'

My stomach flipped. Was he fishing?

'Not really,' I lied. 'He's no Liam Hemsworth. Anyway, we've talked about me. It's your turn. And you should know that going to the gym or any kind of physical exertion doesn't interest me at all.'

'*Any* kind of physical exertion?'

It did not take a genius to work out what he meant and I couldn't help but smile as I felt my cheeks colour slightly.

'Are you stalling? Surely you can think of *something* to impress me.'

'I'm not sure it'll impress you, but I've just had an interview for Mars Mission. The whole application process has been all-consuming, so with that and work, I haven't had time for much else lately.'

I don't know what I'd been expecting him to say but that was probably the absolute last thing. I thought maybe I'd misheard over the band that had set up in the corner or that three cocktails in rapid succession had gone to my head.

'Did you say you've applied to go on *Mars Mission*? As in, the one-way mission to establish human settlement on the red planet?'

He nodded as if I'd asked him if he took sugar with his coffee, but I sat up straighter, almost spilling my drink and knocking my foot—ouch—against the table in the process.

Jay lifted my leg and swung my foot up to rest in his lap. I put my cocktail down on the table, needing my full wits about me as I tried to ignore his touch and focus on the conversation. 'Please explain?'

His replying chuckle went through me again, leaving heat in its wake. 'What do you want to know?'

'Um, the first question would be why? Actually, no, the first question is what do you mean an *interview*? How far into this process are you?'

'I made it through round one, which was an online application and a video where I had to answer some questions and explain why I thought I was suitable. Round two was a medical and an interview.'

'Who was the interview with?' My stomach clenched into a tight knot. No question he'd have passed the medical with flying colours.

'Mars Mission's chief medical officer. I'm still waiting to find out if I'm lucky enough to make round three. Only one hundred applicants will get through.'

Lucky? 'Why on earth would you want to do something like that?'

'Why not?'

'Because it's a one-way trip!' Our paper had done an article about it a few years ago when it was only a twinkle in the organisers' eye. Initially we'd all assumed it was some kind of joke, or worse, a scam. 'That's if you make it all the way. If you get selected, you'll never return to earth, never see your family again. What if you change your mind when you get there?'

I felt claustrophobic simply at the thought.

'That'll be tough luck,' he said. 'Is this shoe making your foot worse?'

'Huh?' Why were we talking about shoes at a time like this?

In reply, he unzipped my ankle boot and slipped it slowly off my foot. I shivered as he ran his thumb over the arch and gently began to massage. For someone who looked and acted so tough, Jay's touch was pure tenderness.

'Are you insane?' I reached for my cocktail again as I tried to regulate my breathing. 'What makes you want to do something so bat-shit crazy?'

He laughed. 'Since I was a little kid I've been fascinated by space and its infinite possibilities. I can't think of anything more exciting than possibly being involved in the settlement of a whole new planet. Besides, it's not really any different from going to live in another country.'

'Except you can't just hop on a plane to come back and visit.'

'No. But I'll still be able to communicate with earthlings through email and video messaging. Apparently we'll even have the internet.'

'Really?' Technology never failed to astound me.

'Ah-huh.' He nodded and went on to explain a little more about the whole mission.

The trip would take between six to eight months, depending on when it occurred, and those on board would only be able to eat freeze-dried or packaged food. There were over 200,000 people as crazy as Jay who had applied for the mission. There were no showers on board, but astronauts would be given wet towelettes for hygiene. Exercise would be rigorous for three hours a day during the journey to preserve muscle mass.

That there was one more reason why I would never volunteer.

'So, do I pass the interesting test?' Jay asked when he'd finally finished telling me everything.

'I'm still making up my mind.'

This seemed to amuse him. 'Shall I get you another drink while you do?'

While these cocktails were to die for, Jay getting me another drink would mean removing his hand from my foot, and I wasn't sure I wanted that.

I smiled and rubbed my lips together. 'Maybe just one more?'

'Your wish is my command.' He carefully moved my foot from his lap back to the table, giving it one final caress as he stood.

I shivered as he headed for the bar.

As Jay waited for someone to serve him, he looked back to me and, even across the room, I could see hunger in his eyes. Something inside me turned molten.

Suddenly I didn't want another drink. I wanted something else entirely.

I couldn't remember the last time I'd had a one-night stand. There were a few in my early twenties, but although my relationships before Christos couldn't be considered serious, they'd progressed beyond the casual hook-up to two-or-three-month type deals. The kind of boyfriends I could take to a work function or who could be my plus-one at a wedding but who I didn't bother taking home to meet my folks. But right now a one-night stand felt like a very attractive option.

As if a mind reader, Jay abandoned the drink mission and stalked back to me. There was only one question in his intent gaze.

I thought of Gralice's theory that the best way to get over someone was to sleep with someone else and my tongue darted out to moisten my dry lips. 'I'm feeling tired. Do you mind walking me back to my cabin?'

'I reckon I can handle that.' He offered his hand to help me up.

'Hang on. My shoe.' I winced as I shoved it on.

'Let's get outta here.'

His hand clasping mine, we weaved through the revellers in our desperation to escape. Ignoring my foot, which was yelling loudly at me to slow the hell down, I hurried alongside Jay to the elevators. There were three elderly women waiting, but neither of us paid them any attention as he turned, took my face between his hands and pressed his mouth against mine. Heat swept through me as I wrapped my hands around his back. His tongue nudged into my mouth. This was no tentative kiss; it felt almost as if he were trying to eat me.

When we pulled apart a few long moments later, the elevator doors were closing in front of us.

'Dammit!' He slammed his hand against the button, but the doors stayed shut.

'Let's take the stairs.'

'Good idea.' He grabbed my hand again, but we only got a few paces before my foot gave way beneath me.

A yowl escaped my mouth and Jay swept me up into his arms. 'You alright?'

'I will be. Hurry,' I said, adding my deck and cabin number so he knew where we were going.

Jay jogged up the stairs like he was carrying a packet of fairy floss—all that working out obviously had its advantages—and was barely puffing when we emerged into the cabin corridor. We hurried past what felt like a hundred other doors and then we were finally inside, every nerve ending in my body buzzing.

'This is not my cabin,' I said, glancing around as he lowered me onto the bed.

'I know.' He peeled off his jacket and ripped his T-shirt up over his head. 'It's mine. It was closer. And you were getting heavy.'

'Are you calling me fat?' My breath caught in my throat at the sight of his bare, tanned, muscled chest. I'd seen it before, sure, but now it was about to be mine. However, if he was making such a judgement on my body, I should probably tell him where to go.

Jay chuckled as he climbed onto the bed and straddled me. 'You are anything but fat, Geraldine, but running with jeans that no longer fit because what I'm carrying turns me on so damn hard was an effort.'

His hands skimmed from my shoulders down my sides as he spoke and I shivered involuntarily. That was a very good answer.

Suddenly my bra felt too tight and my near-see-through blouse like a full nun's habit. There was way too much material between us. I palmed my hands on his hard chest and shoved him upwards.

'Hey!' His brows knitted together. 'If you've changed your mind, you only need to say.'

'Shut up and take off your jeans,' I ordered as I yanked off my shirt and bra in a matter of seconds.

'Holy mother Mary.' Jay's Adam's apple moved slowly up and down as he looked his fill at my breasts.

I glowed. 'Why are you still wearing your jeans?'

He blinked, then stood, kicked off his shoes and rolled his jeans and jocks down his thick thighs till they pooled on the floor.

As I quivered in anticipation, Jay stepped towards the bed. 'Why are you still wearing yours?'

I couldn't answer, so thankfully Jay did the honours. His lips met mine and I moaned as my hands roved over his body.

Although Jay was attractive in a hard, edgy kind of way and I was turned on almost beyond belief, I fully expected the sex to be awkward and unsatisfactory. We were both more than a little drunk and first time sex was never blow-your-socks-off amazing. Maybe I had low expectations but somehow doing it with Jay broke all the rules of what a drunken one-night stand was supposed to be. We talked, we laughed, I may even have cried, but that was because at one stage he forgot about my sore ankle as he grabbed both my feet and put them on his shoulders as he drove into me.

I should probably have left once we were done, but instead he pulled me into his side and we spooned as we fell asleep.

There was no doubt in my mind what this was. It was the best kind of rebound sex I could have hoped for—an 'up yours' to

Christos! Perhaps I was using Jay in the worst kind of way possible but he knew the score and was more than happy to oblige. Although we hadn't verbally laid down any ground rules, we both understood this was a one-night (two or three max, we didn't have any longer) kinda thing, which is perhaps why when we woke a few hours later we went for it again.

'Shit, I only had one condom,' he said, hovering above me.

'Damn.' But no way was I missing out on this. Life was too short. And anyway ... 'It's okay. I'm on the pill.'

Jay was inside me again before I could think about how reckless I was being. I'd thought the first time might have been a fluke, but somehow I came with him inside me a second time, and he flew over the edge only moments later.

'Wow,' he breathed as he flopped down onto my chest.

'I know,' I whispered back, grinning like the cat who'd got the cream *and* the canary. My body felt so utterly satisfied and I ached in spots I wasn't sure had ever ached before.

When my heart rate finally returned to normal, I glanced over at the little digital alarm clock on the bedside table. It was two in the morning and I could feel a very gentle rocking of the ship on the ocean.

'I suppose I'd better go back to my cabin,' I said.

'Stay.' Jay threw a heavy arm over me and drew me into his side. I had no doubt that if our circumstances—or rather our surrounds— were different, he'd be picking up my boots and throwing me out the door, but things felt different on a cruise. I didn't even know where he lived.

'You sure?'

'Yep. With your foot, you don't want to be stumbling around the ship in the middle of the night.'

'Okay.' I bit my lip to stop myself from grinning. 'I'm just going to the loo.'

I climbed out of bed and walked across the room to the tiny bathroom where I flicked on the light, refreshed myself and stared in the mirror.

My hair was in dire need of a brush, but there was a glow in my cheeks that hadn't been there yesterday and ... was that a hickey on my neck? I hadn't had one of those since I was a teenager. I leaned forward to scrutinise it, touching my fingers to the spot where Jay's mouth had marked me, and a thrill ran through my body.

8

My eyes blinked open at the sound of a coffee machine as both the alluring aroma of caffeine and memories of last night came rushing at me.

'Do you want a coffee?' Jay smiled over from the tiny bench where he was playing with the machine, wearing nothing but a fluffy white towel.

I sat up fast, dragging the sheets with me to cover my bare chest. 'What time is it?'

'Nearly eleven.' He started towards me with a mug of steaming goodness and a plate of croissants, but I barely registered them.

'What? I haven't slept this late in years.'

'Relax. You obviously needed the rest after …'

My body quivered at the thought and the sheet fell from my grasp as I accepted the coffee and took a sip. 'What time did you wake up?'

'About seven.'

'What have you been doing all this time?'

'I've been to the gym, done a few laps in the pool, grabbed these.' He nodded to the plate of croissants still in his hand. 'And then came back for a quick shower.'

I picked up one of the croissants and tore off a chunk with my teeth. The buttery goodness all but melted on my tongue. 'These are so good.'

'I know.' From the way he was looking at me, I wasn't sure he was talking about the pastries.

My body heating, I took another sip of my coffee. I'd barely swallowed before Jay reached out and traced my nipple with his finger.

Oh God! I willed my hormones not to react. It was almost noon. Mum and Gralice would be wondering where I was and I shouldn't be wasting precious interview time, but my mind was helpless against my libido. I put the mug on the bedside table and dragged Jay back under the covers.

What difference would another few minutes make?

We were both already starkers and my body was already more than ready to accommodate him. But he didn't seem in any rush, choosing instead to trace his tongue from my lips, down over my collarbone, lingering on both my nipples before venturing lower. And lower.

I cried out and gripped the edges of the mattress as his tongue poked inside me. *Oh. My. God.* Did this man have a PhD in the female form?

Within moments my body was convulsing around his tongue.

A grin on his face like this time *he'd* got the cream and the canary, he crawled back up my body and thrust inside of me. It was the first time we'd done it in straight missionary position but it was anything but vanilla. By the time we were done, my bones felt like liquid, my heart was buzzing and our bodies were both slicked with sweat.

Three times in less than twenty-four hours was a record I hadn't hit since my very early twenties. But it wasn't just the frequency, I couldn't actually recall ever having sex like that before. Sex that made me feel almost like somebody else.

I grinned up at him. 'I think you're in need of another shower.'

'Maybe this time you should join me.'

'I don't think there's room for two in that bathroom, never mind the shower.'

Before he could reply, a knock sounded on the door and I jumped out of my skin.

He climbed out of bed and wrapped the towel back around his waist. 'It's probably the steward come to clean the room. I'll get rid of him.'

'Where the hell have you been?' came a woman's high-pitched voice the moment he opened the door.

'I'm enjoying my cabin, having a holiday. Isn't that what we're supposed to be doing, Kate?'

Who is Kate? I tried to hide under the sheets in case she ventured in.

'You're *supposed* to be spending quality time with your family. That's what Gran and Grandpa wanted when they shouted everyone this cruise. Three days isn't too much to ask, is it Jay?'

'Let me get dressed and I'll come find you.' He went to close the door, but Kate wasn't ready to say goodbye.

'Anyway, there's this woman hanging around and I'm getting a weird vibe about her.'

'What do you mean?' Jay sounded frustrated.

'Everywhere we go, she's there too. She was at dinner last night, the show *and* breakfast this morning!'

'This is a cruise, Kate. It might seem a big ship but there's like two thousand people on it and only so many different shows and places to eat. You're bound to run into some people more than once.'

'I'm not stupid, but—Have you got someone in there? Oh my God, Jay, couldn't you keep it in your pants just this once? Three days,' she said again.

'Actually, it's four days and three nights, but what I do with what's in my pants isn't any business of yours.' There was an edge in his voice and I wasn't sure whether to laugh or cringe as he all but shut the door in the woman's face.

'Sorry about that.'

'Who was she?'

He let out a heavy sigh as he came back to sit beside me. 'My sister.'

'I didn't mean to eavesdrop but ...'

'Kinda hard not to in such a confined space.'

'Did she say she thinks someone is following your family?'

'Yes.' The expression on his face said just how ridiculous he thought this notion. 'Kate's a little paranoid. She's suspicious of almost everyone and very overprotective of her family. It's a miracle she let Sheldon get close enough to impregnate her, but somehow he did and now she's the poster child for helicopter parents everywhere.'

I wondered if her kid had been the one making all the noise last night. 'Who's Sheldon?'

'Her husband. The man's a saint, and I pity their poor child. He's five and she'll barely let him take a shit by himself.' Jay sighed and ran a hand through his hair. 'As much as I'd rather stay holed up in here with you, I'd better go and show my face.'

'I should go and find my mum and grandma anyway.' I took one final swig of coffee and climbed out of bed, not at all self-conscious about my nakedness as Jay helped me collect my clothes.

He dangled my bra on the end of his finger. 'This is cute, but I think I much prefer you without it.'

'Give it here.' I snatched it back and covered up in haste, for fear if I didn't, we'd get distracted and his sister would come knocking again.

'So, what are your plans tonight?' he asked as I shoved on my last shoe.

I picked up the newssheet that had been slipped under the door earlier. 'Let's see, I can't decide whether to go try my luck at karaoke—there's a signed Elvis LP on the table for the winner—go see *Spinout* in the cinema, or watch yet another tribute artist. The choice is killing me, but I definitely don't wanna miss the *Blue Hawaii* party tonight.'

'Pity. I was hoping maybe we could get another drink, but no way I can compete with *Blue Hawaii*.'

'Maybe I *can* sacrifice *Blue Hawaii* for another one of those cocktails.'

His replying grin was lethal. 'Ten pm same place as last night?'

'I'll see you then.'

I couldn't wipe the smile off my face as I headed up a few levels to my cabin and didn't even care about doing the walk of shame in last night's clothes. Jay felt like a gift bestowed upon me so I didn't waste a whole weekend wallowing over Christos's rejection. Although I knew that once I got off the ship and was faced with single life and lonely nights again I'd be a mess, I was thankful for a few days' reprieve.

'*Hola*, Ms Johnston,' Raquel greeted me as I slowed in front of my cabin. 'How are you this afternoon?'

'I'm wonderful, thank you. Have you seen my mother or grandmother this morning?'

'Yes, they went out about nine o'clock for breakfast.'

'Thanks.' I smiled and retreated into my cabin.

After a shower, I dressed quickly and stepped back out into the corridor, figuring that as it was just after midday, I might find the others in one of the ship's eateries. A quick (or rather slow, I still wasn't great on my feet) sweep of all such places didn't reap any rewards, but I was starving, so I grabbed a burger out on the pool deck and sat down to eat and rest my foot a while. Loads of people passed by but halfway through my delicious meal, I still hadn't spotted the three I knew.

So much for them worrying about where I'd been!

It was then that I overhead a couple talking about their afternoon plans. He wanted to go play the pokies but she said she'd like to attend the Elvis cooking show first. *Bingo!* Washing down the last of my burger with Diet Coke, I smiled at a woman who hovered close to collect my empty plate. 'Do you know which deck the Elvis cooking show is on?'

'It's usually held on Deck Seven in the theatre.'

I couldn't work out what her accent was but I liked it. 'Thanks.'

To my utmost surprise the theatre was almost full. I scanned the crowd looking for my mother, grandmother and Rosa, but couldn't see any of them.

'Can you believe it? I hear the Happy Happy Housewife is going to help with the show,' said a woman as she and her friend walked past. 'I wonder if we can get her autograph afterwards?'

I silently sniggered as I searched the theatre once again, looking for a vacant seat. A hush fell over the crowd signalling the show was about to begin and an usher urged me into one of the few remaining seats.

'Tell me, ladies and gentleman,' boomed a voice moments before a man dressed in classic King garb all but ran onto the stage and broke into song. 'Are you lonesome this afternoon? Then never fear, cos Elvis is here, to capture your hearts and your stomachs. And not only are you lucky enough to be spending time with this hunka hunka heartbreaker, Tristen Madden ...' He pointed to his chest and hit the audience with a cheesy grin. 'But today, you are in for double the treat, because I have a special guest. Not only does she look like an angel, walk like an angel and talk like an angel, I hear she cooks like an angel too. Let's give it up for Marie Johnston, otherwise known as the Happy Happy Housewife.'

The crowd erupted into applause as Mum strutted onto the stage. She waved and blew kisses at everyone as if she were Madonna or someone.

The chef guy tossed her a plastic smile. 'Welcome, what a pleasure to have you with us today.'

'Oh, Tristan.' My mother cocked her head to one side and smiled. 'The pleasure is all mine, I loved you on *MasterChef*.'

MasterChef? Was this guy famous?

The woman next to me snorted. 'He got out in the first elimination, how many seasons ago? I'm surprised she remembers him.'

I wasn't sure whether she was talking to me or to herself but I smiled.

'What are we going to make this afternoon, Tristan? Love Me Chicken Tenders? Blue Suede Berry Pie? Meatloaf?'

'Well, Marie, I feel like in this cool weather, we could all do with a little comfort food. What do you think?'

'Ooh yes, nothing I like better than cooking comfort food.'

'Then oh-boy are you gonna love helping me cook Elvis's famous Peanut Butter and Banana Fried Sandwich.'

I cringed at the thought. Although I liked bananas well enough and pretty much lived on peanut butter sandwiches when I was too busy with work to cook, putting them together sounded like a recipe for disaster.

'You better put this on, we wouldn't want you to stain that lovely dress.' Tristan handed Mum a white apron, then did a slow head-to-toe of her as she did it up. 'Seriously, gang, has any other woman ever looked quite as perfect in an apron? I'm feeling all shook up inside.'

Oh my goodness, was that supposed to be an Elvis reference? And was Tristan flirting with my mother? He had to be at least ten years her junior.

She fluttered her eyelashes at him. 'You don't look so bad yourself in yours.'

The burger I'd scoffed for lunch churned in my stomach, and I couldn't help scrunching up my face in disgust as they began to demonstrate how to make what had apparently been the King's favourite sandwich.

'First we need two pieces of white bread. Do you mind popping those in the toaster for me, please, Marie?'

Mum did as he asked and the next step was heating two tablespoons of butter in a frying pan. We heard the sizzle over the speakers.

'Maybe you should turn down the heat there,' she said, peering over the top of chef Elvis's shoulder and directing her attention to the crowd. 'Butter should never be melted on high heat, you know? If it gets too hot the milk solids separate and the butter can burn.' She picked up a wooden spoon and poked it into the butter. 'That's probably ready now ... you should turn down the heat when it's about three quarters melted and stir until it's all the same consistency.'

'Thanks for that fascinating information.' Tristan spoke through clearly gritted teeth but kept his smile plastered on his face. 'Would you like to mash the banana?'

Mum actually winked at the audience as she picked up the banana. Tristan made a crude comment as she peeled it in much the same manner a stripper removes her clothes. She laughed as if it were the funniest thing she'd ever heard, totally playing up to the audience.

Their banter continued as Mum kept interrupting and offering cooking tips. Tristan tried to pretend not to care, but it was clear he was annoyed at the way the audience was lapping her up. I had to admit she did have something special. It was clear to see why her videos got so many views, if you liked that kind of thing.

Once the bread was toasted they spread two heaped tablespoons of peanut butter onto each slice. Two tablespoons of PB *and* two tablespoons of butter—my arteries trembled at the thought. No wonder Elvis died young.

Tristan and Mum bantered and made agonising commentary over every step, dragging out what should have taken five minutes max to a full fifteen-minute ordeal. Halfway through the demonstration the woman next to me started playing with her phone and I didn't blame her—the duo on stage were pretty cringeworthy. When the sandwich was finished and Tristan cut it in half and hand-fed my mother, I wished I still had my phone so I could find refuge there as well. *Damn Christos.*

'That is delicious,' Mum declared. 'And so easy to make. Elvis was definitely onto something.'

Tristan nodded and chuckled in reply. 'Now, Marie, I'm guessing most of our wonderful audience already know who you are, but just in case, why don't you tell us a little bit about yourself?'

'I'd love to.' My mother turned to bat her eyelashes at the audience. 'My name is Marie Johnston and I'm a proud, happy housewife. I've been living in domestic bliss with my lovely husband for over thirty-five years. I love everything about being a wife and mother. A couple of years ago my beautiful daughter Geraldine introduced me to Instagram. At first I only posted photos of the meals I made for my husband, but then friends started asking for the recipes, so I started posting them as well. I guess things just took off after that. I started widening my posts from food to other things.

Now I share helpful hints about cleaning, craft, interior design, child-rearing, health, beauty, and of course, romance.'

'Your husband is a very lucky man,' Tristan said with a wink.

My mother blushed. 'Oh he is, but I'm also a very lucky woman.'

Finally, the torture was over and Tristan announced that tomorrow he'd be back again. 'Same place, same time, but a different Elvis speciality to tantalise your tastebuds.'

There was a rush of people from their chairs. At first I thought they were eager to escape to greener pastures—like maybe a bar for a cocktail—but instead they flocked to my mother. Rosa appeared out of nowhere to manage the crowd. While Mum signed everything from handbags to T-shirts, I moved forward a few rows and plopped myself down in a seat closer to the action.

'Are you waiting for a signature from Marie? Are you a fan?'

It was the woman who'd been sitting next to me in the audience. With short black hair and minimal make-up, she had a no-nonsense vibe about her, wasn't wearing a wedding ring, and simply didn't seem the type to buy into the whole new domesticity scene.

'Oh no.' I couldn't keep the amusement from my voice or deny it quick enough. Did I look the type to enjoy such nonsense? 'She's my mother.'

9

'Really?' The woman's eyes lit up as she thrust out her hand. 'Lovely to meet you. I'm Holly Pearson, a publisher from Bourne Books.'

'Hi.' I grinned, unable to believe my luck as Holly dropped into the seat beside me. A publisher. This had to be a sign! Although I had a few contacts myself, the book industry was as much about who you knew as anything and, even though I had a pretty remarkable subject in Gralice, it never hurt to make another acquaintance. And Bourne Books, an independent publisher, were big in non-fiction and had produced a number of bestsellers in the last few years. I needed to play this opportunity cool, not launch immediately into my pitch, but for the life of me I couldn't think of anything else to say.

In the end I went with, 'What are you doing on the ship?'

Holly frowned slightly. 'I'm here for my sister's fortieth, but cruising isn't really my thing.'

'Mine either.'

'Was it your mother's idea?'

And there was my opening. 'Actually no, we're here with my grandmother as well. You may have heard of her ...' I paused for a metaphorical drumroll. 'Alice Abbott?'

'Good Lord!' she shrieked. 'I love that woman. She's so smart, never afraid to speak out and say what she thinks. My bachelor degree is in science—I kinda fell into publishing—but I still like to stay informed, so I devour her column every month. I just love that she makes science accessible to the masses. And of course I'm eternally grateful for all she's done for women. How peculiar that she birthed a woman like your mother.'

'I know, right? You couldn't get two more different women, but they definitely share the same DNA.'

Mum and Gralice might not share many of the same interests, values or beliefs, but they're cut from the same cloth physically. Both reasonably tall, both golden blondes (although Gralice's hair is now a lovely silver) and both curvy without being fat. I'd followed suit for a third generation.

Holly glanced down at her phone again and I saw Mum's Instagram profile on her screen. 'I can't believe she has so many followers. All we hear about these days is the glass ceiling, women fighting for equal pay, the gender imbalance in parliament, violence against women, and yet, here she is raving about staying at home, taking care of one's husband, doing *craft*, and she has other women hanging off her every word.'

Never mind about Mum, I wanted to say, *let's talk about Alice Abbott*. If only Gralice were here right now and I could introduce them. 'Actually another one of the reasons ...'

I didn't get to finish my sentence.

'Oh look, she's almost free.' Holly sprang from her seat and hurried to the front where there were now only two women speaking to my mother. With a heavy sigh, I stood and followed.

'Hello, Ged. Wasn't that wonderful?' Rosa smiled at us and snapped a photo of the two women and my mother.

'Thank you so much,' they gushed in unison.

'I can't believe we got to meet you,' added the shorter of the two.

'Lovely to meet you both as well.' Mum's smile was as large as her Botoxed forehead would allow. 'Remember that little tip I gave you about the bedroom.'

Ew. I wanted to shove my hands over my ears but resisted, trying to stay cool in front of Holly.

As the women walked off, still giggling with excitement, Holly stepped forward and offered my mother her hand. 'Great show.'

'Thank you. Would you like my autograph?'

'Or a photo?' Rosa added. 'You can tag Marie on Instagram!'

'I'm actually hoping for a little more than that.' She whipped a business card out of her pocket and thrust it at Mum. 'I'm Holly Pearson, non-fiction publisher at Bourne Books, and I was wondering if you'd ever thought about writing a book?'

What the actual?! My mouth dropped open as Mum asked, 'What about?'

Holly smiled encouragingly. 'About your life as a wife and mother, and how other people can achieve the same happiness and satisfaction you have. A how-to guide—very similar to your vlogs and other social media posts, but all collected in a book so your followers can have something tactile.'

'You think that's something people would be interested in?'

Holly nodded. 'The response this afternoon and your numbers online speak for themselves.'

Mum puffed up her chest like a bird trying to impress a mate. 'Aside from my social media posts I haven't had much experience in writing, but my mother and daughter both write, so maybe it runs in the family.'

'Fabulous.' Holly made a clicking noise with her tongue. 'I know you're on holiday, so I won't take too much of your time now, but I'd love to talk to you next week. Are you in Victoria?'

'Yes, Port Melbourne,' my mother replied.

'Well, how about you give me a call when you get back and we'll make an appointment for you to come into the office. You can meet the team and I can give you my vision for your book. I think I can make this *very* worth your while.'

'Can I bring my assistant?' Mum gestured to Rosa.

'Yes, of course.' Holly shook Rosa's hand. 'She's more than welcome. And have you got an agent?'

'Should I?' Mum's eyes were wide.

I gulped. Oh my God, Holly was talking like this was a done deal. I hated feeling like a left-out child, but … *What about my and Gralice's book?*

'Not at all. That's totally up to you,' Holly assured her. 'But I wanted to check I wasn't stepping on anyone's toes. Anyway, we'll talk next week.' With a final nod, she turned and strode out of the theatre.

Mum pressed a hand against her chest. 'Oh my God, I can't believe that just happened.'

You and me both, I thought, as she and Rosa jumped up and down on the spot like a couple of silly schoolgirls.

'Have either of you seen Gralice this morning?'

As if she didn't hear my question, Mum stretched her back. 'This having fans thing is quite draining. My fingers are a little cramped.' But she laughed as if this didn't bother her at all. 'Oh my goodness, I'm going to write a book!'

I smiled through my teeth. 'Do you know where she is now?'

Mum blinked. 'Who?'

'Gralice!'

'The three of us had a lovely coffee and cake together on the pool deck,' Rosa informed me. 'And then we watched the Elvis lookalike contest.'

'It was very funny,' added Mum. 'We laughed so hard that we were starving by the end of it, so we went for lunch. I think I've eaten more in the past twenty-four hours than I did in the whole month leading up to it.'

'Did you have lunch with Gralice?'

They both shook their heads. 'Oh, no, she went for a wander after coffee. We haven't seen her since,' Mum said.

'Seen who since?'

We all spun round to find my grandmother standing behind us.

'You!' I launched at her and gave her a hug.

'How was the cooking show?' she asked as she extricated herself from me.

Mum and Rose ignored the question, telling her instead about meeting Holly Pearson.

'Wow, that's wonderful.' Gralice gave my mother a hug.

Was she *deaf*?

'They want her to write about *new domesticity*,' I clarified.

Gralice's proud smile didn't falter. 'I know. I think it's wonderful that women have the freedom to make the choice to stay at home now if that's what they want.'

What the actual? Had we walked up the gantry and into an alternate universe?

'Anyway,' Gralice said with a smile, 'I've booked us in for pedicures this afternoon. We'll see if they'll let us order in a bottle of champagne to celebrate.'

'Pedicures?' It wasn't that Gralice had anything against pedicures in principle—she believed women should have the right to do whatever the hell they wanted—but I could never remember her painting her nails.

'Yes. Unless you have other plans, Ged?'

'Actually, I was thinking maybe we could get started on your interview?'

She waved a hand at me. 'There'll be plenty of time for that.'

And once again, I knew there was no point arguing.

There were four reclining massage chairs in the salon and four therapists, which meant none of us had to watch and wait. After the required small talk with the lovely women and one man tending to our toes, we fell into conversation of our own.

'We rambled on about ourselves last night,' Gralice said to Rosa, 'but we didn't get to learn much about you. Did you grow up in Melbourne?'

'No, I was born in Brazil.'

'And what brought you here?' Gralice wanted to know.

'My family immigrated to Australia in the mid-seventies when I was eight under the government assistance scheme.'

'That's a big move,' Gralice said. 'What did your parents do when they got here?'

'Not long after we arrived they got jobs running the pub in Stawell. Aside from the few Indigenous residents, we were the only non-white members of the town and it made me the target for bullies all through school.'

'That must have been hard,' I said, wondering if being bullied at school was something Mum and Rosa had bonded over.

She shrugged. 'What doesn't kill you makes you stronger, but I did escape to Melbourne the moment I finished school.'

'Are your family still in Stawell?' I asked.

Rosa shook her head. 'No, Dad died of a heart attack not long after I left, and Mum packed up and headed back to Brazil with my two younger sisters.'

'Do you go back often?' This question came from Gralice.

'I couldn't afford it when I was younger, but now I try and return every couple of years. Mum's getting frail these days. I have contemplated moving back myself a few times, but Australia feels like home now. Saying that, I'm trying to convince Marie to come with me next time I visit. Travelling overseas and looking at how women from other places and cultures live could be a fascinating add-on to her vlogs. I reckon her followers would love it.'

'That sounds like a wonderful opportunity,' Gralice said. 'South America is one of the most spectacular places I've ever been.'

Mum smiled wistfully. 'I don't know ... It does sound fabulous, and I could cook up some frozen meals for Tony I suppose, but I'm not sure we can justify the costs with him not working as much.'

'If it's money you need, I'd be happy to help you,' Gralice offered.

Mum's eyes widened. 'Really?'

'Of course. I've got a little put away, and Lord knows I can't take it with me!'

'And Dad will be fine, Mum,' I reassured her. 'I'll pop in and see him. It won't hurt him to eat takeaway a few nights.'

'That's what I've been telling her,' Rosa said. 'She does way too much for that man.'

Although I did agree to an extent, I didn't like the way Rosa referred to my father as 'that man'. 'Yes, but isn't that her schtick? And why she needs an assistant?'

Rosa chuckled. 'Yes, I suppose you're right. Is it time for a top up?'

We held up our glasses for Scott, the male therapist, to refill. Beginning to relax after my disappointment over the whole Holly-

Pearson-Bourne-Books thing, I let the chair pound my muscles as my therapist, Kia, swept her talented fingers over the arch of my feet. She was good, but not quite as good as Jay. I grinned at the thought, wondering what he was doing right now.

'What are you grinning at?' Mum asked. 'You're looking better than you did Thursday night. The sea air obviously agrees with you.'

I grinned and glowed some more—nothing to do with the sea air. 'Yeah, well, this being on a ship far away from Christos is good therapy. And anyway, I figure it's more his loss than mine.'

It was easy to talk the talk when my body had not yet recovered from its brush with Jay. It might be a different story Tuesday morning when I had to go to work in the same building as my ex.

My three companions cheered.

'It sure is, darling. And who needs a man to have fun?' Mum lifted her glass and downed the rest of her drink.

'Not me,' Gralice and Rosa exclaimed in unison.

I laughed and joined them in a toast.

'While I'm really enjoying this,' Mum mused, gesturing to her champagne flute and her toes, 'I have to admit I had so much fun on stage cooking earlier. I can't remember the last time I went more than twenty-four hours without cooking or baking something.'

Rosa hit her with a bemused smile as she put her glass down on the little table between the seats. 'You really love it, don't you? Where did that passion come from?'

'Certainly not from me,' Gralice said. 'My idea of a gourmet dinner when Sappho was a kid was chops or sausages, maybe with a side of frozen peas.'

'That's when you bothered to cook.'

I hoped Mum wasn't about to pick another argument.

'I have to say,' Gralice admitted with a twinkle in her eye, 'I *was* delighted when the first McDonald's opened down the road.'

Mum looked to Rosa. 'As you can probably guess, I taught myself out of necessity. Believe it or not, eating French fries and chicken nuggets every day gets old after a while, but when Dad met Craig—who is a wonderful cook—Craig encouraged me.'

She went on to describe some of the dishes she'd learned from Craig and the wonderful times they'd had together in the kitchen. Gralice laughed frequently, and threw in some of her own memories from Mum's childhood—like the time Mum, Phil and Craig forgot about the Christmas cake in the oven because they were sobbing over *Bellbird*.

'I came home from a meeting and had to put the fire in the kitchen out. They hadn't even smelled the smoke.'

'Hey, it was the final episode. We were devastated.'

'If I recall, you guys were happy enough when I got takeaway *that* night,' Gralice said with a chuckle.

That must have been the beginning of Mum's love affair with TV, especially soap operas. In my lifetime, she'd been an ardent fan of *A Country Practice*, *The Flying Doctors*, *E Street*, and she still watched *Home & Away* and *Neighbours* on a nightly basis. Dad always got dinner at six o'clock on the dot, so that they'd eaten and Mum had cleaned up before her shows began. No one was allowed to phone her during this sacred hour. Even when Sophie went into labour with Mum's first grandchild during *Home and Away*, Will dared not call her until the episode was over.

I'd rarely heard Mum talking about her childhood in such a candid manner. Most often she referred to how difficult she'd had it, but perhaps the ship was acting as a tonic. Neither Gralice nor Phil were ones to be quiet about their values and beliefs or to be ashamed about who they were. In the early seventies, Phil was one of the first members of Society Five, a gay rights and support organisation, and, in addition to her scientific pursuits, Gralice has always been at the forefront of any protests for women's rights.

As a result of Mum's unconventional origins and home life, she'd found it difficult to make friends at school and often felt lonely and isolated. The parents of her classmates didn't encourage her to spend time with their children, thinking the questionable morals of her parents might rub off on their precious offspring. She was not only left off the guest list for birthday parties, but she was shunned and teased in the playground.

From what I understood, neither Gralice nor Phil had tried to sympathise but encouraged her to rise above the shallow mindedness of her classmates, to shrug it off and refuse to let the bullying shape her. Mum once confessed to me that she used to fantasise about something awful happening to Gralice and Phil so that she could be adopted into a 'normal' family. But there was no reference to any of that now.

Gralice pointed her new, shiny toes out in front of her. 'You know I could get used to this pamper thing.'

'See, Mum? Haven't I been telling you for years how nice it is to take a little time out and do something special for yourself. It's not just for Tony that I stay trim and dress well, it makes me feel good too.'

'If I didn't know better, you two are the absolute last people I would pair together as mother and daughter,' Rosa said, looking from one to the other.

'It sure made things interesting growing up,' Mum said. 'Remember that time I brought a Barbie into the house and told you I wanted to be her when I grew up.'

'Don't remind me.' But Gralice smiled as she said it.

'Mum thought Barbie was the spawn of the devil,' said my mother.

'I wanted to throttle you,' Gralice retorted. 'I felt like I'd failed as a mother.'

Mum laughed. 'But she took it out on poor Barbie instead. She chopped all her long, golden hair off and threw her in next door's rubbish bin. I cried for a week, until finally Dad convinced her that perhaps Barbie was a positive toy for girls.'

'And how did he figure that?' asked Rosa.

'He said that Barbie was the only toy girls had that boys didn't and that she was the star, not Ken. I think he secretly enjoyed playing with them as much as I did.'

'I didn't like Barbie's unrealistic proportions,' Gralice justified. 'I didn't want Sappho growing up obsessed with her weight and appearance at the expense of her brains and everything else, but Phil argued that she only saw her as a play toy and probably hadn't even noticed how wrong she looked.'

'I think I was about nine when Dad bought me Surgeon Barbie. Mum couldn't argue with that and after that he bought me Barbies every Christmas and birthday until I grew out of them.'

'Yet, if I remember, poor Surgeon Barbie wasn't your favourite, you much preferred Babysitter Barbie and her friend the princess.'

Rosa and I chuckled at Gralice's amused tone. Her and Mum's differences had always been a point of contention, but now they were laughing at them too. It made me feel warm and fuzzy all over as I realised this was the first time in a long while I'd hung out for longer than a few minutes with Gralice and Mum together without the rest of our family. It was nice. Maybe Gralice's idea to strand us together at sea wasn't such a bad one after all.

Once we were all done—Mum with her pink toenails, Rosa with multi-coloured ones, Gralice with black and me with a striking red I hoped Jay might comment on later—it was time for afternoon tea.

'What do you make of all this?' I whispered to Gralice as Mum and Rosa strode ahead of us towards the elevators.

'Make of what?'

'The website, the possible book deal. People taking her "Happy Happy Housewife" stuff seriously?'

Gralice touched my arm and her eyes sparkled. 'Did you hear what Rosa called your mother's new interest? Her *career*! It might not be the way I imagined or hoped, but Sappho's finally got a bit of the autonomy I've always wanted her to have. And between you and me, I think she likes it. I haven't seen her smile so much since Phil gave her that Barbie.'

I snorted. Trust Gralice to put a feminist spin on *this*.

10

Following the pedicures, we enjoyed Devonshire Tea as planned and then caught a little sun as we sipped another cocktail out on the deck. We dined together at the waterfront restaurant and I was pleased when Oleg appeared again.

Sadly, Jay's party did not.

'What do you want to do now, Mum?' my mother asked Gralice when we were all utterly stuffed.

Gralice sighed and leaned back in her seat. 'What are our options again?'

Rosa got the daily newssheet out of her large handbag and placed it on the table. 'Well, there's the *Blue Hawaii* party later of course, but before then we could go see tonight's show, watch a movie or try our hand at karaoke.'

'I've never done karaoke before,' Gralice said.

I raised my eyebrows. 'That's because it's mortifying.'

Rosa swatted me with the newssheet. 'Oh, don't be such a spoilsport.'

'Let's give it a shot.'

I almost fell off my seat at Gralice's announcement and the look on my mother's face said she was as surprised as me, but who were we to argue with the birthday girl if she wanted to get up on stage and make a fool of herself?

'I'm only coming to spectate,' I said. *And while away the hours until my hook-up with Jay.* 'Where is karaoke again?'

'In the bar where we were having cocktails earlier.'

The same bar where I was due to meet Jay. I stiffened. Although I guessed it would be crowded by that time, it might make things difficult sneaking off without being seen. Telling myself I had one hundred and twenty minutes to work out a game plan, I followed the others out of the restaurant.

Karaoke had already started when we arrived but we nabbed a table not too far from the stage.

'It must be my turn to buy the drinks,' I said. 'What's everyone having?'

Mum and Rosa had moved on to wine and Gralice wanted a gin and tonic, but I was not going to miss the opportunity for another one of those fabulous cocktails. I wasn't a fan of Elvis tunes when the man *himself* was singing—if I had to sit through other people botching his songs, then a fancy drink was compulsory.

Mum came to the bar to help carry everything. 'Isn't this so much fun? I'm not sure I want to go home.'

'I think Dad would have something to say about that.'

'What can I get you lovely ladies?' asked a mop-headed barman who looked as if he spent a lot of time making his hair look so shaggy.

I placed the orders for the others as I stared at the cocktail menu. I'd lost track of what number I was up to. 'I'll have a pina colada, please. And don't worry about the straw.'

We took the drinks back to our table and commented on the people who were taking turns on the stage. Some of them were ghastly, but others not too bad. When Mum and Rosa had a go singing 'Return to Sender', I found myself laughing rather than cringing. Although Rosa was good, Mum was of the ghastly variety, but they were having so much fun, nobody cared. The hour ticked over and my heart was beginning to thump in anticipation, when Gralice tapped my knee. 'Come sing with me.'

'Oh, no, no, no. I told you I was only watching.'

'Where's the fun in that?'

I glared at Rosa.

'Go on, darling, live a little.' This from Mum. 'You get your singing talents from me.'

'That's why I refuse to take part in this craziness.'

'Come on,' Gralice urged, 'I shouted you your ticket, the least you can do is get up and keep me company on stage.'

'Gifts aren't supposed to come with conditions,' I whined. 'Do you even know any Elvis songs?'

'I heard nothing but Elvis when your mum was a teenager,' she said as she grabbed my hand to haul me out of my seat. 'I'm sure the lyrics are somewhere in the deep crevices of my mind, and don't the words appear on the screen anyway?'

I groaned as we arrived at the edge of the stage where a woman dressed as Priscilla was taking down the names of all the fools who wanted to sing.

'There are three groups ahead of you,' she said apologetically.

Pity there weren't three hundred.

As we waited, I prayed for a miracle. Like the karaoke machine blowing up, or maybe even an iceberg!

'Alright, loves, you're up,' said the woman with the clipboard.

A guy handed us a microphone each, and as I looked out at the crowd my dessert churned in my stomach. Words started scrolling across the bottom of the screen and Gralice started singing. Pitying everyone in the room, I joined her, but I couldn't seem to get in time with the music or my grandmother. Telling myself this would be over in a matter of minutes, I made the horrible mistake of looking out across the crowd.

Jay! He was leaning against the bar and his smirk hit me right in the chest. Where was that damn iceberg?

There was nothing for me but to keep singing—if you could call it that. I might not be doing a very good impression of Elvis but I was giving Cameron Diaz in that old movie *My Best Friend's Wedding* a run for her money.

Finally—thank the Lord—the song came to an end and my hell was over. Forgetting about my sore foot, I leapt off the stage and didn't wait for Gralice as I headed back to our table. I wasn't sure I would ever forgive her.

I snatched my jacket off the seat. 'I'm getting another drink.' This time I didn't bother asking if anyone else wanted one as I made a beeline for the bar.

I held up my hand as I approached Jay. 'Do *not* say a *word*!'

'Word.' The blasted man laughed but thankfully (for his own good) didn't make a comment about my singing ability, or lack thereof. 'Can I get you a drink?'

'You better make it a big one. I'll have what you're having.' This kind of mortification called for more than a pretty drink, it required hard liquor.

He chuckled and turned to make my request to the woman behind the bar.

'Thanks,' I said as the drink landed in front of me and I downed half of it in one go. 'Anyway, how was your day?'

'Good, I spent a lot of the arvo in the gym and—'

'Didn't you go this morning?' I interrupted.

'Yeah.' He spoke as if he didn't understand the question.

'Did you spend *any* time with your family? With your grandparents?'

'We had lunch together and then I sat through this awful Elvis cooking show for my grandmother. Honestly, I've seen everything now.'

'*You* were at the cooking show?' I couldn't believe I hadn't seen him, but the theatre had been jam-packed.

'Yeah. That's forty-five minutes of my life I'll never get back. You should have seen it.'

'I did. My mother was on the stage,' I said before I could think better of it.

'What? *Your* mother is the Happy Happy Housewife?'

'Please don't tell me you'd heard of her before today?'

'Hell no, but my sister wouldn't stop going on about her this afternoon. What is she, some kind of housewife guru?'

'Something like that.'

He raised one of his delicious ginger eyebrows. 'You don't approve?'

'It's not that exactly—I don't understand, more like. She keeps getting recognised, people literally gush over her, and this afternoon a publisher practically offered her a book contract on a plate.'

'And that's a *bad* thing?'

'Do you know how hard it is for real writers to get that kind of opportunity?'

'Can't say I do.'

'Some people write loads of manuscripts and rack up hundreds of rejections before they even get a foot in the door.'

He lifted his glass to his lips and I watched his Adam's apple slowly rise and fall as he drank. 'Are you talking from personal experience?'

'Not yet, but I have always wanted to write a book and I'm under no illusion that writing my grandmother's biography or finding a publisher for it will be easy. Mum never even wanted to get published and suddenly the opportunity has fallen in her lap.'

'Sounds like someone's a bit jealous,' he said with an annoying twist of his lips.

'That's not it,' I scoffed. 'It's just … Never mind. I don't want to talk about this. '

'Fair enough.'

I took a big gulp of my drink, then turned the conversation back on him. 'What *else* did you do today?'

'I went rock-climbing and swam a while before dinner with the family.'

Just the thought of all that exertion exhausted me. 'Are you doing so much exercise because you like it or is it training for the Mars thing?'

'I just have a lot of energy and need something to get rid of it. Most days off I'm out hiking or riding my bike or something, but those options aren't available onboard.'

I thought of a way I could help but first I had a question. 'When you say bike, do you mean push or motor?'

'Both. I like my mountain bike for the challenge and the fitness and I use it on a day-to-day basis rather than pollute the air but I do like my Kawasaki for the thrill and will take it out for a treat on weekends. I can't be sky-diving or bungee jumping all the time.'

'You've been sky-diving?'

'Yeah.' Again as if he didn't understand the question. 'And paragliding, although that doesn't give you such an adrenaline rush after a while. Abseiling's not bad if the height's there, and last year I went to Norway and had a go at ice-climbing.'

I wasn't even sure what ice-climbing was but it sounded dangerous and I knew I never wanted to do it. I'd sing a million Elvis songs in front of a crowd at the Melbourne Entertainment Centre before I did anything as insane as the things Jay seemed to do on a regular basis.

'What's the worst that could happen?' he asked as if reading my mind.

'You could die.' Of course we'd already established he didn't care about little things like that—this was the man eager to take a suicide mission to Mars. This evening confirmed it. We had absolutely nothing in common. Maybe it was time to stop trying to find something and succumb to what we'd already proven we were good at.

I nodded towards his still half-full glass. 'Are you done with that drink?'

'I can be.'

'Your cabin or mine?'

He winked—'Mine's still closer'—then nodded towards my foot. 'Do you need assistance?'

'No.' Grabbing his hand, I started for the door.

Tonight an elevator arrived quickly and we were blessed to have the small space to ourselves. Our lips converged, our hands taking liberties with each other's bodies. I was contemplating slamming my hand on the stop button and getting down and dirty right here, right now, when there was a ping and the doors peeled open. Jay and I sprung apart and I grinned at the sight of my bright orange lipstick smeared across his face.

'Good evening,' he said, nodding politely to the middle-aged couple who were waiting to enter the elevator.

I held in my giggles until we were a few metres away. 'Did you see their faces?'

'No. I was too busy imagining you naked.'

Heat zapped through me and I'd never been happier to see a door in my life. He pressed his room card against the lock thingamajig and pulled me inside.

This time we didn't even make it to the bed.

'Oh my God!' I said a few minutes later when Jay held me, panting, against the door. 'That was …'

'I know.' He carried me across the room and unceremoniously dumped me on the bed.

'Can I get you a drink or anything?' he asked as he properly undressed. It was a sight to behold and it took a few moments for me to remember how to speak.

'Maybe just some water.'

I took off the rest of my clothes and slid under the covers. Jay joined me a few moments later with a bottle of ice-cold water. He unscrewed the lid and handed it to me, watching intently as I drank my fill. 'Better?'

I nodded and pulled him against me. 'Will you miss this if you go to Mars?'

'What? Sex?' He ran his hand over my naked back, resting it on my butt. I shivered.

'Yeah. I know there'll be a gym on the spaceship, or is it called a rocket? But there's no release quite like *this*, is there?'

'No, but if I'm lucky enough to make the final cut, I won't be alone. There'll be female astronauts. And the mission *is* to set up a new colony.'

Jay's words were a stark reminder that this was nothing more than physical for either of us, but I wondered if sex would be different in space. Would the lack of gravity make it better or worse? I'd never been more interested in astronomy in my life!

'Sing for me …'

'What?' Lost in my thoughts about sex in space, I thought I must have misheard him.

He tucked a few strands of flyaway hair behind my ear. 'I want to hear you sing again.'

'Are you insane?' I pulled back a little. 'Or do you *like* being tortured?'

'You weren't that bad.'

'I wasn't that *good* either.'

He chuckled. 'So, if you won't sing for me, tell me what it was like having a diehard feminist and academic for a grandmother and the Happy Happy Housewife as your mum.'

'Well, she wasn't *the* Happy Happy Housewife when I was growing up and I didn't know any different. My grandmother was always the way she was—loud and unapologetic in her fight for women—and Mum was the way she was.'

'Is your grandmother disappointed with the way your mum turned out?'

I thought about the tension between them last night. 'I think at times she feels conflicted. Mum had all the opportunities my grandmother could afford her yet she choose to study domestic science at university. She was going to become a home economics teacher, but she got married young and stayed at home instead of advancing her career. Gralice believes in choice for women, but yes, I think she wishes Mum had more to show for her efforts than a clean house and a happy spouse.'

'You call your grandmother "Gralice"?'

'Yes. It's a combination of Grandma and Alice because back in the day when she became a grandmother, she didn't want to sound like one.'

'That's cute.' He leaned across me to grab the bottle of water. 'Where do you sit on the spectrum then, Ged?'

'What spectrum?'

He unscrewed the lid and took a sip. 'Are you on the 1950s domestic goddess end, are you a man-hating feminist, or are you a modern women who wants to have it all? Love, kids *and* a high-powered career?'

I was unsure quite how to respond to his question and mocking tone. 'Feminists don't hate men!'

He raised an eyebrow and opened his mouth as if to speak but I got in first. 'Do you believe men and women are equal?'

'Not physically. Males and females are made differently. Women go on about wanting to be the same as men but the fact is, our bodies are not the same and we have different physical capabilities.'

I sat up a little and pulled the bed sheets up to cover my breasts. I couldn't have such an important conversation while so exposed. 'Women don't want to be the *same* as men. That's not what feminism is about. Feminism is about gender equality, the same choices, rights and opportunities for both sexes. It's about making everyone—regardless of their gender—feel valued and respected. Do you think women didn't deserve the right to vote?'

'Of course not.'

'What about getting the same wage for the same job? The right to make decisions over their own bodies? To feel safe walking the streets at night? To have an abortion or to say no to their husband? Do you believe that girls and boys in schools should have the same educational opportunities?'

'Yeah, of course I do.'

I grinned, victorious. 'Then you, my dear, are a feminist.'

He shook his head. 'Nah, I'm not. All those things you mentioned, we've got them all now. Women like your grandmother have fought hard for those things, so feminism is an outdated notion.'

I seriously couldn't believe my ears. Spoken like a true white middle-class male wanker.

'The women's movement might be making good progress, but our government is still dominated by men, we still don't have pay parity in most workplaces, there's still an unconscious bias that boys are better at maths and sciences than girls, career mums still do the majority of the housework and kid-wrangling, female authors write women's fiction, whereas male authors write fiction, and that's even before we take into account minority groups, women in some Middle Eastern countries and transgender women. We still need to fight for *their* rights.'

'Agreed, but that's not about feminism—that's about humanity, making sure that every human being on the planet is valued just as much as the next one—but extreme feminism does more harm that it does good these days.'

'How the hell do you figure that?'

'Well, men are damned if they do and damned if they don't. I tried to open a door for a woman last week and she called me a sexist pig. She said she could open the fucking door herself. And what about dates? Do you or do you not offer to buy a drink? Pay for dinner? Once upon a time, paying for your date was seen as chivalrous. Now some women get offended, thinking you think it means they don't earn enough to take care of themselves.'

I laughed out loud. *That* was his argument? He had to be taking the piss or he was one of the worst kind of men's rights apologists I'd ever come across. 'I let you buy me a drink tonight. And yesterday. But I also bought *you* a drink. If you truly did meet a woman who called you a sexist pig for showing her a bit of common courtesy, then you're right, she's a disgrace against feminism, but that's like saying all priests are sex offenders.'

He shrugged one broad shoulder. 'Maybe she was, but I think today's feminism has some serious flaws. Take the whole "Me Too" movement for example.'

'What?! How on earth can you think women standing up for themselves, speaking out against abuse and sexual harassment can be a bad thing? You're a cop, for crying out loud. You must see the worst of it!'

'Yeah, and I don't condone any of it, but there are degrees. Me Too is hugely problematic, if you ask me. It was meant to be about making women feel empowered, when all it's really doing is making them look like victims and criminalising men.'

'It doesn't criminalise *all* men, only those who need to be pulled up on their behaviour. And trust me, there are plenty of them out there. The number of inappropriate comments I've had while just trying to do my job—from other journos and from men I'm interviewing—is disgusting.'

'I'm not disputing that, but there are also plenty of good men. And some guys are now worried about being alone with women they work with for fear they'll be accused of sexual harassment. Women want equal opportunities in the workplace but the fact is, men in senior positions are going to be fearful of hiring women because being alone with them can be dangerous. Behind closed doors, it's always the man's word against the woman and we all know who gets believed.'

'So what?' I threw my hands up in the air. 'We should all just let the patriarchy continue because it's easier that way? I can't believe what I'm hearing. How can you say you believe in human rights yet not feminism?'

'I didn't say I don't believe in feminism per se, I said I wouldn't call myself a feminist and I don't want to be associated with detrimental movements like Me Too. I don't want to be associated with digital witch-hunts that seem to be the domain of third-wave feminism.'

'Digital witch-hunts?'

He nodded and named a few recent prominent cases in which men had been hauled over the coals online for alleged inappropriate behaviour. 'I want to be able to make up my own mind about people and issues but feminists want everyone to think exactly the same way they do.'

'That's ridiculous. Maybe if you'd actually experienced any form of discrimination or abuse in the—'

His expression grew dark. 'You have no idea what I know and what I don't. And quite frankly, as a journalist, I thought you'd be more open to debate and discussion. You say feminism is about every human on the planet having freedom of choice, yet you don't like that my outlook and opinions vary slightly to yours.'

'That's not true!' I shook my head but what was the point debating with him? It was clear he was one of those misogynistic men who was happy to sleep with a woman but would never respect them. No matter what I said, I wasn't going to change his values. His messed-up views on love should have been a red flag but I'd been too consumed with lust to take them seriously.

He raised an eyebrow.

'You know,' I said, wishing my clothes had landed nearer to the bed when I'd hurriedly discarded them, 'I don't have to sit here and argue with you about this.'

'No.' He grinned that infuriating smile and leaned back against the bedhead, locking his hands behind his head. 'You don't. We could have sex again instead.'

My stomach flipped traitorously, but no way was I sleeping with him again. I had more self-respect than that.

'I don't think so.' I flung back the sheet and snatched up my knickers.

'Suit yourself,' came his cocky voice from behind me.

I quickly found the rest of my outfit and as I dressed, I felt his eyes burning into me. It felt like déjà vu from when I rushed out of the hotel last week. Although I didn't believe in the outdated notion of man-hating feminists, right now I wasn't feeling much enamoured with the male of the species.

So much for a bit of a fling to make me feel better.

I was almost at the door when he spoke again. 'Forgotten something?'

I whirled around to find him twirling my lanyard on his finger. I stalked across the cabin and snatched it off him. 'Thanks.'

'Come on, Geraldine. Don't be like this. We don't need to see eye to eye on everything to have fun together, and you can't deny we were having a lot of fun.'

'Whatever we were having, it's over,' I said, and this time I didn't look back as I opened the door and slammed it behind me.

11

I awoke in my own bed, in my own cabin, to the sun blaring through the portholes. It looked to be a beautiful day out on the ocean but I buried my head under the pillow. I couldn't believe we still had another twenty-four hours until we could disembark. If I wasn't such a terrible swimmer, I'd have thrown myself overboard and started towards the mainland, trying my luck with the sharks.

Don't be so miserable.

Jay was only ever supposed to be a distraction to take my mind off Christos, so why was I letting our disagreement get to me? It had to be because I was still recovering from a broken heart. If only we'd left it at a one night stand—the quick rebound sex it was supposed to be—I might have been feeling empowered. But instead I felt almost dirty, and the horrors of Thursday afternoon seemed even worse than they had at the time.

I couldn't believe Christos and I were through. A sound like a cat whose tail had been stepped on escaped my mouth and tears followed accordingly. I threw off the pillow, snatched up a tissue and buried my face in it. The tissue immediately turned black, and I remembered that when I'd fled back to my cabin last night, I'd thrown myself straight into bed, no energy or inclination to take off my make-up. Just fabulous!

There seemed to be only two options at my disposal—I could stay in bed all day, feeling sorry for myself while watching Elvis movies on the TV, *or* I could put Christos *and* Jay behind me and enjoy the last full day on the ship with Mum and Gralice, hopefully finding some time to finally start our interview.

I took my time showering and choosing an outfit—a floral-print maxi skirt, black long-sleeved tee and a white fringed jacket that never failed to boost my mood when I wore it. I wanted something that made me feel good about myself, nothing to do with the fact I might have the great misfortune of running into Jay.

No longer a streaked-mascara mess, I knocked on Gralice's door first and was pleasantly surprised to find her actually inside.

'Well, isn't this a lovely surprise. You forgot to say goodbye last night and I thought we might not see you *quite* so early.'

I ignored her raised eyebrows and the insinuation in her voice. 'Have you had breakfast yet?'

Gralice shook her head. 'No, I was about to see if you and Sappho wanted to go eat now?'

'It's a yes from me.' I injected an enthusiasm I didn't feel into my voice.

'I just need to put on my shoes.'

'Okay. I'll see if Mum's ready.'

'Mrs Johnston is not in there,' Raquel told me as I lifted my hand to Mum's cabin door.

'Oh. Well. Never mind. Have a great day, Raquel.'

'You too.' She hit me with her bright smile and scurried into the storage room.

124

'Is Sappho not ready?' Gralice asked as she emerged from her cabin.

I shook my head. 'She must have already gone to meet Rosa. Maybe we'll see them up there.'

'They do seem to be very good friends,' Gralice said as we walked. 'I think she's the first friend of your mother's I've actually liked since that naughty little Italian girl she went to school with.'

'It's hard not to like Rosa,' I said, realising that I couldn't remember my mother having many friends at all. Sure she'd socialised with the mothers of Will's and my school friends, but I was pretty certain most of those associations had dwindled not long after we'd graduated. She and Dad were members of the local lawn bowling club, but I don't think she saw any of those people outside their Saturday afternoon bowls session. 'And it's good to see Mum doing something for herself for a change.'

'Amen,' said Gralice—the least religious person I knew—as we got into the elevator.

We smiled and made the usual small talk with our fellow passengers and then emerged onto the food court level, but there was no sign of Mum or Rosa.

Luckily, no Jay either.

'Maybe they've gone to the restaurant. Shall we go down and see if we can find them?' Gralice suggested.

'Do you mind if we eat here?' I gestured to my foot, which although much improved still twinged a little when I walked more than a few metres. 'We can find the others later.'

She nodded. 'Of course.'

In great need of comfort, I started with thick fluffy pancakes loaded with mascarpone cream and berries and Gralice began with a bowl of fruit.

'So,' she said the moment we were both back at the table, 'how was your evening with Hot Stuff? I suppose he was the reason you deserted us the night before as well.'

'I don't know what you're talking about. I was just tired.'

Gralice raised her eyebrows. 'I didn't come down in the last shower, Ged, but if you don't want to kiss and tell ...'

I sighed. 'Turns out he was a bit of a wanker.'

She snorted. 'I see. What exactly was the problem? Did he talk too much about himself? Wax lyrical about his ex-girlfriend? Or his mother?'

I could tell her any number of irritating things Jay had said or done during our brief time together, but I chose only the big one. 'We had an argument about feminism.' Then I told her word for word our conversation. 'He just doesn't get it.'

'Sounds like a lost cause,' she surmised when I was finished. 'But was the sex any good?'

I understand it's unusual to talk about such things with one's grandmother, but Gralice and I had spoken about sex long before I was actually doing it.

'I hate to say it,' I admitted, slumping back in my chair, 'but I'm not sure there are enough words to describe how good it was.'

'Well, chin up, girl.' Her eyes sparkled. 'Sounds like a couple of good nights spent if you ask me. I'm guessing he took your mind off the Greek at least a little.'

'Yes, but ...'

'No buts! Stop beating yourself up. Sometimes the best sex of your life is with people you don't even like.'

'Maybe ... but it was good with Christos and I *love* him.'

I sniffed—a fresh wave of pain washing over me—and picked up my serviette to pat at my eyes. Why on earth had I thought putting more mascara on was a good idea? Why had I thought rebound sex might make me feel better? It was nothing more than a temporary plaster over the pain.

Gralice reached across the table and patted my hand. 'Oh, darling, I didn't say it wasn't good with someone you love. If the chemistry *and* the emotion is there, there's nothing better.'

She spoke like she knew what she was talking about. I tried to swallow the lump in my throat so I could ask her if she'd ever felt that way about anyone, but before I could, a shadow fell over the table.

'What are you two looking so glum about?' Mum asked as she lowered herself into the seat beside me. Rosa took the other empty chair.

'Um ...' Mum would likely not approve if I told her about Jay, or she'd start grilling me about his husband potential. And although I suspected Rosa wouldn't judge me, I didn't want her to know what a terrible judge of men I was. It was already embarrassing enough that the first time we'd met she'd heard about my partner dumping me for his *ex*-wife.

Anyway, I was feeling a little better after my chat with Gralice. She was right—two nights of hot sex wasn't anything to pine over; nothing like almost a year and the belief we had a future together.

'Just Christos,' I said with a little shrug.

'Oh, sweetheart.' Mum gave me a quick hug. 'I'm sure you'll find someone twice the man that he was.'

I shook my head. 'I'm done with men. They're way more trouble than they're worth.'

'Amen,' said Gralice again.

'Anyway ...' Mum cleared her throat and pointed to my plate of pancakes. 'Those look good and I've worked up quite an appetite.'

'Doing what?' I asked.

She and her assistant exchanged a look.

'We've been at the gym,' Rosa informed us.

Now I'd heard everything. Aside from the few weeks she got up early to do *Aerobics Oz Style* in front of the telly when I was a kid, I couldn't remember my mother ever doing any kind of workout. She always said a housewife didn't need exercise and had even done a vlog recently about the amount of calories burned during half an hour of mopping, vacuuming or ironing.

But I guess she did have a *public image* to uphold.

'Good for you,' I said, somehow managing *not* to ask if they'd seen a tall, incredibly muscled redhead while they were there.

'Is there anything specific you want to do for our last full day on the ship?' Gralice asked as Mum and Rosa ate.

'We're going to film some video for my YouTube channel,' Mum said between mouthfuls of pancake. 'We've been so busy, we've forgotten all about it since day one.'

'And then we thought we might go watch the Elvis and Priscilla lookalike contests. And tonight there's the Young Elvis Rising Star contest. That should be fun,' finished Rosa. 'Or do either of you have any better ideas?'

I looked to Gralice hopefully. 'Maybe we could spend some time talking about your biography?'

'Okay.' Gralice nodded. 'We can do that for a few hours and meet up for lunch.'

'And shall we try and book one of the special restaurants for our last night together?' Mum asked.

I looked to Gralice for confirmation—it was her cruise after all—but Rosa spoke first. 'We're probably too late now, but the waterfront one is very nice.'

'And I think Gralice has a crush on our waiter,' I teased.

'The Russian one?' Mum looked outraged. 'He's even younger than Ged.'

Gralice laughed. 'I was young once too, you know. Anyway, Oleg's nice eye-candy but he couldn't handle me.'

'I really like your mother,' Rosa said, smiling at mine.

Mum uttered a disapproving 'tsk', but grinned as she did, and then Gralice and I said goodbye and went off to find a quiet place to work.

12

The first two bars Gralice and I looked into were too busy and noisy for her liking, so we continued until we found one deserted except for a lone barman polishing glasses behind the bar.

'This looks good.' Gralice pointed to some leather armchairs over by the window. 'Do you want to sit and I'll get us some coffees?'

Coffee was the least of my worries as I looked around the lounge area. The tables and couches had been pushed to the edges to make room for about six rows of plastic chairs set up with an aisle down the middle. My gaze went to the front of the chairs where a floral archway with the words 'Little White Wedding Chapel' in bold pink print had been set up.

They're going to renew their vows on Monday.

Jay's words from our first proper conversation landed in my head and my belly rolled—not in a good way.

'This looks like it might be set up for a private function,' I managed.

'So?' Gralice shrugged. 'Nobody's even here yet.'

She was right. Also, there were probably loads of people renewing their vows this weekend, and even if the worst happened and this was the setting of Jay's grandparents' special event, who cared? As Gralice said, this was a public area. And why the hell was I so on edge anyway?

If this *was* Jay's grandparents do, and he *did* turn up, one of two things would occur—he'd either ignore me *or* attempt to talk to me. I wasn't sure what would be worse or why I even cared. We were both adults.

So what?

We'd slept together?

Big deal.

But maybe it was just too soon after our argument.

The best thing about a one-night stand was that you generally didn't have to face the person ever again. Sadly, on a cruise the chances of running into your one-nighter were significantly greater.

As Gralice approached the bar, I sank into an armchair and set my laptop on the coffee table in front of me. Although I vowed not to let thoughts of Jay affect me, I may have angled my chair so that if his party did turn up, he might not notice me. It didn't hurt to use some stealth.

'I thought these might be a bit of fun instead,' Gralice said when she returned a few minutes later carrying two tall glasses of what looked to be iced coffee, resplendent with cream, chocolate dust *and* even a straw. Take that, Jay!

'Thanks.' I took a lovely long sip. The bold taste of the coffee combined with a nice, cool sweetness felt like exactly what the doctor ordered to calm my nerves a little.

'So.' I put my drink down, switched on my voice recorder and opened the notebook where I'd started scribbling questions and ideas. 'I'm not sure yet whether to present the book in chronological order or more thematically, but I thought it might be easier to start at the beginning for the interviews.'

'As you wish,' said Gralice.

'Could you begin by telling me a little bit about your childhood?'

'Well ...what exactly do you want to know?'

'What are your earliest memories? You had a brother, right?'

She nodded.

'Were you close?'

'No. My father treated us very differently, which kind of made that impossible. He treated Richard like an adult from the age of about ten, whereas he treated me like a doll to show off to his associates. He wasn't a nice man, but he was a wealthy one and he used his money to get what he wanted.'

'Did your father make money from his bar? Or did he come from a rich family?'

She made a scoffing noise. '"Bar" is far too nice a word for what my father owned and operated. He came from a poor, working class family—his dad worked on the railway—and he was determined to rise above it. I'm not sure exactly what he did to change his circumstances originally. I wouldn't have put it past him to have been involved in something illegal, but by the time I was born, he owned what was essentially a brothel. He pretended he ran a theatre-style cabaret bar but his clientele was almost entirely male and the showgirls were often near-nude with pasties covering their nipples and flesh-coloured underpants that left little to the imagination. There were rooms at the back where patrons could pay for "private dances".' She made inverted commas with her fingers.

'There were plenty of depraved men just like him, happy to pay big bucks for the objectification of women. It made me sick knowing that the roof over my head, the food I ate, the clothes I wore, even my schooling were all paid for from such reprehensible activities.'

I was honestly gobsmacked. All I'd ever known about Gralice's parents was that her father had been a businessman in the entertainment and hospitality industry.

'You can't have known all that as a child though,' I said. 'At what age did you become aware of what your father's business actually entailed?'

'I think I had my suspicions much younger—I never liked the way my father treated my mother—but they were confirmed when Richard turned thirteen and our father took him to "work" to "make a man of him". He told him it was time for him to start learning the family business, and boy did Richard boast to his friends when he discovered what that was. I eavesdropped on his conversations and saw red.'

'What did your mother make of your brother's involvement so young?'

Gralice shrugged, but her tone when she spoke was bitter. 'She was a fan of the saying "boys will be boys" and she liked the lifestyle my father's business gave her. She liked the posh house, the fancy clothes, the nice things, but she wouldn't have dared object anyway. She knew her place as a woman and turned her other cheek when my father sampled the merchandise at work.'

I could tell she wasn't talking about the liquor behind the bar.

'If she did anything that didn't please him—if his dinner was cold, the bed sheets not wrinkle-free, if my brother and I misbehaved— he'd punish her.'

'He abused her?'

She nodded. 'Physically. Mentally. Emotionally. I'm pretty sure sexually as well. He viewed my mother as his possession to do with what he liked. As he did with any woman that worked for him. They all had a use-by date too. The clientele preferred them young. When

I first worked out what he was up to, I swear some of his girls were only a year or so older than I was.'

The thought that I was related to such a man made me ill.

Before I could properly digest this information, we heard voices and footsteps coming into the lounge. I'd almost forgotten about the possible vow ceremony but, although I hadn't suffered any sort of seasickness so far, nausea now swirled in my gut.

I slowly twisted my head to peer around the edge of the armchair like some kind of spy.

And there he was. Standing with about ten other people, gathered around an elderly couple. I sucked in a breath. Hopefully Jay would be so focused on his grandparents that he wouldn't notice me over here in the corner.

I retreated behind my cover, pressing my body deep into the armchair, and exhaled slowly.

'Oh my God! *He's* the guy you slept with?' Gralice spoke too loudly and Sod's Law meant the gathering crowd chose that moment to hush.

I glared at her and lifted my finger to my lips, praying they were all hard of hearing.

Suddenly a shrill voice pierced the air. 'Oh my God, Jay! There she is!'

Crap. I'd only heard that voice once before but it was imprinted in my memory—his sister, Kate. But what did she have against me? Surely she wasn't going to ruin her grandparents' vow renewal ceremony by calling me out as the woman who'd taken Jay away from precious family time? If she had a bone to pick, it should be with the gym—he'd spent way more time there than he had with me.

I sank lower into my seat, hoping an Elvis impersonator would show up soon to start proceedings, but the colour drained from Gralice's face.

And then a woman that could only be Kate appeared beside us. She looked like a grown-up Pippi Longstocking and had a fiery expression to match, her hands perched aggressively on her hips. But it was Gralice she was glaring at, not me.

'What do you want with me and my family?'

I was so stunned that I sat there open-mouthed a few moments.

'Kate. Calm down.' Jay appeared beside her.

'This is the woman I was telling you about. Wherever we go, she's watching us.'

'What's all the commotion?' Another voice entered the fray, this one belonging to the elderly man. 'Alice?' His eyes widened and he pressed a hand to his chest as he looked at my grandmother. 'Is it really you?'

Slowly, she raised herself from the armchair and gave him a bashful smile. 'Henry French. Fancy meeting you here.'

What was going on?

'You two know each other?' Kate looked from Gralice to her grandfather and to Jay. 'I told you she's been watching us.'

'Um, excuse me,' I said, not liking Kate any better than I liked her brother. 'But we were here first.'

'Maybe this time,' she spat, 'but *she's* been spying on my family the whole cruise. And the fact she knows Granddad makes it even more suspicious. What do you want from us?'

Jay opened his mouth but the old man spoke first. 'Kate, calm down. Alice isn't spying on us, are you?'

'Of course not,' Gralice said, indignation in her voice *and* the expression on her face. 'I'm here on the ship to celebrate my eightieth birthday, nothing more sinister than that.'

Henry smiled warmly at her. 'Well, happy birthday, Alice. It's lovely to see you again after all these years. I'd like you to meet my granddaughter Kate, and my grandson Jay.'

'Hello, Kate. Hello, Jay.'

Jay offered his hand and gave Gralice a friendly smile, but Kate's expression remained icy.

'We're on board to celebrate my wedding anniversary,' Henry said, stepping back a little and gesturing to the elderly woman dressed in a sweet, pale pink skirt and jacket—an outfit Gralice would never be seen dead in, but which suited this old dear. She crossed the room with the aid of a walking stick.

Jay rushed over to assist her and when they arrived, Henry put an arm around her shoulder and gazed adoringly at her. 'Alice, I'd like you to meet my lovely wife Shirley. Shirley, Alice is my ... a friend from long ago.'

The two women smiled at each other and shook hands.

'Nice to meet you, Shirley.'

'And you too. If you and Henry are old friends, you're more than welcome to come and join us for the renewal of our vows and enjoy a drink with us afterwards,' Shirley offered. 'I'd love to hear some stories from before Henry and I met.'

Jay chuckled. 'So would I.'

My stomach squeezed and I silently willed Gralice to decline. I didn't want to spend the last day of my cruise hanging out with Jay and his family, no matter how sweet his grandparents seemed.

'Oh, that's kind of you to offer, but Ged and I wouldn't want to intrude on such a special family occasion.'

No, we definitely would not.

'Congratulations to you both.' Alice looked from Shirley back to Henry with what I recognised as a forced smile.

'Thank you, Alice,' Henry and Shirley said in unison, then he added, 'Enjoy the rest of your cruise.'

'We will, thank you. Come along, Ged.'

I gathered up my things and as we left, Jay shot me a cocky smile. 'Bye, Geraldine.'

I didn't reply—glad I'd never given him the go-ahead to call me Ged—and hurried after Gralice.

'I know it's still early but I need a drink,' she said as we approached the elevators.

'Fine by me.'

We headed down a couple of levels to a bar I hadn't been in yet. There was definitely no shortage of drinking establishments on the ship and this one was all done up like something from colonial Australia. I grabbed a couple of beers—cocktails didn't feel quite right for this conversation and it was too early to start on the hard liquor—and joined Gralice at a table in the corner.

'So.' I put the drinks down in front of us. 'Are you going to tell me about Henry?'

She shrugged and drank from her glass, the beer froth gathering on her upper lip. 'There's nothing to tell.'

But she didn't meet my gaze and I knew her too well to believe such subterfuge. 'You know I'll get it out of you eventually.'

She let out an exasperated sigh. 'Fine. Henry's an old flame.' Her voice caught in her throat on this last word and I noticed her hand shaking.

It was so unlike Gralice to be flustered, especially over a man. 'How long were you together?'

'Maybe about a year.' She looked down into the beer as she spoke. 'But we were very young.'

'Did you love him?'

She took a moment, as if carefully contemplating her reply. 'More than I've ever loved anyone since.'

Oh my God. Shivers painted goosebumps on my skin. Her words were so heartfelt, so raw, and her eyes glistened as if she were trying hard not to cry. I could count on one hand the number of times I'd seen my grandmother cry—the first time she met each of her great-grandchildren, and last year when Philip and Craig got married.

I reached across and put my hand on hers. 'What happened?'

'He proposed. And I said no.'

I gasped. I don't know why it was so shocking—Gralice had never made quiet of the fact she didn't rate marriage—but perhaps it was the emotion, the hint of something that looked like regret in her eyes. 'Wow, and what happened then?'

'We broke up. Henry was moving away for work and thought a wife would improve his chances of promotion when he got there. I wasn't prepared to go with him and give up my own work in the university lab to go and be someone's handbag and live-in housekeeper.' She smiled sadly. 'We were both angry—he couldn't understand why I couldn't do this for him, and I couldn't understand how he could ask me to when he knew how I felt.'

While I was proud of Gralice for making such a stand, I imagined Henry must not only have been heartbroken but also aggrieved. Perhaps Jay's antagonism towards feminism had been passed down from his granddad.

'This wasn't the first time you'd seen Henry on the ship, was it?' Was this why Gralice had been acting so weird since we'd boarded the ship?

She looked away, but not before I saw her cheeks colour. *Oh my God*. It dawned on me that it wasn't just since being on the ship that Gralice had been acting out of character but that this whole Elvis cruise had come seemingly from nowhere.

'You knew Henry was going to be on the ship, didn't you?'

Slowly, she turned to meet my gaze again and nodded. 'I've been feeling a little nostalgic lately and I started thinking about him, all the fun we had together … I wondered what had become of him. Whether he was still in Victoria; whether he was even still alive.'

'And how did you find out?'

She huffed. 'I searched for him on the internet. I found an article about him retiring seventeen years ago, and he's even on Facebook. Sadly, his profile is set to private, but not all his family are. I found some profiles with the same surname and one of them posted something about a big family holiday on a cruise ship. They tagged Henry and ...'

'I get it,' I said. Kate's accusation of Gralice all but stalking them was sounding more and more on the money.

'Don't look at me like that. I know how often you young things check out *your* old boyfriends on Facebook.'

She was right—it was one of my and my girlfriends' favourite things to do late at night when we'd had too much to drink. It was always a joy to discover that an ex had got fat or gone bald, or was chief trolley pusher at Coles. I wasn't shocked by Gralice's social media know-how but by the fact she even had someone she'd bothered to go to this much effort for. I'd always seen her as kind of being above the emotions we mere mortals dealt with.

'How come you've never mentioned him before?'

She sighed. 'I guess talking about him was too painful. I've had a long and fulfilled life, but I'm only human. I can't help wondering sometimes what my life might have been like if I'd said yes.'

'Well, Mum wouldn't have been here for a start,' I said, rattled by Gralice's out-of-character, almost melancholy pondering, 'and that means neither would I, nor Will.' I tried for a joke. 'Granted the world could probably have done without Will, but could you imagine your life without me in it?'

She smiled and reached for my hand. 'Life without you wouldn't be worth living.'

I grinned back, feeling even closer to my grandmother than usual. 'The feeling's mutual.' But I had one more question. 'Did Philip know Henry?'

'No. He and I broke up long before I met Philip.'

'So you brought us all on the cruise because you knew Henry would be on the ship?'

She looked down into her beer and nodded.

'What were you hoping would happen? Were you planning on talking to him?'

Gralice was quiet a moment, then, 'I had just one wish ... I wanted to see him one last time.'

'Did you mean for him to see you today?'

'No. Definitely not. I didn't know Henry and Shirley were renewing their vows.' Gralice paused a moment. 'Do you think they look happy, or ...' Her voice drifted off and she looked as if she were fighting tears.

I didn't know what to say. Henry and Shirley had looked at each other with such adoration, and renewing your vows didn't seem like something you'd do if you weren't truly in love. But I wanted to tell Gralice the opposite, so I sat there like a mute, useless lump instead.

'I'm sorry,' she said after a few moments, sniffing and pulling herself together. 'That was a stupid question. I'm acting like a silly old woman and I'm terribly embarrassed.'

'Don't be. Love's nothing to be ashamed of. But if Henry is anything like his grandson, then you probably dodged a bullet.'

She half-smiled and took a swig of her beer. 'Maybe you're right.'

'I'm always right. But why did you bring Mum and me with you?'

'I was hardly going to go on a cruise by myself,' she said indignantly. 'And I wasn't lying when I said I thought it would be a good bonding opportunity. I wanted the chance to spend some time with Sappho.'

'Fair enough.'

'Promise me something, Ged?'

'Anything.' While this insight into another side of Gralice was fascinating, part of me hated seeing her so vulnerable.

'Can you please not tell your mother about ...' She let out a heavy sigh. 'About my ridiculous, silly and childish reason for dragging us all on this cruise? She probably wouldn't understand and—'

'Say no more,' I interrupted. 'My lips are sealed. But can I ask you something as well?'

'Anything. Always.'

'When you said you were ready for me to write your biography, did you mean it or—'

'I meant it, Ged, and I'm sorry I haven't made myself more available to you. I've been ... distracted, but I promise once we're home we can book in regular meetings and I'll give you my full cooperation.'

'Thank you.' I leaned over and gave her a hug and she embraced me more tightly than she ever had before in response.

13

When I walked into the newsroom early on Tuesday morning, I felt like I'd been gone for years and would probably have an Elvis earworm for life. So much had changed since last Thursday, yet, with only a few months to go until a decision was made about Darren's replacement, I couldn't afford to let anything distract me from work.

'Morning, Ged, how was your long weekend?' asked Libby, another reporter with her sights on promotion. 'Darren said you'd gone on a surprise cruise.'

Was that a hint of disapproval I heard in her tone?

'That's right.' I forced a smile as I scanned our open-plan office. No sign of Christos yet, although I knew I wouldn't be able to avoid him forever.

'How was it?'

'How was what?'

'The cruise.' She gave me a bemused smile.

Ah, right. 'It was ... fabulous. I've got some ideas for stories to pitch to Darren.' That wasn't a huge lie. It would be fascinating to take an in-depth look at the not so glamorous side of cruising—the gambling, the mysterious deaths, what it was really like for the crew living for months on end on a ship—and I'd taken a fair few mental notes while on board myself.

'Fantastic.' She gestured towards my desk. 'Looks like someone missed you.'

My insides tightened as I laid eyes on a massive bunch of bright flowers. They were a mix of cymbidium orchids, roses, disbud chrysanthemums and magnolias, with a few creamy white snapdragons to finish it off. Although they were drooping a little, I knew they'd have cost a fortune.

Were they from Christos or Jay?

Stupid to even think they were from the latter. Even if he were the type to send flowers—which I severely doubted—he didn't know where I worked, and why would he be sending them anyway? Perhaps they were from my grandfathers; I wouldn't put it past them to send the bouquet in an effort to try and cheer me up.

'When did they arrive?'

'Yesterday morning.'

That settled it. I'd still been on the ship then, which Phil, Craig *and* Jay had known, so they had to be from Christos. My stupid, traitorous heart lifted. Had he changed his mind about getting back together with Carly?

My hands shaking, I plucked the envelope from its holder and opened it. Libby watched me in the way someone might do if they were driving past a car accident.

Ignoring her, my eyes fell upon the short message: *I'm sorry, Ged. It breaks my heart to break yours. Christos.*

How dare he make such a gesture at work! If he wanted to prolong my agony, the least he could have done was had these blasted blooms delivered to my apartment. And the audacity and arrogance of him to assume he knew how I felt.

My heart was just fine, *thank you very much*.

'Are they from Christos?' Libby asked.

Why was she still lingering?

I scrunched up the 'sorry' and dumped it in the bin under my desk, wondering if everyone in our office knew Christos had gone back to Carly. It would only take one person to get wind of this fact and it would be round the newsroom in no time—we were, after all, experts at spreading news, particularly of the bad variety.

Were they all laughing at me? Or worse, pitying me? Was Libby hoping my heartbreak would distract me from my game? If so, she had another think coming. I wasn't going to hand her the promotion on a platter, any more than I planned on handing it to the other contender, Tom.

'You can have them if you want,' I told Libby, picking up the damn bouquet and thrusting it at her.

'Oh, are you sure? I do love chrysanthemums.'

'You're welcome to them,' I said, switching on my computer, ready to throw myself into work.

'Thanks.'

Beaming, Libby finally headed off to her desk and I took a sip of the takeaway coffee I'd picked up downstairs as I started going through my email. The whole weekend lift-out team had an editorial meeting every Monday to brainstorm, share our ideas and allocate stories for upcoming issues. I'd missed this meeting so was itching to talk to Darren about my possible cruise-ship article. Sadly, his office door was shut and I knew better than to barge in uninvited.

A little while later, Darren swung by my desk, leaning against it as he spoke. 'Good few days off, Johnston?'

A man who'd been in newspapers since God was a kid, he lived his work and called everyone by their surnames. It had surprised us all when he'd revealed his intentions to retire at the end of the year, but rumour had it his wife had threatened divorce if he didn't.

'Fabulous,' I replied and told him about my idea for an article about the not-so-Disney side of cruising.

'I love it.' He ran a hand through his silver-white hair. 'And I reckon you might even be able to stretch that into a series of articles—say, one a week for a month or something. But I've got something I need you to get a wriggle on first.'

I looked up in anticipation.

'Did you hear about the elderly dementia patient who had to have stitches last night after supposedly running into a wall at a Brighton nursing home?'

Although I'd read all the morning papers online in bed while snuggling with Coco as I always did, I'd also been fretting about having to face Christos so I wasn't sure anything had sunk in. I couldn't recall anything about this. 'Of course. Shocking.'

Darren thrust a press release at me.

'I want you to go deep. Talk to this man's family, any other residents who still have the brain power, family and friends of other residents, workers there if you can get permission. No one is buying the "wall" story and the police are investigating obviously, but we all know how hopeless they can be. See what you can find out about if the victim was assaulted by another patient or if it was one of the aged care workers.' He rubbed his hands together. 'This is an expensive care facility; families are paying big money to have their loved ones looked after—play on that angle too. Elder abuse always gets everyone outraged and I'm thinking unless we change prime ministers again, this might make a good cover story for this weekend's edition.'

'I'm onto it.'

A buzz shot through me. With a number of us working on the lift-out, cover stories weren't taken for granted, and even after all these years, I still got a thrill when I was allocated such a gritty subject. If this poor man's injury wasn't an accident, I wanted to make sure the public knew and the culprit got what they deserved. I would be incensed if this was one of my grandparents. And I also wanted to remind Darren exactly what I was capable of.

'Good. Throw in some things about the commission into elder abuse in aged care facilities as well. Maybe some statistics about the number of dementia patients in care. And keep me posted.'

'I will.'

As he stalked away, I took another swig of my now-cold coffee and snatched my handbag off my desk. Usually I'd do a little preliminary research online—see what else had been written about the incident so far—but this morning I jumped on the opportunity to get out of the office, away from a possible run-in with Christos.

I couldn't believe my luck (or rather *un*-luck) when the doors of the elevator opened and there he was. Alone. Every bone in my body went cold. Last time I'd seen him he was buck naked; today he was suitably covered in smart navy trousers and a pale pink shirt, open at the top button. Christos wasn't one for wearing ties, and he was one of the few men I knew who could wear baby pink and have women turning their heads and gawking at him in the street. It had something to do with his dark eyes, dark curls and Greek complexion.

'Morning.' I managed an apathetic tone as I sent a message from my brain to my heart reminding it what an utter wanker he was.

'Hey.' He reached out to drag me into the lift. 'I'm so glad we ran into each other. I haven't been able to stop thinking about you.'

I shrugged him off and all but plastered myself against the opposite side of the lift. 'Weren't you getting out?'

In reply, he pressed the close doors button. 'Did you get my flowers?'

'Yeah, thanks.'

'You're welcome.' Christos didn't seem to notice my sarcasm. 'Why haven't you been answering my calls or text messages?'

'I've been otherwise engaged.' I kept my chin high, half-hoping he'd ask me what exactly I'd been up to as I'd love to see his face if I told him about my escapades on the high seas with a stranger.

Would he be hurt? Would hurting him make my pain any easier?

'Do you want to go get a coffee? Or maybe we can catch up for lunch later?'

I glared at the man who just a week ago I'd thought was the love of my life. Was he for real?

'Um. No. I'm heading off to chase a story and I don't think we have anything to say to each other anyway.'

'You left in such a rush on Thursday. I didn't have the chance to properly explain.'

I glanced up at the digital display that was counting down the levels. It was moving way too slowly, so slowly in fact that I wondered if it was broken. Normally I prayed for a straight run down, but today I was desperate for the lift to stop on the next level and for someone else to join us. Of course the gods didn't listen—they were probably up there right now eating popcorn and Maltesers as they watched the farce that was my life unfold.

'You made yourself quite clear,' I said. 'You and Carly are getting back together. For the kids. But does your *wife* know you enjoyed one last shag with me before breaking it off?'

The elevator doors opened to the lobby and I shot out, not caring about my still-recovering foot, not *really* caring about his answer. Carly was welcome to him.

'Ged, please,' Christos called as I rushed towards the exit. 'I need to talk to you.'

I whirled around and hissed at him, 'Keep your voice down!' I didn't want to cause a scene that would become fodder for water cooler gossip.

'I will,' he implored, 'if you'll just give me five minutes.'

I couldn't resist the pleading expression in his burnt caramel eyes and against my better judgement, I relented. 'You can walk me to the cab rank.'

'Thank you.' He fell in beside me as we stepped outside into the cold. I tightened my thick orange coat around me and prayed there'd be a line of taxis waiting.

'I fucked up Thursday afternoon. I didn't get across what I meant and you didn't give me the chance to explain.'

'I don't think I need a rocket science degree to understand. Honestly, it was a shock, but it's probably best we both forget we ever meant anything to each other and it'll be much easier to do that if we—'

'I can't.' He shook his head. 'I can't do that, Ged. Because I love you.'

'What?' His words stopped me in my stride.

'I *love* you. I miss you. I already miss our conversations, I already miss being together. You're the last person I think about when I go to sleep and the—'

'Don't say that!' My voice caught as I held my hand up, willing him to shut up but at the same time wanting him to continue.

'It's true.'

'And let me guess, you love Carly and the kids too. What do you want? For us all to live together in some weird polygamous situation?'

'No, of course not. And I don't love Carly.'

My heart squeezed in hope.

'Not in that way. Not anymore. I love that she's a good mother, we're friends, we respect each other and we both want the best for our children. Issy's been having a tricky time and has recently been caught with drugs at school.'

'Shit.' I forgot myself for a moment. Isidore, Christo's oldest daughter, was only fourteen. 'I'm so sorry.'

'The school counsellor thinks she's reacting to her home situation. She said divorce is never easy on kids, no matter what you do, and that nest parenting isn't for everyone. When Carly and I tried to talk to Issy about how we can make things better, she screamed that the only way to make it easier would be if we hadn't got divorced in the first place. Her behaviour is really scaring us, Ged. Carly and I have been at our wits' end wondering what to do and so she's proposed we get back together—in name only, until the kids have left school.'

What? That was the most ridiculous thing I'd ever heard and only reinforced my belief that Christos's kids were a little spoilt. 'But Lexia is only five. That's years away.'

'Time flies, and our children are worth the sacrifice.'

'Hang on. What do you mean "name only"? Will you and Carly not sleep together? Won't the kids get suspicious if you don't share a bed?'

'We'll share a bed, but there won't be any sex.'

I found that hard to believe. Had Christos looked in the mirror lately? What if Carly got horny while reading *Fifty Shades* one night and he was just there?

'Both of us have agreed that we can, discreetly, see other people. Of course I don't want other people—I only want you.'

My mouth dropped open. Those four words coming from Christos's mouth turned my knees to jelly and my heart to mush. 'Are you ... I ... Oh my ...'

His lips relaxed into a comfortable smile as he pulled me into his arms and held me close. His arms felt nice, his embrace so right, so comfortable.

But I was so confused.

Thursday afternoon was still so horrifically clear in my head and I felt certain I hadn't misunderstood him. Was he backtracking now or was this what he'd been truly trying to tell me when I'd been scrambling around for my clothes?

'I still want us to be together, Ged,' he whispered into my hair. 'No one works the way we do. The past few days without you have been the worst few days of my life.'

'Mine too.' I blinked back tears and guilt—how would Christos feel if he knew how quickly I'd jumped into bed with someone else? 'But how exactly would this work?'

'Nothing would be very different from how we were before. We can still enjoy our afternoon rendezvous, and I'll still be able to stay at your place every few days.' He winked. 'Us journos are often away for work, but we'll simply have to be more covert about our relationship. As far as anyone will think, I'm married to Carly, but the three of us will know the truth.'

I yanked out of his embrace. He'd caught me off guard but I couldn't believe I was even contemplating such a situation. How low could my self-respect go?

'You're delusional,' I told him, shaking my head. 'You can't sit on the fence where love is concerned. I understand your devotion to your children, but I can't put myself through what you're suggesting. I don't want to be the *other* woman. I don't want to be your sordid secret. I deserve more than that, Christos.'

He blinked, and for the first time since we'd met it looked like he might be about to cry. 'I know you do, Ged. You deserve the world, but this is all I can offer right now.'

I nodded, swallowing the lump that had ballooned in my throat. 'I guess this is really it.'

Maybe I would regret this decision, maybe I'd end up a lonely old woman—with dogs, not cats—but I couldn't live with myself if I accepted his proposition. As far as I could see, Christos would be the only winner in such a situation. He'd have the best of both worlds—a wife and a mistress.

And I wasn't going to be anyone's mistress.

14

Of all the ways to wake up on a Saturday morning, a dog standing over you and breathing into your face was one of the least appealing.

'Ugh, get off!' Shoving Coco away, I sat up and grimaced as her stinky breath turned my stomach. 'We need to do something about your dental hygiene.'

She cocked her head to one side, then leapt off the bed and shot out of my room, her paws scratching the floorboards in her haste. Yawning, I grabbed my mobile from the bedside table and checked the time. Yikes, almost ten o'clock. Even on weekends I rarely slept this late, but I had been burning the candle at both ends recently.

Putting my dog's needs ahead of my own, which involved making a cup of coffee and heading back to bed, I got up and stuffed my feet into my ugg boots. After dragging on my dressing gown, I pottered through the apartment to where Coco, leash between her teeth, waited by the door.

'Sorry, beautiful girl,' I said as I clipped the leash onto her collar. Once outside she made a beeline for her favourite bush.

'Feel better now?' I smiled at her, grateful she hadn't made a mess inside. 'Come on, let's go get you some breakfast.'

But Coco did not want to go back inside.

As I walked towards the building, she yanked the leash in the opposite direction, pulling me towards the gate that led to the outside world. It struck me she hadn't had a proper walk since I'd hurt my foot, which was—*Oh Lord*—over three weeks ago.

What kind of terrible dog owner was I?

Since leaving the ship, I'd become even more of a workaholic. The only good thing about parting ways with Christos was I now had all the time in the world to focus on work and Gralice's biography. True to her word, she'd committed to regular meetings. I'd already filled two notebooks, which I'd started to transcribe and shape into chapters on my computer. Working so hard gave me little time to dwell on the end of my relationship, but the casualty of all this dedication had been my poor pup.

Guilt swamped me, but no matter my remorse, if I went out dressed like this people were likely to assume I was homeless and start throwing coins at me.

'Breakfast, shower, then walkies,' I said, tugging Coco towards the building.

She planted her paws on the ground and refused to budge.

'Please.' I dropped down to my haunches and rubbed her behind her ears in the way she adored. 'You need to let me get dressed first.'

Whether she understood or not, she wasn't on board with this plan. She was a dead weight as I pulled against her lead and, at almost forty kilograms last vet check, I was helpless against her. Frustrated, I looked around for somewhere to secure her. We weren't supposed to leave dogs unattended in the courtyard but what other option did I have?

'Be good,' I told her sternly and rushed inside to get dressed. Worrying she might start barking, I bypassed a shower, coffee and breakfast, but as I pulled on a pair of black leggings, I decided skipping breakfast might be beneficial anyway. I was also one of those people who ate their feelings rather than starved them, so since my break-up with Christos I'd been devouring packets of Tim Tams like they were carrot sticks and my leggings were tighter than I recalled. Coco's intervention had come not a moment too soon.

Back in the courtyard, she went bonkers at the sight of my sneakers as I untied her. 'Come on, you silly girl.'

It was a beautiful sunny morning in Carlton Gardens and there were lots of people out and about making the most of nice weather—parents pushing prams, kids screaming on the playground, folks sitting reading on the grass, teenagers kicking around a soccer ball and other crazies doing some kind of group exercise near the old Moreton Bay fig. While Coco rushed about sniffing at all the gross things she could find, I enjoyed the fresh air and quiet solitude as I took stock of where I was at in Gralice's life story.

We'd covered her childhood and her education at an all-girls private school in Melbourne's inner suburbs, where she'd been forced to take home economics and mothercraft classes. I'd laughed when she told me how she'd almost been expelled for using her sewing skills to turn her school uniform skirt into a pair of culottes. Apparently her father hadn't found it so amusing. It was the first time he'd physically punished her, and the day she attributed to cementing her determination to do something about the inequality between the sexes.

But as much as I was enjoying our chats and loved discovering all these new things about my grandmother, I was also itching to finish the book so I could send it out into the world.

When Coco paused to inspect a patch of grass, I took a moment to peruse the news on my phone. Whenever Christos had been with me on a Saturday or Sunday we'd go through the papers together in bed—this was one of the many things I missed about 'us'. Being single in your thirties was lonely.

'You're on the wrong side of the path!'

I glanced up to see a man jogging on the spot, waiting, presumably, for me to get out of the way. Our eyes met and mine narrowed.

'Well, well, well … if it isn't the lovely and feisty Geraldine.'

My stomach plummeted as I thought of my unwashed face, my unbrushed hair, which I'd hurriedly fingered into a ponytail, and the old baggy jumper I'd thrown on over the top of my leggings in my haste to get back outside to Coco.

Why was it a cruel fact of life that whenever you ran into an ex-boyfriend—not that Jay fit that definition—you were always looking your worst?

'How are you?' It sounded like he thought running into me was the funniest thing ever.

I had no words and surely my eyes had to be deceiving me. Granted I never paid much attention to the frenzied joggers pounding the pavement in my local park, but I was certain I'd have noticed if he'd been one of them. His hair was wet from sweat, as was his grey T-shirt, and his face glistened from exertion, but somehow this didn't detract at all from his edgy attractiveness.

'Cat got your tongue, Geraldine?'

'No!' I recovered, repeating the mantra 'wanker, wanker, wanker' in my head. 'I just can't believe the misfortune of running into you.'

My heart pounded as I spoke. I hadn't thought of him in more than two weeks. Well, not much.

He pressed his hand against his chest as if wounded but his chuckle gave him away. 'Now, now, no need to be so cruel.' Then he dropped down to his haunches and reached out to rub my dog's head. 'I'm guessing this is the delightful Coco?'

I was impressed he remembered her name and also infuriated at the way she reacted to his touch. Her tongue flopped out of her mouth and her eyelids fluttered as she leaned into his hand. *Damn hussy.* I yanked at the leash in an effort to put distance between them. 'I thought you didn't like dogs.'

He pushed to a stand again. 'I never said that.'

I tapped my foot. 'At any rate, we've detained you from your exercise routine far too long and we have pressing matters to attend to also.'

Why was I suddenly speaking like an English dissertation?

'I guess that means you can't spare the time to grab a coffee?'

What? Did he *mean* coffee or was he alluding to a quickie behind one of the bushes?

'I'd love the chance to set a few things straight. I think you may have got the wrong idea about me.'

'What? That you were a misogynist?'

The corners of his mouth turned up. 'Yes.'

Hmm. 'Do you live round here?' I asked, biding time and wondering if him being in the area was an aberration. This park was my and Coco's sanctuary—our little slice of nature in the city, a place where she could sniff other dogs' pee and I could unwind after a stressful day. The possibility of running into Jay would unbalance that.

'Yep, I live on Walter St, in the old milk bar.'

'Really?' I knew it well. 'I thought that building was deserted.'

'Maybe it looks that way from the front, but I've renovated it to my liking inside. What about you? You live nearby?'

I nodded and found myself giving him my just-around-the-corner address.

'I'm surprised we've never run into each other before.'

'Me too.' I took a step back—it was getting harder and harder to ignore his very masculine scent. Would coffee be *such* a disaster?

I was in dire need of a cup and it wasn't like I was going to do anything stupid when I hadn't even showered or brushed my teeth. Hearing him trying to justify his primitive thoughts might even be amusing.

'I've only got time for a quick one.'

His eyes widened as if he were surprised by my acquiescence, but he quickly suggested a cafe nearby. 'How's your foot? You okay to walk that far?'

'It's better now.'

'Great. Well, this place has the best coffee in Carlton.'

I couldn't believe it. He'd named the cafe where I bought my coffee every morning before I hopped on the tram that took me into the CBD.

'How long have you lived round here?' Jay asked as we started towards the cafe.

'On and off for twelve years. I moved out of home and in with my grandmother while I was at uni, and then I went to London for eight years. When I came home I rented a small apartment. You?'

'About five years. I was stationed in the country before that.'

I couldn't imagine Jay doing small-town life well, but I guess most cops did their stint in the sticks. 'Do your family live nearby?'

'My sister lives far too close for comfort, but everyone else is in Geelong,' he said as he untied a black sweatshirt from around his waist and pulled it over his head. 'What about yours?'

'My parents live in Port Melbourne. Dad's parents have both passed, but Gralice, Mum's mum, still lives around the corner in Fitzroy where she's been for almost fifty years, and Mum's fathers are in St Kilda.'

'Fathers?' Jay sounded as if he might've heard wrong.

'That's right,' I said, not about to get into my family history with him. 'Have you heard about Mars yet?

'No, but I should know if I've made it through to the next round soon.'

Once at the cafe, Coco and I sat outside while Jay went in to order our drinks and an egg and bacon toastie for me. He tried to shout me, but I insisted on paying my own way. This was *not* a date and even if it was, after our conversation on the cruise, I wouldn't have allowed it. He returned a few moments later with a number for the table and I wondered what was I doing, sitting here at my favourite cafe with the man who'd both seduced and riled me on the ship.

Coco slouched between us as if settling in for the long haul and Jay leaned back in his seat as if doing the same. 'Funny about our grandparents knowing each other, isn't it?'

I nodded, not wanting to say too much on this issue for fear I might reveal his grandfather was my grandmother's primary reason for going on the ship. 'So, what did you want to say to me that might make me change my mind about you?'

'Right. I kinda wanted to apologise for how we left things. I thought we were having a fun banter, but I do tend to take things to the extreme sometimes, especially when I'm talking about issues I feel strongly about.'

'Like how flawed modern feminism is?'

He winced. 'Look, it's not that I'm against the core values of the women's rights movement, but rather some of the avenues that are being used these days.'

'Like Me Too?'

He nodded. 'I know I went off on a tangent about that but I'm genuinely worried that the mass sharing of small stories about inappropriate behaviour detract from the big accounts of abuse. You can't tell me that rape and wolf-whistles are the same thing, yet Me Too lumps serial sex offenders in the same hashtag as bad dates and sleazy comments.'

'I'm not saying cat-calling is the same as rape,' I retorted, 'but neither can you tell me that kind of behaviour is okay, because it often leaves women feeling vulnerable and unsafe. Yes, there are huge differences between the two acts but there are also dangerous similarities.'

'I'll give you that,' he said with a single nod, 'but I also think resources would be better focused on genuine cases of sexual misconduct and really helping the victims and their families in cases of domestic violence. How does posting online about how someone once wolf-whistled at you get to the core of the issue we *all* want to address. We need to be protecting the kids, women and men that are trapped in situations of real abuse rather than wasting precious resources on the odd sexist remark.'

'But how do you define "real abuse"? At least we're attempting to break the culture of silence, raising awareness and stimulating important conversations about male accountability—hopefully serving to reshape people's opinion on what is actually acceptable.'

'But is public shaming more important than real ethical reflection and action? Is a hashtag on its own enough? I think it's dangerous on many levels giving it too much power. People start to believe that real problems can be solved by mass comment, when what we really need is action at a deeper level.'

I wanted to argue simply because I don't like admitting defeat, but he had some valid points. 'No movement is perfect, but Me Too is also only one aspect of feminism. The overall goal is men and women working towards awareness of what is acceptable behaviour and what is not, of making the world a fair and safe place for all, regardless of gender, and there's still a lot of work to be done in that area.'

'Now that I will agree with,' he conceded.

I grinned, feeling victorious. 'So whether you'll admit it, there is still a place for feminism today and I think you do actually fit the definition of a feminist.'

He chuckled. 'Maybe I just don't like labels or being put in a box.'

A waiter arrived at our table before I could respond to that, delivering two steaming mugs and a chunky toasted sandwich that oozed cheese out its edges. My mouth watered just looking at it.

'Thanks,' we said in unison and then the waiter retreated.

Jay lifted his mug to his mouth and downed what looked to be half his drink in a matter of seconds, but when I tasted mine, I screwed up my nose.

'What's wrong?

'Does your coffee taste okay? I think the milk might be off in mine.'

'Mine tastes great, but we don't have the same milk.'

'Oh?'

'My milk is soy. I'm vegan.'

'Really?'

'It's cheaper, and healthier— the research is undeniable—but even more important are the environmental factors. Farming for meat has such a detrimental effect on the planet.'

'So what happens to farm animals if we all go vegan? Are you suggesting we just let them die out?'

'I can't see *everyone* going vegan—but how is that any worse than breeding them specifically to kill them?'

Jay had a point.

'And,' he went on, 'do you know how much grain we produce and how much land space that takes up so that we can feed all these beasts humans feel entitled to eat? Let's just say it would go a long way towards helping fight poverty in the third world.'

'Maybe, but why would you care about any of that if you're going to Mars?'

'I care, Geraldine. For one, it's a slim hope that I'll actually make the next round, never mind the final cut. And two, I still believe in preserving the earth and what we have, even while believing we need to start exploring other alternatives.'

I swallowed another bite of my sandwich, then smiled. 'So a bit like feminism?'

'How do you figure that?'

'Even though a lot of good work is being done, there's still a long way to go.'

The corners of his eyes crinkled. 'When you believe something, you don't back down, do you?'

'Is everything okay here?' our waiter asked before I could reply. I'd been so enthralled in our conversation I hadn't even noticed him reappear.

'Yes, thanks.' I totally forgot about my coffee until he'd gone.

'So,' I said, 'do you work round here as well? Are you at the Fitzroy or Carlton Police Station?'

'Neither. I'm with SOG—Special Operations Group.'

SOG responded to critical incidents like hostage situations, armed offenders and bomb threats. They were highly trained, highly skilled officers prepared to put their lives on the line in high-risk situations. It was exactly the kind of role I could imagine Jay in. And, annoyingly, it only made him more intriguing.

'And how are things with your ex?' he asked, possibly to detract the conversation from his work. From what I understood, SOG officers weren't supposed to say much about what they did. Trade secrets or something. Still, it surprised me how much he appeared to have gleaned (and remembered) from our brief conversations on the cruise.

'They're well and truly over. I'm trying to keep busy and not think about him.'

'Good idea.' Jay smiled and warmth travelled from the top of my head right to my toes.

I told him about my mother's book deal going ahead, that my brother and sister-in-law had just announced they were having their third baby in four years, and that I was making good progress on Gralice's biography. Although I didn't think we had anything in common, we'd managed to make conversation that didn't feel awkward despite the fact we'd seen each other naked.

When his phone beeped, alerting him to a text message, I looked around while he read it and was astounded to see that lunch was now being served. How had we managed to talk for so long?

He pushed to his feet. 'I'm sorry, that was work—I'm going to have to go.'

'No worries.' I smiled. 'This was only supposed to be a quick drink after all.'

He nodded and as he slid his phone into his pocket he reached down to ruffle Coco's fur with a 'Bye, girl' then straightened. 'Well, this was fun. You have a great rest of the weekend.'

What? That was it? No exchange of numbers or suggestions to see each other again? I couldn't help being a little disappointed and wasn't sure whether I liked this polite, well-behaved Jay or the one who'd infuriated me on the cruise better.

'Yeah, you too,' I replied as he turned and swaggered off down the footpath.

15

Coco couldn't believe it when I clicked her leash to her collar and took her for *another* walk. After my weird morning with Jay, I'd showered and dressed, and was now ready for an afternoon with Gralice. As we walked the short distance to my grandmother's house, I found myself on edge, wondering if I might run into him again. Now that I knew we lived in the same suburb, I'd never be able to run down the street to the supermarket to buy a carton of milk without first making sure I looked presentable.

Sure, he'd seen me at my worst this morning, but that didn't mean I ever wanted to repeat that situation. I didn't want Jay to be questioning his sanity about sleeping with me in the first place, I wanted him to be fantasising about doing it again.

Not that I *ever* planned on going back there, but it irked me that he hadn't even asked for my number this morning. Then again, I guess it wasn't surprising considering his stance on relationships. *Well, buddy, you don't need to worry about me. I am well and truly done with men.* In fact, if nuns didn't have to wear full body armour—was that even still a requirement?—then I'd probably join a convent. It would also solve the problem of having to see Christos at work.

As I let myself in to my grandmother's place in Fitzroy, I recoiled at the stench. Her house never smelled of candles or baking like my parents' place, but it didn't usually smell this bad either.

I dropped my bag, keys and Coco's leash to the floor. 'Gralice?'

'In here.'

I followed her voice down the hallway to the spare room, which apparently contained a bed for guests that hadn't been seen in decades because the room had been overrun with scientific journals and other books.

Gralice wasn't much for sentimental possessions but bought on average a book a week and never parted with any of them, thus had a library to rival the local public one. Most of her collection was non-fiction—in addition to thick scientific tomes, she had all the famous feminist texts, books about philosophy and psychoanalytic theory, body image, reproduction, religion and politics—but there were also the usual classics and pretty much every novel ever nominated for a significant literary prize in her lifetime.

'You look shocking,' Gralice said, jolting me from my thoughts of her past.

'Gee, thanks.' In old clothes that hung on her body, she was hardly looking like a supermodel herself, but she'd been so funny about her age lately that I decided not to mention it. 'And it's lovely to see you too.'

I kissed her on the cheek, once again getting a whiff of that peculiar smell. Was it the old-person aroma I'd heard about or had the movement of the old books and papers polluted the air?

'I'm serious, Ged. You're looking rather sallow.'

'I'm fine. Just tired.'

'Would you like a coffee?' she asked, pushing herself to her feet. Her flexibility was pretty impressive for an eighty-year-old woman.

The taste of this morning's caffeine disappointment still lingering in my mouth, my stomach turned at the thought of trying again. 'Do you have any Diet Coke?'

'Does a bear shit in the woods?' Gralice asked and I smiled. Everyone had a vice—my grandmother's was Diet Coke; oh and whiskey. Sometimes she even enjoyed the two of them together.

We headed into the kitchen, and as Gralice retrieved a treat for Coco from her 'secret' stash in the pantry, I grabbed two cans from the fridge, put one down on the table and cracked open the other while I went to the front door to collect my laptop bag, taking a tentative sip. Thank the Lord, it hit the spot.

'So, why were you late?' Gralice asked as she joined me at the table.

'Um ...' I contemplated telling her about running into Jay but decided against it, due to her association with his grandfather. 'I overslept my alarm and then got stuck in to housework. The apartment needed a good clean and I lost track of time.'

She took a swig from her can and looked at me as if she wasn't sure whether to believe me.

'So, what's with the piles of books?' I said, deflecting. 'Have you got someone coming to stay or something?'

She shook her head and sat at the counter on one of her stools that had been fashionable in the 1970s and were now back in vogue due to their vintage chic appeal. That wasn't why she still had them—she'd simply never needed to replace them and didn't care about keeping up with current trends. 'I've decided to sell my house and all the clutter makes it look smaller than it actually is, so I'm taking the opportunity to get my things in order.'

'You're going to sell your house?' I'd never known her to live or want to live anywhere else. She'd always said she'd be carried out in a box. 'But where will you go? You're not planning on moving in with Mum and Dad, are you?

'Fuck no. Can you imagine? I haven't really given it that much thought. Maybe I'll check myself into one of those homes while I still have the ability to pick a good one.'

'No.' The thought of Gralice in a depressing nursing home left me cold. Besides, she'd probably offend all the other residents with her coarse language. 'You don't want to live in one of those places. Even the good ones feel like asylums—trust me, I've recently written an article on them. And there's nothing wrong with you! This is crazy talk.'

'I don't want to be a hassle or a burden when I'm gone. You always hear horror stories about old people dying and their poor families having to pack up all their crap. This way you lot won't have to do anything but distribute my riches between yourselves.'

Gralice was clearly trying to make a joke. She wasn't poor, but by no means was she a millionaire either. She'd worked hard all her life, but she'd spent what she had on raising Mum, and then later on travelling, and of course there were the books. A habit like hers wasn't cheap. Saying that, she owned her little house and it now would be worth at least ten times what it was when she'd bought it in the seventies.

But I didn't care how much her house was worth if it meant living in a world without *her*.

'You'll never be a hassle,' I said, reaching across and putting my hand on hers. 'And you shouldn't have to move out of your home.'

'It's only bricks and mortar, Ged, you know I'm not sentimental. Anyway, enough about my de-cluttering, aren't you here to grill me about my fascinating and fabulous life? Where did we leave off last time?'

Before I could reply my phone rang. 'Hang on a sec.' I dug it out of my handbag and my heart hitched a beat when I saw my father's name on the screen.

I frowned at Gralice. 'It's Dad.'

'Well, are you going to answer it?' She sounded slightly anxious. My father and I got along well enough, but we didn't have the kind of relationship where he called me up just to chat.

I nodded and pressed accept.

'Ged. Thank goodness you answered.'

'Is something wrong with Mum?'

'No. Well, not exactly. I am a bit worried about her.'

'Why's that?'

'It's Rosa. I think there's something suspect about her.'

'Really? Has something happened to give you this feeling?'

'It's not one big thing exactly, but lots of little things. I don't know that we can trust her. I'm sure she's charging your mother far too much for whatever it is she's supposed to be doing and I'm uncomfortable with her spending so much time in our house.'

I thought Dad was probably simply a little put out about Mum's Insta-fame and Rosa's subsequent arrival in her life, which had upset *his* routine.

'I'm sure she's perfectly trustworthy. We spent four days with her on the cruise and I didn't get any strange vibes.'

Ignoring my attempts to placate him, he begged, 'Can you do some digging for me? Use your contacts to see if you can find anything untoward about her?'

I didn't know what kind of contacts he thought I had, but my job meant that I often had to do a little PI work—usually the extent of which was an internet search with the occasional trawl through old newspapers on microfilm. Only because I enjoyed this investigation process, wanted to be able to tell Dad he needed to tame his imagination, and also because he'd probably keep pestering me until I agreed, I promised I'd find out what I could.

'Thank you, Ged. You're an angel.'

Gralice laughed as I shoved my phone back into my bag. She'd obviously understood the gist of my conversation.

'What do you think of Rosa?'

'Seems nice enough. Very efficient and easy to be around.'

I nodded. 'Yes, poor old Dad, he's not used to having to share Mum. Anyway, enough about him.' I pressed play on my little voice recorder. 'Can you tell me about your decision to move out of home?'

'Ah, that's right. Such a liberating moment.'

'How old were you?'

'Seventeen, I think. Yes, that's right. I'd finished school and was at secretarial college, which my father saw as the only worthwhile option until I "settled down". I wanted to go to university and study science, but he thought that a frivolous waste of time and money for a girl, and so I decided to get my secretarial certificate and get a job, so I could save to pay for my own tertiary education.

'Dad was constantly making reference to me getting married and having babies and always on the lookout for a "suitable" husband, but I had no plans to get married unless it was my decision. And I wanted to experience life before I ever did such a thing. But he was always bringing sons of friends and associates home and telling them lies about how great I was in the kitchen, when I was far more interested in taking the new-fangled appliances apart and examining how they worked than actually using them. One day I finally snapped. I told him to stop wasting his time because I was never going to marry anyone, never mind anyone *he* deemed suitable, and he lost it.'

'What do you mean "lost it"?'

'"Do you think I'm going to support you forever?" he roared and then laughed when I retorted that I planned on supporting myself.

"Go on then," he called my bluff. "Move out. Stand on your own two feet. You've got far too high an opinion of yourself, Alice Abbott, but let's see how long it is before you're crawling back to Daddy for a handout." I packed up my bags and I left.'

'And what did you do next? Where did you go?'

'Well, first I went to the corner store, bought a packet of cigarettes and smoked the whole damn lot of them in almost one sitting as I tried to ignore the voices in my head telling me I was off my rocker, asking me where I was going to get the money, not only for food, but for somewhere to stay. That day as I wandered around the city, pondering my next move, I saw a sign at a boarding house: *Free room in exchange for domestic duties.*' Gralice smirked. 'The irony wasn't lost on me but I couldn't believe my luck. I wasn't domestic in the slightest but how hard could making beds and washing dishes be? Doing such tasks to give me freedom and independence was totally different to being barefoot and pregnant in the kitchen doing them for some man.

'And,' she winked, 'as much as your mother likes to go on about the skills of domesticity, it's not rocket science. I managed, and although it was almost unheard of at that time, I took any jobs I could get to pay my own way through university.'

We spent a little time discussing some of those jobs and while I was fascinated by everything Gralice said, I found myself stifling a yawn.

'Am I boring you?' She chuckled.

'No, not at all. I just don't think I've had enough caffeine today,' I said, and took another sip of my Diet Coke.

16

'What are you up to today?' Jay asked as he pulled on his T-shirt. How he felt the need for any further exercise after our night of exertion between the sheets was beyond me.

'Lunch at my mother's. It's a celebration of her book deal.' Thank God I didn't have to be there for another few hours as there was no way I was ready to vacate my bed just yet.

'Sounds like fun.' He grinned wickedly as he sat down on the edge of the bed to put on his running shoes.

'Not sure about fun, but lunch with my family is always amusing.' Not that he would ever find out.

This was the second time this week that Jay and I had seen each other and, by seen, I mean purely in the biblical sense. There'd been no dates and less conversation than we'd had at coffee. Last Wednesday evening, merely a few days after we'd run into each other in the park, I'd been sitting on an uncomfortable plastic chair at my local Thai restaurant waiting for takeaway and scrolling through my phone when someone sat down beside me.

Even before he leaned close and whispered—'We must stop running into each other like this'—I knew who it was. My body knew him. His shadow and his scent. My mouth went dry as an involuntary shiver rolled down my spine.

Doing everything I could to keep my demeanour cool, I slowly turned to meet his gaze. 'Good evening, Jay.'

It was raining out and his hair was wet, his skin still glistening in the artificial light of the restaurant, reminding me of the moment I'd seen him climbing out of the pool. Only this time he was fully clothed in jeans and a black hoodie.

'It is indeed.' He shook himself a little. 'How are you not soaking wet?'

I pointed to the row of umbrellas lined up against the wall. 'I've been living in Melbourne long enough to always be prepared.'

He chuckled. 'I knew you were much more than a pretty face.' There was a moment's silence between us before he added, 'I was kinda hoping I might run into you again.'

'Really?' I suddenly felt a little giddy. 'Are you lacking people to argue with in your life?'

'No, but not all of them give me as much pleasure as you do.'

I wasn't sure if it was what he said or the way he said it, but either way my cheeks burned and they weren't the only part of me. What should I say to that?

'Order for Johnston,' barked a Thai woman behind the counter. I looked up to see her holding a white plastic bag, steam coming out of the top of it.

'That's me.' I shot to my feet as Jay nodded.

I crossed to the counter to collect my food, thanked the woman and turned back to him. 'Well, I guess I'll see you round.' It was on the tip of my tongue to ask if he wanted to take a table in the restaurant and eat together, but he got in first.

'Or we could take dinner back to your place and catch up properly?'

My insides fluttered. Unlike when he'd suggested coffee in the park, this time I had no uncertainty about what he was insinuating. Part of me thought it would be fun to turn him down, to see if he'd put any effort into convincing me. My nights had been lonely the past few weeks and the thought of a little human companionship was impossible to resist.

I tightened my grip on the plastic bag. 'Your place or mine?'

'This time yours is closer,' he said as he stood. 'Do you want me to carry that?'

I pushed his hand away, a spark shooting through me at the touch. 'I can carry my own dinner, thank you very much.'

'Of course you can.' His deep chuckle reverberated through me as he opened the door for me to go through.

My apartment was a three-minute walk from the restaurant; we managed it in two and a half.

'Nice place,' he commented as I let him inside and Coco greeted us in her usual enthusiastic manner. It was only when she'd calmed down and I was about to ask him if he wanted to eat on plates, that I realised, 'We didn't wait for your order.'

Jay shrugged and took a step forward, closing the gap between us. 'To be honest, I'm not that hungry for food anymore.'

If there was a dial to operate my libido, his words and the heat in his eyes would have cranked it almost as far as it could go. Despite the fact I'd been hungry enough to contemplate chewing off my own arm on the way home from work, I suddenly wasn't that hungry anymore either. My Thai dinner languished uneaten on the kitchen bench as I grabbed Jay's hand, hauled him into my bedroom and ravished him. Or maybe he ravished me.

To be honest, it's all a bit of a blur. I've discovered that thinking straight is impossible when his tongue and/or fingers are anywhere near me.

I do remember what happened afterwards though. Jay had taken it upon himself to open the obligatory post-sex conversation about what 'this' meant to each of us.

'I really like sleeping with you, Geraldine.'

'The feeling is mutual.'

'I'd like to do you again—over and over—but I don't *do* relationships.'

I'd silenced him with a finger on his lips. 'I know. And it's not a problem, because neither do I anymore. Besides, the only thing I like about you is your body anyway.'

That was not completely truthful now I'd got to know him a little, but it made him smile.

'So what you're saying is you're happy with my naked body being at your beck and call but you won't start fantasising about white dresses and diamond rings?'

I'd made a face. 'Hell no. And you better not either.'

'I think you're pretty safe there.'

We'd agreed on a friends-with-benefits arrangement. And I felt very modern, very liberated, having decided that giving up men didn't mean I also had to give up sex. Besides, seeing Christos at work would be so much easier to handle if I knew I could see every inch of Jay's naked body outside of it. And sex was good exercise, wasn't it? Doing it regularly might help me get rid of some of the padding I'd collected since Christos tore out my heart and trampled it.

By the time I'd woken Thursday morning, Jay had gone. The only evidence that what had happened hadn't been a very sordid dream was the musky scent of him on my pillow and his phone number scrawled on the back of the takeaway receipt on my beside table. With a chuckle, I'd picked up my mobile and created a new contact called *Sex-on-Tap*. As he didn't have my number, I knew the ball was in my court, but I waited until late last night to message him: *I have needs, do you feel like helping me meet them?*

His reply was almost instantaneous: *I can be there in 10.*

There were no endearments or hugs or kisses in our messages and I'd fully assumed he would stay a few hours and then disappear into the night again, so it had been a bonus when I'd woken this morning with his hard-on pressing into my back. There was something so indulgent about morning sex.

Shoelaces tied, Jay stood. 'Want me to take Coco out for a pee before I head off?'

My dog, who'd been lying on the floor by the bed, lifted her head at the sound of her name. 'That would be wonderful,' I said and then snuggled back under the covers as the two of them left my bedroom.

'What did you bring?' Gralice asked as she climbed into my car, holding a newish-looking plastic container, a delicious fruity aroma emanating from within.

'What do you mean?'

'Sappho said she was too busy so asked if we could bring a plate of something to share.'

'Shit.' I was so used to Mum cooking that her request must not even have sunk in.

'You forgot, didn't you?'

I'd had other things on my mind this morning but I refrained from mentioning those. 'We'll have to stop somewhere on the way. What did you buy?'

'I *made* a pineapple upside-down cake.'

'You did *what*?' I could not recall Gralice ever cooking any kind of cake in my lifetime.

'I found the recipe in one of the books Sappho must have given me for Christmas when she was a teenager, trying to give me not-so-subtle hints about how to be a better mother. It actually wasn't that hard.'

I shook my head. My mother too busy to cook and my grandmother taking up baking! What was wrong with the world?

Twenty minutes later as I parked on the verge in front of my parents' house, my grandfathers arrived in a taxi. They greeted us and Craig offered to carry my contribution.

'Hmm ... this smells delicious,' he said, taking the box of gourmet sausage rolls I'd picked up from a bakery.

Phil meanwhile took Gralice's container and air-kissed both her cheeks. 'How are you?'

'I'm fine.' She patted his hand and then started up the garden path ahead of us.

I looked at Phil. 'What was that about?'

'What was what about?'

'You asked Gralice how she was.'

He and Craig exchanged a look. 'Yes,' he said slowly. 'It's called being polite.'

'It's just ...' I lowered my voice even though she was already inside, no doubt being accosted by her great-granddaughter for the lollies she always brought. 'She's been acting a little odd lately—packing her things, selling her house—and she seems fixated on getting old.'

'None of us are getting any younger,' Craig said, putting a comforting arm around my shoulder. 'There's no point pretending otherwise.'

'What are you three jabbering about out there?' came my mother's high-pitched voice from the front porch.

'Come on, Ged.' Phil nodded towards the house. 'We don't want to keep the lady of the house waiting.'

Heaven forbid.

'Great-Gran-pa Phil. Great-Gran-pa Craig. Aunty G!' Charlotte ran at us down the hallway then paused, not sure which one of us to hug first. I scooped up my niece and covered her in kisses.

'Hello, gorgeous. Love those funky jeans you're wearing.'

Charlotte didn't appear to care about my compliment. 'I'm going to be another big sister.'

I laughed.

'I know, congratulations,' I said, carrying her into the kitchen. 'That's super cool. That means I'm gonna be another aunty.'

Before Charlotte could wrap her head around this, we were swamped in the usual hug-and-hellos from the rest of the family. As Craig and Phil deposited the food on the bench, I lowered my niece to the floor and my mother linked her arm through mine.

'You remember Holly Pearson,' she said.

The publisher and I commented how nice it was to see each other again. I hadn't known she'd be at Mum's celebration, especially on a weekend; they must be seriously excited about *The Happy Happy Housewife*. Maybe after a few drinks, I'd find the courage to talk to her about Gralice's biography.

Holly gestured to a young woman with purple hair, a vintage dress and facial piercings. 'And this is Jessica Shepherd, one of our best publicists at Bourne. She's got some great ideas for marketing your mother's book.'

'Fabulous.' I beamed, wondering how one could market a book that wasn't even written yet.

'Can I get you a drink, sweetheart?' Rosa joined us, waving a bottle of champagne and carrying four empty flute glasses in her other hand.

'Yes, please.' I kissed her cheek. 'And it's good to see you again.'

'You too.' She smiled at me as she passed me one of the flutes and poured liquid gold into it. 'And I have to say you're looking much better. I hope you've stopped pining after that stupid man.'

'What man?' I winked and lifted my drink to my lips.

Mum called my granddads over next. As she introduced them to Holly and Jessica, I went to sit next to Dad, who was looking a little lost in his usual position at the head of the table.

'Hullo, sweetheart.'

'How are you today? Isn't Mum's book exciting?'

He snorted and tightened his already crossed arms. 'I wouldn't know. She's barely told me anything about it. She's far too busy *working* with Rosa. That woman's here so much she may as well move in.'

'Aw, Dad.' I wrapped an arm around him. He had to be the only one of my family who wasn't enamoured with Mum's assistant. 'The fuss will die down soon and everything will go back to normal, I'm sure.'

'I didn't have any clean underwear this morning. And there was no milk for my coffee.'

The thought of my father's dirty jocks turned my stomach. Perhaps it was time he learned how to wash his own clothes? I decided not to suggest that now for fear it would put him in a worse mood.

Besides, Mum and Dad's arrangement worked for them—I took in my father's gloomy demeanour—or at least it always had.

'Anyway,' he leaned in close, 'what have you found out about her?'

'Sorry to disappoint, Dad, but I haven't found anything.' *And* I had done a thorough search—there was actually one incident of drink driving in her early twenties, but as that was over thirty years ago and she'd probably matured a lot since then, I decided it didn't make her a threat to my mother and it wouldn't do any good to mention it to my father.

Who among us hadn't done something stupid in our errant youth?

His shoulders sagged. 'Nothing? Perhaps she's changed her name or something. I tell you, that woman is hiding something!'

'So, what did you cook us, sis?' Will asked as he lowered himself and Oliver into the seat next to me. I was grateful for the interruption.

'Sausage rolls.'

He raised an eyebrow. '*You* made sausage rolls?'

I shrugged. 'Cooked, bought—they're almost the same thing. I've been busy.'

'You forgot, didn't you?'

'Well, I'm not used to needing to cook when we come here. What did you make, or did you leave that task to your lovely pregnant wife?'

'I gave my lovely pregnant wife a lie-in this morning, while I whipped up a lasagne. It probably won't be up to Mum's standards though.'

'I'm impressed. I didn't know you could cook, big brother.'

'There's a lot you don't know about me.'

'And most of it I probably don't want to,' I retorted.

'So how's your book coming along, Ged?' Will asked as Holly and Jessica approached.

I gave him an appreciative smile. So much better that he raised it than I did. 'Really good.'

'You're writing a book?' Holly looked intrigued. 'What's it about?'

'It's a biography about Gralice—I mean Alice's life and work.'

'Sounds fascinating. How much have you written?' she asked.

'I've got a rough draft of the first five thousand words, but I've done an outline of what I want to cover. Alice and I are almost halfway through our first round of interviews.'

'I'd love to read the manuscript when you're done. I'm not sure it's quite right for Bourne, but I have a friend at University Press and they've recently launched an imprint solely for biographies of groundbreaking women.'

I tried to contain my excitement. 'Wow, that sounds great.'

'No worries. I'm fascinated to learn more about the amazing woman who raised Marie. Oh, and the men.' Holly winked at Craig and Phil.

'Will you read me *Where Is the Green Sheep?*' Charlotte asked, interrupting the conversation as she climbed into my lap.

'It would be my pleasure.' I didn't want to look over-eager with Holly anyway. As Charlotte snuggled in, my heart swelled with love. Being an aunt to these little people had to be the best unpaid job in the world.

After two more stories, Mum tapped a teaspoon against her champagne flute.

'Attention, everyone. I want to thank you all for coming to celebrate this monumental occasion, I honestly never thought I would write a book but ... here we are.'

As she giggled and smiled at Holly and then Rosa, I took another sip of my drink. If she was this annoying when the book hadn't even been written, I could only imagine how painful she'd be if she ever finished and saw it on real-life shop shelves. And I only had to listen to her go on about it occasionally—*poor Dad*. I gave him a sympathetic knee squeeze as Mum went on (and on) about the exciting things being planned for *The Happy Happy Housewife*.

A lot had happened in the past four weeks. Mum and Rosa had been working with a web designer to redesign her website. The *Women's Weekly* had expressed interest in running a story on 'Australia's Favourite Housewife' and there'd even been a couple of morning TV breakfast shows wanting to interview my mother. Maybe *I* should write an article about her?

'*Wake Up, Melbourne* have even mentioned the possibility of Sappho having her own weekly segment,' Rosa announced, smiling proudly.

Mum sniffed and reached out to hold her assistant's hand. 'I couldn't have achieved any of it without you. Shall we show everyone our sample merch?'

'Ooh yes.' Rosa hurried off into the living room, which had recently been transformed into Mum's office—another bone-pick of my father's—and returned with her arms full.

'We're going to start with these,' Mum explained as Rosa thrust us something white with pink and green polka dots splashed all over it.

I unravelled mine to discover it was an apron that looked far too fancy to ever wear while actually cooking. There was a full skirt, and the bit that went over the chest had a white ruffle around it. In addition to the bright retro pattern, there was a cartoon image of my mother on the front. Her hair was coiffed in a perfect 1950s Lucille Ball do, her arms flung out to the side as if she were singing 'The Hills Are Alive', one leg kicked up behind her, bright red heels on her feet to match her lipstick, and what I thought was an old-fashioned vacuum cleaner beside her.

'We're going for a 1950s housewife look,' Mum said, touching a hand to her hair. 'For a bit of fun.'

'I love it.' Holly popped her apron over her head. 'Something like this image could also work well on the book cover, don't you think, Jessica?'

The publicist nodded. 'We should show it to the designers.'

'I'm so glad you like it.' Mum beamed. 'Rosa has almost finished setting up our online shop and we'll sell these and all sorts of other branded products like mugs, tea towels and other kitchen implements.'

I wondered when she'd have time to write the book with everything else on her plate, but neither Holly nor Jessica seemed to be worried about this small detail.

'This has been such an unplanned but wonderful adventure and each and every one of you has played a part in my journey ...'

Mum went on but I zoned out, letting my mind wander. If she didn't shut up soon I was liable to die of starvation.

Finally, she appeared to run out of words and Rosa declared it was time for a toast. 'Has everyone got a full glass?'

'Don't you want some?' my mum asked Sophie. 'I know you're pregnant, but surely a little sip won't hurt.'

Sophie shook her head. 'Thanks, but I'll stick with soda water. My tastebuds go AWOL when I'm pregnant and I can't stomach alcohol or, sadly, coffee.'

Every bone in my body froze as a terrifying possibility landed uninvited in my head. *My* taste buds had been wreaking havoc lately, not approving of all the things I usually delighted in. My lungs ached and my head spun as I let out a slightly hysterical laugh.

'You okay, Ged?' Craig asked.

'Fine,' I managed as I reached for my glass of water and gulped down a few big mouthfuls. 'Just swallowed something the wrong way.'

Thankfully no one else appeared to notice as Rosa launched into a spiel about how clever and talented my mother was, and then finally it was time to eat.

'This is such a lovely idea,' Holly exclaimed, smiling around the table. 'You should do a chapter in the book about pot-luck family get togethers. Even the best housewives deserve a day off every now and then.'

My father harrumphed and shovelled a forkful of Craig's potato and chicken curry into his mouth. Everyone laughed, except him, baby Oliver—who'd started grizzling in Will's arms—and me, who couldn't stop thinking about the possibility I might be pregnant.

No, I was on the pill. I'd even had a period a week or so ago. Just because my sister-in-law went off coffee when she was growing babies didn't mean I would. There had to be some other explanation.

Still, the rest of the afternoon dragged. I was lost in my own little bubble of terror, analysing the past few weeks of my life, which now I thought about it also included weight gain, unusual tiredness and a heightened sense of smell.

Needing to put this ridiculous possibility to bed, I detoured via the pharmacy after dropping Gralice off and bought a pregnancy test. As I let myself into my apartment, the little cardboard box carried in a white paper bag felt like a ticking time-bomb in my hands.

Coco jumped at me in her usual way, but I barely even acknowledged her as I headed into the bathroom. Ripping open the packet, I yanked out the little stick and read the instructions. They were simple enough, and it seemed wrong that something that could alter the course of my existence was so easy and would give me an answer in a matter of minutes.

Every bone in my body quaking, I pulled down my knickers, sat myself on the loo, and peed on the little stick in my hand.

17

It was official. I was definitely, without a shadow of a doubt, one hundred percent Up The Duff!

It was now one week and one day since I'd sworn at the PREGNANT staring up at me from the white little stick in my hand. What had happened to the one or two blue lines that had been the way of the few tests I'd done in my early twenties? Those tests had been far kinder; first you got one little line that told you the test was working, then you got a few minutes' reprieve until the next line might appear to inform you your life was about to change irrevocably. Luckily, I'd never seen two blue lines.

But this time ... not even one line flashed up at me. Instead, after less than ten seconds, the P-word appeared, large and bold in the little result window. I'd gasped, flung the test stick across the bathroom and immediately vomited into the toilet bowl.

How could this be happening?

I didn't want to be pregnant. I didn't want to have a baby. *Did I?*

But before I could even wrap my head around this, another even more horrific thought struck. Who the hell was the father?

Wiping my mouth, I forced myself to my feet, washed my hands and went to fetch my pocket-sized diary. Call me old-fashioned, but I still liked to keep my appointments and special birthdays, et cetera, on paper so it was easy to flick through and look ahead to what was coming. This time, however, I snatched the little book from my handbag and flicked backwards.

The last period I'd recorded was over seven weeks ago.

Seven?

I was sure I'd had one since then, but I didn't seem to have noted it down. And, now that I thought about it, that period hadn't lasted more than a day, maybe two max, and had been very light. If the home pregnancy test was correct, could what I'd assumed was my last period actually have been what I'd heard pregnant women call 'spotting'?

Oh Lord. I pressed a hand against my stomach but not in that endearing way that *happily* pregnant women did. They were always touching their stomachs as if to make sure their bump was still there—mine was in an effort to try and stop myself vomiting again.

A wine would be nice right about now.

I'd retrieved a nice bottle of pinot gris from the fridge and poured half a glass when I remembered pregnant women weren't supposed to drink alcohol. Another curse fell from my lips as I lowered the bottle onto the kitchen bench. Not only had the alien growing inside me ruined me for my great love—coffee—but now I couldn't drink wine either.

I really wasn't feeling much affection towards this 'thing' right now.

Then again, having a calming glass of vino wouldn't make a difference if I wasn't going to continue with the pregnancy anyway.

I lifted the glass to my lips and took a sip, waiting for the calming effects to come.

They didn't. My usually favourite drop tasted sour on my tongue and something I could only define as guilt caused my chest to burn. My mother and my sister-in-law often complained about 'mother guilt' but surely it didn't start this early in pregnancy?

How far along was I anyway? After pouring my drink down the sink, I flopped onto the edge of the couch and told myself to calm the hell down. If I worked out exactly how pregnant I was then maybe I'd be able to work out who the sperm that had got me into this predicament belonged to.

'How do you tell how many weeks pregnant you are?' I asked Siri.

'Okay, here's what I found on the web for how do you tell how many weeks pregnant you are,' came her immediate reply.

Honestly, how on earth did anyone get by before Siri and Google were invented?

The helpful websites she directed me to weren't all that helpful. According to one pregnancy and birth e-zine, there was no way to know for sure exactly when you ovulated or conceived, so a pregnancy was dated based on your LMP instead. Not up with the lingo, it took me a moment to work out that LMP stood for 'last menstrual period' but only a few more seconds to find the due date calculator that informed me I was expecting an Australia Day baby.

Perhaps that was a bad omen. Who wanted to have a baby on a date fraught with such political controversy and sadness for so many Australians?

The site was a virtual font of information, but it couldn't tell me the one thing I wanted, needed, to know. I'd last slept with Christos smack bang in the middle of what was apparently my 'prime ovulating window', but the problem was that during that time I'd also had my first tryst with Jay.

Coco skidded past me, jolting me from my catastrophic thoughts, and I looked up to see she had something white and thin between her teeth. She halted a few feet away, gave me a precocious look and started to chew vigorously.

'Oh my God.' I leapt to my feet and threw myself at the dog, but she scooted out of my reach and ran towards the bedroom.

'Give that here. You've got my baby in your mouth!'

Baby! My heart thudded, that one word reverberating around my head as I chased my dog around my room. What did *I* know about babies? What would I do with one? My one-bedroom apartment might be okay while it was tiny, but kids grew fast. My niece and nephew seemed to double in height every time I saw them. And they had so many toys and little shoes. Where would I put all that stuff?

I was thirty years old. I'd managed to get a degree, hold down a job; I had a roof over my head and a supportive family—so why did this feel like such a disaster?

The answer came down to one thing. Not only was I unsure I wanted a baby and not in a relationship with the father, I didn't even know who he was.

I'd never felt more stupid in my life.

And what about work? The promotion? Due to the timing, if I decided to have the baby I could kiss the job of editor of the weekend lift-out goodbye. Announcing I was pregnant and needed to take maternity leave at the same time Darren was due to retire would not be my finest career move. No way Libby would allow herself to get into this predicament, and there was no risk of Tom getting pregnant and stuffing up his chances of promotion.

It was an effort, but I finally caught Coco and wrangled the stick from her clutches. Screwing up my nose, I wiped her slobber off it with my sleeve and checked the result hadn't changed. It hadn't, but maybe there was an error and I was getting all worked up for nothing.

I'd only bought one kit because I'd been so certain it would come up negative, but now I wished I'd invested in a few more. Deciding I needed professional confirmation before I worked out my next move, I'd gone online and booked an appointment with my doctor for the next day and then sent an email to Darren saying that I wouldn't be at work as I'd come down with some ghastly stomach bug.

'Congratulations, you're definitely pregnant!' had not been the words I'd been hoping to hear from Dr Grannich, who'd been my go-to doctor since my early twenties.

Was she effing kidding?

'But I can't be. I'm on the pill.' I clutched my handbag in my lap, feeling like I'd been told I had nine months to live.

I'd convinced myself that the doctor would give me some other explanation for the positive result on the home pregnancy test. Perhaps there'd been a recall on a faulty batch but the packet I'd bought had been missed by a new, probably adolescent, incompetent employee at the chemist.

'I know you are, but the progestogen-only contraceptive pill, even when taken accurately, is only ninety-nine percent effective.'

'What? I thought that statistic was only to cover companies' arses.'

Dr Grannich smiled sympathetically. 'There are a number of reasons why your contraception may have failed. Do you always remember to take it at the same time?'

'Yes.' I kept my pills next to my toothbrush and popped one every morning before I cleaned my teeth.

'Well, perhaps you were sick during your cycle or … drank too much?'

I shook my head, ignoring the thought of all those cruise cocktails—if they were responsible, would that mean Jay was the father?

'If you threw up at all that could have prevented the pill from doing its job. Of course there are a few less likely reasons. Some medications can affect it—antibiotics, laxatives … there's even a herbal detox tea that has been found to …'

The rest of her possible explanations fell on deaf ears. Whatever the reason, it didn't matter now.

'So you're absolutely sure? There's no mistake?'

'You're pregnant, Geraldine. I guess the question now is what you want to do about it? If you're planning on having the baby, we need to start you on folate tablets ASAP. I'll also run some bloods to check your iron and other things, and I can refer you to an obstetrician or the public hospital—you'll need do a dating scan to confirm your due date. Will you go public or private for the birth?'

Birth? I shook my head. I couldn't think that far ahead.

'Dr Grannich,' I began, my cheeks burning at what I knew was going to be the most mortifying conversation of my whole life.

'Yes?' she prompted.

'Is there a way to find out the father of a baby before birth?'

Her big brown eyes widened. '*Oh*.'

I grimaced. 'Preferably without either possible party knowing.'

Even though I'd already read everything I could find in answer to this question into the wee hours of the morning, I asked on the remote chance Dr Grannich was privy to something the internet was not. Google didn't know everything!

'Do you not know who the father is, Geraldine?' she said after a few long moments.

I thought for a smart woman this was a pretty stupid question, considering, but shook my head. 'It's definitely one of two guys.' I didn't want her to think I was a total floozy. 'You see, I *was* in a long-term relationship but we broke up and I kinda had rebound sex with someone else.'

Oh Lord, I wanted an earthquake to split the floor and suck me under it. I'd always admired the well-dressed, incredibly poised Dr Grannich and somehow this conversation made me feel like I'd let her down. A tear slipped down my cheek and, before I could even try and stop them, more followed in rapid succession. I wasn't usually such a crier but in the past twenty-four hours I'd leaked more than the *Titanic*.

Dr Grannich reached for the drug-company branded tissue box on her desk and offered it to me.

'Thanks,' I managed as I yanked one out and tried to mop up the salt water streaming down my face.

'It's going to be okay,' she said. 'You're only about seven weeks pregnant. You have time to wrap your head around this and work out what you want to do. It is possible to find out who the father is before you give birth, but I'm afraid it will be tricky to do so without at least telling one of the possibilities.'

The doctor's tone was kind, sympathetic, and not judgmental at all, or if she was judging me, she didn't let it show. Perhaps this wasn't such a rare occurrence? Maybe she had plenty of patients as foolish as me.

'There are several methods for obtaining samples that can determine paternity. You can have chorionic villus sampling at eleven to fourteen weeks' gestation or an amniocentesis at a later date, but both these tests come with a small risk of miscarriage. There's another safer option as well, but—'

'I read about non-invasive prenatal paternity testing. Is that what you're talking about?'

'Yes, we'd take a small sample of blood from you and compare the DNA in your blood with DNA collected from the alleged father— this can be in the form of a cheek swab, a strand of hair or a blood sample. This offers an accurate result from about the tenth week of pregnancy, but it takes up to two weeks to get the results and I have to warn you it's not cheap.'

The cost was the least of my problems. It would be impossible to get a blood sample or a cheek swab without Christos or Jay knowing, unless I got them very, very drunk, but a strand of hair might be achievable.

Dr Grannich put paid to this line of thinking. 'A signature of consent is required from all parties for the test to go ahead, and besides, the cheek swab is preferred testing material. DNA is easier to extract from swabs than from blood.'

'Right.' I nodded, sweat pooling at the back of my neck.

Perhaps I could simply text Sex-on-Tap this request: *Hey, you know all that great sex we had on the ship? It might have sparked a baby. How do you feel about giving me a swab from your cheek to see if said baby is yours?*

My skin tingled almost painfully. A baby was not part of our friends-with-benefits arrangement any more than it was part of *my* arrangement full stop.

'Do you think one is more likely?'

I'd been pondering this question since peeing on that ghastly stick. One minute I'd manage to convince myself that the baby was Christos's, but the next I felt certain it was Jay's, and I couldn't imagine him being overly ecstatic with the news. One little silver lining in this very dark cloud was that if Jay *was* the father of my baby, at least I now knew where to find him. Imagine having to tell my child that all I'd known about his/her father was that his name was Jay?

Whoever the father—or rather the unsuspecting sperm donor, as I was now calling him—a baby changed everything. How could I keep having sex with Jay when I was possibly carrying another man's child? And how could I see Christos at work knowing what I did?

I had visions of them both being in my birth suite, holding a hand each, directing me how to breathe and then shoving each other out of the way at the business end as the baby popped out and they tried to see if it had red or black hair. Maybe my friends and family would place bets on the result. Of course this was a ridiculous scenario because it involved both unsuspecting sperm donors wanting to be the winner, whereas Jay would probably be stoked to lose this competition.

Considering his stance on relationships, I was pretty certain fatherhood was not in his ten-year plan, which, if he got *his* way, involved immigrating to Mars.

Holy fuck—Mars! If Jay was the father and if he got picked for the space mission, my baby—our baby—might never get to know him. I would have to tell him/her that being part of a new civilisation was more important to his/her daddy than he/she was. Or would finding out he was going to be a father make him reassess his application? And if so, would he spend the rest of his life resenting me and the baby for trapping him? *Argh!*

How had I got myself into such a bloody mess?

'Geraldine!' Dr Grannich's sharp voice jolted me from my nightmare. 'I know this is a shock but it's not the end of the world. You only need a sample from one of them to work out what's what. That is … if you want to continue with the pregnancy?'

I loved her for not calling this *thing* a baby, but that was the million dollar question. This could be my only chance at motherhood ... but did I want it? Suddenly nothing in my life felt so black and white. Yet would it be fair to some innocent kid to land me on them? What did I know about motherhood? Sure I managed to keep my dog alive, but a baby was on a whole other level.

Would knowing who the father was make a difference? Would it make my decision any easier? *Should* it?

'How long do I have to decide?'

'Terminations are allowed on request in Victoria up to sixteen weeks, so you don't need to rush into any decision. Take time to think over your options, talk to someone you trust about your situation, or I can refer you to a counsellor if you'd prefer?'

'Okay. Thank you.'

I'd left Dr Grannich's office with three things—the business card of a counsellor, a referral to an obstetrician, and the advice to come back if I made the decision to terminate.

All that had been a week ago and I still had no idea how I felt about this opportunity. My body had had eight days to get used to being hijacked by a tiny stranger and the possibility of imminent motherhood, but it was still a shock every time I remembered I was pregnant and I still wasn't any closer to making a decision.

I'd been holding off confiding in Gralice or Mum because getting pregnant accidentally made me feel like a fool; both of them had put a lot of thought and planning into their journeys into motherhood.

Although I was grateful I had the choice so many women who had gone before me hadn't or had risked their lives to make, this didn't make my decision any easier. Part of me thought I was crazy to even contemplate single motherhood, but another part of me felt excited by the possibility and the thought that I would have this in common with Gralice. Then again, our situations weren't exactly the same. Gralice had the support of her baby's father, whereas there'd been no planning whatsoever in my situation and I had no idea how much practical, financial or emotional reinforcement Christos or Jay would offer.

I'd have the assistance of my family. My father, brother and granddads would be ecstatic. Mum might be disappointed that a grandchild of hers was going to be born out of wedlock, but once she recovered from that shock, I knew she'd be as besotted with my baby as she was with Charlotte and Oliver and, that although we might disagree on a lot of things, she'd be a practical support as well. While none of the unusual circumstances would bother Gralice in theory, I couldn't help wondering how she'd feel if the father of my baby turned out to be Jay, if it meant sharing a great-grandbaby with her long-lost first love.

The obvious people to talk to about my dilemma would be Christos and Jay. A voice in my head kept asking how I could make a rational decision when I didn't know how either of them would feel about the situation, but I felt that I needed to wrap my head around pregnancy and possible motherhood before I went down that path. I didn't want their possible support or lack thereof to sway this monumental decision.

Christos and I had succeeded in ignoring each other since his proposition on the footpath. I tried to focus on the job but couldn't think about anything besides my predicament. This past week I'd written the shabbiest article for the lift-out about Australia's most famous exports—it was surprising Darren hadn't rejected it—and my work on Gralice's biography had fallen by the wayside. I'd gone to ground, not seeing anyone outside of work: not Gralice, not Mum and definitely not Jay.

He'd messaged twice asking if I wanted to 'catch up'—once I'd ignored him and once I'd told him I was busy.

Occasionally I even pondered the possibility of not telling either of them at all. Legally I had no obligation to do so—my body, my baby—but morally I wasn't sure. Did the unsuspecting sperm donor have a right to know, and more importantly, did my child? And, all that aside, could I financially do parenthood alone? At least I had a steady job, which came with reasonable maternity leave, but if I chose to have this baby I could kiss goodbye to the possibility of promotion, and a time would come in the not too distant future where I could no longer hide my pregnancy. Even if I ghosted Jay, Christos might start asking questions.

If I didn't talk to someone soon my head was going to explode! The counsellor's card was still burning a hole in my pocket, but quite aside from the fact I wouldn't be able to get an appointment immediately, I needed to talk to someone I trusted.

There was only one thing for it.

I dragged myself off the couch. 'Come on, Coco, we're going to visit Gralice.'

Deep down I knew my grandmother wouldn't judge me and I trusted her opinion more than anyone else in the world. I might only be eight weeks pregnant but I felt as if I had a ticking bomb inside me.

It was time to make up my mind before I lost any more of my sanity.

18

It was after dark and raining heavily by the time I got to my grandmother's house.

'Gralice,' I called as I dropped my bag on the floor and Coco rushed down the hallway. I followed to find my grandmother in the bathroom, perched on the edge of the bathtub, leaning over the toilet bowl and clutching her stomach.

'Ged!' She looked up in surprise as Coco nudged her with her big wet nose. 'What ... are you ... doing here?'

Her complexion was pasty, her normally well-groomed hair limp and oily and, once again, I smelled that awful odour in the air. Only this time I knew my olfactory senses weren't playing games—it was vomit! My eyes went to a row of pill bottles near the sink.

I pulled Coco away and shut her outside in the hallway. 'What's wrong with *you*? And don't even try to tell me "nothing".'

'I ...' Gralice let out a heavy sigh. 'I've got cancer, Ged.'

'What?' My stomach turned to rock as a bitter cold flooded my limbs. Those were three words you never wanted to hear coming out of a loved one's mouth. For a second, I thought I must have heard wrong.

She couldn't have *cancer*—it defied all sense and logic. She was too strong, and although she'd been a smoker once, she'd given up long before I was born. I couldn't recall her having so much as a cold more than twice in my whole life.

'I need some water.' Gralice began to push to her feet and I rushed forward to assist her.

As my fingers closed around her arm, I felt bones and realised she hadn't simply lost a few kilos, but what felt like a third of her body weight. A lump formed in my throat as guilt filled my heart. I'd been so consumed with my own issues that I'd ignored the niggling feeling that something wasn't quite right with my grandmother.

Cancer. It was a terrifying word—so oppressive and malevolent— but these days it didn't have to be a death sentence. Plenty of people recovered and lived to tell the tale. Gralice would be one of these survivors.

I exhaled, trying to calm myself as I led her into the dining room, assisted her into a chair, and then went into the kitchen. I poured us each a glass of water, wishing once again that I could drink something stronger.

'What kind of cancer?' I asked once she'd drank her fill.

'Gastric,' came her one-word reply.

So many questions battled in my head. 'How long have you known? How did you find out?'

'I started to feel off a few months ago,' she confessed. 'At first I thought I was suffering indigestion as I kept getting pain in my stomach, and I often felt bloated even when I didn't eat much at all. I started to lose weight but put it down to my lost appetite. Then the vomiting began, and didn't get better after a couple of days, and then I saw blood when I went to the toilet. That's when I went to my doctor. He immediately sent me off for an endoscopy. The biopsy results revealed the cancer.'

Her words left me numb. This could *not* be happening. 'What stage is it?'

'Four. It had already spread to my liver, and they've also found a spot on my lung.'

Oh God. I grabbed my glass of water and downed half of it in one big gulp, then reached out and took hold of Gralice's hand, unsure whether I was trying to take or offer comfort.

'Why didn't you tell me?' I whispered, fighting tears once again. 'I should have been here for you.'

'This isn't about you, Ged. I needed time to come to grips with the news myself.'

I wanted to be angry—rage was easier to face than fear—but how could I hold this against her when I'd spent the last week trying to *come to grips* with my own life-changing news?

'So what happens now? Were those pills in the bathroom part of your treatment? Do you have to have surgery, or will you just have chemo? When were you planning to tell me? Do Phil and Craig know? Does Mum?'

'Only my doctor and medical team know. And I'm not having chemotherapy or any kind of treatment. The pills are painkillers and anti-inflammatories to make me as comfortable as can be.'

'What do you mean you're not having chemo? Surely they can do *something*. You should see another doctor, get a second opinion.'

But with her next words, Gralice landed one of the biggest blows of my life. 'I've chosen not to have treatment. I'm too old for all that palaver.'

'What?' As a scientist, surely she'd want to make the most of modern medicine. 'Don't be ridiculous.' I refused to listen to such a defeatist attitude. 'You can't just *choose* not to try and get better. What about me? I need you. We all do.'

Gralice squeezed my hand. 'Ged, my girl, I love you, but I need to be selfish now. I don't want to put myself through something that will only give me a few more months—months where I'd be in and out of hospital, losing my hair and feeling sick from all the chemicals being pumped into my body. That's no way to live. But I'm okay. I've accepted my fate. I've had a good life, I have a beautiful family and a lot to be proud of. This is it for me. We all have to go some way. Cancer is mine.'

We sat in silence for a few long moments, still not wanting to believe this was actually happening, I said, 'How long have you got?'

'It's not like having a baby. They can't even give you an estimated date of death, but Dr King says I'll be unlikely to see Christmas.'

'*Christmas?*' My blood went cold. That was just over six months away. Too soon. *Way* too soon.

'No.' I tugged my hand out of hers. 'I can't accept this. You have to try *something*. A few months is better than nothing.' If I sounded hysterical it was because I was.

'Whether you accept it or not, this is my decision and I hope you'll come to understand and support it.'

'But—'

'No buts, Ged. This is why I've kept from telling you. I knew you, Sappho and Will would try to convince me to change my mind but I'm not going to.'

'That's why we went on the cruise, isn't it? It's why you suddenly want to spend as much time with Mum as possible. Why you're sorting through your stuff, packing up your house?'

She nodded. 'Facing death causes you to take stock of your life. I haven't got many regrets …' Her voice trailed off a moment. 'But I do wonder about Henry, and one of my biggest regrets is that I haven't got the relationship with Sappho that a mother and daughter should. I see it so clearly now. All her life I've tried to force my views and my values onto her; I've looked down on her decisions and that has caused distance between us. I can't change the past, and so I want to try to get to know her a little better in the few months I have left. But I didn't want her spending time with me out of guilt.'

'I understand, but ... you have to tell her soon. She's so busy with *The Happy Happy Housewife* stuff but if she knows she doesn't have forever with you, I'm sure she'll make you a priority. You don't want her to have regrets and guilt after you've gone either.' My heart ached that I was even saying these words. 'And I know you probably don't want to admit it, but you're going to need us in the coming months.'

Gralice extracted her hand. 'I'll tell her when I'm ready, Ged. And I'd appreciate you keeping quiet until I am. I don't need you or anyone else trying to take over. This is my death and I'm going to do it my way.'

I squeezed my eyes but couldn't stop the tears from pouring. Gralice snatched a couple of tissues from a box on the table and held them out to me.

'Thank you.' I took them, sniffed and blew my nose. As much as I wanted to argue, I knew if I pushed her it would only cause a rift.

'Now,' she said when I finally pulled myself together. 'What's up?'

'What do you mean?'

'I didn't think we had a date to work on the biography tonight and usually when you drop by out of the blue in the evening, you've got something on your mind. Is it work?'

I blinked. I'd almost forgotten that I'd come, not only to tell her about my pregnancy, but also to ask her wisdom and advice.

Yet, was now really the right moment? And maybe Gralice's devastating news had made my decision for me anyway.

It was hard enough to imagine motherhood, but facing it without my grandmother by my side? That was almost impossible. Then again, would the prospect of another great-grandchild give her reason to live? To fight? My heart swelled with hope and I opened my mouth to tell her my news when another thought deflated it.

Was wanting to give Gralice reason to live good enough reason for me to decide to become a mother? And what if it only made her sad that she wouldn't get to see my baby born? Then there was the Jay/Henry scenario …

Now I felt even more confused than I had when I'd arrived.

'I just felt like seeing you,' I lied.

Her lips curved upwards. 'Aw, Ged. It's always a pleasure seeing you and I'm sorry I had to deliver such bad news.'

'Don't apologise. I love you. I'm glad I know and want to be here for you.' I sniffed again, wishing she'd told me earlier when there still might have been a chance of treatment working. 'Promise you won't shut me out and try to do this alone?'

'Promise. And I love you too.' Gralice cleared her throat—she'd had enough mushiness for one night. 'Now, have you eaten? I don't have much in the cupboard as my appetite has shrunk to near nothing with this fucking cancer, but we could order you in a pizza or something.'

I was famished—near-starvation seemed to be a constant state for me these days—and although a pizza probably wasn't the healthiest of options there was no way I could go home and cook something nutritious after this. Besides, I couldn't bring myself to leave her yet. After tonight, I wasn't sure I ever wanted to let her out of my sight.

After we'd placed an order, I cracked a Diet Coke from Gralice's fridge while we waited for the delivery.

'So, what happens now? Are you in pain? What *can* you eat?'

'I've got a palliative care team helping me deal with my symptoms and they manage my pain. In addition to my doctor, I'm seeing a cancer specialist to monitor the progression of the disease, a physiotherapist, and also a dietician to make sure I don't starve to death before the cancer takes me.'

I winced, but Gralice's blunt words shouldn't have shocked me. She'd always been a matter-of-fact person.

'Casey, my dietician, has got me onto smoothies, which I can sip slowly.' She nodded towards the blender on her bench. 'I chuck a whole load of fruit and veggies in that and she gave me some protein powder to add. It's not as bad as it sounds.'

Gralice changed the subject after that. 'Have you seen much of Christos?'

'No. Thank God, he seems to have given up on the idea of us having an "affair" and we've perfected the fine art of pretending the other one doesn't exist.'

'The audacity of the man!' She shook her head. 'To think he thought you'd be happy with such an arrangement. Speaking of work, has Sappho actually written any of her book yet?'

I chuckled, or at least I tried, but I was finding it almost impossible to think about anything else but the Big C invading my grandmother's body. 'I'm not sure, but I guess a lot of the book will be made up of stuff from her previous blog posts. It's not like she needs to do a ton of research.'

Which reminded me of all the background research I still had to do on Gralice's biography. Although I'd been eager to get it out into the world as soon as possible, I realised that now not only did I need to get everything from my grandmother before it was too late, but she might not ever get to see her book in print.

Was cancer going to be the final chapter of Gralice's biography?

My heart grew heavy. I didn't want to think about life without my grandmother. How much more could things irrevocably change in such a short time?

'I'm going to the bathroom,' I said, needing to pull myself together.

I returned a few minutes later to find Gralice and Coco curled up together on the sofa, an episode of *Sex and the City* playing on the TV.

'Is this the one where Samantha declares she's a lesbian and Charlotte says she's not, she's just run out of men to sleep with?'

She grinned. 'It sure is.'

'Ooh, that's a good one.'

For all the flack the TV show had received in recent years about not being very feminist, it had always been one of my and Gralice's favourites and she would argue till she was blue in the face that this classic provided a positive take on female liberation. It gave women a voice, showed the power of female friendships, it challenged ageism, made being a single woman and in charge of your own life not only acceptable but almost desirable, and, most importantly, celebrated women taking ownership of their own sexuality. And to hell with the slut-shamers!

But no matter all this, right now Carrie and the girls felt exactly like the comfort food I needed, and so I snuggled up on the other side of my dog to watch, until the doorbell rang signalling the arrival of the pizza.

'Are you sure you don't want any? Can I get you something else?' It felt wrong sitting here stuffing my face when Gralice hadn't even had one bite.

'I'm fine. I had some soup earlier.'

We watched another couple of episodes in comfortable silence before a yawn escaped my mouth.

'It's getting late, you should go home. You don't want to be falling asleep at work tomorrow.'

But I didn't want to leave Gralice. 'How about I help you into bed and stay the night? I can even call in sick to work tomorrow if you want?'

Darren was liable to sack me if I took any more sickies, or at least look upon Tom or Libby more favourably for the promotion, but that was the least of my problems right now.

'Don't fuss, Ged. I'm sick but I'm not a total invalid yet. I can still look after myself and, quite frankly, would like to put myself to bed for as long as possible. So if you don't mind …'

'Okay, okay. I'm going,' I held up my hands as I pushed myself up off the couch, 'but only if you promise me you'll call me any time—day *or* night—if you need *anything*.'

'I promise.'

Gralice walked me to the door, I kissed her goodnight and headed to my car. I'd barely put on my seatbelt when the tears started to fall. Coco, sitting on the passenger seat, reached her paw across and placed it on my thigh. She knew I was sad, even if she didn't know why, and her gesture did offer a level of comfort.

By the time we got to my place, the tears were easing again.

As we approached my apartment building, I noticed a dark lump sitting on the front step and wondered if it was the homeless guy I sometimes bought coffee for. However mean-spirited it might be, I wasn't in the mood to deal with him tonight. Sucking in a deep breath, I reached into my bag to see if I had a few coins to spare.

But, before I could find any, the lump looked up and I realised it wasn't the homeless guy after all.

19

My steps faltered as my gaze fell upon the two suitcases beside my father. Coco was delighted to see him—an outing *and* a visitor all in one night, it was a doggie's fantasy! Me? Not so much. I wanted to be alone to lick my wounds.

'What are you doing here this late at night? And what's with the suitcases?' I asked, as Dad struggled to his feet to avoid Coco licking him all over his face.

He finally met my gaze and I saw his eyes were bloodshot. Had he been crying? My dad was a bloke's bloke, a product of the generation that subscribed to the belief men didn't show emotion. I'd never seen so much as a tear sneak down his cheek.

I reached out a hand to touch his arm. 'What's wrong? Has something happened to Mum?'

Please God don't let her have cancer too.

He harrumphed. 'I've left your mother.'

'What?'

'She's having an affair.'

'When on earth would she have time to have an affair?' My mind flickered to the celebrity chef on the ship. Was all that flirting more real than I'd imagined?

'Pretty easy to find the time when it's with her assistant,' he spat.

I couldn't help but laugh. He had to be mistaken. His wife—my *mother*—was the straightest person I knew, the absolute last person on earth I would ever expect to come out of the closet.

'Mum and Rosa are just friends, and colleagues. They may be spending a lot of time together at the moment because of the book and everything but that doesn't mean—'

'I found them in bed together, Ged.'

'Oh my God!' The words spewed out of my mouth as my stomach revolted at the image. Not that *I* had anything against lesbian sex, but no one wanted to think about their parents having sex together, never mind with other people.

I couldn't believe she'd cheated on Dad with anyone, never mind a *woman*!

He nodded glumly. 'Didn't I tell you there was something dodgy about that woman? I'd started to have my suspicions that something was going on, but I told myself I was being ridiculous. After what I saw ... I can't live another day in denial. I don't think I'll ever be able to look Marie in the eye again.'

You and me both. But before I could say anything, my handbag vibrated and I tugged out my phone, glancing down at the screen to see I had ten missed calls from my mother and a number of text messages:

Have you seen your father?

Call me!

Where are you?

I need to talk to you. Now.

Shoving the phone back in my bag, I chose to ignore one parent in favour of the one in front of me. 'Come on, let's go inside and I'll make you a cup of tea.'

Coco pushed ahead of me as I let us into my apartment and Dad dragged his belongings behind. This was another one of those moments where tea didn't seem adequate and I cursed *Thing* for my forced teetotalism. It was on the tip of my tongue to offer Dad something stronger—if anyone needed alcohol right now, he did—but then he wouldn't be able to drive home.

Another more shocking thought followed rapidly on the heels of that one. The suitcases meant he wasn't *going* home—at least not tonight. It wasn't that I didn't adore my father, but I didn't have the emotional capacity right now to deal with his devastation on top of everything else, and I didn't have the space for a house guest. The couch was barely big enough for an afternoon nap and no way he was having my bed in my current needing-to-sleep-twenty-hours-a-day state.

I was going to murder my mother.

'Have you told Will about Mum?' I asked tentatively; it would be far more sensible for him to land on my brother and sister-in-law. Their house might not be mammoth but at least they had a spare room.

'No. He and Sophie have enough on their plates. You don't mind me coming here, do you?'

'It's fine,' I lied as I willed the kettle to hurry the fuck up. While it took its sweet time, I grabbed a packet of Tim Tams from the pantry. Thank God chocolate wasn't on the list of things pregnant women were forbidden. Having to forgo alcohol and soft cheese was bad enough, but if the powers that be added chocolate, the population would die out pretty damn fast.

'I can't believe it,' Dad said, leaning against the kitchen counter as if he might collapse any moment. 'Thirty-seven years together and it's come to this. My wife leaving me for a *woman*.'

I wondered if he'd be any less upset if he'd found Mum with another man. 'Aren't you the one who walked out on her?'

'You don't expect me to stick around after walking in on that, do you? A man has to have *some* pride.'

'No, of course not.' I certainly didn't condone adultery and had always believed that commitment meant something, however you chose to express it.

'I shudder to think what the folks at bowls are going to say,' he added glumly.

'Let's not worry about anyone else right now,' I said, opening the Tim Tams and shoving them at him as the kettle started to whistle. 'You need to work out what you want to do. Have you spoken to Mum about this? Maybe it was a mistake? A one-off. Maybe she didn't enjoy it. Maybe ...'

'The reason I went into the bedroom was because I heard her screaming. I'd come home earlier than planned and I thought someone was attacking her.' He dropped his head into his hands. 'She's never screamed that way with me.'

La-la-la-la. I wanted to put my fingers in my ears. Instead I snatched up a biscuit, shoved it into my mouth and turned my attention to making tea.

'Let's take these into the lounge room.'

He nodded, picked up the rest of the Tim Tams and followed me like a forlorn puppy.

I dipped a biscuit in my tea. 'So, what did you do when you ... found them?'

'I froze a few moments, too stunned to believe what I was seeing, but then I told Rosa to get the hell out of my house. When your mother went after her, I grabbed two suitcases and started packing. I contemplated throwing all Marie's things out onto the lawn instead—that's what you're supposed to do, aren't ya? But I just wanted to get out of there. Being in that house … where I'd found the two of them … I just couldn't.'

'Fair enough.' I was still in shock and couldn't think straight. 'How long do you think this has been going on?'

'Lord only knows. Probably since before that blasted cruise Alice made you all go on. I never bought that excuse about Marie having so much work to do that Rosa needed to go along as well. From the moment she walked into my house, I knew she was trouble. As was that blasted blog thing. Your mother changed when she started making internet friends and I'm telling you, not for the better!' He held up his teacup. 'You got anything stronger than this?'

I got to my feet—'I'll see what I can find'—and returned a minute later with a near-empty bottle of bourbon that belonged to Christos.

'How's this?'

'Perfect.' He all but snatched the bottle from my grasp and poured a large measure into his tea.

'What are you going to do now?'

'I'm going to get very, very drunk and then I'm going to pass out on this here couch.'

'Don't you have to work tomorrow?' He wouldn't want to let his lollipop kids down.

'Dammit.' He put the teacup on the coffee table and his head fell into his hands.

'I actually meant what are you going to do going forward? Do you want to try and work things out with Mum?'

He looked up and his lower lip wobbled again. 'I'm not sure she'll want to. First I lose my job and now I've lost my wife. What have I got left?'

'You've got us, Dad. Me and Will.'

'Thanks, sweetheart. But I think I'd like to be alone for a bit. Do you mind?'

Mind? However sorry for him I felt, I was ecstatic. In the past few hours I'd had enough shock, drama and heartache for a lifetime, and I wasn't sure how long I could sit here consoling him. 'Of course not. Let me get you set up in here.'

I fetched an extra pillow from my bed and a spare blanket and returned to the lounge room where I found Dad had resorted to drinking straight from the bottle. Thankfully there wasn't much left in it.

I tucked the blanket over him like he was the child and I the parent. 'Are you going to be alright?'

'Yes. I can sleep anywhere, sweetheart.'

'Okay then, goodnight. I'll see you in the morning.'

I went into my bedroom and immediately texted my mother: *Can't talk right now. Dad here. Meet me for lunch tomorrow. Midday. Cafe next door to work.*

I did not finish with the 'x' I usually did.

20

The morning dragged as I counted down the minutes until my lunch-time powwow with Mum. Darren had asked me to work on a story about the national anthem after a teenager had refused to stand and sing it at her school assembly and subsequently been suspended for her actions. While I was outraged and agreed that 'Advance Australia Fair' was extremely problematic, I was not giving the story the attention it deserved because I was more outraged at my mother.

Less than twenty-four hours with the sad sack that was Dad and, although in theory I was on *his* side, I now wanted to kill them both. When I should have been writing, I deep-dived into everything I could find about later-in-life lesbianism instead.

In addition to the articles on the famous women who'd come out of the closet—Portia de Rossi, Liz Gilbert of *Eat Pray Love* fame and Cynthia Nixon, who played my fave character from *Sex and the City*—there were plenty about non-celebrity women like my mother. Apparently, this was a rising phenomenon worldwide and researchers had come up with a number of reasons why this might be the case.

One school of thought was that hormones played a part, that menopausal changes sometimes stimulated a heterosexual woman's interest in exploring same-sex attraction and that this wasn't so much coming out of the closet as becoming sexually awakened. Another big one was that non-heterosexuality was now far more socially accepted than when women currently post-menopausal were young, with lots more same-sex relationships being portrayed in the media and mainstream entertainment. This gave them permission to admit to something they hadn't felt safe or comfortable enough doing before.

And something that particularly struck a chord was that this was an age when women often started thinking about themselves and their needs after years of putting kids and family first. Was that what had happened to Mum? In pursuing another interest, she'd fallen into a career, but had she also inadvertently found something else she didn't even know was missing from her life?

Or maybe it was a combination of all of the above.

Finally, the time arrived where I could leave the office and go face my mother with my myriad questions. I hustled downstairs and into the cafe next door like a woman on a mission.

'Ged!' She ambushed me the moment I stepped inside, throwing her arms around me and squeezing tight. 'I'm so glad to see you. I was terrified you'd be angry and refuse to talk to me.'

Oh, I'm angry, I thought as I yanked myself out her embrace and scrutinised her. It was the first time I'd seen her without Rosa in weeks, and while she still looked like the woman who'd raised me and had recently become an internet sensation, there was also something different about her.

Oh Lord. It suddenly struck me. She had that look of someone who'd just had sex, that post-coital glow. My hopes that this was some grave misunderstanding fading fast, I led her over to a table in the corner, where hopefully we'd be out of sight if anyone from work came in or—probably more importantly—my mother's crazy fans.

What on earth would *they* make of this latest revelation?

I cut straight to the chase the moment we sat down. 'Since when are you a lesbian?'

Mum turned a bright shade of tomato. 'Please, Ged, keep your voice down. We don't need to air all our family business in public.'

I raised my eyebrows. This coming from the woman who aired everything in her life on a daily basis on the internet. 'Fine, but this is all a bit of a shock. What's going on? Dad seems to think you are having an affair. With Rosa?'

If this sounded like a question it was because I was still clutching desperately to the hope she would tell me he was mistaken, or at least what he'd seen was a one-off she now regretted immensely.

'I am.' Her hand rushed to her mouth to cover it as if she couldn't believe what she was saying.

'Hi there, ladies.' A cheerful server with golden curly hair piled up on her head like it was one of the desserts appeared beside us with a little notepad and pen. 'Are you guys ready to order or would you like me to run through today's specials?'

'We'll have the soup of the day,' I told her without even bothering to ask what it was.

'Good choice.' She smiled as she scribbled on her pad. 'And would you like some drinks?'

'Water will be fine, thank you.'

'Actually,' Mum piped up, 'I'd love a flat white. Skim milk, no sugar.'

As the waiter retreated, I met my mother's gaze once again. 'How long has this been going on behind Dad's back?'

'Don't say it like that!'

'How else am I supposed to say it? You cheated on him.'

She had the good grace to look guilty, her chin dipping towards her chest as she replied. 'It just happened.'

As if that was a reasonable excuse!

'How long?' I prodded.

'Well, we'd been getting close for a while, but we consummated our feelings on the cruise and have been together ever since.'

A light bulb went off in my head. 'You didn't go to the gym at all, did you?'

She blushed again.

'How did this start?' I asked, pushing aside the image of what alternative exercise they'd been doing. 'Have you ever had these kinds of "feelings" before? Have you always been a lesbian? Or has this come as much of a surprise to you as it has to us?'

'I'm not sure I am a lesbian, sweetheart, but I know I care a lot about Rosa and am definitely attracted to her. There was one very brief dalliance with your friend Ashley's mum at the school fundraising fashion parade. It was just a kiss and I wrote it off as us both having had too much cheap wine, but until recently it was probably the best kiss of my life.'

I grimaced, remembering Ashley—a quiet tomboy, however much that sounded like an oxymoron. To think, all these years I'd thought my mum as boring as white bread and butter when she'd been kissing other mums in secret! All this certainly sounded like lesbianism to me, but it wasn't surprising that she wasn't comfortable with shouting this from the rooftops, considering how her unconventional upbringing had affected her and made her a target for bullying over the years.

'Maybe I'm bisexual?'

This almost sounded like a question, as if she wanted me to inform her about her sexual preferences when the truth was I didn't want to be thinking about her and sex at all.

'Okay …' I took a deep breath, trying to wrap my head around everything. 'Look, maybe this isn't what it looks like. Maybe you're simply mistaking the first real friend you've had in years for something more? Maybe you're having a midlife crisis?'

Or maybe I was clutching at straws!

'I don't think so. Rosa makes me feel like I'm alive. Like finally my life has purpose and meaning. We connect mentally, emotionally and physically. I've never met anyone like her and it's certainly never been like this with your father. I always thought I was asexual. Sex with Tony was always a bit of a chore. He tried his best, but I gritted my teeth, thought of England and hoped it would be over quickly. Thank God it usually was. But with Rosa—'

'I get it.' I held up my hand; I did not need the clandestine details to understand and her actually sharing them was so far out of character it was unnerving. 'So, is *Rosa* a lesbian?'

'Oh yes, darling, didn't you know?'

Well, now that I thought about it in hindsight, maybe there were signs but, due to my mother's association with her, the thought hadn't even crossed my mind.

'So, what happens now?'

She frowned as if she didn't understand the question.

'Between you and Dad. Do you want to officially go your separate ways? You need to work this out because he doesn't deserve to be messed around.'

Her face fell. 'How is he?'

'He's devastated, Mum. What do you expect?'

She recoiled at my harsh tone. 'I never meant to hurt him. This wasn't something I planned. It just happened.'

'A *month* ago. You should have told him the moment you realised you had feelings for Rosa. Sneaking around behind his back, letting him find out the way he did ...' I shook my head in disgust. 'It would have been bad enough if he'd found you in bed with another man, but this betrayal is on a whole other level. He's heartbroken and angry, but also mortified and embarrassed. He's worrying about what people are going to say and wondering if he's ever really known you at all or if you've been lying to him, to *us*, all these years.'

'I haven't been lying,' she said emphatically. 'I loved your father. He's a good man. When we met I was desperate to have a secure family life. He gave me that and I'll always be grateful to him. But lately I've been wondering if this is really it. Life had meaning when you and Will were at home and Tony and I had things to talk about, but, now we're empty nesters, having children and grandchildren in common isn't enough. There's so much silence because neither of us have anything to say to each other. *The Happy Happy Housewife* gave me something to be excited about, but then I met Rosa and she's shown me that I don't have to settle for simply existing anymore. She's challenged me to embrace and experience life. I don't want to hurt your dad, but I want to be free to be my true self. Can you understand that, Geraldine?'

I sighed and nodded, my chest cramping at the realisation this wasn't just some phase. Mum was speaking in a tone I'd never heard before; she sounded like a different woman. On the one hand I was happy for her, but I was also still angry and devastated for my father. I couldn't help wishing she could have taken up pottery or something instead. That she could have found meaning in a hobby rather than adultery.

Perhaps it was my fault, as I'd been the one to introduce her to the world of social media. Right now I felt like kicking myself because I knew that if she wasn't looking after Dad, someone else would have to. And, as the only daughter—however wrong it might be—I suspected that role would fall to me. Already that morning I'd made him eggs on toast and told him to make sure he had enough money for lunch when he asked me what I was going to make him.

'Dad,' I'd said as I grabbed a banana for my own breakfast, 'I don't even make lunch for myself.'

For a moment, I'd thought he was about to start crying again and I told myself to be kinder to him, that he'd suffered a massive blow. Not long after mine from Christos, I could certainly sympathise— our situations might not be exactly the same, but part of me felt cheated too. However, I knew my patience would wear thin fast.

'Dad can't stay with me indefinitely,' I told Mum now. 'If you're going to be with Rosa, you guys are going to have to work out what you're going to do about the house, your joint finances, whether or not you're going to get a divorce.'

She visibly flinched and I knew she would struggle with that no matter how much she wanted it. Divorce, in Mum's old-fashioned, conservative head was something that brought shame and gossip, thus should be avoided at all costs. But she couldn't have her cake and eat it too.

'I suppose we'll have to sell. Neither of us can afford to buy the other out. It'll be sad to say goodbye to our home though … it holds so many special family memories.' She blinked, her eyes watery. 'All those Christmases, the laundry door where I measured you and Will as you grew up, the pets buried in the backyard …'

I found myself reaching across the table and squeezing Mum's hand. She was right; I'd always imagined my parents would grow old together in the Port Melbourne house. Had this drama not come immediately on the heels of me finding out about Gralice's illness, it might have felt more traumatic to be facing their separation at the grand old age of thirty, but divorce wasn't fatal in the way cancer could be.

Mum sighed. 'I guess all that will take time though. Rosa and I have been talking about going to Brazil so I can meet her family. We might even spend a few months there. I could work on the book without too many distractions.'

The book about how to be the perfect wife.

I struggled not to snort at the irony, but then I thought about Gralice. Mum couldn't run away to Rio, or wherever Rosa hailed from, when her mother had only months to live.

'You can't go,' I blurted, before realising Gralice would kill me if I told her about the cancer, but how would my mother feel if she missed this last chance to spend time with her own? And, Gralice desperately wanted the chance to heal the divide between them.

Mum blinked. 'Why not?'

'Because … Because I'm pregnant. And I need you around for moral support.'

Her mouth fell open and her eyes stretched wide as if I'd just told her I was joining a cult or had won Saturday Night Lotto.

'Surprise!' I threw my hands up in the air and almost hit our waitress as she returned with the coffee. In her effort to jump out of my way, liquid splashed out of the cup and over her apron. 'I'm so sorry.'

'It's fine.' She grinned again but it didn't seem quite as genuine as the last time. 'I'll get you a replacement.'

'Don't worry about it. I'll have that one,' Mum said, reaching out to take it.

'If you're sure.' Once-smiley waiter retreated again and Mum and I stared at each other.

This was the first time I'd said those two words out loud and they sounded even more shocking and terrifying than they did in my head. 'Would you please say something? It's not like you thought I was a virgin, and I haven't murdered anyone or anything. I'm merely having a … I'm with child!'

'I'm sorry. I'm just surprised. This is wonderful news.'

She stood and came around the table to hug me. I squirmed a little and couldn't quite bring myself to say 'thanks'. How had I told Mum before I'd told Gralice? The world had gone bonkers.

'How far along are you?' she asked, when she finally pulled back.

'About eight weeks.'

'And how does Christos feel? I suppose a baby will complicate his decision to get back together with Carly. Does this mean you two—'

'No. Definitely not.' I shook my head. 'I haven't told him yet because … well … I'm not sure if I'm having the baby, and also … it may not actually be his.'

'Who else's could it be?' Mum exclaimed loudly.

I pressed a finger to my lips, but before I could explain she continued, 'I might not be a mathematician, but you said you're eight weeks along and you only broke up with Christos about a month ago.'

'Five and a half weeks.' Not that I was counting.

'Were you seeing someone else at the same time?'

'No, I met a guy on the ship and—'

'You *slept* with someone on the ship?!'

I thought Mum's outrage a little cheeky considering what she and Rosa had been up to. Not to mention I was a grown-up and single. 'Yes. It wasn't anything serious. Just a bit of fun.'

'A bit of fun that might have resulted in a baby!' She pressed a hand against her chest and for a second I thought she was going to do the sign of the cross. 'Do you even know who this man is?'

'Calm down, of course I do. I made sure I knew his name before I let him look up my skirt, Mother. His name's Jay. He's a policeman.' I thought she'd like that. 'He's not my type but he's fit and healthy, so good genes, I reckon.'

I decided not to mention that we'd been casually seeing each other, as this might give her a false sense of hope, or tell her about the Mars thing, as this would make her think him insane.

'I see. And how are you feeling? Have you had any morning sickness?'

'I'm exhausted and feel constantly nauseous but I've only thrown up once.'

'Poor love.' She reached across and patted my hand. 'Ginger ale helps with that. I'll buy you some. I drank gallons when I was pregnant with you and your brother, but my morning sickness passed by the end of the first trimester so with any luck, you'll only have a few more weeks of discomfort.'

'I've already discovered the benefits of ginger, dry crackers and peppermint tea.'

'Ooh, can I get a selfie of us to put up on my vlog? My followers are going to be so excited when they hear I'm having another grandchild!'

'No way.' She was not exploiting me and Thing to get more views and I couldn't risk her followers finding out before Christos and/or Jay. 'Anyway, as I said, I'm not actually sure I want to go through with the pregnancy.'

She seemed to have missed this point in the confusion about the sperm donor. I braced myself for the lecture telling me that of course I'd have the baby—motherhood was the most rewarding job in the world, yadda, yadda, yadda—but it didn't come.

'It is a big decision,' she said instead, warmth and understanding in her voice, 'and one only you can make. How will it affect your chances of promotion?'

'Legally, it shouldn't affect it at all, but the timing is pretty much the worst it could be.'

'I know how much you wanted it.'

'Yes.' I nodded, surprised that she rated this. 'And I didn't think I wanted children, so this should be an easy choice, but now I've actually got to make it, I'm not so sure. What if this is my one chance at motherhood and I reject it?'

Once-smiley waiter chose that moment to return to the table with our steaming bowls of cauliflower soup. We paused our conversation, thanked her for our lunch and ignored it the moment she left.

'Motherhood is very rewarding,' began my mother, 'but it's also a massive commitment and a great deal of hard work. The off-chance you might regret not having a baby is not a good reason to embark on it. Especially single motherhood—it's not something you should enter into lightly. Dad might not have been much help in a practical way but he was always there for all of us emotionally. He took care of us, I never had to worry about whether we'd be able to afford a roof over our heads or food on the table.'

'Are you saying I should have a termination?'

'I didn't say that.' She picked up her soup spoon. 'I want you to do whatever is right for you, and I want you to know that whatever you decide you'll have my full support.'

'Thank you.'

'I wonder if there's any way to tell who the father is before the baby is born?'

'There is.' I nodded and told her about the DNA sample test.

'Will knowing who the father is make a difference to your decision?'

'I don't know.' Part of me hoped the baby was Jay's because that would be far less complicated on some levels. Especially if he zoomed off to Mars. Whereas if Christos and I became co-parents,

I'd never be free of him. I wasn't sure my heart could take that. It was bad enough sharing air at the office; every time I saw a glimpse of him I was reminded of what we'd had and what I'd lost.

'It shouldn't, should it?'

'Time is on your side,' Mum said, sounding more matter-of-fact and more Gralice-like than she ever had before. 'You're not showing yet. And not to be pessimistic, but you're not past the safe mark either. Remember, I had two miscarriages between Will and you. Why don't you mull it all over a little longer? You don't need to tell anyone else until you are ready. Your secret's safe with me.'

I thought this might be the first secret we'd ever shared and I wondered if she would also refrain from telling Rosa. A vision of them in bed snuggling up together, discussing my dilemma post sex, landed in my head. *Ugh.*

'Yes, that's a good idea. And what about you? Have you told the others yet?' By 'the others', we both knew I meant Gralice, Phil, Craig and Will, and I guessed the answer was no because I hadn't had frantic texts or phone calls from any of them, but she couldn't keep them in the dark forever.

Mum put down her spoon again and clutched the pearl necklace around her neck. 'No. I called you because I suspected Tony would go to you. You've always been Daddy's little girl, but I suppose I'll have to face my parents and Will soon. I doubt your father will want to be the bearer of the news.'

This was an apt assumption. When he'd left to go help the kiddies cross the road this morning he'd been muttering about making a voodoo doll of Rosa.

'I don't think you need to worry about telling Gralice about your—' I struggled to work out how to phrase whatever this was. 'She might be surprised but she'll also be supportive, and so will Phil and Craig, obviously. Will might take time to come around, but … we're adults now.' At least I was trying to act like one. 'Whatever happens, we'll cope.'

I wasn't sure I believed this. Will was going to be devastated and I didn't feel at all confident about coping with what the next few months had in store, but I said what my mother needed to hear.

'Thank you, sweetheart.' Mum reached across the table and clutched both my hands. 'I'm so lucky to have you as my daughter.'

I forced a smile. 'Lucky' was the last word I'd use to describe anything that had happened to me lately. In a matter of a month my life had become a soap opera—one in which I'd been forced to take a starring role when I didn't even want to watch the show.

21

'Are you alright, my love?' Mum squeezed my hand. She and Rosa were sitting on either side of me on uncomfortable plastic chairs as we waited for someone to call my name. As I'd suspected, Mum had told her lover, but I didn't mind. They'd both been a massive support over the past few weeks but Will would be furious if he knew how accepting I'd been of Rosa. And Dad would probably never speak to me again. I still didn't agree with Mum's adultery, but life wasn't black and white and I wanted to move forward, not dwell on the past.

'Yeah, but I really need to pee.' My heart was thumping so wildly I swore they could hear it and the hand Mum had taken hold of was so sweaty it probably betrayed my reply. My full bladder was making me uncomfortable but it wasn't responsible for my anxiety. 'Thanks for coming with me.'

'We wouldn't be anywhere else,' Rosa said, taking hold of my other hand, which had been resting on my stomach.

It was still pretty flat, but an ever-so-slight bump that I already had to accommodate when choosing outfits was visible. Despite the initial shock, my pregnancy had taken a back seat for a couple of weeks while I'd dealt with (or rather survived) all our other family dramas, but I sometimes found myself talking to Thing about all that was on my plate.

'I think your grandmother is having a midlife crisis,' I'd say when I'd gotten off the phone to my mother, or 'Gralice wasn't looking that great today, was she?' when we were walking home from an interview session. I chatted to Thing in the morning when I was trying to work out what to wear to work, and sometimes I even asked what it felt like for dinner. 'Pasta or beans on toast?' I'd discovered Thing had a penchant for beans and I couldn't even bring myself to care about all the extra gas this created. At work I spent as much time out of the office as I could, and at home the only ones affected by my bean-frenzy were Coco and my father, who, despite the fact my mother had 'temporarily' moved in with Rosa, seemed to spend a lot more time at my apartment than he did at his house. It was driving me batty.

But, one complication at a time.

'Geraldine Johnston?' Finally a woman in white summoned me.

I leapt to my feet, then swayed a little as dizziness hit me. Mum and Rosa steadied me.

'You okay?' asked the woman, crossing over to me quickly.

I nodded, ignoring the plague of wasps (these were no butterflies) that had taken up residence in my stomach.

'Great. Well then, I'm Helena Clarke, your sonographer for today. Let's take a look at your baby.'

'This is my Mum, Marie, and her ... assistant, Rosa.' The world at large still had no idea their relationship was more than professional and I didn't want to be the one to break that news. 'Can they come too?'

Helena smiled. 'Yes, of course. Lovely to meet you both.'

Mum took my hand again as we followed Helena down a short corridor into a dimly lit room. An examination table took pride of place in the middle with a computer screen and the ultrasound machine beside it.

'It might be easier if you take off your coat before you get on the bed.'

I did as Helena suggested and then climbed onto the bed.

'Can you lift your top up a little? I'm going to smooth some gel over your stomach—it might be a little cold,' Helena warned as she waved the ultrasound wand above me.

Sucking in a breath, I pulled up my shirt and Helena put a paper towel over the waistband of my trousers then pushed them down a little, revealing my naked, ever-so-slightly rounded belly. As the ultrasound wand touched my skin, I squeezed Mum's hand and held on tightly, the squirminess in my stomach like no nerves I'd ever felt before. I turned and focused on the screen. Within seconds a grainy black-and-white image appeared.

I gasped as I gazed at the weird-looking creature. It was shaped much like the beans I'd been enjoying on a near daily basis, but I could make out a head, very much out of proportion to the body and two tiny legs. 'Where are the arms?'

Helena chuckled, moved the probe slightly and pointed to the screen with her other hand. 'They're there, don't worry. It's just hard to see from this angle at this stage. Now, let's get some measurements and confirm your due date.'

'Ultrasound images are certainly more sophisticated than they were when I was having babies,' Mum mused. 'Thank you for letting us share this with you, darling.'

I forced a smile, worried that she was getting too attached to something that wasn't born yet and, more to the point, might never be.

And then a woh-woh-woh-woh-woh sound filled the room.

'Oh my God. Is that the …?'

'Heartbeat? Yes, it is.' Helen smiled as she finished my sentence. 'And it's nice and strong. Exactly what we want to hear.'

My own heart stilled. I couldn't take my eyes off the image, but within seconds it grew blurry as they filled with tears.

If there'd ever been any doubt I was keeping Thing it evaporated in that moment. That heartbeat was so strong, so loud, so real, and I felt a sudden connection and an urge to protect what was in my body like nothing I'd ever felt before.

I would die for that heartbeat.

Whether or not I had Jay's or Christos's support, I didn't care. It would be me and Thing against the world and I couldn't wait to meet her, or him.

Forty weeks felt forever away, yet at the same time I was terrified of going into labour any earlier and sacrificing my baby's health. Not to mention everything I needed to organise and achieve before D-day. Clothes—tiny ones for Thing and maternity ones to accommodate my increasing girth—a cot, a pram, a car seat, maternity leave, a birth plan, a hospital, a *name* … the list seemed endless but I didn't feel overwhelmed.

If I could grow a baby that possessed such a beautiful strong heartbeat, what couldn't I do? I was in awe of how amazing and powerful women were. Thanks to Gralice, I'd always believed women could achieve anything we wanted if we put our minds to it, but now I felt almost invincible.

'So … was I right about the dates?' If I'd somehow miscalculated and was more pregnant than I thought, I'd know Thing belonged to Christos.

Helena nodded. 'Spot on. You're currently twelve-and-a-half weeks; due date is January twenty-sixth, although don't hold me to that.'

My heart sank. The truth about my baby daddy would have to wait a little longer. 'Can you tell if I'm having a girl or a boy?'

'Not at this stage.' Helena yanked a few tissues from a box beside the computer and wiped the gel off my stomach. 'But if you want to find out, we'll be able to see at your next scan.'

'Okay. Thank you.' I bit my lip to try and tame my grin. 'Do I get a photo?'

'Of course. I'll print them off while you get dressed. I imagine you might want to go to the toilet. I can give these to your mother so you don't have to hold on any longer.'

'Thank you.'

'I guess this means you're keeping the baby?' Mum asked with a wide smile as I emerged from the bathroom a few minutes later and she handed me a strip of black-and-white photos.

'Ah-huh.' I gazed down at Thing. At my *baby*. 'I'm going to be a mother. A *mum*!'

'Congratulations,' Mum and Rosa said in unison and pulled me into a group hug.

'Are you going to tell the others now?' Mum added.

'I guess so.' I stroked my stomach affectionately, finally ready to shout my impending motherhood from the rooftops. 'They might start to notice when I begin to gain weight.'

Mum and Rosa chuckled as we started out of the building.

'And what are you going to tell them about the father, sweetheart?' Mum's question killed my joy a little.

Over the last few weeks, I'd almost managed to convince myself that Thing had been conceived by immaculate conception. But, of course, my family would want to know this significant detail. *Dammit*.

I could just imagine Will finding my predicament hilarious—he'd dine out on this story for *years*. Phil and Craig would be supportive,

Dad confused, and Gralice? Well, let's just say, considering Jay's relation to Henry, it might be easier on her if Christos was the father.

'Actually, I think I might hold off until I know who the father is.'

'So, you are going to find out?'

'I don't think I could live with myself if I didn't. I owe it to my baby to find out the truth.'

But my gut clenched at the thought of confronting either of them. Was this how the Virgin Mary had felt when she'd had to tell Joseph she was pregnant?

We said our goodbyes and as they headed off, I pulled my mobile out of my bag. Deciding it would be easier to have this conversation with Jay, who knew about Christos, rather than my ex, who knew nothing about my fling, I tapped out a message to Sex-on-Tap before I could chicken out: *Hey, can you come round to my place tonight?*

Jay would assume this was a booty call, but I could hardly break this news to him via text. I half-expected him to ignore me as I'd been doing to him the last couple of weeks or, if he did respond, tell me he was busy. But his reply came almost instantly: *8pm?*

I glanced at the time—it was almost five. Three hours to go, which would give me plenty of time to check in on Gralice, before heading home to get ready for Jay.

22

I found Gralice resting on the couch, but she roused when I came into the house. 'Oh, this is a lovely surprise. Did we have an interview scheduled?'

'No, I just wanted to see you. How about I make us a cup of tea?'

'That would be lovely.' Although she smiled, there was irritation in her tone and she may as well have hung a 'KEEP OUT' banner over her head.

Slowly, she rose to sitting position, but it was clear she wasn't feeling well at all. She looked worse than she had for a few days—her skin was almost grey and her eyes a little sunken. It was like she was fading away before me.

She went into the bathroom while I fiddled about in the kitchen making toasted cheese sandwiches as well as the tea. We watched the news together while I scoffed down three sandwiches and Gralice nibbled at hers. I felt reluctant to leave her alone but couldn't cancel on Jay, so made her promise to call me later if she needed anything.

She rolled her eyes, told me to stop being a fusspot, and sent me packing.

My nerves multiplied as I headed from Fitzroy to Carlton. Was I right to choose Jay to ask for a sample? Neither of my options appealed, but Christos was already a father and so might freak out less about the possibility of a baby.

Nope, I'd made my decision now—Jay was coming over—so I tried to come up with the perfect delivery.

Hi Jay—how do you feel about babies?

Jay—nice to see you again. Can I have a swab from your cheek? Why? Oh, I'm helping my niece with a school assignment. Yes, she's only three, but she's very advanced for her age.

Hey, Jay—funny story. You know how I told you I was on the pill, well, apparently, it's only ninety-nine percent effective and …

Jay—is that short for anything? I wondered why I'd never contemplated this possibility before. Was he really a Jayden? Or a Jamie? Or a Jason?

Argh. What did his name matter? I'd only need to know this detail if he *was* the father and I needed the full shebang for Thing's birth certificate.

By the time I got home there was only forty-five minutes until Jayden/Jamie/Jason's arrival and, after taking Coco out for a quick pee then shaking her dog biscuits into her bowl, I dashed around the apartment trying to make it presentable. I didn't know why I was so anxious about making everything look nice—Jay didn't give me the impression he was an interior design connoisseur and it wasn't like he'd give two damns about anything else when I told him why I'd summoned him. But then again, this was going to be one of the most important conversations of my life. For Thing's sake, I couldn't stuff it up.

With fifteen minutes until his ETA, I jumped in the shower. Although it didn't really matter how I looked, considering, I wanted to feel my best. There wasn't time to wash and blow dry my hair, but I threw on a clean pair of black yoga pants and my favourite jumper. I drew the line at make-up but swiped a layer of tinted moisturiser over my face.

And then the intercom buzzed.

My heart leapt into my throat as I followed a barking Coco through the apartment. My finger shaking, I pressed the button that would let Jay into the building, then took a deep breath and counted to ten before opening my front door.

He was already standing there—those long, muscly legs and incredible fitness meant that what would take someone else thirty seconds he did in less than ten. And he didn't even look puffed.

Coco jumped up at him, giving me a few moments to collect my thoughts. Jay caressed her neck and she writhed with pleasure.

'I missed ya, gorgeous girl.' For someone who didn't see the point of pets, he was certainly very affectionate towards mine.

Finally, he looked up. He towered above me but our eyes met as he looked down. 'Well, well, well, long time no see. I thought you must have changed your mind about us.'

'No, I—' While a little voice inside my head screamed at me to tell him I was pregnant, the words died on my tongue.

'It doesn't matter.' He kissed me on the cheek, then held up a bottle of champagne. 'Do you have fancy glasses? We're celebrating!'

Cheek kisses should be chaste, yet this one felt anything but. And ... *Hang on.*

'What are we celebrating?' I blurted as my heart thumped a tattoo.

His lips twisted into a grin as he stepped inside, kicking the door shut behind him. 'I got accepted into the third round of Mars Mission. You're looking at one of the final hundred!'

My already small apartment shrank around us. The air felt lacking in oxygen and I could feel my stomach tying itself in knots.

'Isn't it fantastic?' Jay picked me up and swung me around. Coco barked and I thought I might actually be sick.

'Put me down.' Once my feet were flat on the floor, I found some words. 'Wow … That's … I'm … speechless. You must be …'

'I'm not sure it's sunk in yet,' he said, making his way into my kitchen. I followed on shaky legs as he started opening and closing cupboards. 'Where are your glasses?'

'Um.' I opened a cupboard and retrieved two champagne flutes— the last time I'd used them was when Christos's divorce came through and we were toasting his new-found freedom.

As I placed the glasses on the bench, Jay tore off the gold foil at the top of the bottle and expertly popped the cork. The label told me he'd splurged, but I panicked as he poured the amber liquid. I couldn't drink champagne—Thing was nowhere near legal—but how could I deliver my news when Jay was practically jumping up and down in my kitchen with excitement over his? Way to kill a guy's joy!

'Here you are.' Still grinning, he handed me a glass, his fingers brushing against mine.

I tried to ignore the heat that shot through my body at his touch. 'Shall we take these into the lounge room and toast your good news there?'

As I turned to go, I felt Jay's palm in the small of my back. It was such a patriarchal and possessive gesture, but I couldn't help liking the way it made me feel.

There was a potted Devil's Ivy (that I miraculously hadn't yet succeeded in killing—I didn't get green thumbs from my grandfathers) next to my couch and I made sure I sat near it.

'So.' I forced a smile as I tried to relax into the couch. 'Congratulations.'

'Thanks.' He lifted his glass towards mine and we clinked.

'Mars, hey? What happens next?' I hoped I didn't sound hysterical.

This was good news. I should be happy for him. Crazy as it was, this was what Jay wanted. But all I could think about was how Thing would feel if its father buggered off to outer space.

'Next round is gonna be tough. I'll have to embark on a series of group challenges across five days, and people will be eliminated throughout the selection period, so that they end up with only forty candidates moving into the next round. We don't know much at this stage, but there will be both indoor and outdoor challenges testing us on team work, problem solving, trust ...'

He went on, but I barely heard a word.

What would the children at school say? Would they think it cool that Thing's dad was off starting a whole new civilisation or would they think it weird? And would it make our child a target for bullies? Kids were cruel. I knew how badly Mum had suffered due to her unconventional-for-the-era parents, and look how that had turned out. I couldn't help feeling that maybe a father who put Mars before his family would also give reason for kids to tease.

Envisioning raising a red-haired child with a whole host of abandonment issues, I stared at my glass, wishing I could take a sip.

'I still can't believe I've made it this far and been chosen out of over two hundred thousand initial applicants.'

'It's amazing alright. When does this challenge thing take place?' I asked, trying to sound half as interested and enthused as Jay was.

'Not exactly sure yet. Probably sometime next year.'

'And what does your family think? I can't imagine Kate being overly enthused.'

He chuckled. 'You know my sister so well. But they don't know yet. When I said I just found out, I literally meant I *just* found out. You're the first person I've told.'

My stomach did a summersault, but I forced a smile and lifted my glass to my lips, pretending to drink.

'I cannot wait to find out who my fellow candidates are.'

No doubt they'd all be as insane as him. How could any *normal* person be so excited about the possibility of dying on a foreign planet? If they even made it that far. The odds would probably be better if he jumped out of a plane sans-parachute.

Jay talked more than he'd ever talked before and I listened as best I could, asking questions when necessary and smiling a lot to compensate for how I felt inside. If I wasn't possibly pregnant with his child, I might have been excited for him. His passion was undeniable, no matter how crazy I thought the whole Mars thing.

But I could kill that excitement with two little words.

'Can I use your bathroom?' Jay asked.

'Sure. You know where it is.'

While he was gone I poured all but the last few drops of my champagne into the plant. 'Enjoy,' I whispered, thinking how dire my life had become when I was jealous of a plant. I was going to have to tell Christos instead. With any luck the baby was his—however painful that might be for me—and I'd never have to complicate Jay's world.

'Looks like you need a top up,' he said, when he returned a few minutes later.

I smiled and held out my glass as he filled it.

'Anyway, enough about me. You must be sick of hearing about Mars.'

'Not at all. It's fascinating.'

He laughed. Obviously I was a shit liar.

'I'm sorry, I'm really happy for you, it's just ...' What could I say?

'You look tired.' He reached out and stroked his thumb down my cheek.

'I've had a stressful few weeks.'

'What's wrong? Is it work? Has your ex been giving you a hard time?'

'Not exactly—although he did proposition me for an affair.' I snorted and quickly filled him in on Christos's proposition.

'The guy sounds like a dick. So, if not him, what's bothering you?'

'It's family stuff.'

'I might not be the best listener, but I'm happy to try. What's been going on?'

And because talking seemed a safer option than crawling into his lap, I said, 'Can you keep a secret?'

'Like no one else.'

So, I started with the news that my parents were getting a divorce. 'You promise you won't tell anyone about this.' I did not want to be responsible for ruining Mum's new career, even though I thought she might be on borrowed time where that was concerned. Sure, Australia at large had voted 'yes' and embraced alternative families, but I wasn't sure Mum's target audience were so progressive and they might have something to say if they discovered their guru was a soon-to-be divorcee shacked up with her female lover.

'Geraldine,' he said, taking my hand when I hesitated, 'you have my word. I'm not a gossip.'

So I told him everything. Mum's affair with her female assistant, my brother's fury, my father's devastation, and the fact I felt smack-bang in the middle of it all. 'Will's wrath is fuelling Dad's self-pity and woe. I'm trying to stay neutral and not take sides, but ...' I sighed. 'It's exhausting.'

'And I thought my family was a mess.'

I let out a half-laugh at Jay's words, but there was nothing funny in what I told him next. 'And to make it all worse, my grandma has cancer.'

Tears I never meant to cry in front of him threatened.

'Shit. I'm sorry.' He squeezed my hand.

'Thanks.' I sniffed, trying to rein in my waterworks. 'It's just a shock. Gralice isn't only my grandmother, she's one of my best friends, and this doesn't even seem real because I can't imagine life without her. So, I forget about it, and then suddenly I remember, and I ache so much that it hurts to breathe.'

The fight was lost. A tear slipped down my cheek, but Jay wiped it away with the pad of his thumb.

'Sorry. I've put a downer on your night.' Maybe it would have been better if I'd told him about the baby.

'Don't apologise,' he whispered, then leaned in close and kissed me on the lips.

Oh Lord. Alarm bells rang inside my head; little voices screamed at me to pull back. This wasn't a good idea on so many levels, but it felt so good that I ignored them all. The damage was done; it wasn't like I was going to get pregnant again.

Jay pulled me onto his lap and as I straddled him I felt the bulge in his jeans. I wanted him more than I'd ever wanted anything before. He took my face in both his hands and deepened the kiss. I groaned as his tongue danced with mine and I tugged up his sweatshirt, desperate to feel his smooth, hot skin. As my hands travelled up his bare chest, he moved his mouth lower, kissing my neck, and then he yanked my jumper and T-shirt over my head in one swift move. His lips closed around my nipple and the lace of my bra wasn't the only thing that grew wet.

'Oh, Jay.' I writhed above him, and when he groaned I slid my hand between us, unbuckled his jeans and slipped it inside. He felt hot and hard and oh-so-good.

All rational thought fled.

I needed him. Now.

And judging by his breathy reply he felt exactly the same. 'Pants. Off.'

Right then, Coco started barking and we stilled at the sound of a key turning.

'Hello, love,' called Dad as he stepped straight into the lounge room. 'Geez. Oh. Sorry, sweetheart.'

Jay's eyes widened as they met mine. 'Who the hell is he?'

'My father.' I cringed, mortification washing over me as I snatched up my jumper, shoved it back over my head and climbed off Jay. 'Dad, what are you doing here?'

'The pub had some quiz night thing on tonight and I needed some company,' he explained, and I couldn't help noticing his words slurred a little. 'But sorry, I didn't know you already *had* company.'

Jay was standing now and looked as if he wanted to murder my father. He could take a ticket and get in line.

'Where did you get a key?' I asked, certain I'd never given him one.

'I took the spare from the pantry last time I was here.' He looked to Jay and gave him a sheepish smile. 'Hi.'

Jay nodded but didn't return any kind of smile.

'Dad, this is Jay. He's just a ... We were just ...'

My father's face reddened. 'No need to explain yourself, you're a big girl. I'll be off again, shall I?' He swung his car keys on his fingers.

As much as I wanted to tell him 'yes, bugger off', I couldn't send him back to his car when I already suspected he'd driven here over the limit.

'It's fine,' Jay said, probably thinking the same. My father was lucky he didn't arrest him on the spot. *Could* SOG cops still make regular arrests? 'I'll go.'

'Dad, go put the kettle on while I see Jay out.'

My father did as he was told, and I stepped up close to my friend-with-benefits. 'Really sorry.' And perhaps I didn't simply mean about this evening.

'Take care of yourself,' he said, leaning forward to kiss me on the cheek. 'Remember, you're just as important as the rest of your family. Let's catch up soon.'

I nodded and saw him to the door.

As mortifying as our interruption had been, it was probably a blessing in disguise. Could I really allow myself to keep sleeping with Jay under the circumstances?

23

The door of the cafe opened and I looked up to see Christos entering. As he glanced about and loosened the black scarf around his neck, I tried to ignore the kick in my belly at the sight of him. No matter how much he'd broken my heart, he was still as devastatingly handsome as ever.

I waved and caught his eye. He came over and there was an awkward moment—*Do I stand? Do we shake hands? Nod? Kiss cheeks?*

'Hey, Ged.' He decided on a smile. 'You're looking good.'

'Thanks.' It was like we were strangers meeting for the first time on a blind date.

'Have you ordered?'

I gestured to the mineral water in front of me—I'd given up the Diet Coke when I'd decided Thing was here to stay. 'I ate earlier, but you go ahead if you like.'

'Maybe I'll just grab a coffee.'

'Good idea.'

Christos went to place his order and returned a few moments later with a takeaway.

'Well, I must admit your email threw me for six,' he said as he shrugged out of his coat, draped it over the back of his seat and sat.

It had been ten weeks since the hotel fiasco and we'd spoken to each other a grand total of twice since. Once when he'd tried to proposition me for an affair, and a couple of weeks later when he'd tried to apologise and ask forgiveness, suggesting maybe we could be friends instead.

I don't think so, mister!

'I didn't think you'd ever talk to me again. How's your family?'

'Yep—they're all great,' I lied, 'but I'm not here to chat. I'm pregnant.'

'What?' Christos jerked his head back and the coffee he'd lifted to his mouth splashed over the rim and onto his pale blue shirt. 'Are you serious?'

'No. I thought it would be a funny joke. Of course I'm serious.'

Wanker, I added silently.

'Okay. Well.' He puffed. 'This is big news. You're not planning on having it, are you?'

My hackles rose. 'I wouldn't be telling you if I wasn't. I might have been undecided about having kids but I'm sure I want this one and—'

'Relax.' Christos held up his hands as if I were holding a gun on him and let out a long breath. 'This is wonderful news. Sure, it complicates things a little, but a baby is never a mistake. My kids aren't always easy, but they've brought me the greatest joy in my life and I cannot be unhappy about the prospect of another one.'

Of course, he assumed Thing was his and, petty as it might be, it brought me great pleasure to set him straight. 'Actually, there's a possibility the baby isn't yours.'

His thick, dark eyebrows squished together as he lowered the coffee cup to the table. 'I ... but ... what? How far along are you?'

'I'm almost thirteen weeks. I had my first ultrasound yesterday.'

'But we only broke up ten weeks ago?'

'Yes. And I was devastated. That weekend I went on a cruise with Mum and Gralice and I ... I had a lot to drink and ... I met this guy.'

He lowered his head but not in time for me to miss the hurt that flashed across his face. It should have felt good to see him feeling a fraction of the heartache and betrayal I had, but weirdly, it didn't.

'So, you're having a baby and it could be mine but it could be this bloke's instead?'

'Yep.'

'How do we find out?'

'There's a prenatal paternity test we can do—it compares a sample of foetal DNA from my blood with a sample from you. Your sample can be a fingernail or some hair or even blood, but apparently a swab from inside your cheek works the best. I ordered this kit online so we can get your sample right now and then I can go get bloods and we should have the results within a couple of weeks.'

Christos didn't say anything a few moments, then he cleared his throat. 'What's this other guy like?'

'It doesn't matter.'

'Do you ... do you love him?'

'No.' I scoffed. 'I barely know him.'

'Okay. But who do you *want* to be the father?'

I didn't need to think about this question. Logically, he was the better option. 'You.'

He nodded. 'Do you have a photo?'

'Yes.' Thing's ultrasound pics had become a permanent fixture in my handbag over the past twenty-four hours—I liked to dig them out and stare at them sporadically. 'Do you want to see?'

'Yes, please.'

I retrieved the little strip of black-and-white photos from my handbag and pushed them across the table to him. My heart stilled as I watched him pick them up and scrutinise them. Was he looking for similarities between his children and this tiny bean-like creature?

'New life is a true miracle.' He lifted his head to look at me and his eyes looked misty. 'How have you been feeling? Any morning sickness?'

'I've had a bit of nausea but only thrown up once, and that was right after I found out I was pregnant, so that could have been down to shock.'

'I fainted when Carly told me we were pregnant with our first.'

I found myself smiling. 'The most depressing part is that I can't stand the taste of coffee anymore and so I've got nothing to combat the bone-numbing tiredness. I'm hoping my love of it returns once Thing is born, otherwise I'm not sure how I'm gonna deal with all those sleepless nights.'

'*Thing*? You're calling the baby Thing?'

'I can call it what I like,' I snapped. Initially, when I wasn't sure whether I was keeping it or not, Thing had seemed like a good, impersonal way to think of the baby, but then it had kinda stuck and now I thought of the nickname quite fondly. 'I don't know if it's a girl or a boy so—'

'It's okay,' he interrupted. 'Thing has a nice ring to it, and I can hardly pick on *your* choice—the names Carly and I used for our three were much crazier.'

'What were they?'

'Well, we called Isidore "Vegas" because we were supposed to be going there for a holiday but then Carly got pregnant and it was put on hold. Phoenix was due on Christmas Day so we called him "Jesus". We're getting our comeuppance for that now as he's as un-Jesus-like as you could get. Satan would have been a more accurate nickname.'

'He's not *that* bad.' Phoenix had severe ADHD but I actually preferred him to the girls on the few times I'd met Christos's kids. Sure he was cheeky, but at least he wasn't whiny like Isidore and Lexia.

'He was always on his best behaviour with you for some reason.'

That made me swell with happiness—maybe I was a natural born mother after all. 'And what about Lexia, what did you guys call her?'

'Guinea Pig, because Phoenix desperately wanted one and so we decided to try and trick him that the baby was his new pet.'

'And how'd that work?'

'Well, he certainly treats her like an animal sometimes.'

I laughed, wondering how he'd treat another sister or brother. If Christos were the father, his children would be Thing's siblings. Would they dote on Thing due to the age gap—there'd be almost six years between the baby and Lexia—or would they resent it for taking more of their father's time?

'Have you any ideas for a proper name once Thing is born?'

I feigned shock. 'You mean you don't think Thing is appropriate? I thought you said it had a nice ring to it.'

He chuckled in the way he'd often done when we were together. Christos was so easy to be with and we'd spent hours talking nonsense in each other's company, but I couldn't forget what he'd done to me. Mortification and hurt washed over me as I recalled stumbling from the hotel room not so long ago.

'I should be getting back to work,' I said, digging the DNA testing kit out of my bag and putting it on the table. 'Would you mind taking the swab now so we can get this sorted?'

He stared at the package on the table as if it might leap up and bite him.

'I've read the instructions. It seems pretty straightforward—maybe you could do it in the bathroom?'

'Okay.' He picked up the package, then stood. 'Back in a minute.'

I tapped my fingers on the table as I waited for his return, thinking how weird this conversation had been. He'd taken it much better than I'd expected and I couldn't help imagining how different things might be if we were still together and I *knew* my baby was his. Having just passed the 'safe' mark we'd probably now be announcing it to our friends and family in some cutesy way on Facebook—normally I hated that kind of thing but I'll admit pregnancy hormones seemed to warp my senses.

'Here you are,' he said, when he arrived back at the table and handed back the package. 'The swab is in there, all sealed. I guess now we wait.'

I nodded as I put the test kit carefully into my bag and stood. We both needed to get back to work and I didn't want to spend any more time with Christos—it was too confusing for my poor heart. 'I'll—'

He spoke at the same time. 'I want you to know, Ged, that if the baby is mine, I'll support you both—financially, emotionally and practically. Obviously, this might mean reassessing my home situation, but Carly and the—'

'Thank you,' I interrupted, 'for not freaking out about this, but I think we're getting ahead of ourselves. I'll call you as soon as I have the results and if the baby's yours, we can work out how to go forward. But this won't change anything between us.'

'Of course it will. You've got to be sensible. How are you going to navigate single parenthood of a newborn with a career? Us being together again would make sense and—'

'*No*, Christos,' I said firmly, before I really lost the plot. I was outraged that he would question my ability to cope with work *and* motherhood. His wife was an ear, nose and throat doctor and, until recently, had managed to be a single working mother every second week. Not to mention the fact my grandmother was one of the forerunners of women who did both.

'*If* you are the father, the only type of relationship you and I will ever have is a co-parenting one.'

I wasn't sure who I was trying to convince more—him or me.

24

'Coming up after the break, we speak to influencer Marie Johnston about new domesticity—the craze currently taking the world by storm.'

It was clear from the expression on her face what Melanie Myers, one of the hosts of *Wake Up, Melbourne*, thought of this movement, but her co-host Paul Moretti supported it.

'I think it's a wonderful thing,' he said, smiling cheesily as he ran a hand over his thick, dark, gelled hair, 'getting women back into the kitchen. Lord knows I wish my wife would take a leaf out of Marie's book and spend a little more time in ours.'

'Careful, Paul,' Melanie said, 'or Angela might not only be evicting you from the kitchen but also the house.'

As he chuckled, the producers cut to an ad break and I thanked God the show was almost over. Although it was now almost 9 am—Mum's was the last segment—we'd all had to get up *before* the break of day in order to take up our positions in the live audience. I'd swooped Gralice up at an ungodly hour and then we'd met Mum and Rosa at the cafe next to the TV station. She'd been looking very glamorous in a 1950s dress with *The Happy Happy Housewife* apron over the top. Her hair and make-up were impeccable as well—perhaps another one of Rosa's many talents—and I'd felt frumpy beside her in my almost-too-tight jeans and face that only had a layer of tinted moisturiser on it. Even that had been an effort at five-bloody-o'clock in the morning.

We hadn't seen Mum or Rosa since they'd been ushered into the green room and we'd been shown to seats in the audience.

'Do you think I have time to sneak to the bathroom?' I whispered to Gralice who was sitting beside me. Next to her were Phil and Craig, holding hands and glancing around the studio as if they couldn't believe they were here. They weren't the only ones. I couldn't quite believe Mum was doing this, considering her current domestic situation. On the other side of me sat Holly Pearson, who'd come along for moral support. I wondered, would she feel so supportive if she knew that her new star author wasn't exactly who she was claiming to be?

Gralice glanced at her watch. 'I wouldn't risk it if I were you, Sappho will kill you if you miss her five minutes of fame.'

I pressed my knees together and tried to think of something, *anything*, but the burning sensation in my bladder. It was ridiculous how often I needed to pee. What I'd read about early pregnancy told me this was completely normal—something to do with extra blood flow in my kidneys—but that didn't make it any less annoying.

'Do you have a UTI?' Gralice asked, a little too loudly for my liking.

'No,' I shot back, 'I've just drunk a lot of water this morning.'

I still hadn't told her that I was pregnant because I was waiting till I'd be able to tell everyone who the father was. It was the first secret I'd ever really kept from Gralice but the past few weeks had been crazy enough without me adding this extra element of drama.

The day after I'd met Mum in the cafe all hell had broken loose. She'd tried to talk to Dad about how to broach the subject of their separation with the rest of the family, but he'd locked himself in my bathroom and flat-out refused to enter into any discussions about anything. So she'd taken it upon herself to break the news.

As predicted, her parents had been supportive. I think Gralice was secretly pleased by Mum's new lesbianism, but Will was anything but. Almost two weeks later he was still acting like a two-year-old, refusing to speak to our mother at all. I wasn't sure whether he was more upset by our parents' separation, the fact Mum had cheated on Dad, or about her coming out, not that she'd done that to anyone outside of our immediate family.

She was still vlogging and posting on social media as if nothing had happened. It was a good thing Dad didn't have Instagram or Facebook or he'd have been even more of a grumpy bear, and, surprisingly, Will hadn't taken to his account to fume in the manner most people did these days when they had grievances. Sophie had made some vague post about people not being who you think they are, but no one had cottoned on to what she was really talking about.

The past week and a half had been hellish. Dad seemed to spend most of his time glued to the couch, eating junk food, watching daytime television and mourning the loss of his comfortable existence. He appeared to have given up the Uber driving and when I'd asked him about this, he'd said something about taking compassionate leave. But I think it was as much to do with the fact that driving interrupted his increasingly frequent evenings at the pub. Although I did feel sorry for him, I also found him a bit pathetic, but Will thought I was being harsh. He and Soph were one hundred percent on Dad's side—easy when they didn't have to deal with him—whereas I was the dutiful daughter stuck in the middle.

'Ooh look. Your mother's coming on.' Holly dug her elbow into my side and I looked up in time to see Mum giving us all a little finger wave as she crossed to the bright blue couch.

'Welcome back, everyone.' Melanie turned her saccharine smile to the camera. 'Lucky last today, we have with us Marie Johnston, a suburban mother who has taken the internet by storm. Welcome, Marie.'

Mum beamed at Melanie. 'Why thank you, it's such an honour to be on the show. I watch it every week while I'm doing my ironing.'

'Or perhaps we should all call you the Happy Happy Housewife? That's your handle on Instagram, isn't it?' asked Paul. 'And you also have a very successful YouTube channel, is that right?'

'Indeed, I do. I had no idea when my daughter introduced me to Instagram a year ago that there was a whole other world inside my smartphone, but now I have over a hundred thousand followers across all my platforms and I've been contracted to write a book.'

Paul whistled. 'No offence, but I thought only young women peddling beauty products and gym memberships had that kind of popularity.'

'Oh, I'm all for beauty products, Paul, but the wonderful thing about new domesticity is that it makes the need for gym memberships redundant. When you're living an active life at home—gardening, cooking, cleaning, doing the groceries—you burn calories without having to pay for it.'

'Can you explain what new domesticity means?' asked Melanie.

Mum batted her eyelashes towards the camera. 'Basically it's about reclaiming housewifery and reviving the lost domestic arts—things like jam-making, knitting, growing your own vegetables, sewing your family's clothes. It's about embracing traditional homemaking and putting your role in the home before all else. For years people have been saying these tasks are demeaning for women, that we've been treated like slaves by husbands and children, but the truth is, running a home properly and taking care of one's family can be the most rewarding thing in the world if you ignore the naysayers.'

Kudos to her, she didn't mention my father at all—she presented the whole house*wife* thing as being much more about taking pride in one's home than doing so for a man.

'We'll get to the book later,' Melanie said, her smile thin as she shot Paul a supercilious look. 'But how did this all begin?'

Mum explained how she'd begun by posting photos of my dad's dinners and other household things she made. 'The post about the plastic bag holder I sewed out of tea towels was very popular, as was the one about how to get sweat stains out of the underarms of men's shirts.' And how from there, her following rapidly grew. She spoke about hashtags and sharing and going viral, and I had to admit she sounded very tech-savvy.

'But the absolute best part of all of this is the women I've met online and in person—they come up to me on the street—tell me how *The Happy Happy Housewife* has inspired them to live a better, more fulfilling life, and how their families are also much happier now they're taking the time to nurture and care for them properly.'

She almost had me convinced and visualising a life of domestic bliss—although the image of my spouse was blurry—until I remembered *her* broken family. I wasn't sure how she could sit on national TV and talk like this, but nobody else appeared to see a problem. Holly was positively beaming at the reaction from the rest of the live audience—not that *she* knew the truth either—and Gralice, Phil and Craig looked proud as punch of their girl.

Me? I still needed to pee and that felt more urgent than anything else.

'I can see the benefits for the husbands and the children,' Melanie said, 'but why do you think women are loving new domesticity so much?'

'So many of them are feeling disillusioned with the fast and stressful pace of modern life. Women are tired of being fed the lie that you can have it all and do it all. Maybe it's true, maybe you can, but not without some important things being sacrificed. New domesticity gives women the permission to follow their primal instincts, without feeling less of a person for doing so.'

Paul grinned at Mum's explanation, but Melanie merely raised her eyebrows. 'Don't you think this could be a dangerous trend— men might take advantage. They could start dominating workplaces again and making things difficult for women in the workforce. We're still fighting for equal pay and here you are advocating a step back in time?'

'Oh, Melanie, I think you're getting a little worried about nothing,' Mum said dismissively. 'Just because a large number of women are embracing new domesticity, doesn't mean all women will.'

'Hmm.' Melanie didn't sound convinced. 'And Marie, am I right that your mother is the acclaimed scientist and feminist activist, Alice Abbott?'

'That's right.'

'Ms Abbott has spent her life petitioning for better rights for women in the workplace and in the home ... how does *she* feel about what you're advocating?'

'Oh, you'd have to ask her that yourself,' Mum replied with a smile, not mentioning that Gralice was sitting in the audience. 'But, as feminism is all about choice, and new domesticity is about women making the decision to put domestic duties first and enjoy the rewards of being a full-time housewife, then I'd say she'd be hard pressed to have anything bad to say about it.'

'Bravo,' Paul said, and the audience also applauded. 'Thank you for coming on the show today, and I'm sure viewers will be delighted to know that we are welcoming Marie to *Wake Up, Melbourne* as a regular. The Happy Happy Housewife will be stopping by once a month to give us all some tips on how to live better in domestic bliss. We're looking forward to it, aren't we, Mel?'

'Oh yes.' Melanie smiled tightly. 'I can hardly wait.'

'Shall we go out for brunch to celebrate my television debut?' Mum said when we congregated in the foyer ten minutes later.

'That sounds splendid,' Phil said, wrapping his arm around Mum and pulling her into his side. 'You were such a super star.'

'You were.' Holly grinned. 'This book is going to be a mega hit, and the regular gig on weekend TV will make promoting the book even easier, but I'm so sorry I can't join you for brunch. It's my niece's first birthday and I'll be banished from the family if I miss it.'

Mum gave Holly a hug. 'Of course, family must always come first.'

'Speaking of family, where was Tony this morning?'

Mum looked momentarily startled. There was a brief uncomfortable silence where I thought she might confess, but when she didn't I jumped in to try and save the moment. 'Dad's not well today.'

'Oh, that's no good,' Holly said with a frown. 'Do tell him I hope he's better soon.'

Mum nodded. 'We will, but thanks so much for coming to support me. I hope you couldn't tell how nervous I was.'

'Not at all. You're a natural,' Holly said and the rest of us had to agree. Perhaps Mum should have pursued a career in acting because she was certainly doing a very good job of it now.

We said goodbye to Holly and made our way to a hotel about five minutes down the road, which Rosa said did the best brunch she'd ever had. Gralice looked exhausted by the time we arrived but I knew better than to say anything.

Our waiter led us to a table in the corner of the restaurant with a view onto the Yarra River. Once we'd ordered, we spent a few more minutes recapping Mum's television debut and then her expression grew sombre.

'I wish Will, Sophie and the kids could have been here. Do you think they'll have watched on the TV?'

Phil, Craig, Gralice and I exchanged looks. While Will still wasn't talking to Mum, he frequently spoke to the rest of us, venting his fury about what he saw as her abandonment of our father.

Our silence spoke volumes and Mum sighed. 'I guess they might need a little more time.'

Rosa put her hand on top of Mum's as she tried to distract her. 'Did you show everyone your cover concepts for the book?'

Mum's eyes lit up, her sorrow momentarily forgotten. 'No, not yet.'

'You have cover concepts already?' From what I'd always understood, things moved at a glacial pace in publishing.

'Bourne Books are so excited about the book, and they thought it would make a great gift for Mother's Day so they want to release it next April, hence why things are moving quickly. While Marie finishes the manuscript, they're getting a start on design, et cetera,' Rosa explained as Mum searched her phone for the images.

'Here they are. They're only concepts at this stage but they're going to do photos of me for the cover instead of that model.' She passed the phone to me and Phil leaned over to take look at the same time. The concept was a woman with curlers in her hair, standing in a pale pink wallpapered living room, smiling at the camera as she ironed a man's shirt.

'Very retro,' I said, passing the phone down to Craig so he and Gralice could take a look. They agreed, although I couldn't imagine any modern woman willingly buying a book with an iron on the front.

Our food arrived and there was a lull in conversation as everyone began to eat, all except Gralice who merely picked at her scrambled eggs.

'Things serious between you two then?' Phil smiled as he caught Mum and Rosa exchanging a tender smile.

They nodded, and if we were alone I was sure they'd have sealed this with a kiss, but they refrained from any public displays of affection. I'd seen them together few times in the past week or so when I'd managed to engineer us all spending time with Gralice, and I was getting used to Mum and Rosa's *togetherness*. In public they acted purely professional but in private things were different. They couldn't keep their hands off each other and it was clear to see they were soul mates.

Another half an hour passed with varying topics of conversation until I noticed Gralice fading—she tired so quickly these days and I still couldn't believe no one else had noticed.

'I think I'm gonna make a move, sorry, Mum,' I said, collecting my handbag from the floor. 'I've got work to do this arvo. Do you want me to give you a lift home, Gralice?'

'If you're not ready to go yet, we can drive you?' offered my mother.

Gralice blinked—obviously guessing my sneaky plan—and for a moment I thought she was going to refuse, but in the end she nodded. 'Yes, I've got things to do.'

Rosa frowned at Gralice's plate. 'But you've hardly touched any of your meal.'

'I had a big breakfast,' she lied, pushing back her chair to stand.

'You're actually looking a little pale,' Mum said, and Phil and Craig also looked a little concerned.

Finally! I held my breath waiting for my grandmother to come clean.

But she didn't.

'I'm fine,' she said, rising from her seat. 'Thank you all for a lovely morning.'

Then, she kissed them all goodbye and I followed after her, dumbfounded.

The moment we were out of sight, Gralice slowed her pace—she puffed and looked as if she'd just run a half-marathon. I led her over to a public bench where she could sit while I went back to fetch the car.

'Don't you think that would have been a good time to tell them about your ... about your cancer?' I still found it difficult to say the word.

'Now *isn't* the time. Can't you see how happy Sappho is at the moment? I don't remember ever seeing her as carefree and joyful before. I don't want to ruin that.'

'You can't hold off forever and there's never a good time for such devastating news, but don't you think having Rosa and being so happy will help Mum through this?'

I tried not to sound so desperate, so pleading, but I was feeling the pressure of having this knowledge that the rest of my family did not. I wanted us to be able to support Gralice and each other through the tough months ahead.

'Mum's right, you are looking pale and they're already starting to suspect something. You're only going to get worse. Sooner or later you won't be able to hide it from them, and then how do you think they're going to feel?'

'I'm not going to get much worse,' she said quietly. 'I refuse to put myself, you, or any of my family through the crippling, independence-robbing final stages of cancer.'

It took a second for the meaning of her words to register, and then a cold terror filled my lungs.

'Oh my God. Are you going to …?' I couldn't bring myself to say the words but it was clear from the look in her eyes that she understood.

I expected her to immediately deny it but instead she slowly nodded. 'It's the logical decision. I'm sure you don't want to watch me suffer any more than I want to endure it. Do you?'

And that felt like a trick question, because of course I didn't want her to suffer, but selfishly, I wanted as much time with her as possible. Christmas had seemed way too soon to lose her but the thought that Gralice might decide to end it at any moment made me want to shake her.

At the same time, it made perfect sense. As a woman of science and someone who'd always advocated for human rights, I knew she strongly believed that a person should be able to make the decision to end their life if they were terminally ill.

My grandmother had been independent and forward thinking her whole life; the surprising thing wasn't this confession, but that it had taken me so long to work it out.

25

I sighed as I switched off my computer and gathered my things to head home for the weekend. My whole body felt heavy with exhaustion. Wasn't this fatigue supposed to bugger off in the second trimester? I wasn't sure I even had the strength to walk the short distance to my tram stop. For a fleeting moment I contemplated calling my father and asking him to come get me, but I guessed by now he'd already be on his second or third beer at the pub.

'Got any plans for the weekend?' Libby asked as we headed for the elevators.

'Walking my dog, visiting my grandmother ...' I didn't have the energy to pretend to be doing anything more exciting or work-orientated. All I wanted to do was sleep, although I did hope to find some motivation to work on the book.

Libby screwed up her face. 'Sounds, fun. *Not*. I'm going skiing with my new guy, although I'm not sure how much skiing we'll be doing—there are rumours the resort isn't paying their staff award wages.'

If she was right, that could be a mammoth story for her, but I couldn't summon any of the jealousy or angst this should bring me. I had more important things on my mind, like when I'd find out who my baby daddy was. The DNA testing company had said we'd get the results after anywhere from seven to fourteen days so I was on tenterhooks every night when I went through my mail.

'Enjoy.' I said faux-cheerily.

'I'm gonna pop to the loo. I'll see you Monday with a full report.'

As Libby changed directions, I continued on to the lifts and Christos sidled up beside me. I hadn't spoken to him since DNA Thursday, as I was now mentally referring to it.

'Hey.' He smiled as he shoved his hands in his pockets. 'Long week.'

'Yep. Got much planned for the weekend?' It wouldn't hurt me to be civil to Thing's possible father.

'Carly and I are taking the kids to America for a couple of weeks. Lexia is desperate to go to Disneyworld and we thought it would give us all a chance to reconnect as a family.'

'Oh.' I blinked. Why did this feel like a slap in the face? 'Great.'

'I wouldn't go, under the circumstances, but we don't want to let them down.'

'It's fine.' And I meant it. As if I would ever begrudge three kids a trip to visit Mickey and Minnie—or whoever it was they were into these days.

The lift pinged open and I wasn't sure whether to be happy or annoyed that we were the only people in it.

'I'm guessing you don't have the results yet,' Christos said as we started to descend.

I shook my head.

'Right. I'll keep my phone on while we're away so ...'

'I'll message you as soon as I know,' I promised. And then because we still hadn't got to the ground floor—why did it feel like the elevators went so much slower when I was stuck in one with him?—I asked, 'Have you told Carly about …?'

'Yes.' He nodded, surprising me. 'I told you we're not together-together anyway, *and* if the baby is mine it was conceived before we decided to reunite. I wouldn't say she's happy, but she understands that we'll have to deal with a new family member if need be.'

'You don't have to *deal* with anything!'

The idea of Thing visiting Carly and Christos's house and Carly possibly treating our child like a bad smell did not sit well with me.

He touched my arm and I tried to ignore the sparks that shot through me. 'I'm sorry, that came out wrong. I—'

Thankfully the doors opened at level two before he could finish his sentence and about five people from marketing piled in around us. I yanked my arm from his and refused to meet his gaze as the lift continued downwards.

'Goodbye. Have a good holiday,' I said with a brittle smile as we all spilled out into the lobby.

'Thanks, Ged.' He wandered off in the opposite direction with his head hung down.

As I walked the short distance to my tram stop, my phone beeped with a message.

'Watch it, lady,' chided some guy as I halted on the footpath and stared at the screen.

The message was from Sex-on-Tap—from *Jay*—who I hadn't heard from since I'd messaged him *that* night apologising for the intrusion of my father.

No worries, he'd replied. *Message me when your complications have settled down a little.*

259

Of course, my complications were about as complicated as ever, so I'd fought the impulse to contact him and tried to ignore the disappointment in the pit of my stomach when he didn't reach out again. I told myself this was a good thing—if he did I'd have to tell him about the baby when there was really no point unless I knew whose it was.

But now here he was—well, a message from him on my phone—and I was no closer to knowing anything.

Hey. Work has been insane this last week—I've been working practically 24/7—but I've got the evening off and wondered if you wanted to help me unwind. Jay.

Yes, cried my hormones, *that's exactly what we want. Let's help each other unwind.* But I shook my head, reminding myself what a terrible idea that would be. Seeing him again and not telling him about the baby would be as good as lying and only make things worse if it was his. But if I told him, he was unlikely to end up feeling very unwound and I'd probably end up feeling worse than I already did.

I inhaled deeply. Call me chicken, but within a week I'd know the truth; that wasn't long to put him off.

So sorry, I typed as I started towards the tram again, *I'm sick.* It wasn't *that* much of a lie—the nausea still hadn't left me entirely. *Maybe another time?*

I typed and deleted the last line three times until I finally pressed send before I could second guess my decision. There wasn't supposed to be so much angst in a friends-with-benefits arrangement, but I guess Thing had complicated that slightly, even if Jay was none the wiser yet.

What would happen between us if Christos was the father? I couldn't imagine Jay wanting to continue our arrangement once I had a newborn, and I'd probably be too busy anyway. But maybe he'd be happy with the occasional bonk before I popped. Apparently some men were turned on by pregnant women.

Yeah, right, said a little voice inside me, *you reckon Jay's gonna be one of those guys?*

I climbed onto the busy tram full of Friday afternoon commuters eager to go out and kick up their heels or get home and kick off their shoes. I was definitely in the latter category.

By the time I reached my stop, Jay still hadn't replied and I tried to ignore the disappointment. He could have at least told me to get well soon or something. Just because I wasn't available for the horizontal mambo didn't mean he couldn't be nice.

With a heavy heart and tired feet, I walked the short distance to my apartment and tried to give my dog half the enthusiasm she greeted me with. I took her outside and let her amble round the courtyard as I didn't have the motivation to take her out for a walk and couldn't risk running into Jay. When she'd sniffed all there was to sniff, I lured her inside with the promise of dinner. While Coco munched on her favourite biscuits, I changed into my PJs and made myself a nutritious meal of beans on toast, which I ate in front of the TV.

I got out my laptop, intending to work on Gralice's biography, but I must have fallen asleep because I woke up sometime later to a chorus of Coco's barks and the buzzing of my intercom. My thoughts immediately went to Dad and I groaned. No way was I in the mood to deal with a few hours of his lamenting Mum's new-found lesbianism while I threw a load of his dirty clothes into my washing machine. I did feel for him and kept vowing that I'd teach him some of the basic household tasks that he was so hopeless at but had decided it would have to wait until I reclaimed that energy.

'Any time now,' I said, smiling down at my slightly curved belly. After the embarrassing episode with Jay I'd confiscated Dad's key, so maybe if I pretended I wasn't home, he'd eventually move on. But the buzzing and the barking continued, and it was giving me a headache.

I heaved myself off the couch and went to the door. 'Who is it?' I snarled through the intercom.

'Jay.'

I caught my expression in the hallway mirror as my stomach turned itself inside out. You know that face from the old movie *Scream*? I was doing a perfect imitation.

'I told you, I'm sick,' I said in a fake-feeble voice when I finally recovered from the shock.

'That's why I'm here. Buzz me up, I brought supplies.'

Supplies? My hand lifted of its own accord and hit the button that would let him into the building. Oh Lord, what was I getting myself into?

I opened the door and Coco shot out to greet him, returning a few moments later looking pretty damn proud of her find.

'Ugh, you do look sick.' Jay made a face as he gave me the once-over. 'Stomach bug, cold or flu?'

'Um ... stomach.'

'Lucky I bought lemonade then. Back to the couch.'

He pointed his finger in said couch's direction, but I didn't immediately cooperate. 'But what if you get sick?'

'It's been such a week at work that a few days off would be a blessing. But ... it won't happen. I never get sick. Now, you, couch, before I get cranky.'

'You're very bossy,' I said, but started towards the couch nevertheless.

'You ain't seen nothing yet, baby.'

'I'm not your baby,' I said as I shut my laptop and put it on the side table next to the couch.

'Don't get your knickers in a knot, it's a term of endearment.' Jay grinned, then upended a whole pile of stuff from two large recycling bags onto the coffee table.

Alongside the lemonade was a packet of tissues (the soft, expensive variety), cough mixture, cold-and-flu tablets, dry crackers, ice-cream (the gourmet, expensive variety), microwave popcorn, some DVDs, two paperback novels and a tattered-looking board game. He'd gone to a lot of trouble and he must have spent a fortune on the pharmacy items.

'Don't look so shocked. We're friends remember. This,' he gestured to the coffee table, 'is what friends do for each other.'

It was cute he thought us friends and I had to admit I *was* happy to see him.

'There better not be any Elvis movies in there.'

'I want to make you feel better, not torture you.'

With a smile, I reached across and picked up one of the novels, something called *The Scholar* by Dervla McTiernan. 'Are these *yours*?'

'Don't look so surprised. Just because I'm fit, incredibly good-looking and have a great body doesn't mean I'm a blockhead.'

I raised an eyebrow, smiling.

'And, that's a good book,' he added with a wink.

'I know—I've read the one before it and have been meaning to get this, but I've been so preoccupied with work and Gralice's biography lately that I haven't had time to read for pleasure.'

'Well, tonight you're taking a break from all that.' He nodded towards my laptop. 'I've been worried about you burning the candles at both ends.'

He'd been worried about me!

'How's things going with your family?'

I sighed. 'Not good. Dad is rapidly turning into an alcoholic, Mum and Rosa are getting closer by the day, my brother is still angry, and Gralice ...' I bit my lip to try and stop myself from crying but also from confessing all.

'What is it?' Jay asked, his voice full of concern.

And, against my better judgment, I told him. 'Gralice is planning to end her life herself before the cancer really takes hold.'

'Wow. How do you feel about that?'

'Utterly confused. If you'd asked me before this what I thought about euthanasia and assisted suicide, I'd have told you adamantly that I believed in a person's right to die with dignity, but ...' I sighed. 'It doesn't seem so clear cut when it's so close to home. I'm on edge constantly. I can't think about anything else—it's affecting my work, my sleep, my book. I keep thinking about her doing it. Each time I see her, I keep wondering if it will be the last time. Will she leave us letters? Part of me wishes I didn't know, part of me totally understands her decision and wants to support her and another part feels guilty because I'd rather have her with us longer, no matter how ill she gets.' I placed a hand on my stomach. 'It makes me sick just thinking about it.'

'All those emotions seem totally reasonable to me, but if it's any help, I think your grandmother's decision is a bold and brave one. We spend so much money these days prolonging life, and I'm not saying we shouldn't spend it on people who want to live longer, but if they don't, we should respect that.'

'I know ... and in theory I agree, but she's my grandmother. I don't want to lose her.'

He nodded. 'I get that. And that sucks balls no matter how it happens. I wish there was something I could say to make you feel better. No wonder you're not feeling well when you're dealing with all this.'

'Thank you.' I half-smiled, reached out and squeezed his hand. It was good simply to be able to talk about it with someone.

'Happy to be of service.' He stood. 'Now, can I get you a glass of lemonade or anything else before I take Coco for a walk?'

'You'd do that?' My heart squeezed for two reasons—it was such a sweet offer, but it would also mean him leaving.

'Sure. Sometimes I take the dog belonging to the little old lady who lives next door to me for a run when she's not feeling up to it. What do you say, Coco, wanna go to the park?'

He helped little old ladies!

Of course, Coco said 'yes'. At least she jumped up and did her crazy dog dance around him.

Jay laughed. 'I'll get you that drink and then you rest while we're gone.'

I nodded as Jay picked up the ice-cream and lemonade and went into my kitchen as if it were *his* kitchen. Was this really happening? My friend-with-benefits, the possible father of my baby, had come over knowing there wouldn't be any sex on offer. I felt awful for lying to him when he was being so damn nice—friends didn't lie to each other—but I was already feeling so bad and I couldn't bring myself to make things even worse.

He returned and placed a glass of lemonade on the coffee table. 'Have you eaten? Would you like me to grab something while we're out? Or I could make you some soup?'

My brow crept up of its own accord. 'You read *and* cook?'

'I'm a man of many talents, Geraldine.'

While Thing liked the sound of soup and I liked the sound of Jay slaving away over a hot stove, that would only increase my guilt.

'I'm not up for eating,' I lied.

'Okay.' He leaned over and kissed me on the cheek before he and Coco went off for their jaunt. I opened the book to page one, resisting the urge to rush into my bedroom and make myself look more presentable. While he was gone I read about two pages—but I read those pages about ten times because I couldn't concentrate.

'How was the walk?' I asked as I let dog and man back inside.

'She sniffs a lot, doesn't she?' Jay unclicked Coco's leash.

I laughed as she went over to the couch and slumped down in front of it. 'Yes, and it appears to be exhausting business.'

He smiled. 'How you feeling?'

Confused. 'The lemonade helped a little.'

'Good. Now, ready for me to beat your arse at Game of Life?'

'You're staying?'

'Well, you can't exactly play by yourself, and Game of Life always makes me feel better when I'm sick.'

'I thought you didn't get sick.'

'I don't, but when I was a kid I often faked it to get off school.'

'That I *can* believe.' I shuffled over to make room for him on the tiny couch beside me. 'Go on then, teach me how to play.'

'You've never played Game of Life?'

I shook my head. 'But don't think that means you're going to win. I'm very good at board games.'

Half an hour later I was losing dismally. I was an *athlete* (which Jay thought hilarious) living in a teepee with no kids and only ten thousand dollars to my name. Meanwhile Jay was a brain surgeon, living in a mansion with four kids, a very sexy wife and millions of dollars of paper money.

'This game is depressing. If I can't even hold down a relationship in a board game, how am I ever supposed to hold down one in real life?'

Jay snorted. 'Why would you want to?'

'Okay, out with it. What happened to you that made you so negative about relationships? Did your parents go through a bitter divorce when you were a teenager? Did the girl you loved all through high school marry someone else?'

'Got it in two.'

'What?'

266

'Well, almost. My parents weren't married in the first place, but you were pretty close to the mark on the next question.'

I blinked. 'I'm sorry. I shouldn't have said anything.'

'It's fine. It was over a decade ago now. We went out most of high school and I proposed far too young. I was a stupid besotted kid. Anyway, we got married and about a year after the wedding I found her in bed with my best friend.'

I gasped but Jay just chuckled.

'Pretty clichéd crap—thank God I'd stood firm on my resolve not to have kids. I've been happily alone ever since. It's better this way. If you don't put your heart on the line, if you don't expect anything from anyone, you can't get hurt and they can't let you down.' He nodded towards the board. 'It's your turn to spin the wheel.'

Knowing this was Jay's way of telling me the personal chit-chat was over, I swallowed the further questions I desperately wanted answers to and spun.

'How long does this game go for?' I asked about fifteen minutes later when I was still no closer to living my best life. 'Can't I get hit by a milk truck or something?'

He laughed. 'Wanna watch a movie instead?'

'Yes.' I dived on the DVDs and was surprised to discover he'd brought three of my favourites: *Charlie's Angels*, *The Italian Job* (the most recent one) and *Indiana Jones and the Raiders of the Lost Ark*. Maybe movies were the thing we had in common?

'So, is Jay short for anything?' I asked as he settled back beside me on the couch while *Indiana Jones* loaded on the DVD player.

'Nope. Just boring old Jay.'

He was anything but boring. 'I like it. And most of my friends call me Ged. You're welcome to as well if you'd like.'

'Thanks,' was all he said in reply, before pressing play on the remote.

But I couldn't concentrate on the movie any more than I could concentrate on the book or the board game. I was enjoying hanging out with Jay way more than I should have been when we were both fully clothed, yet at the same time I couldn't relax because I knew I was keeping this massive thing from him. But I didn't want to tell him because I knew the moment I did, things would change between us.

This would change.

Still how could I let *this* go on without saying anything?

I resolved to tell him the moment the movie was over. Right now Marion was freaking outside a burning building because she'd just shot and killed someone and there was no way I could interrupt such a critical scene with such an important confession.

I woke up some time later to a silent apartment. The TV had been switched off, the lights dimmed, and I was curled up on the couch with a blanket over the top of me. I couldn't even remember the movie ending.

'Jay?' I called as I dragged myself into a sitting position.

The only answer I got was Coco raising her head from where she was lying on the floor next to the couch. She gave me an irked look as if she could have done without the interruption.

I snatched my phone off the now-empty coffee table and checked the time. It was two o'clock in the morning and it looked as if Jay had tidied up all evidence of our night before he'd left.

Dammit. I slumped back and let out a deep sigh.

He was gone, and I still hadn't found the guts to tell him.

26

'Thank God, she's gone. I'm never moving from here again,' I announced as I flopped down onto Gralice's couch. Every bone in my body ached and the skin on my hands was red-raw from scrubbing, despite the fact I'd been wearing plastic gloves most of the day. 'I don't know how Mum finds so much joy in that and does it on a daily basis. I'm definitely not cut out for new domesticity!'

Gralice laughed as she lowered herself into her favourite armchair. 'You and me both, but I have to admit, although she's a hard task master, this place is looking better than it has in years.'

It was almost six o'clock in the evening and Mum and Rosa had just left. For the last ten hours we'd been working our fingers to the bone getting Gralice's house ready for the first open inspection tomorrow afternoon, in which a bunch of strangers would traipse through, picking the place to pieces. I shuddered at the thought. No wonder selling a house was up there in the top five most stressful life events—yep, I'd once written an article about *that* as well. But any potential buyers would be hard pushed to find anything to complain about here.

Gralice and I would have been happy with a quick tidy tomorrow morning and a surface polish, but Mum had refused to rest until every speck of dust had been eliminated. She was one of those weird people who got a kick out of cleaning. But this time she also had an ulterior motive, as Rosa was filming every part of the home inspection preparation for the vlog. No longer able to utilise my father across all her social platforms—or her adorable grandchildren, thanks to Will banning her from seeing them—she'd had to get a little creative over the past few weeks. There'd been a lot of home-decorating tips, and the next big thing was a 'selling your house' special, which would not only include her finest spring-cleaning tips but also portray her in a good light as she assisted her elderly mother to downsize.

If Gralice wasn't sick I was certain she wouldn't be having any of this nonsense, but then again, if Gralice wasn't sick she wouldn't be selling her home. I couldn't believe Mum still hadn't twigged to what was going on, but she was so hung up in the throes of a new relationship, Dad's and Will's wrath, the vlogging and the writing of the book that she probably wouldn't have noticed if World War Three kicked off right in front of her.

'How are you feeling about all this?' I asked Gralice.

'About what?'

'About selling your home? It's a big thing when you've lived somewhere as long as you have. You must have lots of memories between these walls. It would be natural to be a little emotional right now.'

I know I was. Once Gralice's house changed hands, it'd be one more thing she could tick off her list of loose ends. One step closer to her being ready to say goodbye.

'It's a house, Ged. People get far too attached to physical things.' She tapped her chest. 'My memories are in here and the only possessions that matter to me aren't really mine at all—they're you, Sappho, Phil, Craig, Will, the kids.'

I pursed my lips together to stop from bawling at her words and forced myself to say something that had been weighing on my mind.

'You're right—you are *my* prized possession, Gralice. I love you more than anyone else in the world and although I never want to say goodbye, and I know it will hurt more than anything ever has, I also know watching you suffer will be a hundred times worse. So, I want you to know that I understand and respect your decision to end your life when the time comes.'

'Thank you. That means a lot.'

'And,' I continued, although my mouth went dry and my heart shook with the knowledge of what I was about to say, 'when the time comes ... if you need help—'

My grandmother interrupted. 'Oh, Ged. You are an absolute gem, but I would never ask you any such thing.'

'You're not asking. I'm—'

She silenced me with the lift of her finger. 'Remember there's now a legal drug available to terminally ill patients in Victoria. This is not going to be some barbaric death—in fact it will be much more peaceful than the alternative. I've already spoken to my doctor, I know what's involved and when the time comes I will do it myself.'

'Can I at least be with you? I can't bear the thought of you being alone.'

Gralice hesitated a moment. 'Let me think about that, okay?'

Knowing this was the best reply I was going to get right now, I nodded.

'Right,' Gralice clapped her hands, 'you must be starving after all that hard work, shall we do Uber Eats?'

It was a deliberate attempt to change the subject, but I needed a moment before I could reply.

'Actually, there're home-cooked meals from Mum in the fridge,' I said eventually. She'd been providing me with nutritious dinners ever since she found out I was pregnant, because she didn't trust me to take care of myself. On the one hand, it was infuriating, but on the other, she was a very good cook. She'd delivered the latest batch this morning and had reminded me when she left not to forget to take them home.

'In that case, let's heat something up.'

'What do you fancy?' I asked, my head stuck in the fridge. 'Lasagne? Curry? Shepherd's pie?'

My mouth watered and my stomach groaned just uttering these words, but Gralice said, 'You choose. I'm not eating much anymore.'

Ignoring the twinge in my heart, I grabbed a container labelled butter chicken and threw it in the microwave. While it heated, Gralice made a cup of tea and I got plates and cutlery out of the cupboards.

'What's this?' I asked as my eyes landed on an old Arnott's biscuit tin in the corner of the bench.

Gralice turned to see what I was referring to and smiled wistfully. 'Just some old photos I uncovered while sorting through all my things. I thought they might be useful for your book, or jog my memory at least—it's getting a bit rusty these days—and I'd forgotten some of them even existed.'

Of course, that piqued my interest big time. 'Can I take a look?'

She nodded, but I'd already lifted the lid in excitement. Inside were loads of black-and-white prints.

'They're not in any particular order but some have comments on the back.'

The first image was of four women, all wearing flares and tight T-shirts with the symbol for woman and the letters W.E.L. in the centre of it. I knew WEL stood for the Women's Electoral Lobby, of which Gralice was a founding member. She was the tallest woman in the photo and was wearing a bandana on her head and what looked to be a pair of men's sunglasses.

'You were so cool,' I said as the microwave dinged. I ignored it.

'Past tense?'

I smiled. 'Who are the other women in the photo?'

She sidled up to me and peered at the photo. 'That's Bee next to me in the middle. She passed away in the eighties of liver disease. On the left is Ronnie, who you know, and ...' she frowned and shook her head, 'I can't for the life of me remember the last woman's name. She wasn't a member long.'

The next photo was another group of mostly women—some pushing prams—and some kids marching through the streets holding balloons and banners showcasing the WEL logo, but there was even a man in their midst. 'What were you protesting?'

Gralice turned the photo over to reveal the date 1975 on the back. 'Ah, that must have been our International Women's Year march—the UN declared it. That was the beginning of International Women's Day.'

'Why have I never seen these before?' I demanded as she handed it back.

'I'd forgotten about them, to be honest.'

'Is that Mum?' There was a girl at the front of the photo with long blonde plaits and a sullen expression. Opening this box felt like stumbling on a pot of gold.

'Yep.' A smile danced on Gralice's lips. 'She hated me for making her go to those things.'

'And, oh my God, is that Phil?' He was wearing bell-bottom pants, a too-tight sweater, and his dark hair was longer than I'd ever seen it.

'Sure is. He was always very supportive of WEL—that's how we met.'

'Really?' I frowned, confused. 'But didn't WEL form in 1972?'

'I *meant* I met him through a mutual friend—one of the women, an academic also at the university—who was one of the other founding members of WEL. But we knew each other long before the organisation began.'

She drank some tea, but I was far too invested in these magnificent photos to worry about eating or drinking. These images were going to take Gralice's biography to a whole other level. The only problem would be choosing which ones *not* to include.

A wonderful idea popped into my head. In addition to writing the biography, I could pitch a feature to Darren about the history of WEL and interview some of the women, like Gralice, who were involved, asking them to reflect on how feminism had grown for better or worse over the past fifty or so years.

'Would you mind if I used some of these for an article as well?'

'What about?'

Her eyes lit up as I told her. 'That's a fantastic idea—Tom and Libby will be green when they hear about it. One step closer to that promotion for you.'

I half-smiled and focused back on the photos, thinking about them in terms of which ones would work best in the lift-out. The demonstration photos were my favourite. I loved the slogans the women carried, such as 'My womb is not state property' and 'Machines are turned on by men *and* women!' In some ways these girls looked like a bunch of hippies but they'd been women changing the world.

The next two photos were stuck together. Carefully, so as not to damage either, I pulled them apart and looked down at the second:

a picture of Gralice and a very handsome young man in a navy suit. They both looked so young and carefree.

Her eyes grew wide as if she'd seen a ghost but she quickly recovered.

'How did that get in there?' She went to take it off me, but I held it close to my chest.

'Is this Henry?' I teased. He looked nothing like Jay. 'Or is this another beau you failed to mention?'

'Give that here,' she demanded tersely.

Unsure whether she was embarrassed or simply didn't want to dwell on the past, I went to hand it over but noticed there was an inscription on the back.

Alice and Henry—Bank Dinner January 1964.

No, that couldn't be right. My grip tightened on the image.

Mum was born in October 1964.

I suddenly remembered something Gralice had said on the ship when I asked whether Granddad Phil had been friends with Henry: *No. Henry and I broke up long before I met Philip.*

My blood went cold.

None of this made sense.

'Give me the photo, Geraldine.' There was an edge to her voice and she *never* called me Geraldine.

'I was under the impression you and Henry broke up some years before Mum was born, but this photo says otherwise.' I kept my voice calm, desperately wanting her to tell me someone must have made a mistake with the date.

'I don't want to talk about this.'

'I think we need to.'

'Nonsense—and I'll keep those photos for myself if you don't respect my wishes!'

But in that moment, I didn't care about the photos, her *wishes* or even her biography. The nausea that had calmed over the past week returned with vengeance.

'Yes. You. Do. Because I'm pregnant.'

'What?' She blinked. Her posture stiffened again. 'How pregnant? Why didn't you tell me?'

That was rich considering she'd kept her cancer a secret from me and was still hiding it from most of our family. And also, beside the point.

'If Phil isn't Mum's father, who is? *Please* tell me it isn't Henry?'

Please let her have conceived in a rebound fling, like the one she'd encouraged me to have.

Her already pallid complexion turned paler as she touched her hand to her throat. 'Is Jay the father of your baby?'

My chest contracted—the terror on her face was confession enough.

I leapt up from my seat, startling Coco awake, and ran into the bathroom where I promptly threw up into the toilet bowl. My body shuddered as rage and shock and fear tore through me. Suddenly it all fell into place—there weren't any photographs of Mum and Phil when she was a baby or toddler. I'd always assumed this was because fewer photos were taken back then, but this made so much more sense.

There weren't any because he wasn't her father.

And if Henry was Mum's biological father that meant Jay and I were …

I couldn't have a baby with my cousin!

Gralice appeared and I flinched as she tried to hold my hair back out of my face. 'Leave me alone.'

If I wasn't currently indisposed I would have fled her house—I couldn't bear to look at her.

'Please, Ged, let me explain.'

But any explanation would be too late if Jay *was* Thing's father.

'Just go,' I shouted and hurled into the toilet bowl again.

She relented and eventually my stomach calmed, but I sat there on the cold, hard tiles of the bathroom floor, shaking and hugging my knees to my chest as I tried to process what I'd discovered.

If Phil wasn't Mum's biological father, then he wasn't my grandfather either. My heart squeezed at the thought. I adored Phil. The thought we weren't truly related broke my heart and it would devastate my mother.

Anger and confusion flooded my body as everything I'd ever believed about my grandmother and my family crumbled around me. She was a liar—she'd lied to Jay's sister on the ship and she'd lied to my mother her whole life. The woman I'd loved and respected most in the world had lied to all of us.

But she wasn't the only con artist among us—Phil and Craig were also guilty of deception. No wonder my mother didn't see a problem pretending to the world she was somebody she was not, when the three people who'd raised her had extremely questionable morals. Unless …

I pulled myself off the floor, splashed water over my face and went out to Gralice. I found her out in the hallway, muttering something to herself as she paced up and down.

'Does Craig know?'

'Of course he does. There's nothing those two don't know about each other. Phil told him not long after they met. He understands why we did what we did.'

Part of me still wanted to run, but if I did I wasn't sure whether I'd ever want to come back and there were so many questions I wanted answers to. 'Would you like to tell *me* why that was exactly?'

There was no warmth in my voice and I could tell my tone hurt Gralice but I couldn't bring myself to care.

'Yes, shall I put the kettle on again?'

'I still haven't drunk my first cup,' I said as I strode past her into the kitchen and sat down at the table again. Gralice joined me a few moments later and I could barely bring myself to look at her. This would have been shocking enough if I wasn't possibly pregnant with Jay's child, but now … What was I going to do if Jay was the father?

Having a father who absconded to Mars would be the least of Thing's problems—I could only imagine the schoolyard taunts if they found out her/his parents were related, so closely, by blood.

'Can I get you anything to eat?'

I glared at my grandmother; as if I could eat at a time like this. 'Is it true that Henry is Mum's real father?'

She didn't meet my gaze but nodded.

I shook my head in disgust. 'Were you still with him when you found out you were pregnant, or had you already broken up?'

'I realised I was pregnant about a month after we broke up. My periods had always been irregular, so the first sign was when I fell asleep in the middle of the afternoon one day. When it happened again the next day, it was Bee who asked me if maybe I was pregnant. I was almost three months by the time a doctor confirmed it.'

'But weren't you on the pill?' Fat load of good that had done me, but still.

'No, Henry and I were always careful but at that stage the pill was only available to married women and it came at great cost due to its large "luxury" tax. Making the pill available to *all* women at an affordable price was one of the first things I rallied for.'

Of course, I was super proud of my grandmother's involvement in this and other important causes, but I hadn't realised how close to home they were for her. If the pill had been readily available and abortions legal, Mum might never have been born.

'How did you feel when you found out you were pregnant?'

'Terrified. I'd never wanted a baby. I couldn't believe how stupid I'd been. I'll admit I considered trying to terminate the pregnancy, but Bee knew of someone who had died from a backstreet abortion and I wasn't going to risk that. Neither was I prepared to risk my health by drinking bleach or shoving a crochet hook inside me.'

I cringed at the thought and placed a protective hand on my belly—this was all sounding very, very familiar. Our stories were much closer than I'd imagined.

'So you decided to have the baby? I'm guessing you never told Henry?'

'No.' This one-word confirmation was barely more than a whisper and something akin to guilt shadowed her expression. 'I knew if I did, he'd support me—he'd probably have been over the moon—but his support would have meant marriage and that felt like locking myself in a prison cell and throwing away the key.'

I'd always admired Gralice's staunch independence but now I wasn't so sure. It felt unfair that she'd assigned a role to Henry without ever giving him the chance to disprove it, and that was quite aside from the fact she'd robbed him of being Mum's father.

'Even if you didn't want to get married, don't you think he had a right to know he had a child? Don't you think Mum had a right to know her real dad?'

'Things were different back then,' Gralice said, her tone defensive. 'Henry wouldn't have allowed a child of his to grow up out of wedlock—I would have had no choice but to fall into a role that I wasn't ready for, a role I wasn't sure I ever wanted. I chose to give Sappho life and I embraced motherhood as best I could. I'm proud of what I've achieved. I'm glad I had Sappho, I'm glad she led to you and Will, and, however hard it's been at times, all these years later I've never regretted that decision.'

'So am I,' I said, 'but what about Henry's rights? What about Mum's? How could you have lived with such a lie?'

Granted, I'd considered keeping my pregnancy secret from the possible fathers, but that had been a fleeting thought in the shock of the moment. I'd almost immediately realised how wrong and unfair that would be to both the father and my child, but Gralice had remained unwavering in her deception. For fifty-five years.

'All I can say is it felt like the right thing to do at the time. Especially after ...'

'What?'

She sniffed. 'After I decided to have the baby I thought maybe I *should* tell Henry, but when I went to find him, I saw him with someone else. I found out he'd moved on to a new girl—Shirley, as it turns out—within weeks of us breaking up. He wanted to get married, and the fact he found someone else so quickly broke my heart.'

'Oh.' I blinked, unsure how I felt about this. I could understand how hurt Gralice would have felt, but did that make everything else she'd done okay?

'How did Philip come into the equation?'

About to drink, she lowered her mug back to the table but kept a firm grip on it. 'When Sappho started school, she began to notice other kids had two parents. I'd never mentioned a father to her. I probably should have told her that hers was dead, but I couldn't bear to break her little heart. I didn't know what to say, so I kept avoiding her questions. And then one day when Philip—who I'd met through a mutual acquaintance—was visiting, she asked if *he* was her father. We were such good friends and he was there so often that I guess it was an obvious choice for her. He and I exchanged looks and no words were necessary. I knew what he was offering, and I gladly accepted it. Philip and I had become close friends fast and

I'd already shared my and Sappho's history with him. We shared the same values and vision for the world. From that day forward Philip became Sappho's father and she was young enough that she accepted it fully.'

'So, you guys did meet through a mutual friend before WEL was established?'

'Yes.' She nodded slowly as if wondering at my stupid question and then realisation dawned in her eyes. 'Oh, I see. No, I didn't lie about that. I promise you, aside from Sappho's real father, everything you know about me is true.'

I refrained from commenting on that. 'But Philip and Mum, they're so alike in so many ways. I've never doubted their connection.'

Gralice smiled sadly. 'To Philip, Sappho *is* his daughter. He's always loved her as his own and provided for her well. We haven't spoken in decades about the fact he isn't biologically her father. Sometimes I think he's forgotten the truth himself.'

'Wow.' I didn't know how to feel about all this. On the one hand Philip was a true hero, taking on someone else's child, loving her and caring for her as if she were his own, but on the other hand he'd enabled Gralice's lie.

If he hadn't offered to become Mum's father, then perhaps the truth would have come out years ago. Then again, Gralice's other option was telling Mum her dad was dead; at least this way she'd given my mother a father figure. Although not the traditional father figure, and one who had been the cause of a lot of childhood bullying and angst in my mother's life. I wondered now if this had led to her ignoring or suppressing her own feelings towards her own sex. If this was the case, Gralice and Phil had even more to answer for.

'Have you *ever* thought about telling Mum?'

My grandmother rubbed her lips together. 'Only recently. When I realised I wasn't going to be around forever, I started questioning things. The guilt that I'd always ignored, telling myself I'd made the right decision, grew stronger. I suddenly wondered whether in making a stand for what I believed in, I'd short-changed my daughter.'

'That's why we went on the cruise! Oh my God, were you planning on telling both Mum and Henry while we were stranded at sea?' My eyebrows rose as I imagined the drama that could have ensued.

She nodded. 'But then while we were on board, Sappho talked about her childhood memories of Philip and Craig; I knew I couldn't take that away from her. And maybe I couldn't do that to Phil either. I realised that telling the truth wouldn't do anyone any good, but it could cause a lot of pain. It would hurt Sappho, it might compromise her relationship with Phil and Craig, and if she wanted to get to know Henry, it could also cause great hurt and unrest in his family. And what if he didn't want to know her after all these years? I might inflict pain, and for what? To ease my own guilt?'

Not to mention the fact Gralice could die before Mum ever forgave her.

My stomach ached. I wasn't sure what to think, and how could I face Mum, knowing this massive thing about her, and not say anything? Had this lie been responsible in part for the chasm between my mother and hers? How could you be truly close to someone if you were keeping such a massive secret from them?

I resolved there and then to be completely honest with my child— from the moment he or she could understand, they'd know the exact circumstances surrounding their conception and exactly who their father was.

But if Jay is that person …

Any softening I'd been starting to feel towards Gralice evaporated. Angry tears pooled in my eyes as I pushed back my seat and stood.

Gralice looked up and her tone was almost pleading as she spoke. 'Are you going to tell your mother?'

'I don't know.' I shrugged. 'She knows about my pregnancy and she knows Jay might be the father.'

'You told your *mother* and you hadn't told *me*?'

'I didn't want to hurt you unnecessarily by telling you about Jay due to his connection with Henry.' The irony was that although I'd kept quiet to protect her, I no longer cared so much about her feelings. 'Christos has done a DNA test—I should get the results this week. Let's hope he's the father, but if he's not ... I can't ... I obviously can't go through with the pregnancy and Mum will want to know what's caused my sudden change of heart.'

'Oh.' Gralice's shoulders slumped.

I blinked as tears started to fall. 'And you might have been able to live with such a massive secret, but I'm not sure I can.'

With those words, I swept all my belongings up into my arms and fled.

27

I was on the tram on the way to work the following Tuesday morning when my phone rang. I frowned at the unknown number on the screen. Usually I let such numbers go to voicemail, but something told me to answer this one.

'Good morning.'

'Hello. Is that Geraldine Johnston?'

'Yes,' I said warily and then my heart froze as the woman identified herself as someone from the DNA testing company. 'I'm sorry to have to tell you,' she continued, 'but we were unable to determine a result using your first samples and will need to repeat the test.'

'What do you mean? *Why* didn't it work?' The few people around me gave me a funny look as my voice rose, but I didn't care what any of them thought.

The voice on the other end of the phone remained calm. 'Unfortunately, in a small number of cases, there isn't sufficient foetal DNA in the mother's blood to provide an accurate result, which means the foetal fraction is too low to offer a reliable analysis.'

'So you don't know who the father of my baby is?' I reached out to grip a pole as dizziness overcame me. I *needed* those results. Now!

'Not yet, but I'm going to courier you a new testing kit, so it should get to you today, and as soon as we receive the samples we'll make your test a priority.'

'Hang on. What do you mean samples? I thought you said it was *my* blood that wasn't sufficient?'

'Yes, but we need everything again—your blood, and samples from the potential father to make sure it all goes smoothly. We do apologise for the inconvenience and of course—'

'So you've said,' I grumbled, unable to curb my rudeness.

I gave her my work address for the courier, then disconnected before she could hit me with another less-than-genuine sounding apology. My head fell forward to rest on the pole. I really wished I had a seat right now, but it was peak hour and I didn't look pregnant yet, so nobody was about to give up theirs for me.

Thinking I'd have to talk to Christos again at work, I remembered that he wasn't back from America for another couple of weeks. *Dammit.* I couldn't wait that long. The past two days since Gralice's revelation had been torturous enough. Sunday arvo and Monday had dragged; I'd ignored her messages and stayed late at work in case she tried to visit me at home. Part of me wondered if she might have decided to come clean with Mum and I'd half-expected a distressed phone call from my mother but there'd been no such call.

It wasn't unusual for Mum and me to go a few days, sometimes even a week, without talking and she was currently busy with the book, but what would I say to her when she did check in? She was sure to ask about my pregnancy, but every time I thought about it my stomach revolted and I found it difficult to breathe.

The sooner I knew the truth the better.

There was only one thing for it. I was going to have to tell Jay.

As the tram stopped near work, I negotiated my way off with all the other commuters and stepped out of the thoroughfare. My fingers trembled as I tapped out a message.

Are you free tonight? I need to see you.

Someone's obviously feeling better.

And then he added a wink emoji. An emoji. From Jay! This was not good.

It's my day off so message me when you're home from work and I'll come over.

My stomach churning, I continued on to the office and somehow managed to make it through the morning. Midafternoon I was trying to focus on writing up an article about how screens might be responsible for Australia's epidemic of teenage anxiety and depression—thankfully most of my research had been conducted via phone—when a package was delivered to my desk. The envelope and label were nondescript so as not to draw attention, but I immediately knew it was the new DNA test.

Darren chose that exact moment to walk past my desk. 'You're looking a little green.'

I shoved the package into my handbag and tried to force a smile. 'I'm fine.'

He glanced towards my bag. 'How's the article going?'

'Good. I'm almost done.'

He nodded. 'Excellent. Well, when you've filed it, take an early mark. I know you were here till late yesterday and we're under control. If anything else comes up, I'll email and you can work from home.'

Not wanting him to think I wasn't one hundred percent committed to work, I went to object but thought of the package and the fact Jay said he had the day off. The sooner I told him, the sooner he could give me a swab, the sooner I could send it back and the sooner we'd get the results. 'Okay, thanks.'

I finished my article, emailed it to Darren and headed home. Well, not quite home.

I'd passed Jay's 'milk bar' house a million times before and never paid the building much attention. As I'd told him, I'd thought it was deserted—it certainly looked ramshackle from the outside, with the paint peeling off both the veranda posts and the sign at the top of the building. Two newspaper logos and the words 'Macca's Milk Bar' were only just still visible. There were shop windows on either side of the door and both were covered with dark curtains. I couldn't find a doorbell and my hand shook as I pounded on the wood.

Just when I thought he must be out—no doubt pumping iron at the gym—the door peeled open a fraction.

'Ged?' His surprise turned into a grin and he opened the door properly, revealing a spacious but sparsely furnished living room. 'Well, hello there. This is a pleasant surprise.'

Despite the fact it was July, he wasn't wearing a shirt and his black trackpants hung low across his hips. For a moment, I forgot why I was there, and also another pertinent fact—that we were *related*. I had no right to drool over his bare chest. It had been one thing when I didn't know we were cousins, but now ... What kind of sicko was I?

'Are you in the middle of something?'

He shook his head and tried to cover a yawn. 'No, I worked until the early hours so was asleep.'

'Oh, I'm sorry. I can come back later if—'

'No.' He grabbed my hand, yanking me into the house and right into his body. 'Stay.'

And then he dipped his head and covered my mouth with his. Alarmed, I pulled back and palmed my hands on his chest.

Jay frowned as he looked down at me. 'Geraldine? Are you okay? Are you still sick?'

I shook my head as my mouth went dry but somehow I managed to speak. 'I'm pregnant.'

He stepped backwards as if I'd pushed him and the colour drained from his face. 'What the hell?'

I flinched. 'It's okay. It might not be yours.'

'You've been sleeping with someone else?'

I don't know why he sounded so offended—it wasn't like we'd agreed to be exclusive or anything. 'No, but I'm fourteen weeks. The timing of conception makes you and my ex both a possibility.'

'*Fourteen weeks?*' He glanced down at my stomach. 'How long have you known?'

I swallowed. 'A while.'

'And you didn't think to mention this when we were fucking?'

'I haven't slept with you since I found out and I wasn't sure I was going to keep the baby, so I …' My explanation died on my tongue. Nothing I could say made any sense and I didn't think he'd take kindly to me telling him that I'd been enjoying spending time with him and didn't want to ruin that.

'I thought you were on the pill,' he said, accusation loud and clear in his tone. 'I would never have slept with you if I'd thought otherwise. I don't want children.'

'If you were that opposed to the possibility of procreation you should have kept it in your pants! I don't expect anything from you—I'm not even sure I'm keeping it anyway.' Although it pained me to say this, how could I if he was the father? 'But I need a cheek swab, so I can eliminate you.'

'A cheek swab?'

I nodded and explained how the prenatal paternity DNA testing worked.

'Why aren't you asking the other guy?'

'I already have, but there was a problem with the test and now he's away on holiday with his wife and kids.'

Jay's eyes widened and his jaw was tense. 'If you're not gonna keep it, why do you need to know who the father is?'

'Because ... because I haven't made up my mind yet.'

'Where's this test then?'

'It's in my bag,' I said as I dug inside to retrieve the envelope.

I could tell he was angry at me—for being pregnant in the first place, for not telling him as soon as I knew or for telling Christos first, I wasn't sure. Probably a cocktail of all three. I could only imagine how he'd react if I told him the rest of my news, but I wouldn't do that to Gralice. No matter how angry and betrayed I felt, the truth about Mum and Henry wasn't my truth to tell.

And then it hit me. I knew next to nothing about DNA testing. Even if we were lucky and the results showed Jay not to be the father, would they also reveal that we were related?

'You know ...' I began, starting to shove the package back in my handbag, 'maybe I should just wait until Christos comes back.'

What more would a couple of weeks hurt? I wasn't even showing yet.

But Jay shook his head and held out his hand. 'I don't think so. Let's get this sorted once and for all.'

It was impossible not to obey the stern expression on his face and if I resisted he'd only wonder why. My hand shaking again, I offered the test kit to him.

'What do I have to do?' he asked gruffly.

'There's some little sticks in there to swab inside your mouth and plastic test-tube containers to put the swabs in. Once you're done we'll need to fill in the form with your details and your consent.'

Without a word, he took the kit, turned and strode into the kitchen where he ripped it open and spilled the contents out on the bench. Although I'd seen him naked, taking DNA from the side of his mouth seemed weirdly intimate and, not wanting to make him any more uncomfortable than he already was, I looked everywhere but at him.

His place could have been the blueprint for bachelor pad (*before* a guy moved in and messed it up). The floor was polished concrete and the walls different shades of brown. The front door opened straight into the living room, and this led into an open-plan kitchen-cum-dining room. I guessed the bedroom was down the back. I probably wouldn't be getting a look in there now, but if this main area was anything to go by, I could imagine. There was no clutter anywhere. The marble coffee table had nothing on it bar a remote, the two matching brown leather sofas were devoid of cushions and a massive TV took up most of one wall.

The only truly personal touch was a framed photograph beside the television. For a moment I forgot myself and curiosity got the better of me as I ventured closer to take a look. It was of a woman—early twenties at a guess —and a little boy and girl. The woman had a gaunt face and dark circles around her eyes, the look of someone terminally ill, or maybe she was just weary. Both kids had bright red hair and a smattering of freckles across their noses. The boy was particularly cute, although even at a young age the expression in his eyes said life pissed him off.

'Is this you?' I asked without thinking as I reached out to pick it up.

'Yes.' Jay's one word answer was terse and seemed to say so much.

I immediately put the photo back in its place, remembering what exactly was happening here.

He gave me the evil eye as he took a final swab and shoved the test stick into its plastic tube. His stance and the expression on his face emanated tension and displeasure. This Jay seemed so far removed from the one who'd played Game of Life with me when he'd thought I was sick; it was like there were two different people in that smoking-hot body.

Ugh! Stop. Related, remember?

I stood there awkwardly, not saying a word until Jay crossed back to me, holding the package as if it were a dirty nappy. 'How long till we know?'

'A few days to a week—the company said they'd hurry the results as they stuffed up the first one.'

He nodded once. 'You know … if it … if it shows that the baby's mine and you insist on keeping it, then financially I'll take care of you, but this is not going to change anything for me.'

What I should have said was that I didn't *need* his help, thank you very much, but instead I found myself asking him, 'Why?'

He rolled his eyes. 'Because legally it's required and I'm not a complete and utter bastard.'

'No. Why are you so adamantly against being a father? Lots of men don't want to have kids because they don't want to sacrifice Friday nights out with the guys or weekends playing video games, but I don't think that's your reason. What is it exactly that makes you so terrified of getting close to anyone? So terrified you're prepared to move to a whole other planet?'

'I'm not terrified of anything, Geraldine. And even if I was, I wouldn't need to explain it to you. This was never supposed to be anything more than sex.' He stepped past me and opened his door. 'Now, if you don't mind.'

Cool air whooshed into the room. I shivered and, annoyingly, tears prickled my eyes, but I refused to cry in front of him. For a while I'd been starting to think that maybe he was a nice guy masquerading beneath a tough exterior, but I guess I'd been mistaken. Stupidly, my heart ached at this realisation.

As I left Jay's place—the new sample safely in my bag—I prayed to a God I was pretty sure I didn't believe in that my ex-boyfriend was the father of my baby.

28

I screwed up my nose when I let myself into my parents' place—it smelled as if something had died in there and looked as if someone had ripped off the roof and dumped a ton of rubbish inside. Will obviously hadn't been exaggerating when he'd called and told me how badly our father was coping alone. I know he'd been visiting Dad a bit and trying to help, but he was busy with work and the kids, and I felt a bit guilty for not having done my bit.

'Dad?' I called, navigating through empty beer bottles and pizza boxes.

I found him asleep on the couch, the TV blaring in the background. He reeked—an awful combination of beer and body odour—and appeared to have grown a beard since the last time I'd seen him. It was ten o'clock in the morning and I feared he hadn't made it to bed last night. In fact, if the pillow and throw rug were anything to go by, he probably hadn't made it to bed in a while.

'Dad.' I shook his shoulder. 'Wake up. It's Ged.'

It took a bit more shaking and shouting before he roused, blinking as he tried to sit up. 'Am I late for work?'

I assumed he meant his lollipop duties as last I'd heard he was still on a break from the Uber driving.

'No. It's Saturday.' Thank God; he'd terrify the kids in his current state.

'Ah. Good.' He flopped back into the couch and closed his eyes again.

'Oh, no you don't.' I yanked at his arm. 'It's time to get up and face the day.'

'I can't. I don't want to. And I've got nothing to do anyway.'

'What happened to Saturday afternoon bowls?'

'I haven't been since your mother left—I can't bear to think what they'll all be saying.'

'No one's saying anything, as far as I can tell,' I told him. 'Mum is still posting about being a housewife, so maybe you should just go along and act as if everything is normal too.'

'I think I'll just order in a pizza and watch the football.'

'No!'

He startled at my loud objection.

'Enough is enough, Dad. You can't go on like this.'

'But ... I don't know how to live without Marie. We've been married thirty-five years.'

'I know, but you're going to have to learn as I don't think she's coming back.' My words might have been harsh, but life was full of surprises and they weren't all good ones—I should know. 'She definitely won't have a change of heart with you looking and smelling like you do now. And what would she think of this pigsty?'

'You think she might have a change of heart?'

My own heart went out to him and I felt a tad guilty for my lack of sympathy. He hadn't asked for any of this, any more than I'd asked for my current complications.

'I'm sorry, Dad, I don't think so. She's moved on, and it's time you started to think about doing the same. You need to clean yourself up and the house.'

He looked at me as if I was crazy.

'I'll help,' I said, knowing how much of a mammoth task this must seem to someone like him, 'but I'm not doing everything for you. I'm going to teach you how to take care of yourself.'

He looked terrified at the prospect and I wasn't exactly enthralled with the idea either, but we were both going to have to grin and bear it.

'Step one: Have a shower. Wash your hair. Shave. And put on some clean clothes.'

He nodded and slowly heaved himself off the couch. I tried not to screw up my noise as I got another whiff of his BO. Once I heard the bedroom door click shut, I surveyed the damage trying to work out where the hell to start. It was hard not to feel resentment towards my mother as I picked up a pair of my father's dirty jocks and tossed them in the laundry. Unsure of what else I might find lingering in the lounge room and not wanting to find out, I decided to begin in the kitchen.

It wasn't as bad as it looked because Dad didn't know how to cook so almost everything he ate came out of a packet. There were empty tins and cartons everywhere, but it didn't take long to toss them all into a bin bag. Next, I wiped the surfaces, loaded the dishwasher and checked the fridge to see what we might be able to cook for a late breakfast. There was literally nothing bar a bunch of condiments left over from Mum's time, a carton of eggs and a near-empty bottle of milk.

Miraculously, both were still in date, so I whipped up some scrambled eggs. There was no use trying to teach him to change his ways on an empty stomach.

When Dad returned to the kitchen he wore the suit he'd been wearing the night of Gralice's birthday.

'Why are you wearing that?'

'Um …' He shrugged sheepishly as he glanced down at his outfit. 'It's the only clean thing I have.'

Since he'd stopped bringing his dirty clothes around to my place, I'd assumed he'd been taking care of at least that himself. Apparently not.

'Why haven't you done any washing?'

'I don't know how to use the machine. I tried to learn once when Marie was sick, but she got angry when I mixed the whites with the colours, and so …'

His voice trailed off and I shook my head, disgusted at both my parents for allowing things to get this dire. 'Well, you're going to learn today. But first, eat that.' I gestured towards the eggs and toast I'd put on the kitchen table for him. 'And then we're going shopping.'

'Shopping?' Fear filled his voice as if I'd just told him we were going sky-diving.

'You can't live on pizza and beer forever. We're going to get the basics and I'm going to help you cook up some dinners for the week.'

He didn't look any less terrified but sank into his seat and devoured his scrambled eggs. While he ate, we wrote a shopping list together.

'That was delicious, thanks, Ged.' He popped a kiss on the top of my head as he dumped his plate and cutlery into the sink.

'Oh no,' I said, 'they don't go there. Put them in the dishwasher and once we have a load, we'll wash them all together.'

For a moment I thought he was about to object but he nodded and did as he was told. I smiled my approval.

'Now, go collect your dirty clothes and we'll put them in the wash before we go out.'

I met my father in the laundry a few moments later on his second trip there and my eyes widened at the mountain of clothes already on the floor. We were going to be here all bloody day.

'Let's start with these,' I said as he turned around, presumably to fetch more. 'Find the items you use most frequently and load a bunch of them into the machine first.'

'Don't we have to sort them or something?'

'Don't worry about sorting colours like Mum did. I've never had time for that and the world hasn't ended because I mix lights and darks. The important thing is getting you some clean clothes.'

'Okay.'

I stepped aside as he loaded the washing machine and then I showed him how to measure the powder into the slot and set a cycle going.

'How long will that take?'

'About an hour. Long enough for us to go do the grocery shop.'

Again, his face went pale, but I gave him an encouraging smile and ushered him outside. Not sure if Dad still had alcohol in his system, I drove us to the local supermarket. As it was Saturday it was quite busy, but I still made Dad push the trolley, hold the list and select all his own items. It took longer than I'd imagined but finally he paid for his purchases and loaded a week's worth of food into the car.

'I'm knackered,' Dad said once we'd carried all the bags inside and dumped them in the kitchen. 'Is it time for an arvo nap?'

'Not even close.' Although I quite liked the sound of one myself—pregnancy was draining *without* all the added complications I had to deal with. 'First, we need to put everything away, then we need to hang out the washing, put on another load and—'

I stopped when I saw the look on his face. One step at a time. 'How about we put away the shopping, you can make us some sandwiches for lunch and then we'll have a half-hour break before getting stuck in to the rest?'

My father looked as if he wasn't sure whether this was a good deal or not. After I directed him where to put everything, he surprised himself by making us both rather delicious chicken and salad sandwiches. We made small talk while we ate—neither of us wanting to talk about Mum—and went outside to hang the washing. My mother would have a coronary if she saw the way my father hung his jocks (not to mention everything else) but it was none of her business anymore and I was simply happy that he was making an effort.

Next, I attempted to teach him to cook a lasagne. I'd chosen this as it was relatively easy and we could make a big enough batch that it would last him for a few meals. As we cooked, I found myself relaxing and enjoying myself for the first time in almost a week. It was a relief to have something to focus on other than the results of the DNA test and Gralice's revelation. I hadn't seen her since, and without her or Jay occupying my evenings, they were pretty long and lonely.

'How you going with that cheese sauce, Dad? Keep stirring, you don't want lumps.'

He nodded, his eyes trained on the spoon as it circled the bubbling cheese mixture in the saucepan. 'Who'd have thought something so simple was such a skill?'

'You know women love a man who can cook,' I said with a teasing grin.

'You think your mother will be impressed?'

I sighed. 'Mum's not the only woman on earth. And she's moved on, so maybe you could think about seeing other women as well.'

He looked half-terrified, half-horrified at the thought.

'Never mind,' I said, 'the idea of me teaching you all this is that you don't need a woman in your life, but you never know what might happen down the track.'

By the time the meat and the cheese sauce were ready to assemble with the pasta sheets, I seriously needed to take a load off my feet, but I talked him through the assembly and he was pretty pleased with himself when we put the baking dish into the oven. Perhaps you could teach an old dog new tricks after all.

'Now, there's just one more thing you need to do before you can relax.'

'What?' he asked, his expression wary.

I laughed. 'Well, we can't sit down to dinner in such a dirty house, so you need to do a quick vacuum and mop.'

There was just one problem—my father had no idea where these two things lived.

29

The letter was waiting for me when I arrived home Monday night. I collected my mail from the communal hall and flicked through the mostly windowed envelopes as I walked the short distance to my apartment. As I approached my front door, I could already hear Coco jumping up against it and barking her happy bark, but my steps faltered as my gaze fell upon the final envelope. Express post!

I knew immediately it was the results from the DNA paternity test.

My heart began to thump so hard and fast it almost drowned out my dog's noise. I fumbled for my key and opened the door. She burst out and made a beeline for the exit to the courtyard. I pulled the door shut again and hurried after her. The moment I let her outside, I ripped open the envelope, the others falling out of my grasp and scattering on the ground around us.

While Coco did her business, I sucked in a breath and read.

By order of Geraldine Johnston we were requested to perform a prenatal DNA paternity test.

It listed both myself and Jay as the individuals who were examined, his cheek swab against the foetal DNA from my blood. I scanned quickly over the explanation of how the test had been carried out. There were a lot of scientific words and number codes that I didn't understand and didn't care for—all I needed was the conclusion.

And there it was: *Based on our analysis, it is practically proven that Mr Jay French is not the biological father of Ms Geraldine Johnston's foetus.*

Is *not*?

My knees gave way and I crumbled to the ground. Coco rushed over to check I was okay and as I reached out absentmindedly to run my fingers through her fur, I read that line another three times just to be sure. And then I started crying.

This was *good* news for so many reasons. It meant I could continue the pregnancy, and we'd already established Christos was the better candidate for father. Now Jay could go to Mars without feeling guilty. Not that he *felt* guilty or would have changed his plans for a baby anyway, but now at least he wouldn't feel obligated to pay child support. Without a doubt he'd be overjoyed by this news, and I should be too. I *was*. On one level.

But the knowledge that this meant I'd have no reason to see Jay ever again put a tiny and ridiculous dampener on it. Now that I was gonna be a single mum, who knew if I'd ever have sex again?

I'd barely finished scolding myself for this selfish thought when another struck. I *might* see Jay again if the truth came out about Gralice and Henry.

My heart jolted as I once again looked down at the letter to take a closer look, but I couldn't find any information about Jay and *me* sharing DNA or whatever it was that would confirm we were blood relatives. Perhaps they didn't provide anything unless specifically requested. Perhaps if I were a scientist like Gralice I wouldn't need it spelled out for me. The numbers in the columns compared on the page would be obvious if I knew what I was looking for, but perhaps it was a blessing I didn't.

I still wasn't sure how I felt about the revelation—whether telling Mum and Henry was the best and fairest thing to do or not—but at least this way, even if Jay demanded to see the results, I wouldn't be the one to break the news to him. Thank God I hadn't freaked out and told him of the possibility the other day.

'Are you okay?'

I startled at the sound to find one of my neighbours staring down at me and quickly folded the letter and shoved it in my pocket as I scrambled to my feet.

'Yep. Fine.' I smiled too hard, but thankfully the middle-aged gent and I had never said more than hello or goodbye to each other and so he didn't pry, nodding instead as he continued on his way.

'Have a good evening,' I called, letting out a deep breath as I ushered Coco back inside. I tossed some biscuits into her bowl, then poured myself a glass of apple juice and took it into the lounge room to work out my next move. Obviously, I had to tell Jay and Christos. And my mother would want to know, as would Gralice.

My jaw tensed and an angry heat flushed through my body at the thought of her. I was still furious about her secrets and lies and didn't feel as if I owed her anything at the moment, but I couldn't avoid her forever. Especially not when she was so sick. Not wanting to think about that, I checked my phone to see what time it was in Florida. 5 am. Due to my current exhaustion levels, I'd likely be asleep by the time it was an acceptable hour to call, so I shot Christos a text message instead.

Got the results … the baby's yours. Enjoy the rest of your holiday and we'll talk when you get back.

Next on my list was Jay. I downed the rest of my apple juice, wishing it was wine. I don't know why this was so hard, but part of me didn't want to tell him. I was glad not to have to do it face to face because I didn't think I could handle seeing his joyful relief, but I could visualise it anyway. And the thought he'd be ecstatic *not* to be linked with me forever hurt way more than it should. Cursing my crazy, stupid pregnancy hormones, I did what I had to do.

FYI—I got the results of the paternity test. The baby isn't yours.

Less than thirty seconds later, I had a response: *Good news. Best wishes.*

Best fucking wishes?

If I had just *one* wish it would be that I'd never met Jay French. I threw my phone across the room, startling Coco who'd settled at my feet.

'Guess that means we won't be hearing from him again,' I told her.

And this was a good thing. Just because he wasn't Thing's father didn't alter the other sickening fact.

We were related.

I'd slept with my cousin and I most definitely shouldn't want to do *that* again.

As Coco nuzzled me with her nose, I started to cry. I told myself they were happy tears, but then why did I feel so bereft? I was still sobbing a few moments later when my phone started to ring from where it had landed in the corner of the room. My bet was on Christos having seen my message, but I wasn't in the mood to talk to him right now.

The ringing stopped and I snuggled into Coco, but less than ten seconds later it started up again. Once more I waited for it to stop, but it rang a third time. Then a fourth. When it started for a fifth, I hauled myself off the couch and snatched it up, annoyed.

There were five missed calls from my mother. Not Christos. Before I had the chance to worry, the ringing started again.

'What's up?' I asked as I accepted the call.

'Thank the Lord. Why on earth weren't you picking up the phone, Geraldine?'

'I was having a shower,' I lied. 'Why? What's wrong?'

'It's your grandmother.'

My heart turned to ice.

Oh Lord—please let her not have ended it all while I'd been avoiding her. She wouldn't have done that to me. *Would she?*

'What about her?' I whispered, terrified of the reply.

'She's in the hospital—apparently she has cancer!'

Relief washed through me and giddy tears welled up behind my eyes.

'Oh my God,' I said, trying to mask the fact that I already knew.

'I know … it's a terrible shock to us all. First I heard of it was when Dad called me this afternoon. He'd gone round to visit her this morning and found her with a raging fever. He and Craig took her to the doctor and they've admitted her because she has some kind of infection. I can't believe she hasn't told any of us about this illness. Apparently, she's *chosen* not to have treatment. Can you believe that?'

Considering I'd had almost two months to digest the news, I could, but that wasn't the worst of it.

I hopped in an Uber and cried most of the way to the hospital—I think I terrified the driver, but I couldn't help myself. Quite aside from the pregnancy hormones, my mind was a maelstrom of emotions. I'd barely had time to digest the news that Christos was Thing's father and now I was facing another crisis.

What kind of infection did Gralice have? Was it bad? It had to be for her to have been admitted to hospital. But how bad? I didn't know much about illness and cancer, but I knew doctors didn't admit patients for nothing. They must be concerned, and my heart squeezed with guilt at the fact I hadn't checked in on her for days, and all the while I wondered if this hiccup would bring forward her plans.

Now that the others knew she was sick, they'd be mollycoddling her something chronic; this would drive her wild. It was exactly what she'd hoped to avoid.

'Ged!' As I got out of the Uber, I heard my name and looked up to see Will coming from the hospital car park.

'I just can't believe this,' he said, sniffing as he pulled me into a hug. 'I kinda thought Gralice would outlive us all.'

'Me too.' I tried to swallow the lump in my throat as we huddled together on the pavement a few long moments.

'Come on, no point standing around out here all night. Gralice needs us.'

I nodded and then—holding hands like Mum used to make us do when we were kids—we made our way inside and were assaulted by the universal hospital aroma, a nauseating combination of latex, bland food and strong disinfectant.

We found Gralice in a private room with Mum, Phil, Craig and Rosa in attendance. Phil and Craig, wearing matching solemn expressions, occupied two plastic chairs and Mum was sitting on the bed, holding Gralice's hand, but she leapt up when we entered. Will rushed to our grandmother, but I hung back and greeted her and our grandfathers with a hug. Mum's eyes were bloodshot and her cheeks damp.

'Oh, Ged.' She squeezed me tightly. 'Thank you for coming. Maybe you can talk some sense into her.'

Had Gralice *told* them her intentions?

'Sappho,' Phil warned, 'leave it.'

'It's too late for that,' came Gralice's stoic response before I could work out what exactly they were talking about.

I turned to look at her properly and my heart broke. To say she looked awful would be an understatement—I almost didn't recognise her with her gaunt face, dark shadows around her eyes and tubes attached to her hand. It had been just over a week since I'd seen her and in that time she appeared to have halved in size. The horrid, pale blue hospital gown did nothing for her either—she looked very much her full eighty years—and I imagined how depressed she must be having to wear it. I'd been grappling with remorse already, but that gown pushed me over the edge. My anger forgotten, I stepped up to the bed and took hold of her hand.

'I'm so sorry.' If only I hadn't stopped visiting, I might have noticed some signs or symptoms and been able to get her treatment before whatever infection she had got this bad.

'What on earth do you have to be sorry about?' snapped my mother. 'This isn't your fault. Apparently Gralice has gastric cancer and is selfishly refusing treatment.'

'Sappho,' Phil warned again, 'this is Alice's decision and she needs our love and support, not our anger.'

'I'm sorry. It's just such a shock.' My mother sobbed and Rosa pulled her in for a hug.

Will raised his eyebrows but refrained from making comment. Instead, clutching Gralice's other hand, he spoke softly. 'Are you sure you've thought this through? Don't you know how much we all need you?'

'Yes.' She gave him a sad smile. 'I'm sorry I didn't tell you, but I … I guessed you might not understand my decision. It may seem selfish to refuse treatment, but anything they can offer me will only prolong the agony.'

Gralice coughed and we all rushed to pour some water into a plastic cup. She took a sip from the straw, then addressed us all, her voice wavering as if each word were a struggle. 'I've had a good life—no point wasting precious medical resources on me when there are younger people who need them even more.'

I held my breath, wondering if she'd tell everyone that not only did she plan on forgoing treatment, but she intended to end it all before she became a so-called burden. But of course she didn't.

'That's very noble of you,' Rosa said.

Will shot her a glare.

'Can I get anyone anything to eat or drink?' she offered, and I guessed this was more to give her a reason to escape than because any of us needed sustenance.

'Thanks.' Craig smiled up at her encouragingly. 'I'd love a flat white.'

Phil, Mum and I all put in an order, but Will politely declined. With Rosa's retreat, some of the tension in the air dissipated.

'Have you thought about natural treatments? Sophie has a friend who's a naturopath and she swears by—'

Gralice shook her head at my brother. 'My cancer is too far gone for that. I just want to spend what time I have left with my family.' Her expression pleading, she looked in turn to everyone in the room, finally landing meaningfully on me. 'Is that too much to ask?'

Despite the lump in my throat, I joined the others as they shook their heads.

'So, why exactly are you in here today?' Will asked. 'What kind of infection have you got and what are they doing about it?'

Phil answered for her, relaying what the doctor had told them earlier—due to Gralice's weakened immune system the chest infection she'd caught was much more dangerous for her than it was for a healthy person. The doctors had run tests this afternoon to try and identity exactly what germ was causing the infection, but while they waited for results, they'd prescribed a strong course of antibiotics.

'And are those going to make you better?' Will wanted to know when Phil had finished.

'Well, they won't cure the cancer, if that's what you're asking. And it depends on what exactly the infection is as to how well the treatment will work,' Gralice said, 'but hopefully I'll recover enough to go home in the next day or so.'

I let out what I hoped was an inaudible sigh of relief.

Everyone was quiet a few moments, presumably registering that even if she recovered from this, it would only be a temporary reprieve. Our matriarch was dying and our world was about to change irrevocably.

Hating the sad silence and feeling like we all needed a little light in the dark, I cleared my throat. 'So, I have an announcement.'

All eyes turned to me.

'I'm having a baby.'

While Mum smiled knowingly, the others gaped at me in obvious shock.

'Holy shit, sis!' Will was the first to break the stunned silence as he charged around the bed and pulled me into the second hug of the day. 'Sophie said she thought you might be pregnant after last time we saw you, but I told her she was delusional.'

'Well, you can tell her you were wrong and she was right.'

'It happens occasionally.' He shrugged, grinning. 'Massive congrats.'

Phil cleared his throat as he and Craig stood. 'Do the great-grandfathers get a hug as well?'

'Of course.'

'And me.' Mum joined in the group hug.

'So, Christos is the father?' asked Gralice from the bed.

I turned and smiled at her. 'Who else could it be?'

'That's wonderful news, darling.' She sounded a little choked as she pressed her hand to her chest.

'Thank you.' I rushed over to envelop her in my arms, wishing I never had to let go. But she was not much more than skin and bones now, and my heart tore a little more. She was only going to get worse, and I understood how daunting that must be for someone who'd always been so strong and independent.

'Well, well, well, what's happening here?' Rosa asked when she returned with a takeaway tray of coffee cups and everyone was still gushing over my news.

'Ged's pregnant,' Will told her and then lowered his eyes as if remembering he was supposed to be harbouring a grudge.

I smirked as Rosa put the drinks down and threw her arms around me. 'Congratulations, honey.'

'How far along are you? Sophie will be cross if I don't return with all the details.'

'Fifteen weeks. I'm due on Australia Day.'

'Wow—you sure kept that quiet a while.'

'I had my reasons,' I said.

A cuddly-looking nurse with a grin that looked like it was permanently etched into her face chose that moment to enter. 'Visiting hours are over, I'm afraid,' she said apologetically. 'I'm going to have to ask all of you to leave. Mrs Abbott needs her rest.'

'It's *Ms* Abbott,' informed my grandmother.

We let out a collective sigh. None of us were ready to go, but we took turns saying our goodbyes, promising to return the next day.

'Thank you both for coming,' my mother said as we congregated downstairs a few minutes later. 'We're all going to need to be there for Gralice over the coming months and I hope your feelings towards me—'

'Mum,' Will interrupted, 'we'll be there for Gralice.' Then he surprised us all by pulling her into a hug. 'And you're still my mother even if I'm not sure I know you anymore.'

It was as good a truce as we were going to get right now and a step towards reconciliation. I felt proud of my brother for putting his resentment aside.

I guessed seeing Gralice so feeble had shocked all of us into taking stock of what mattered. I looked around me—these guys, as well as Gralice, Dad, Sophie and the kids, mattered to me more than anything else. These were the people who would come together and offer me the practical and emotional support I needed when Thing was born. These people were my family and that was more than just a blood thing.

'Thank you,' Mum whispered, tears in her eyes as she and Will came apart. 'I just can't believe this. I know Gralice and I haven't always seen eye to eye on everything, but I do love her. So much.'

'I know you do,' I said, taking my turn to draw her into a hug.

'She's always been so strong, so independent, so clever, and I've never told her that I do admire that. Now I'm going to lose her and I … I just want more time.'

I told everyone I was waiting for an Uber, but the moment they'd all gone their separate ways, I went back inside and snuck into Gralice's room. She looked to be already asleep and, not wanting to wake her, I was about to retreat when she opened one eye.

'Ged? Is that you?'

'Yes,' I whispered.

She inclined her bed with the little remote and patted the spot beside her. 'Come here.'

I perched precariously on the edge of the bed.

'Stop treating me like china,' she scolded. 'Come close.'

Relaxing a fraction, I snuggled in and rested my head on her shoulder. We sat quietly for a few moments and then she asked, 'So is Christos really the father of your baby?'

'Yes.'

'Thank fuck.'

I smiled—it was nice to know that beneath this frail old-lady exterior my unconventional grandmother still existed.

'I'm so sorry about the other day,' she began, 'it was wrong of me to ask you to keep such a big secret from your mother, and if you really think it's for the best she knows then I'll tell her. I don't want to have anything come between you and me.'

'It won't,' I promised. 'I've had time to think, and I don't think you should tell her. You're right ... some things are better left unsaid.'

Now that Thing was safe, it didn't feel like such a big deal—after all, none of us were perfect. We all had things in our past we weren't proud of or regretted, but that didn't mean we should go around trying to rewrite history. The way I saw it, there was a whole lot more damage than good that could be done by telling Gralice's secret after all this time.

At least her cancer and my pregnancy were now out in the open, and this way I wouldn't run the risk of having to deal with Jay again. I could just imagine his wrath if I were responsible for dropping this bombshell on his family.

'Are you sure?'

'Yes. You're right, Phil is Mum's dad and he and Craig will be my baby's great-grandfathers too.'

'I can't believe you're having a baby,' Gralice said. 'That kid is damn lucky she's gonna have you for a mother.'

I chuckled. 'What makes you so certain it's gonna be a girl?'

'Great-grandmother's intuition.'

I blinked back tears. The sad truth was that, girl or not, Gralice would likely never meet Thing.

I was thankful for the very dimly lit room, which meant she didn't see my face. I'd always idolised her, kept her on a metaphorical pedestal above everyone else. But now that I knew she wasn't as perfect and infallible as I'd always imagined, I weirdly felt even closer to her. I made a silent vow that my baby would hear all about the wonderful things that Gralice had achieved in her life and the positive voice and influence she'd been for generations of women. I would talk so much about my grandmother that my child would feel as if they'd actually known her themselves.

30

I was now almost nineteen weeks pregnant. The nausea had vanished, my exhaustion no longer crippled me, and I'd become one of those women who was constantly caressing her bump. While it still wasn't obvious when I was fully clothed, I'd already invested in a maternity wardrobe and when I was naked you could most definitely tell. Not that anyone except my obstetrician had such intimate access these days, but still.

The past month had flown by, and while part of me wanted time to speed up as I was super excited to meet Thing, another big part wanted it to slow right down. With each passing day, Gralice grew weaker and we were one step closer to the inevitable. She'd recovered from the infection enough to come home, but she was noticeably ill now. The naps she'd never had before occurred at least two or three times a day and even her smoothies seemed an effort to consume. Her house had sold for a great price at auction and she now lived with Phil and Craig.

In my granddads' two-storey terrace in St Kilda, the bedrooms were upstairs, so they'd set her up in the living room downstairs. While she hated being treated like a patient, even she had to concede that going up and down the stairs was too much for her. We got her out of the house and into the fresh air as much as we could, but Coco and I spent most of my non-working hours sitting on the couch chatting with my grandparents and gleaning wonderful tidbits to enhance the biography. Craig had even set up a small desk for me so I could work there and the book was coming along nicely.

Mum, Rosa, Will, Sophie and the kids were frequent visitors—Dad even came around occasionally, although not at the same time as my mother and her 'assistant'. It was good to spend time with them. I'd been so busy with work the past few years that I hadn't made as much effort as I should have where my family was concerned and doing so now was probably the only positive thing to come out of Gralice's illness.

Mum would often entertain us with extracts from her book, which I had to admit was well written and very entertaining. I tried my best to forget what I'd discovered about Henry, to live my life as I would have if I hadn't found out, and to write my book in the same manner. Most of the time this was easier than I'd thought it would be; only occasionally did I feel a prickle of guilt about harbouring this massive secret about Mum's life. But then, I'd witness a moment between her and Gralice, or both of them with Phil and Craig, and knew I'd made the right decision.

Mum had told her followers about the cancer and also about my pregnancy, and both topics were providing plenty of fodder for her vlogs. I tried not to get annoyed about this—Mum was Mum and she didn't mean any harm. We all had different way of dealing with things; my mother's was to share it with strangers and take comfort in their comments and likes.

Mine was to focus on the book and my pregnancy. These days when I wasn't at work, writing, or with my family, I was surfing the net. I'd joined a couple of Facebook groups for pregnant women due the same month, and one for single mums. Apart from a very heated discussion about when was the right time to return to work, I enjoyed the camaraderie. I'd also been doing a *lot* of online shopping. Sometimes I merely window-shopped, but do you know how hard it is to resist buying baby stuff? Electronic swings. Baby kneepads. Infant cologne. White noise makers. You could even buy wipe warmers, so their little butts didn't get cold during those middle of the night changes. And the shoes. Goodness me. I knew Thing wouldn't be able to walk for ages, but they were just so cute!

Both Gralice and Mum told me that I don't need half of it, that babies require surprisingly little, and maybe they were right, but I wanted to be prepared for all eventualities. And, already feeling guilty about Thing's less than ideal beginning, I don't want she/he to miss out on anything.

Christos wasn't behaving much better than me. Not long after he returned from Florida we'd sat down together and had a long heart to heart about the baby, how we were going to negotiate co-parenting considering his complicated situation. He was very supportive—promising financial, practical and emotional support— and the conversation had been very civil, but being near him still hurt, so now we mostly we corresponded via emails, through which he let me know everything he'd bought.

So far, thanks to him, I had a car seat, a cot, a pram, and a changing table that I wasn't sure would fit in my apartment. Maybe he was just excited, but I think he'd been buying stuff to help him deal with the guilt that he wasn't going to be as hands-on in the early days as he had been with his other children. I was planning on breastfeeding and therefore we'd agreed our baby would stay with me full-time to begin with.

Needless to say, things were a little awkward whenever we ran into each other at work, but I figured I should be happy that he at least *wanted* to acknowledge our child's existence and be a part of their life. Yep, Thing had definitely lucked out with the results of the paternity test. In the name of self-preservation, I did my utmost not to think about Jay, so you can imagine my panic one day last week when Darren announced we were doing an article about a local cop who'd been selected as one of the candidates for Mars Mission.

'Would you like to take this one, Ged?'

My words had tripped over themselves as my reply tumbled from my mouth. 'Me. Space. Hate. Not. Probably. Best.'

Darren had looked at me weirdly, and rightly so because career-wise it probably wasn't smart to be turning down such an opportunity, but the chances of me getting the promotion now were slim to none anyway. I knew the statistics—it was an indisputable fact that pregnant women were often overlooked in favour of others. There was no way the paper was going to give this senior position to anyone who was almost nine months pregnant. And it wasn't like I could cry out discrimination because Libby and Tom were equally good candidates for the job. The worst part was I wasn't sure how I would juggle such a demanding career with single motherhood anyway. I hated myself for even thinking such a thing but everything seemed so daunting right now.

Libby, delighted with my refusal, had rushed to offer herself up instead. Apparently, she'd wanted to be an astronaut when she was little and was more than willing to meet Jay on the weekend, which was the only time he was available. I'd have to try very hard not to pepper her with questions but in the end my worry was unwarranted. She'd walked into the office on Monday morning as if the carpet were clouds and hadn't stopped raving about her interview subject since. I suspected they'd slept together and wondered what had happened to the guy she'd been on the ski trip with but suppressed the urge to ask. What did it matter to me what Jay or Libby did with their time?

To prove my care factor was zero, I decided not to read the article that would be published in tomorrow's lift-out. I told myself I was not even remotely tempted to take a peek, but when Darren congratulated Libby about it being one of her best pieces of work—he even suggested it might get a Walkley nomination, *please*—I felt my resolve wavering. I'd just clicked into the shared file on the computer where I could take a look, when all hell broke loose and I forgot all about the article.

'Hey, Ged.' Libby landed beside my desk, her eyes sparkling as if she'd just uncovered the next big story. 'Have you seen Twitter this morning?'

'No. Why?'

'Isn't your mother the Happy Happy Housewife?'

'Yes. Why?' My chest squeezed at the gleam in Libby's eyes. Something told me I wasn't going to like what was coming.

'I think you should take a look for yourself.'

A slight chill lifted the hairs on the back of my neck as I opened Twitter on my computer. Behind me, Libby hovered annoyingly.

It took mere seconds to discover what had her so excited. There were hundreds of comments from Mum's so-called supporters over the past few hours, calling her out for cheating on her husband and thus not practising what she preached. What seemed to have begun with a couple of probing comments had been fuelled by others saying they'd noticed an obvious absence of my father in any of her content and then one person posting a photo of Mum and Rosa looking very chummy indeed at a cafe last week. *Eek*. Who'd have thought my mother would attract this much public attention—in these days of smartphones and social media everyone was a member of the pap.

Some of the comments were downright nasty—it looked as if people who didn't even follow Mum had gotten on board. 'Fraud' and 'Fake' were two of the nicer names she was being called. And somehow, someone had got wind of the fact her real name was Sappho. *Bloody trolls.*

'So, is it true?' Libby asked excitedly as I clicked on the hashtags #happyhousewifefraud and #sapphobynamesapphobynature, which were currently trending, and found even more disturbing tweets. '*Is* your mother a lesbian?'

No comment, was how I wanted to reply but I knew this would be taken as confirmation. And, I didn't want to confirm or deny anything until I'd spoken to Mum, so I minimised Twitter on my screen and shot my colleague a look. 'You shouldn't believe everything you read online. And haven't you got work to do?'

I turned away from her, hoping she'd get the message that I wasn't going to discuss my mother. And I did have work to do. Gralice, or rather Alice Abbott, had announced her cancer in her latest magazine column, also informing her readers that it would be her last, and Darren had tasked me with the job of writing a feature about her life. Luckily, I could pretty much do this in my sleep, so the moment Libby retreated, I clicked back into Twitter.

I could only imagine how my mother, a people pleaser, must be feeling about this public attack, but most of what the trolls were saying was true. It was only surprising it had taken this long for someone to cotton on.

And there wasn't only Mum's feelings to think about. Dad would be horrified; his bowling friends might not be big on social media but they'd hear about this for sure. And then there was Holly Pearson.

Apparently, all publicity was good publicity, but I wasn't sure she'd agree in this instance and Bourne Books had already invested a lot in my mother and her brand.

I wished I hadn't buried my head in the sand where Mum's public image was concerned. I should have cautioned her when she'd come out to us all that this might affect her new-found career, but I'd just found out about Gralice's cancer *and* my pregnancy so hadn't been on my game. I needed to talk to her, but there was no privacy in the office so I grabbed my phone and headed downstairs.

Mum answered on the second ring.

'Oh Ged, I guess you've seen the drama online?' It was a rhetorical question and she sounded like she'd been crying. 'I don't know what to do. Everyone is turning against me. I've lost twenty thousand followers from Instagram in the last hour and Holly has called; she's coming around in half an hour to *talk*. I don't think she's very impressed.'

No shit, Sherlock.

'What does Rosa think?'

'She thinks we should come out publicly, and if people can't accept that they're not worth it, but Ged ...' She sucked in a breath. 'I've worked so hard over the past year to build what I have and ...'

Mum started to cry and I had no idea what to advise her.

'Perhaps don't rush into anything. Speak to Holly and see what she says. Don't respond to any of the comments online until you've devised a plan of attack.'

A shadow fell over me and I looked up to see Christos.

'Look, Mum, try to stay calm. I'll get away from work as soon as I can. Love you.'

'I saw you rush off. Are you okay?' Christos asked, reaching out to touch my arm.

'I guess you've heard about Mum?'

He nodded. 'Is it … true?'

'Yep.'

'Wow. I thought your mother was straighter than the Queen.'

I half-chuckled. 'How do you know what Liz does behind closed doors?'

He raised an eyebrow and I fought the urge to bury my head in my hands.

'You're not looking so great.'

'Geez, thanks.'

He ignored my sarcasm and wrapped an arm around my shoulder. 'Come on. Let's go get a hot chocolate or something.'

As tempting as that sounded, I needed to get back inside and finish my article.

'I don't think so.'

'You know …' He offered a lingering, weighted look. 'I'm here for you if you ever need anything and I can be a good listener.'

'I know you can.' Many a time we'd talked into the early hours of the morning. He'd always been interested in my career, my friends and my family, but I couldn't risk letting myself get close to him again. 'Thanks. I appreciate that, but I just need to talk to Mum.'

'Okay.' He flicked me a resigned smile. 'Well, if you don't need anything beforehand, I guess I'll see you at the ultrasound next Friday.'

'Yep.' At least that was *something* to look forward to.

All eyes were on me when I returned to the office. It was obvious what Libby and my other colleagues had been discussing while I was gone, but I pretended I didn't notice any of them as I sat back down at my computer. I fielded calls from Will, Dad, Gralice, Phil and Craig, each one delaying my article a little longer. Finally, I turned it in, made my excuses to Darren—knowing I was pushing my luck lately—and left.

I'd only been to Rosa's place in Glen Waverly once before, but I remembered the address, so gave that to my Uber driver. Thankfully he wasn't chatty, allowing me to catch up on Twitter while we drove. Nothing had calmed in the past couple of hours, if anything the attacks on my mother were getting more vicious. She hadn't responded, and while I thought this a good thing, her silence was upsetting her loyal followers who wanted to know what was going on.

When we arrived at Rosa's red-brick unit, I thanked the driver and had barely climbed out of the car before my mother—sobbing, dragging a suitcase in one hand, her other arm full of stuff—emerged from inside.

'You're making a very big mistake,' Rosa called from the door, lifting her hand to greet me in a very distracted manner.

'What's going on?' I looked from one to the other.

'She's going home to your father,' Rosa informed and then shut the front door with a bang.

'What?' I gaped at my mother. She was a sight. Mascara streaked her cheeks and her normally neat hair was tousled as if she'd run her hands through it too many times.

She sniffed as she beeped her car unlocked. 'I made a horrible mistake. Can you open the boot for me?'

Too stunned to do anything else, I did as told and she leaned over and let everything she was carrying tumble in, then picked up the suitcase and threw it in as well. She walked round to the driver's side and climbed into the car, and I did the same on the passenger side, hoping to find out what the hell she was doing.

She started the car and reversed out of the driveway and when it was clear she wasn't about to volunteer anything, I asked again, 'What's going on?'

Mum cleared her throat and focused on the road ahead as she navigated the midafternoon traffic. I noticed her hands were shaking on the steering wheel and wondered if I should offer to drive. 'I'm going home to your father. I don't know what came over me these past few months. I feel terribly ashamed for walking out on my family and—'

'You didn't walk out on your family. Will and I are grown-ups and you weren't happy with Dad. You probably didn't handle any of this the best way …' *Starting with the adultery.* Although now wasn't the time to bring that up. 'It would have been better to be honest with your followers from the beginning, but now you have to focus on the future. I know this whole Twitter fiasco has upset you, but you can't let what some strangers think ruin your life.'

'It's not just strangers,' Mum admitted, another sniff.

'Will's coming around. He loves you. We all do.'

'Holly told me if I'm no longer the Happy Happy Housewife, there can't be a book and I'll have to pay back the advance.'

I cringed. I knew it wasn't massive, but it wasn't insignificant either. 'Have you already spent it?'

'Some of it, but that's not the problem. I've never had my own money before in my life, Ged. My vlogging has given me such joy and purpose but also an independence I didn't even realise I craved. I can't bear to lose that again.'

'So, you're going to keep it by going back to Dad and swapping one lie for another?'

'Our marriage was not a lie,' she scoffed. 'I love your father. We're good together. He's a good man. I just hope he'll forgive me for this … this hiatus.'

'What about Rosa? I thought you loved her.'

She hesitated just a second. 'We were spending so much time together and I just lost my head for a little bit. Your father and I have been married for such a long time that things became a little stale between us. We started taking each other for granted, and the first person who showed me a little bit of attention ... well, I was flattered and that confused me.'

My mother was full of surprises. If I'd been shocked by her coming out of the closet in the first place, I was even more so by her shutting herself back in. Did she really expect me to believe this after I'd seen the way she was with Rosa?

'So, what are you going to do?' I asked, deciding not to push her yet.

'Well, if Tony will forgive me, I'm going to ask my followers to do the same. I'm going to explain I made a mistake and I'm utterly sorry about it, but that marriage is worth fighting for and I'm going to do everything I can to make mine work.'

I wasn't sure my father or the *Happy Happy Housewife* groupies would be prepared to accept this apology, and I kinda hoped they wouldn't, which might force Mum's hand. But twenty minutes later when we knocked on Dad's door, he welcomed her back with open arms.

'Wow,' Mum said as she glanced around. 'You've kept things in good order.'

He beamed. 'I've done my best. Ged's been helping me a bit.'

The house wasn't as pristine and neat as when my mother lived there but it was a damn sight better than when I'd intervened a month ago. Dad had slowly been getting himself together. In between work and visiting Gralice, I'd made sure to check on him at least twice a week, each time teaching him another simple meal he could cook for himself. So far, in addition to the lasagne, he'd learned to cook shepherd's pie, steak and chips, poached eggs and a basic chicken pasta. I'd been impressed with his determination and dedication to learn, not only cooking, but everything else that Mum once did for him, so I was kinda disappointed that he was so quick to forgive and forget.

Then again, love was a strange thing, and if there was one thing I knew it was that my father loved my mother. I just wasn't so sure about the other way around. I hoped Mum knew what she was doing—for both their sakes.

31

'Hey, Ged.' Christos kissed me on the cheek and smiled down at my bump. 'You're looking gorgeous as usual.'

'Please don't say things like that.'

It was going to be hard enough sharing a child with my ex-boyfriend without him muddying the waters with flirty compliments.

He shrugged. 'It's the truth.'

'Well, sometimes the truth is better left unsaid,' I retorted and then hurried into the ultrasound clinic.

Christos caught up to me as I was registering at reception.

'Sorry,' he said as we went to sit on the uncomfortable plastic chairs to wait our turn. 'But it's hard being near you and not acting on my feelings. I miss you.'

His words sparked a warm glow, but I immediately extinguished it. This was so messed up. No matter how much he professed to miss me, he'd hurt me when he'd chosen a life with Carly and his other kids over a life with me. Besides, since then I'd experienced the touch of another. Jay might not be Mr Right—I didn't need a Mr Right—but he'd reminded me there were other options. And I deserved more than a man who was only ever going to be half-invested in me.

I leaned back in the seat and crossed my arms over my growing belly. 'How are Carly and the kids anyway?' What I meant was *Does Carly know you're here today and what have you told your three other offspring about ours?*

He sighed loudly. 'They're okay. Things have been a bit tense since I told her about us.'

'There is no us,' I said, clenching my jaw.

'You know what I mean. She wants to know how it's going to work when the baby arrives. She's worried about how our kids are going to handle it.'

'What about *our* child?' I said, unable to keep the irritation out of my voice. 'Our son or daughter is going to be branded with being the child of an affair, so forgive me if I'm more worried about that.'

Christos simply nodded and awkward silence followed. We certainly weren't like the other lovey-dovey pregnant couples sitting around us.

'So,' he said less than a minute later; he could never stand conflict. 'Do you want to find out the sex?'

'Yes. Gralice thinks I'm having a girl and I want to be able to tell her whether her intuition is right.'

'Knowing your grandmother, she probably is. How is she? What about the rest of your family?' I guess he thought it safer talking about my family dramas than our joint ones. 'It's been a big week for your mum.'

Although the major newspapers hadn't published anything about her yet, a number of online women's sites had and, because of me, everyone at work had taken it upon themselves to keep up to date with the scandal. My mother was the hottest topic around the water cooler at lunch time.

'Dad and Will are happy, Mum's pretending to be, and her followers seem to have bought her explanation and apology hook, line and sinker.'

Less than twenty-four hours after the news of Mum's lesbian love affair broke online, she was back at home, making dinner for my father and Instagramming the evidence. What was even more startling was the openly honest and self-deprecating vlog she'd posted, which had immediately become her most watched video ever. I'd thought she might try to pretend the thing with Rosa was a big misunderstanding but she surprised me by confessing that she had indeed cheated on her beloved husband. There'd even been tears in her video as she'd spoken about the shame she felt for taking her life partner for granted, for disrespecting his love, and how grateful she felt that he was prepared to give her a second chance.

I guess her confession and her request that her followers also find it in their hearts to forgive had made her seem more real and accessible, because in the end this 'scandal' had only elevated her profile. The positive and encouraging comments came fast and furious and her social media numbers had grown even higher, which had of course appeased Holly and Bourne Books.

Mum had declared that this 'short break' would only make her marriage stronger. She'd promised that over the coming weeks she'd share her efforts to repair the cracks in her marriage and asked her followers to contribute their stories and any tips they had for such success. So many other women had come out of hiding to tell tales of their own affairs and/or their fantasies of having them.

'You don't sound so sure?' Christos said now.

'I don't know what to believe about anything or *anyone* anymore.'

While Mum was all over-the-top positive and happy in her videos, I wasn't buying any of it. Dad was stoked about not being alone anymore, dining on all his fave meals again and not having to worry about running out of clean jocks, but were either of them actually *happy*? I had my reservations and Gralice agreed, but whenever either of us tried to talk to Mum about it she shut us down. The closeness the three of us had developed over the past few months seemed to have gone again, and now Mum was just taking care of all of us on autopilot.

Thinking about all this was making me cranky, so I was super happy when a stocky, balding man appeared on the edge of the waiting room and called my name.

'That's us.' Christos leapt to his feet.

'No, that's *me*,' I corrected, my jaw clenched.

We had a different sonographer today, who assumed Christos and I to be an item. 'Mum, jump up there on the bed,' he said as he held his door open for us. 'Is this your first baby?'

'It's Ged's first, but my fourth,' Christos informed, pride in his voice.

'Ah, so this isn't Dad's first rodeo, but it's nice the two of you can have a family together.'

I was about to put him straight, but Christos spoke over the top of me. 'Thank you, we are so excited and can't wait to find out what we're having.' There was probably was no point going into all the gory details with this poor guy anyway.

'Right. Let's get started, shall we?' Bald sonographer beamed and clapped his hands together—he seemed very enthusiastic considering he must do this day in day out.

I lifted my top and tried not to be self-conscious about baring my skin in front of Christos. It wasn't like he hadn't seen all this and more before, but it felt weird considering current circumstances. I tried to relax but the sonographer chose that moment to squeeze cold gel all over my skin and I gasped instead.

'Guess I didn't warm that up enough,' he chuckled. 'Okay, what have we here?'

'Hopefully a baby,' Christos said, and I laughed despite myself.

'Yes, definitely one of those,' said the older man, moving the wand slowly over my belly. Once again that lovely woh-woh-woh-woh-woh sound emanated from the computer and I couldn't help but smile.

'That's the heartbeat, right?'

The sonographer nodded. 'And it's lovely and strong.'

It really was the most splendid and beautiful sound in the whole wide world. I glued my eyes to the screen as the image became clearer. Last ultrasound Thing had been barely more than a jelly bean but this time ... 'Oh my goodness, look at its little head.'

'It's not *that* little.' The sonographer clicked a few buttons on the computer and a ruler appeared on the screen. 'I'd say you're having a big bubba.'

'Just how big?' I asked, anxious at the thought of having to squeeze anything out of my vagina. As a teenager I'd had enough trouble getting a tampon up there!

Again he chuckled. 'Don't look so worried—you'll be fine. The female body is made to do this and yours is taking very good care of this little one. Now, did you say you wanted to know the sex?'

'Yes, please,' Christos and I said in unison.

The sonographer moved the wand a little lower and the legs became the focus on the screen. 'What do you see between those little pins?'

As Christos peered at the screen, he leaned over me a little, and I got a whiff of the Abercrombie & Fitch cologne I'd always loved on him.

Ignoring it, I scrutinised the part of the screen between my baby's legs. 'I can't see anything.'

'Exactly,' proclaimed the sonographer as if he were a magician pulling a bunny out of a hat. 'That's because you're having a girl.'

'Gralice was right,' I said, although I wasn't sure anyone would have been able to make out my words as a flood of happiness burst from my eyes, immediately clogging up my throat. And I glanced at Christos to find him also blinking back tears.

'A little girl,' he whispered as our gazes locked.

In that moment I forgot we were no longer an item and found myself linking my fingers through his, taking comfort from the warmth of his hand. I wondered if our daughter would have dark, curly hair like his or straight, golden blonde like mine.

'I want to call her Gralice.' I shook my head and chuckled. 'I mean Alice.'

He nodded through the tears. 'Great idea.'

'Alice is a lovely name,' said the sonographer before finishing his checks and measurements, chatting like a sports commentator as he did. I hung on his every word, feeling a glow of pride as he told us how well Alice was growing. She had all ten fingers and all ten toes and I marvelled over every tiny bit of her.

It was only when the sonographer announced he was done and printed off a lovely strip of photos for us that I realised Christos and I were still holding hands. A lump formed in my throat as I thought about how different this could have been if only I'd conceived a few months earlier.

No way Christos would have agreed to some kind of fake home scenario with Carly if I'd *already* been pregnant with his child. Then all these experiences wouldn't be bittersweet. We wouldn't be exchanging emails about the best car seats and baby monitors, we'd be lying in bed at night talking about them instead. A wave of sadness washed over me—I missed that intimacy so damn much.

I extracted my hand and climbed off the table, thanking the sonographer as he passed me the photos.

'You're very welcome. And good luck with the next few months.'

'Let me buy you dinner,' Christos said as we headed out onto the street.

I frowned. 'It's not even five.' Not to mention the fact I didn't think it a good idea.

He smiled in a way that made me feel as if I'd swallowed warm marshmallows. 'Okay. How about a drink then?'

'I can't drink, and don't you have a family to be getting home to?'

'Carly's taking the kids to a movie, and I was thinking of hot chocolates. That cafe that does the ones with the real shaved chocolate on top is just around the corner.'

Damn, he knew my weak spots. By talking chocolate, he might as well have been talking dirty to me and I was helpless to resist. My mouth watered. What harm would it do to sit for a little longer with him?

'Okay. But I can't stay long. I've gotta visit Gralice tonight and I need to collect Coco first.'

'Oh, I'd almost forgotten about Coco,' Christos said as he gently placed his hand on my back and directed me down the footpath towards the cafe. 'How is she?'

'Frustrated with me as I'm not walking her nearly as much as I should lately.'

He chuckled. 'Maybe you should hire a dog walker.'

When we arrived, Christos insisted I sit while he ordered and, because it was the end of a long week and my feet were aching, I relented.

I was gazing down at the photos of the ultrasound when he joined me at the table a few minutes later. He shifted his chair closer so we could look together.

'I reckon we made a pretty adorable baby.'

'How can you tell? These 3D images might be good, but they're not *that* good. Maybe a pretty adorable alien?'

Our eyes met and held a few long moments. Although we'd been joking around, the air suddenly felt lacking in oxygen. I wondered if he too was thinking about *how* we'd actually made this baby.

'So … I hear you interviewed Shaun Wally the other day,' I said, needing to talk about something neutral, needing to forget how good we'd been together.

'Yeah, not that I had to do much interviewing. The man loves the sound of his own voice. The article will be in tomorrow's paper.'

'I'll check it out,' I lied, because I had no interest whatsoever in playboy cricketers.

'You worked on anything interesting lately?' he asked and as we spoke about work we slipped into our old habit of easy conversation.

The drinks arrived—along with a large slice of warm coconut cake Christos decided we needed—and I found myself more relaxed than I imagined I should be sitting with an ex who was also the father of my baby. So relaxed, in fact, that when Christos picked up the fork, dug into the cake and offered it to me, it was the most natural thing in the world to lean forward and let him feed me.

I moaned as the sweet flavours melted on my tongue.

'Good?' he asked with a grin.

I nodded, my mouth still full of cake.

He sighed and got a serious look in his eyes. 'I know you don't want to hear this, but I've missed you, Ged. Maybe you were supposed to get pregnant to give me clarity and make me see sense.'

I swallowed quickly. 'What are you saying?'

He ran a hand through his thick hair, then scooped up my hand. 'I want us to be together. You, me and Alice … a family.'

I blinked. 'But what about your other three children? What about your arrangement with Carly?'

'It was a stupid arrangement anyway. Carly and I … we fight all the damn time and the kids aren't silly, they can see that. I don't want them to think that's what a normal relationship is like. They might be upset if Carly and I break up again, but we'll get them counselling if need be, and when they see you and me together, they'll realise I made the right decision. You and me, Ged, we're the real deal.'

I couldn't believe what I was hearing but couldn't shake the thought that maybe he wouldn't be asking to get back together if I wasn't pregnant with his child. If it had turned out Jay was the father, would Christos still be declaring he wanted to be with me?

My toes curled in my shoes at the thought of Jay—it felt so long since I'd last seen him, but I still thought about him far too much. Despite having washed my sheets, I swore I could still smell his musky scent on my pillow and it drove me to insomnia.

At my hesitation, Christos spoke up. 'Is it the other guy?'

'What?' I felt my cheeks heat.

'The guy from the cruise—do you have feelings for him?'

'No,' I spoke firmly and shook my head. Even if I did have feelings for Jay—which I did *not*—I could never act on them; I needed to focus on the future. On me and Alice. Obviously that future would involve Christos on some level due to the fact he was Alice's father, but could I dare to hope that the future I'd once dreamed of was also possible?

'I'm wary,' I admitted. 'You hurt me when you chose Carly over me, and now I can't be sure whether you really love me or if you're only suggesting this for the sake of our baby.'

'I didn't *choose* Carly over you.' The words rushed from his mouth and he gripped both my hands tightly. 'I was trying to do the right thing by my family. It broke my heart, it broke *me* to hurt you, to leave you. You've got to believe me. My three kids mean the world to me but so do you, and now so does *our* baby. I love *you* and I want to make a life with all of us.'

I sighed, desperately wanting to believe him. We had been good together and the only reason he'd split with me was because he was trying to be a good father. Now that I felt the love for our own child—a tiny person I already knew I'd do anything for—I realised his decision wasn't black and white. And he'd never stopped caring about me, never stopped desiring me, or so he said. I thought of my mother and how being 'shared' between Gralice and Phil had affected her ... Sure single mums and broken homes were two a penny these days, but did I want that for my baby, for *our* baby?

Maybe I should give him a second chance, maybe I owed it to our daughter. It wasn't as though I didn't like Christos—up until a couple of months ago I *had* been envisaging spending the rest of my life with him—but I was scared. Scared of being hurt again.

And also, if I was honest with myself, scared of being taken advantage of. Motherhood in itself was something I was now looking forward to, but I knew how easy it could be to get trapped in traditional gender roles within the home and no way did I want to become my mother, or at least who she'd been while Will and I were growing up.

I didn't want to lose myself, to sacrifice my hopes, needs and desires because I was too busy keeping Christos and our baby happy.

'Ged?' he prompted. 'What do you say?'

'If we did get back together,' I began, my tone tentative, 'what would our relationship look like?'

His brow creased. 'What do you mean?'

'How would we work together in the home and as parents? I don't want to stop working, I—'

He laughed as if this was a preposterous notion. 'Of course not. I'd never expect that of you.'

'Maybe not, but in order to make sure my career doesn't flounder, I'd need to know you are willing to do your bit. I want us to be equal partners and equal parents—I don't want to do any more of the housework than you do. I know sometimes we'll have to make sacrifices for Th— for Alice's sake, but I want us both to make them.'

'Ged.' His voice was warm and his smile genuine as he squeezed my hands again. 'I'm totally supportive of your career—your professional goals and dreams are just as important as mine. Whatever issues Carly and I had, we were always on the same page regarding our careers. We worked together, and I expect to be just as involved in our child's life, in their schooling and everything, as you are. We're lucky in that our workplace is the same so we can look for childcare near the paper or we can hire an au pair or something. But whatever we decide, I promise you, we'll make those decisions together and we'll ensure that they work for all three of us. So ...' He pinned me with his eyes. 'What do you say? Do you want to get back together?'

'Okay,' I heard myself saying, almost unable to believe the word coming out of my mouth. But it was true, he was a great dad— very hands on and very supportive of Carly's career. Maybe with us working together my dreams of a promotion were still possible. Even if this one didn't work out due to the timing, I could apply for something else at a senior level following my maternity leave.

A massive grin burst on his face as he leaned in close and pressed his lips to mine, but I didn't allow the kiss to develop. We were in a public place and as far as anyone knew he was still with Carly, but more importantly, things were moving too fast.

'I need us to take things slow,' I said, holding up a hand. 'I need you to move out of your and Carly's home and work out proper custody arrangements with her going forward. We can start seeing each other again, but I'm not ready for us to move in together just yet.'

'Okay.' His shoulders slumped, but I wasn't going to be pressured into rushing.

'You sort things out at home and then call me. We'll take it from there.'

He nodded and stood, offering a hand to help me out of my seat. I wasn't so large that I needed such assistance yet, but I took it anyway.

'Goodbye, Christos.' I hitched my handbag onto my shoulder.

'Goodbye, Ged.' He offered me an optimistic smile as I turned and walked out of the cafe.

32

'Why are we here?' I asked Christos as we pulled up in front of my grandfathers' place.

We were supposed to be going to see a movie. I wasn't overly enthusiastic at the prospect to be honest, but Christos was making an effort for us to do things together as a couple and I didn't want to seem ungrateful. I *was* grateful, I just wasn't interested in the latest Marvel movie.

'I ran into Phil when I bought you those flowers the other day.' He smiled at me as he turned off the engine. 'I mentioned we were going and he said he and Craig wanted to see it too, so I suggested a double date.'

I frowned, wondering why this was the first he'd mentioned it, and also surprised by my grandfathers' desire to see the movie at all. Like me, they weren't big superhero film buffs.

'You should have told me—we can't leave Gralice alone.' This wasn't her type of movie and she probably wouldn't cope with the outing anyway. Two hours in a movie theatre didn't seem like much but it didn't *take* much to exhaust her these days.

'I think Phil has organised your mother to come over. She'll be fine.'

Kinda annoyed at his blasé attitude, I unclicked my seatbelt and climbed out. The least I could do was say hi and see how she was before we went to the movies without her.

I hurried up the garden path and entered the house without knocking.

'Surprise!'

'Oh my God!' At the sound and sight of all my family and friends, I jumped back and crashed into Christos as he came up behind me. Chuckling, he leaned in close and whispered his own 'surprise' into my ear.

I was gobsmacked and for a few moments just stared into the living room. Gralice was sitting up in her recliner, a conspiratorial grin on her face and the room was filled with flowers and pastel-coloured balloons.

'Oh my God.' I looked around at the many faces smiling back at me. Libby was there along with a few other colleagues from work, a couple of old school friends, my dad's sister and my cousins, Will and Sophie with Oliver in her arms and Charlotte hanging upside down off the back of the couch. I promptly burst into tears. Pregnancy meant waterworks were always a possibility.

I took a few seconds to pull myself together before starting around the room, greeting everyone and thanking them for coming. When I got to Gralice, I whispered, 'I can't believe you didn't tip me off about this.'

When Mum floated the idea of a gender reveal party a few weeks back, both Gralice and I had adamantly argued against the idea. So, she'd mentioned the possibility of a baby shower instead and I'd promised her I'd think about it.

'I was sworn to secrecy.' She winked, clearly happy to have been taken into Mum's confidence.

'How are you feeling today?' I asked, stooping to hug her.

'Much better for seeing you.' As I pulled back, she reached out and put her hand on my stomach. 'How's our girl today?'

'Little Alice is great.' I smiled as my grandmother's mouth fell open.

She took a moment to speak, blinking slowly when she did. 'Y-y-y-you're g-going to call your baby Al-Alice?'

'Yes,' I whispered. 'I think it's perfect, don't you?'

'I ...' Her eyes glistened with unshed tears and she nodded.

'So far, she's proving to be just as lively as her namesake,' I said as I tried to lighten the mood a little. 'She kicks all the time and keeps me awake all hours of the night.'

'You couldn't tell,' said Sam, one of my friends from uni, 'you look like you were born to breed. You're positively glowing.'

'Thank you.' I squeezed Gralice's hand as I stifled a laugh and tried to graciously accept the clearly fraudulent compliment—I was so huge I couldn't believe I still had seventeen weeks to go. My feet were already swelling after a long day and if it wasn't the baby's kicking keeping me awake at night, it was the heartburn. While apparently some women did pregnancy really well, I was not one of those people. But the sign of a good friend was someone willing to lie through their teeth to make you feel better.

'I know, isn't she gorgeous?' Christos placed his hand in the small of my back and I blushed, embarrassed by all the gushing.

'Good to see you again too, Christos,' Gralice said as he kissed her on the cheek. 'You better be treating my girl right.'

'I'm doing my best.'

And I had to agree that he was. It had been almost a month since we'd decided to try again; he'd moved out of his and Carly's house that very night and was temporarily staying with his parents. The kids were living with Carly in the family home, but he had them for dinner every Wednesday night and they stayed with him alternate weekends. So far so good. Isidore, Phoenix and Lexia seemed way more comfortable with this arrangement than they'd been with the 'nest'. I still hadn't seen them since the split, but next weekend we planned to have our first 'family' dinner together and I was looking forward to it.

Christos and I still hadn't consummated our second-time-around. He'd been very patient, saying he'd wait until I was ready, and although I wasn't entirely sure how we were supposed to navigate my bump, I felt as if that day might be getting closer.

'Anyway.' Christos cleared his throat. 'We might love you and leave you, so the party can get started.'

'Good idea,' my mother agreed.

'We?' I asked, ignoring her.

'Phil and Craig, your dad and Will. We're gonna make ourselves scarce and go get a drink. Have our own little celebration.'

While I felt a little awkward at the fact they felt the need to leave—it was Christos's baby as much as it was mine so why couldn't he enjoy the shower?—the pub on the corner made much more sense than a Marvel movie.

As the door closed behind them Mum forced me into a chair in the middle of everyone. It was decorated like a throne, with helium balloons tied to the back of it.

'Frank!' She raised her hand and clicked like she was summoning a waiter. Within seconds her new assistant appeared beside us—I hadn't even noticed him when I'd entered the room.

'It's *Franc*, Mum,' I reminded her as he asked what she needed.

I'd met Franc last weekend and immediately wanted to squeeze his cheeks and offer him lollies. Maybe it was my maternal instincts kicking in or maybe it was because he looked about fifteen. He was actually twenty-two and gay, so as not to cause Dad any anxiety (at least that was my and Gralice's theory), and his name was pronounced exactly like the wedding coordinator from *Father of the Bride*. I wanted to ask him if Franc was his real name but thought I'd wait until we were better acquainted.

'Are you getting all this on camera?' Mum barked.

Franc blinked a number of times in quick succession. 'I'm sorry, I didn't think you'd want me to film until we started.'

'We've started.' Mum spoke through gritted teeth and rolled her eyes indiscreetly at me as Franc lifted the camera and started it rolling.

'We're not gonna play any silly games, are we?' If I had to sniff baby food in a nappy and guess the flavour, I was liable to kill someone.

'No. We're going to play *many* silly games. My daughter doesn't have a baby every day—I want to get my money's worth. But first, presents.' Mum clapped her hands in excitement and glared at Franc. 'Can you bring the gifts over to Ged?'

'Um ...' He glanced at the camera in his hand.

'I'll get them.' Sam leapt up and collected the first present from an elaborately decorated table by the window.

'This one's from me,' she said as she returned and handed me a full basket. 'I wasn't sure what to get so I went for a selection. There's some things for you, some for baby, and even a Daddy Diaper Duty tool belt for Christos.'

'Thank you.' I laughed at the belt, which had pockets for baby wipes, nappy cream, baby oil but also a pair of gloves, a facemask, goggles and tongs.

I felt surprisingly emotional as I unwrapped the rest of the gifts. Although I was having a girl, there was *almost* no pink in sight among the gifts—everyone knew my hatred of the colour after my mother dressed me in nothing but cotton candy colours for the first ten years of my life.

It took almost half an hour to unwrap and gush over all the gifts and when I was almost finished I had more swaddle blankets than I could possibly need, a baby book I'd probably never fill, dozens of tiny clothes and a few pamper items for me as well. Mum's gift came second last.

'You shouldn't have bought me anything,' I chastised. 'You've already done enough by organising this shower.' Not to mention all the other little things she couldn't resist buying on an almost daily basis. If she kept it up, no way there'd be room for the baby in my apartment.

'Don't be silly.' Mum thrust a large *pink* parcel at me. I peeled back the wrapping and gasped at the sight of the most beautiful bag I'd ever seen.

'Oh my goodness!'

'You like it?'

'I love it.' And that was the truth. Our tastes didn't usually align but this tote with its black-and-white geometric pattern and brown leather handles was very stylish and exactly what I'd have picked for myself. Part of me wondered if Rosa had chosen it before they'd gone their separate ways. I made a mental note to send her an email and ask. I'd checked in with her a couple of times since she and Mum broke up because I missed her, but also wanted to make sure she was okay. She wasn't—there were signs of heartbreak in everything she said, but wallowing was not her style and neither was begging, so she was making the best of things and focusing on new clients.

'Baby bags have certainly improved since my day,' Mum said.

Gralice nodded. 'I wanted to burn that ghastly handmade patchwork one you carried around with Will and Ged.'

Everyone laughed and I put the bag aside as Sam delivered the last gift. I tore back the wrapping paper to reveal a stack of books. There were some of my old faves from childhood—*The Very Hungry Caterpillar*, *Spot the Dog*—and also more recent ones that Charlotte adored—*Where Is the Green Sheep* and *The Wonky Donkey*—but it was the book on the very bottom that cracked me up. *Go the Fuck to Sleep*.

'That one's for you,' Gralice said, 'but if she's anything like your mother was as a baby, you'll need it. That, and a good stash of gin on hand.'

Some of my friends who didn't know Gralice well looked appalled, others obviously thought she was joking, but I knew better, and I loved her for it.

'Thank you.' I put the pile of books on the floor and rushed over to hug her. 'This is my favourite present,' I whispered as my eyes prickled with tears again.

She squeezed me back as tightly as she could before clearing her throat. 'Now, haven't we got some games to play?'

When I pulled back I saw her eyes were watery as well. I was going to miss her so damn much.

'Frank,' Mum hollered. 'Have you got the items for Feed the Baby ready?'

'Um.' He looked at the camera in his hand.

Mum sighed theatrically. 'Didn't I give you the schedule? I told you to have all the props for the games ready on time and why is there still gift wrapping all over the floor? I asked you to collect it as Ged unwrapped everything.'

Franc looked as if he were about to cry.

'Mum, he's not a superman. He can't film *and* do all that.'

'I'll get the props.' Again, Sam leapt up and left the room.

'Right.' Mum's tone was almost manic. 'We need eight volunteers.'

'What are we volunteering for?' asked Libby.

'You'll find out soon enough,' she replied, 'but the winning duo gets a bottle of champagne each.'

Libby, ever competitive, shot her hand up in the air—'I'll do it!'—and a number of others followed. There was only a small collective groan when Mum announced they were about to feed each other baby food while blindfolded. By the end of the game everyone was laughing so hard they were crying, even those with pureed apple smeared all over their faces, and Libby was very pleased when she and Ameerah (a woman who worked with Christos in Sports) were declared the winners.

Next came a few less messy games, and finally we all had to try and make a baby out of play-dough. Mine was dismal; it looked something like a creature Jay might find on Mars. My innards squeezed at the thought and I quickly pushed him out of my mind.

While I had to admit the games were rather fun, my favourite part of the day was afternoon tea. It was so lovely to spend time chatting with people I hadn't seen in a while and getting tips and advice from those who'd travelled this path before me.

When the house was finally empty of guests, Mum flopped down into a plush floral armchair as if she'd just run a marathon and glared at her new assistant. 'Well, don't just stand there, make yourself useful and get me a cup of tea.'

Franc nodded, retreating into the kitchen like a mouse dashing away from a cat.

'You're way too harsh on that poor boy,' Gralice tsked.

Mum sighed. 'He interviewed well and his credentials were good—he has an actual degree in social media—but I have to feed him every little thing. He has no initiative. I might have to look for someone else.'

I suspected no matter who she hired they wouldn't cut the mustard, simply because they weren't Rosa, but I bit my tongue.

Franc delivered tea, not just for my mother, but for all of us and then made himself scarce, beginning to clean up while we sat and chatted. As Charlotte scribbled in her colouring book and Oliver fell asleep in my arms—resting his head on my bump—Gralice yawned. Although she'd barely moved from her recliner, the events of the day had clearly exhausted her.

I glanced at my watch, wondering when Christos would return. I was contemplating giving him a call when there was a loud kerfuffle outside. The front door opened and my brother stumbled through—clearly drunk—with Christos following, clearly even drunker. Craig and Phil were singing 'When I Fall in Love' loudly at the top of their voices. Dad appeared to be the only sober one among them, which, considering his near alcoholic state recently, was both a surprise and a blessing.

'How was the baby shower, love?' he asked me.

'It was wonderful. Looks like you guys had quite the celebration as well.'

'Yes, I'd better put the kettle on. Coffees all round for this lot, I think.'

While Dad went off to organise this, Christos managed to make it over to me, only twice banging into the extra chairs. He stooped down and flung his arms around me, almost crushing poor Oliver in the process. 'How's the beautiful muvvar of my bay-bee?'

'Get away.' I shooed him off as if he were a pesky mosquito and stood to give my nephew back to Sophie.

'I think I'd better be getting these guys home,' she said, giving Will a stern look. 'Someone's going to have a sore head tomorrow.'

'More than one someone I'd say.'

I helped Sophie bundle the kids into the car because it was clear my brother was going to be no use at all, and then went inside to deal with my own drunk, only to find him passed out on the sofa.

Shaking my head, I let him rest while I helped Dad and Franc return the house to some semblance of normal.

'Will you be okay with these two?' I asked Gralice, referring to my grandfathers who were currently sitting at Phil's piano singing show tunes from the fifties.

She smiled warmly in their direction. 'We'll be fine. They're not as drunk as they sound, but will you be okay getting Christos home?'

'I'll help her,' Dad offered as he collected Gralice's cup and took it off to the kitchen.

I took my grandmother's hand. 'Today was surprisingly fun, wasn't it?'

'You know it's the first baby shower I've ever been to.'

'Really?'

She nodded. 'Something to tick off my bucket list, I guess. And yes, it was fun, I just wish ...' Her voice trailed off, but I knew exactly what she wanted to say.

Gralice wanted to live long enough not only to meet my daughter but to be a great-grandmother to her as well. A rough lump swelled in my throat; I would absolutely give anything for that to happen, but it had been almost six months since her diagnosis and Christmas was rapidly approaching.

She was sick enough that I thought she'd have taken things into her own hands by now, yet here she was, not great, but still living the drama with all of us.

Was she hoping for a miracle? Did she just want a little more time with Mum? Or was she trying to hang out long enough to meet her namesake? I guessed it was probably the latter, and part of me loved her for this but another part of me knew it was a sacrifice. I glanced around to check everyone else was still occupied and was about to ask her outright, but she got in first.

'Are you happy?'

I frowned, startled by her question. 'What do you mean?'

She glanced towards my slumbering boyfriend. 'You and Christos, is it the real deal?'

I answered without hesitation. 'Yes, of course. We had a little bump in the road but he's so supportive. He's the one I want to be with and—' I placed a hand on my bump. 'Have a family with.'

Right now, I wasn't that enamoured with Christos—possibly because I was jealous of him being able to celebrate our baby with alcohol while I had to abstain, but at least he was excited. And obviously things weren't ever going to be the same as when we were first dating, but I reminded myself that this kind of comfortable relationship was what I'd wanted.

What made a relationship more real than a baby?

'Okay.' She patted my hand. 'Just make sure you're being true to your heart.'

'I am,' I promised.

'Good.' Gralice smiled wistfully. 'If only I could believe the same of your mother.'

I glanced over at Mum, who was still slumped in the armchair but now drinking straight from one of the leftover champagne bottles. 'She'll be alright,' I said. 'She's just had a lot to deal with lately.'

I wasn't sure I believed this any more than my grandmother did.

Once the house was almost back to what it looked like before, my dad helped me get Christos into his car. I was annoyed that I'd have to drive him home and catch an Uber back to my place.

'You could just stay with me,' he said with a slur as I leaned in through the passenger door and clicked his seatbelt into place.

It was clear he had one thing on his mind, but I wasn't about to re-consummate our relationship when he smelled like a brewery.

33

I was in the State Library doing research for Gralice's biography when my phone vibrated on the desk in front of me. Heartburn filled my chest as I glanced down at the screen to see it was my grandmother. Ever since I'd found out about her cancer, every single call from her made me anxious. Even though logically I knew she was probably just calling to chat, I gathered up my things and quickly headed out of the building where I'd be free to talk.

The phone had stopped buzzing during the time it took me to get outside, so I leaned against a pillar and called her back immediately.

Never one for gratuitous greetings, Gralice cut straight to the chase. 'I need you to come over.'

My heartburn intensified. 'Are you okay? Has something happened?'

'I'll explain everything when you get here.'

'Okay. I'm just at the library so, traffic allowing, I can be there in just over half an hour.'

When I arrived exactly twenty-nine minutes later, I saw Mum's and Will's cars out the front. Inside I found Gralice sitting up in her recliner, Phil in one of the two floral armchairs and my mother and brother sitting together on the sofa as if they were waiting for a school principal. There was a sombre mood in the room, as if someone had died.

Was Gralice about to give us a living reading of her will or something? Worse, was she about to confess all and give each of us a final goodbye? Either way I felt in dire need of an antacid.

'What's going on?' I asked as Craig came in from the kitchen carrying a tray of tea and biscuits. He sat it on the coffee table and proceeded to pour tea for everyone into floral bone china cups.

'No idea.' Mum glanced suspiciously at Gralice as she picked up a teacup. 'But, as we're all here now, maybe you can tell us what this is all about?'

Gralice cleared her throat and looked straight at my mother. 'Are you happy, Sappho?'

Mum blinked. 'What kind of question is that?'

'Because I don't think you are.' Gralice chanced a quick glance at Phil.

'And we agree,' he said taking hold of Craig's hand. 'These last few weeks since you returned to Tony it's been like watching a butterfly retreat back into its cocoon.'

'It's been devastating to see,' Gralice added, fiddling with a large ring she wore on her non-wedding finger, now so loose it was more like a finger-bangle.

'What?' Mum looked outraged. 'I'm ... I'm ...' She stammered to find the right words. 'Tony and I are just taking time to find our feet again, but we'll get there.' She glanced down into her tea and I noticed her fingers were shaking around the fancy cup.

'I'm not sure whether you really believe that or if you're purposely lying to yourself,' Gralice said, 'but I can't stand by while you deny your true self—your true love—without doing something about it.'

Oh no, a shiver scuttled down my spine as I had a sudden premonition of what was to come.

'What do you mean her *true* self?' Will scoffed, a biscuit halfway to his mouth. 'Her true self is being married to Dad, a mother to us and a grandmother. Just ask all her hundreds of followers.'

'I think you'll find it's hundreds of *thousands*, William,' Gralice corrected, 'not one of which I give a damn about. What I care about is my daughter, and it's time to tell her the truth.'

Oh God. My heart thumped. Was this how Jay felt when he knew there was a bomb about to explode and there was nothing he could do about it?

'What truth?' Mum asked, her voice a little shaky.

Gralice let out a deep sigh. 'Fifty-five years ago, I was madly in love with a man called Henry French. He was kind, noble, intelligent, funny—everything I could have ever hoped to have in a life partner, so different from the man who had raised me and my brother. We were on the same page about almost everything, except he wanted to get married and I did not. When Henry proposed, I turned him down. I chose my principles over my heart, and I lost him. I cared too much about my work and also about what people might think about me. I believed others would see my agreeing to get married as turning my back on my beliefs, which I'd already been loud and vocal about. I wanted to be seen as a strong independent woman who could take care of herself and who followed her dreams. But sometimes I wonder if, in choosing what I thought mattered, in fighting for what I believed in, I sacrificed too much. I have—'

'Hang on,' Will interrupted, a frown creasing his brow, 'but Mum's fifty-five.'

He'd always been the maths brain of the family and it was all he needed to say.

Our mother gasped, horror flashing across her face as she looked from Gralice to Phil and back again. The truth was out without anyone actually saying the words. 'Oh my God. Is this Henry person my father?'

Gralice, Phil and Craig nodded glumly in unison.

'But ...' Mum shook her head, looking as if she was on the verge of tears. 'I don't understand.'

So, Gralice told her everything, and while I'd heard this story before, it wasn't any less confronting the second time around, perhaps because this time I was witnessing Mum hearing it. Watching her in pain as she learned that much of what she believed about her life had been a lie was excruciating.

'Nobody else has ever come close to making me feel the way Henry did,' Gralice admitted. 'I should have married him and given us the chance ... the chance to be an equal partnership. I've lived with this remorse all my life, and I don't want you, my precious daughter, to die with similar regrets. If you can look me in the eye and tell me you're back with Tony because that's what you truly want in your heart, I'll accept it.' She looked to Phil and Craig. 'We all will, but if there's any doubt, if you have *any* lingering feelings for Rosa, you need to think very carefully about what you're sacrificing by denying those feelings.'

'I ... I can't believe what I'm hearing.' Mum pressed her hand against her chest, totally ignoring the reference to Rosa. 'Are you saying I could have been raised in a happy family with one mother and one father rather than in a circus that made me the laughing stock of the school? You stood by, knowing kids were teasing me because my dad was a fag, when it wasn't even the truth!'

I winced as I saw the hurt flash across Phil's face but Mum barrelled on.

'Are you saying I have a father out there somewhere who would have loved me, if you'd just given him the chance? That I could have had brothers and sisters and ...'

'Yes, and I'm sorry,' Gralice said when Mum's words finally dried up. 'I know that will never be enough, but don't make the same mistakes I did. Don't forsake your truth, don't lose the true love of your life for something that won't mean anything in the end. All those followers you have online—they might make you feel special—but Rosa—'

'Don't tell me what to do! How to feel!' Mum sprang to her feet, and the look in her eyes had me fearing for a moment that she was about to lash out physically at Gralice. Phil and Craig leaned forward as if ready to intervene, but her attack was merely verbal. 'You're despicable. I don't know how you've lived with this secret, this lie. I always thought you cared about your work and your causes, even your students, more than me, and now I know it's the truth. I will never *ever* forgive you for this.'

She snatched her handbag off the floor.

Phil stood and reached out. 'Darling, I know you're upset but—'

'And you! You're as bad as she is,' Mum snarled. 'Was it all a bit of fun to you? You weren't man enough to have a baby yourself so you—'

'That's enough!' Craig shot up. His voice, louder and sharper than I'd ever heard before, rose over the top of Mum's. 'I won't have you standing here in my house abusing my husband.'

'That's fine, because I'm leaving, and I won't be coming back.'

Gralice's face crumbled as Mum stormed out of the house, slamming the door behind her. I knew what it must have taken for her to make this decision. She and Mum were finally mending rifts, but she'd risked all that because she thought it was the best for her daughter. I knew she hadn't done this lightly, but I wished she'd given me a little advance warning. Maybe together we could have come up with another, less drastic plan to make Mum reassess her relationship situation.

I felt torn between staying and comforting Gralice or rushing after my mother, who'd just had the biggest shock of her life.

'You go after Sappho,' Phil said, reading my mind. 'She won't want to talk to me right now.'

'Okay.' I grabbed my bag and hurried to the door.

Mum's car was shooting out the driveway as I emerged outside and she almost took out the letterbox in her haste. I sped after her, not sure what I'd say when I caught up.

She shot through an amber light and I cursed as I slammed on my brakes. It seemed to take forever but finally the light turned green and I continued on, pulling over a few minutes later when I saw her little yellow hatchback parked on the side of the road.

'Oh, Mum,' I said, slightly out of breath as I opened the passenger door and climbed in beside her. She was hunched over the steering wheel, crying. I put my hand on her shoulder. This was new to me, having to take care of her, but weirdly it made me feel closer to her than ever before.

There was a long period of silence—well, aside from her sobs—before she finally lifted her head. 'Phil's not my father.'

'Not biologically, but he's always treated you like a daughter. Family is about more than DNA. He loves you like you're his own and, I know you're angry but, Gralice loves you too. She's not perfect. None of us are. She made a mistake. All of us do.'

But apparently it was too early for such platitudes.

'A *mistake*, Geraldine, is putting the rubbish out on the wrong day or using plain flour when the recipe called for self-raising. A *mistake* is turning up late to an appointment because you got the time wrong. Lying to your daughter her whole life about who her father is cannot be regarded as a mistake. My mother didn't make a mistake, she made a cold, calculated decision to put her wants and dreams above her daughter's. Above mine. I would never do anything like that to you.'

'It might seem that way,' I began, 'and I promise I'm not trying to make allowances or excuses for her, but it sounds like she lost something too when she chose not to marry Henry. It sounds like she very much regrets that decision now. She's trying to make things right, before it's too late.'

Mum snorted. 'Too late? I'm fifty-five years old. The damage is done. I don't even know who I am.'

Okay, so maybe she needed a little more time.

I'd been angry when I first found out, but that was more due to the fact I might have conceived a baby with my secret cousin. Once that possibility had been eliminated—*thank God*—I'd been able to see things differently, but this affected my mother so much more.

Although I understood her fury, I honestly didn't know what to say to begin to make her feel better, but I tried. 'You are a kind, caring, talented, smart, wonderful woman and mother, and—'

'I don't even know who my father is,' she interrupted. 'Did she say his name was Henry? For all I know he's dead and he never even knew I existed.'

A lump formed in my throat. Should I tell her about Jay? Should I tell her that I knew for a fact Henry *was* alive and it wouldn't be too hard for me to help her track him down? Would she *want* to meet him? And if she did, how would he take the news? What if he didn't want to have anything to do with her?

There were so many questions whirling through my head and yet no sure answers.

I would risk my mother's wrath if I admitted that I'd already known Gralice's secret for some time, but maybe it would be better to come clean now, rather than let the betrayal fester and grow.

'He's alive,' I told her, bracing for the fall-out. 'And I know how to find him.'

'What?' Her eyes widened as she looked at me like I was a stranger speaking in tongues. 'How?'

I swallowed and began. Her eyebrows moved closer and closer to her hairline and the anger in her eyes became more visible with every sentence, but I pushed past the fear and gave her every last detail, apologetic about the part I'd played.

'It's okay.' She grabbed my hand and brought it up to her chest. 'This is *not* your fault. Gralice put you in an impossible position. She should never have asked you to keep such a thing from me, she should never have lied in the first place.'

Relief that Mum wasn't raging at me washed over me and I hoped perhaps in time I could help her come to see things from Gralice's point of view. To maybe even find it in her heart to forgive her. Although immediately a little voice inside my head reminded me our time wasn't infinite. I fought the urge to stand up for my grandmother because any attempts to reunite them would perhaps be better left until Mum had some time to calm down.

'Thank you,' I said instead. 'I'm sorry this has happened to you, but I'm here for you whatever you decide to do. Do you think you might want to reach out to Henry?'

I felt a ridiculous little kick of excitement at the possibility of seeing Jay again. Of course, he'd be furious when he heard what Gralice had done to his grandfather—and I couldn't imagine Christos being pleased by the idea of me contacting Jay either—but I wouldn't let either of these possibilities stop me from helping Mum.

With a heavy sigh, she let go of my hand. 'It's too soon. I've only just found out that Phil isn't my real dad, I need time to digest all of this before I decide about Henry.'

'I understand. But about the other stuff Gralice said?'

Mum frowned. 'What stuff?'

I swallowed, feeling as if I was betraying my father. 'About Dad and Rosa and your feelings for both of them.'

She took a long time replying. 'I think I might need a little time to wrap my head around that as well.'

355

After Mum assured me she wasn't going to do anything silly, I returned to my car and headed back to Phil and Craig's to check on Gralice. She was sleeping when I arrived.

'How is she?' I whispered.

Phil replied in an equally low voice. 'She cried herself to sleep.'

Oh God, what a mess. 'I'm guessing she told you I already knew about Henry being Mum's dad.'

My granddads nodded.

'Did you agree with her that this … this confession was a good idea?'

'We talked long and hard about it,' Phil said, 'and although we worried about how Sappho might take it, we couldn't think of any other way to shock her into seeing sense.'

'I just wish you'd given me a little warning.' I looked around. 'Where's Will?'

'He had to go home and help with the kids,' Craig informed me.

'Really?' I couldn't help feeling irritated he'd bailed on all the drama. 'Did he say anything about all this?'

'He was angry, but I don't think for the reasons he should be,' Phil said. 'He's angry that Alice and I are interfering in your parents' marriage. He thinks we're encouraging feelings in Sappho that aren't there because of our own feelings.'

I rolled my eyes; perhaps it was a good thing Will had left after all.

'Did you find Sappho?' Craig asked.

I nodded.

'How is she?' Phil's voice was shaky.

'She's understandably in shock, but we had a good talk and I'll check in with her again tonight.'

'Did it work?' Phil asked. 'Has it made her think about who she wants to be with, do you think?'

'To be honest, Granddad—' Could I still call him that? 'I don't think that's the first thing on Mum's mind right now. She's confused and doesn't know what she thinks or feels about any of it, but when she drove off, she wasn't going in the direction of home. I think she may have been heading to Rosa's.'

Both Phil's and Craig's eyes lit up and I understood their hope. Gralice and Phil's confession would be for nothing if Mum didn't admit and face up to her true feelings—feelings that to the rest of us (except Dad and Will) were as clear as day.

'Can I get you a cup of tea or something to eat?' Craig asked.

I wanted to go home to my quiet apartment, snuggle up with Coco on the couch and try to unwind for a bit, but I thought perhaps I should wait until Gralice woke up so we could debrief. 'A cup of tea would be lovely.'

We went into the kitchen so as not to disturb Sleeping Beauty and once again Craig did the honours. He and Phil tried to make conversation, asking me about work, about my pregnancy, and whether I'd decided on a colour scheme for the non-existent nursery, but none of us were fully invested in the conversation.

When an hour later Gralice still hadn't woken up and I was struggling to contain my yawns, Phil said, 'Go home. We'll tell Alice you were here, but she obviously needs the rest, and it looks like you do as well.'

I didn't even pretend to put up a fight. 'Thank you. I should take Coco for a walk anyway. She's been cooped up since early this morning.'

My grandfathers walked me to the front door. 'I'll call Gralice tonight,' I promised as I hugged them goodbye.

I was asleep on the couch when Christos buzzed me to let him in late that afternoon and although I'd been slumbering an hour or so, I didn't feel any less fatigued.

His face fell when I opened the door to him. 'You look ghastly.'

'Gee, thanks,' I said, already turning back towards the couch.

'Have you forgotten we have a dinner booking for half an hour?'

'I'm sorry but I'm not in the mood to go out.'

Christos liked eating in fine dining establishments and once upon a time I had too, but half the stuff I couldn't eat at the moment and, even more disappointingly, I couldn't drink any wine. Even if I hadn't had such a shit day, what was the point in having to put on make-up and high heels if I couldn't reap the culinary rewards?

Christos lifted my legs so he could sit beside me on the couch. 'What's the matter?'

Where the hell should I start?

'Gralice called a family meeting today and told Mum that Phil isn't her father.'

'Wow,' he said when I'd finished explaining everything, 'but why tell her now? Is your grandmother trying to ease her conscience or something before she dies?'

I flinched at his last words. 'No, she told Mum because she regrets not following her heart. She's never forgotten or stopped loving Henry and she doesn't want Mum to make the same mistake.'

While I was at it, I told him about the Jay connection—I'd had enough of harbouring secrets for a lifetime. 'So, I hope you'll forgive me if I say I'd rather cancel dinner.'

He nodded. 'Of course. How about I order us in some takeaway?'

No sweeter words had ever been uttered. 'That would be wonderful.'

While Christos called the local Indian restaurant, I phoned Gralice and promised to keep her informed about Mum. Next, I called my mother, but it went straight to voicemail. I left a message saying I hoped she was okay, that she could call me any time but if not, I'd try again tomorrow.

The takeaway arrived, and Christos and I sat together on the couch stuffing our faces as we watched *Sister Act* on the TV. It was the perfect choice because I'd watched it so many times I didn't need to pay too close attention, yet it still made me laugh, which was exactly what I needed. I was smiling at the Pope giving the nuns a standing ovation when Christos suddenly spoke.

'I think it's time for us to move in together. If I'm here 24/7 or you're with me, I'll be better able to support you.'

My heart froze. 'I'm not living with you at your parents' place!'

'That's not what I had in mind. I could move in with you while we look for something together?' He placed a hand on my belly and smiled. 'Something big enough to accommodate all three of us.'

'You mean all four of us,' I said, gesturing to Coco who was lounging on the floor by our feet.

'Yes. Exactly. What do you say?'

I hesitated. Was this what I wanted? My brain said yes, but something niggled inside me. The lure of having a room I could actually make into the nursery I'd been fantasising about was strong, but I didn't want to make such a big decision in my current frame of mind.

'Can I give you an answer tomorrow? I can't think straight tonight.'

'Of course. You've got a lot going on.' Christos leaned in closer and the hand on my belly crept a little higher. My insides squeezed as he cupped my breast and whispered, 'How about I try and take your mind off all that?'

And, although I was emotionally exhausted, I finally let him.

34

The phone call from my mother came five days later, when I was at work writing an article about Victoria's ghost towns. 'I want to meet my father, Geraldine.'

I blinked, unsure why this came as a surprise. Mum had been very quiet for a few days. I checked in with her on a daily basis, and each time she'd told me she was doing okay, still mulling everything over. Her online accounts had been quiet too, with no vlogs and only a couple of Instagram posts of cakes she'd baked. I'd seen Gralice daily, and to say she'd gone downhill terribly since the weekend would be an understatement. Craig and Phil's house had always been such a lively and happy place but now it was as if a storm cloud had set up permanent residence above it. My grandfathers said Gralice spent much of her time napping and they were gravely concerned for her mental health as well as her physical.

I knew she'd tried to speak to Mum, but I also knew all her attempts had been ignored. Phil and Craig had also tried to reach out, but she'd refused to talk to them either. Whenever I broached the subject of her parents with my mother, she flat out refused to enter such discussions and I worried that if they didn't talk soon, Gralice would decide the emotional pain was worse than the physical pain and end it all.

All my life I'd felt torn between Mum and Gralice on some level, but this ... this was worse than ever because this wasn't about differences of opinion, this was about matters of the heart. I loved them both and this rift between them was tearing me to pieces.

'Geraldine, are you still there?'

'Yes. Sorry. So, you want to meet Henry?'

'Yes. Are you still willing to help me?'

'Of course.' I swallowed. 'How do you want to do this?'

'Well, I'm guessing this is going to come as a bit of a shock to him, so I want to break the news as gently as possible. I'd like to meet him, but don't want to cause any problems with his wife or other children.'

I agreed—it would be best to avoid as much hurt as possible.

'So I was thinking maybe you could talk to your friend.' My stomach twisted at her mention of Jay. I was fairly certain he wouldn't classify us as friends anymore and he was going to be shocked to discover we were cousins. 'Ask what he thinks the best way to tell Henry is. You can tell him I'm prepared to do a DNA test—why should he believe Gralice's word? We already know she's a liar.'

I ignored this last bit, hoping that if Mum did meet Henry and it wasn't too much of a catastrophe, perhaps she'd be ready to begin the healing process with Gralice and Phil. Surely one lie—albeit a rather big one—shouldn't overshadow all the good in those fifty-five years.

'Okay. I'll talk to Jay and let you know how it goes.'

'Thank you, darling.'

My hand shook as I disconnected the call and I couldn't for the life of me remember what I'd been writing about. All I could think about was the fact I was on the brink of seeing Jay again.

Should I engineer a 'random' meeting—if I hung out at the park long enough, he was bound to turn up—and just casually drop into the conversation that my mother was his grandfather's illegitimate first child? Or should I send him a message requesting an audience? He might assume I wanted a hook-up and quite possibly just ignore me. Eventually, I decided the best course of action was simply to turn up at his place and try my luck.

For the rest of the day, I did my best to focus on my article—it was fascinating how many spooky stories there were about regional Australia—and when it was finally time to knock off, I packed up my things and headed home. I wasn't chickening out, but taking Coco to Jay's with me would be a good way to break the ice. Even if he no longer liked me, I was sure he'd be happy to see my dog.

A feeling of déjà vu washed over me as we approached his house—it seemed destined that this place was to be the setting of monumental conversations for us. Although my scalp prickled at the thought, another part of me was a tad excited at the prospect of seeing him again. I wondered if this was how someone felt before they were about to go bungee jumping or sky-diving. Perhaps I'd ask him.

As I rapped on his front door, my heart thumped loud and fast. Of course, he might not even be home, so I might be getting myself all worked up for nothing. I'd barely had this thought when the door swung open and Jay stood there wearing nothing but a pair of black shorts. The sight of his bare chest flustered me.

'Geraldine?' He screwed up his face as if his eyes were deceiving him.

I shook my head, trying to rid it of the sight of Jay nearly naked, and spoke in an over-the-top chipper tone. 'Yep, it's me. Hello again.'

Coco was jumping up at Jay, demanding attention. He absentmindedly reached out to ruffle her fur, but his eyes went to my belly. By my calculations it had been eleven weeks since we'd last seen each other and my abdomen had almost doubled in size since then. He probably found the sight of me grotesque, but I wasn't here to please him.

'You look ...'

'Fat?'

He shook his head. 'Pregnancy becomes you.'

Those were not at all the words I'd expected to fall from his lips. 'Well, thank you,' I said eventually. 'I'm having a little girl.'

'Congratulations.'

'I read the article about you,' I said, in an aim to fill the awkward silence.

'Did you?' He almost smiled. 'I thought they might have sent you to interview me when I agreed to do it.'

Did that mean he'd *wanted* to see me?

Another few moments of awkwardness followed and then we both spoke at once.

'Why are you here?'

'Can I come in? There's something I need to talk to you about.'

Jay's posture grew rigid and he yanked his hand from Coco's fur. 'You haven't discovered the baby's mine?'

'No.' I almost laughed at his terror. 'It's nothing to do with the baby.'

'Okay.' He stepped back, curiosity scrawled across his face. 'Come in then.'

Jay closed the door behind us and headed into the kitchen. I followed to find him at the sink filling a large stainless-steel bowl with water. He placed it on the floor and Coco immediately began lapping it up.

'Can I get you something to drink? Do you wanna sit here?' He gestured to the bar stools at the kitchen counter. 'Or should we go into the lounge room?'

'Either. But do you reckon you could put a shirt on first?'

'There was a time you liked my bare skin.'

He raised an eyebrow. Was he flirting with me? Oh God, he had no idea how inappropriate that comment was, but I *did* know better.

'Relax,' he said after a few moments. 'Make yourself at home and I'll be back in a minute.'

I perched on one of the stools, but in my current state it wasn't very comfortable, so I migrated to the lounge room and sat on his brown leather sofa to wait. True to his word, he returned less than two minutes later, thankfully fully clothed.

'So, what's this all about?' he asked as he lowered himself onto the couch beside me, leaned back and rested his arm way too close to my shoulders.

I took a deep breath and cleared my throat. 'You know how my grandmother and your grandfather know each other?'

His brow creased a little and I could tell he was thinking back to that day on the ship. 'That's right.'

'Well, they were more than just friends. They were an item. A pretty serious item. In fact, your granddad proposed to her.'

'Really?'

I nodded.

'And she turned him down?' He sounded both offended and confused.

'It's a long story but the short answer is yes. So they broke up, but not long after that she discovered she was pregnant. With my mother.'

'Are you saying my granddad was the father of her baby?'

I nodded.

For the first time since we'd met he appeared to have been rendered speechless. 'How long have you known this?' he said eventually.

It would be easy to tell him I'd only found out a few days ago, but I was through with lies. 'I've known since the day I asked you for the paternity test, but my mother only found out last weekend. She's decided she'd like to meet Henry. Your grandfather,' I added stupidly as if he needed me to join the dots for him.

I braced myself for Jay's anger, but 'I see' was all he said.

'Look, I understand this is a shock, which is why we decided it best to talk with you first. Mum doesn't want to cause trouble for Henry but she's understandably curious, and due to his age, she doesn't want to wait forever.'

'I understand.'

After a pregnant pause, I said, 'So how do you think Mum and I should go about this? Should she send him a letter, phone him or—'

'I'll tell him. Have you got a photo or something?'

Dammit, I didn't think to bring one. Then I remembered her online presence. I dug my phone out of my bag, opened Instagram and found a recent selfie she'd posted. 'Here.'

Jay nodded. 'Send it to me.'

'Can you see any family resemblance?'

'Oh, yeah, she's got the famous French nose and chin alright.'

'So how do you think he'll react? Will he agree to meet her?' Although I still wanted Phil and Craig to be my baby's great-grandfathers and to teach her all about flowers as they had done me, I was curious to meet this mysterious side of my family. 'Or do you think he'll be too angry?'

'Henry's not that kind of person. If I were him I'd be furious at your grandmother for what she's done, but he'll probably find it in his heart to forgive her. And even if he is angry, he won't hold that against your mother.'

I had to fight the urge to stick up for Gralice. Although I understood the anger, I couldn't help feeling protective. 'What about *your* grandmother?'

'She'll be okay. This was before her time *and* long ago. She loves Henry and won't want to make this any harder for him than it already might be.'

She sounded like a saint, but I couldn't help feeling a little resentful of this stranger. I guessed technically she must be my step-grandmother, but no matter how lovely, she'd never come close to Gralice in my heart. Once again, I felt tears imminent at the thought of losing her and said the first thing that came into my head to distract myself.

'So, how about that? You and me are cousins.' I grimaced. Possibly it would have been better to ignore this fact, but now that it was out there, it couldn't hurt to have some ground rules. 'Let's agree never to speak of our intimacy again.'

We did *not* want this to become some mortifying story people shared at family Christmases.

Jay snorted and shook his head. 'We're not related, Geraldine.'

I was outraged. 'I assure you Gralice is not lying—you said yourself there's a family likeness. But Mum's prepared to do a DNA test if need be.'

'I believe you. That's not what I meant.'

I frowned. 'Huh?'

'Henry's daughter Sally and her husband Tim are my foster parents. Sal and Tim took Kate and me in after we'd been in numerous different foster homes apart for years.'

'Why were you in foster care?' I blurted, the journalist in me asking the first question that came into my head.

His expression darkened a few long moments and I was about to apologise—it was none of my business—when he said, 'Because my mother was murdered by her drug dealer.'

'Oh God.' This made me feel sick on so many levels. 'What about your father? He wasn't around to help?'

'He was her drug dealer, so he was in jail.'

If I'd been shocked by the beginning of his story, this part left me reeling. I got the feeling Jay wasn't the type to want pity so I had no idea what to say. I glanced over and my heart went out to the little kids in the photo frame next to his TV. Maybe this explained a few things about Jay. He'd not only lost his mother to domestic violence, but likely had to deal with the stigma that came being the son of a criminal—of a drug dealer *and* murderer. I could only imagine how many times as a child, and even as an adult, people had asked him about his mother. What had he told them? Had he had to repeat this horrific story, over and over again?

I wondered if that's why he'd chosen to go into the police, to even the score or something. It also explained why he was so prickly about all men being swept under the banner of bad. Did he fear he might be cut from the same cloth as his father? Maybe Kate wasn't the only one suffering a form of paranoia.

'So it wasn't Henry's daughter that was murdered? Or *his* son that went to jail?' I asked, needing to wrap my head around this but trying to remember I wasn't interviewing someone for an article. This was Jay's life, his flesh and blood.

'No,' he scoffed. 'Henry's family are as pure as they come. I was thirteen and on the brink of going off the rails when we were finally placed with them. Kate was eleven. They brought us back together. They treated us like we were their own and welcomed us into their family. Henry and Shirley became the grandparents Kate and I never had—our own parents had been estranged from theirs. Henry took me fishing and he and Tim would take me to footy games; they gave Kate and me the normal life we'd always craved. The life all kids *should* have. If it wasn't for Sally and Tim, for Henry and Shirley, who knows what would have become of me.'

Quite aside from the tumultuous childhood with their parents, I could only imagine what kind of experiences Jay and Kate might have had in foster care before Henry's family took them in. Everyone had heard horror stories of foster kids being abused or simply left to their own devices, not receiving any of the love children need to flourish. Perhaps that was Jay's story—at worst he might have suffered abuse, but at best he might not have been exposed to love, stifling his ability to connect emotionally with others. This probably had a lot more to do with shaping him than the betrayal of his high school girlfriend but maybe that betrayal had cemented his feelings of unworthiness.

Suddenly a random thought struck. 'But you've got Henry's surname?'

He nodded. 'Sal and Tim wanted to adopt us but because my father was still alive, it couldn't happen. Kate and I took it upon ourselves to start using "French" and both of us changed our name as soon as we were old enough. We certainly didn't want our father's name.'

I knew Jay wouldn't appreciate pity, but I struggled to control the emotion welling in my throat. 'Did you ever visit your dad in prison?'

'The state made us go once a month until we were sixteen. It was awful—he killed our mother, for crying out loud. But I stopped the moment Kate was old enough not to go either. We haven't seen the scum since and I'll be happy if I never have to see him again.'

'I don't blame you,' I said, and wondered if part of the reason going to Mars appealed was because it meant he'd be able to completely leave all this past behind. 'I can't believe you were forced to go visit your father. That's terrible.'

'It was a good reminder of what I didn't want to become. Along with the kindness of Sally and Tim, never wanting to end up like him or my mother helped keep me on the straight and narrow.'

'I bet your mum would be proud of the people you and Kate have become.'

368

Whether my words made him uncomfortable or he realised he'd shared more than he wanted to, Jay clammed up.

'Anyway, how've you been?' He cleared his throat and rubbed his bare feet against Coco's fur. She'd made herself at home and was stretched out in front of his couch, quite at home. 'Pregnancy going well?'

Instinctively, I put a hand on my stomach. 'If only I could eat soft cheese and drink wine, it'd be a party.'

He laughed. 'I'll buy you a bottle when you pop.'

Was he just making conversation or was he serious? Did this mean we were gonna be friends now—like real friends, without the benefits—or was he just being kind because we were family?

But you're not, said a little voice in my head.

Caught up in Jay's confession about his childhood, I'd almost missed the key point in all of this—we *weren't* related!

I had to admit this was more than a bit of a relief, but it also complicated things. The inappropriate attraction I felt whenever Jay was in close proximity was now not so inappropriate, at least not in the way I'd thought.

'I'll hold you to that,' I said, trying to make light banter when the mood in the air felt anything but light. Did he feel it too?

'How'd the father take the news?'

Guilt pricked at the thought of Christos, who'd be waiting at the apartment for me—he'd officially moved in three days ago. 'Good. He's been very supportive.'

'I'm glad to hear it.'

I smiled. 'Thanks.'

Now I'd delivered my news and made my request, I should probably make my exit, but I found myself reluctant to leave. It was so lovely to be sitting here with Jay again—I'd missed his company more than I cared to admit.

'And how've you been?' I asked, prolonging the inevitable. 'Any further progress with Mars?'

He shook his head. 'Just a bit of boring paperwork—it'll be a while before things start to happen. Everything moves slowly in the space world. Anyway, are you sure I can't get you something to drink?' When I hesitated, he added, 'Something *non*-alcoholic.'

Part of me desperately wanted to say yes, but I thought about how Christos would feel and declined. 'Thanks, but I'd better head home. Coco will be getting hungry.'

'Of course.' Jay stood quickly. 'I'll call Henry and be in touch.'

'Thank you.'

Outside in the early evening air as Coco and I headed back to my apartment, I reflected on the conversation. It hadn't gone at all as I'd imagined—it had been far better than I could have hoped for. So why was I feeling so confused?

35

Mum called numerous times throughout the day asking if I'd heard from Jay. The answer was always no, and to be honest I was almost as antsy as she was—I'd even taken my phone into the bathroom with me at work.

'We need to be patient,' I'd told her. 'It's been less than twenty-four hours since I spoke to Jay; he might not have had the chance to see Henry yet.'

It was easy advice to give but harder to follow. On my tram ride home, I'd kept my phone in my handbag so I wouldn't be tempted to call or text him for an update. I arrived to Christos holding a wineglass full of apple juice and Coco jumping up at my knees.

'Good evening, gorgeous.' He took my bag, kissed my cheek and thrust the glass towards me. 'How was your day?'

'Fine.' I took a sip while giving Coco the effusive greeting she desired. My nose twitched at the aroma of something spicy. 'What's that smell?'

He grinned. 'I cooked up a moussaka. I hope you're hungry.'

'Famished.'

We'd only been living together four days and it still felt weird coming home to another person in my space, but there were definitely perks. Christos had been off work today and he'd obviously made the most of his free time. Quite aside from dinner, the apartment was cleaner and tidier than it had been in weeks.

'Good, I was thinking we could start checking out some places on the internet over dinner. I had a bit of a look today and came up with a short list of houses I think you'll like, within our location and budget. But first, I've run you a nice warm bath. Come on, I'll help you undress.' He wiggled his eyebrows suggestively.

What was with men? That was the downside of having a live-in lover—things like relaxing bubble baths came with expectations. Couldn't he see that getting down and dirty was the last thing I wanted to do when I was twenty-six weeks pregnant and just home from a long day at work?

'That sounds lovely, but I have to take Coco for a walk first.'

'Does she have to have a walk *every* day?'

'Yes. But perhaps you could take her while I have that bath?'

'Okay.' He didn't sound enthused, and part of me felt bad sending my poor pup out with my grumpy boyfriend, but I wanted that lovely bath in peace.

'Thanks. You are the best.'

'Don't you forget it,' he said as he grabbed Coco's leash.

Resigned to the fact I wasn't going to hear from Jay today, I sank down into the tub full of warm bubbles and willed the water to wash away my stresses. I was halfway to achieving my desired state of relaxation when the intercom buzzed.

Dammit, Christos must have forgotten his key.

Dragging myself from the bath, I wrapped a towel around myself, stalked to the front door, pressed the button that would let him into the building and opened the door.

But it wasn't Christos and Coco who appeared.

'Jay?' Shock almost had me dropping the towel, which due to my bump was already less than adequate.

'Well, hello there.' He didn't even try to hide his slow perusal of my body, and the smile that formed on his lips told me that despite my pregnant state, he still found me attractive.

A jolt of pleasure shot straight to my groin. 'What are you doing here?'

'I spoke to Henry.'

'Oh, right.' In the moment that whole thing had totally slipped my mind. 'What did he say?'

'Do you think I could come in?'

'Um ...' I didn't know if that was a good idea, but neither was having a serious conversation while one of us was practically naked. 'Sure. Come in. I'll just go throw on some clothes.'

'Don't feel you have to get dressed on my account.'

At his deeply suggestive tone, a dangerous heat flushed through me.

'Take a seat,' I said firmly, closing the door behind him and fleeing into my bedroom where I selected the most frumpy clothes I could find.

It was only when I heard the front door open again and Christos exclaim, 'Who the hell are you?' that I realised I'd forgotten to mention his presence to Jay.

'I'm Jay. Who the hell are you?'

'You're the guy from the cruise ship? Ged's new cousin?'

'Cousins?' I heard Jay cackle.

Oh God. I glanced at the window, contemplating climbing out and making my escape. I didn't know why I was so worried—it wasn't like I'd done anything wrong. I'd merely forgotten to mention to Christos the non-family revelation when I'd come home last night. But when I emerged into the living area, I knew I had reason to be.

While Coco was doing a silly dance around Jay, he and Christos were eyeing each other off as if they were two medieval knights poised for battle. I rushed to stand between them and looked from one to the other.

'Christos, this is Jay, he's come to talk to me about Henry. And Jay—' My stomach twisted into a knot. 'This is Christos, my ...'

'Boyfriend,' he supplied, wrapping his arm around me possessively.

I tried to ignore my irritation at his gesture. 'Yes. That's right,' I said, almost apologetically. Why did it feel like by living with Christos I was cheating on Jay?

'You're back with him? After everything he put you through?'

'Hey, watch it.' Christos puffed up his chest and stepped forward slightly. 'Our relationship is none of your business.'

I put a warning hand on Christos's chest—there was no way he'd beat Jay in a fight if it came to that. 'Jay's here to discuss Mum and Henry. Christos and I were just about to have dinner—he's made a delicious moussaka. Maybe you could join us? We can eat and talk.'

Both men looked at me like I was insane, but hey, maybe if they sat down and got to know each other, some of the tension and suspicion might be diffused.

Christos was the first to speak. 'I suppose there's enough for all of us,' he said with a shrug.

Jay shook his head. 'Thanks, but I've already eaten, and this won't take long anyway.'

'Maybe you could go serve dinner while I talk to Jay,' I suggested. If they were determined to act like macho opponents in a ring, it might be easier if we had this conversation one on one.

'Okay.' As he retreated to the kitchen, Christos kissed my forehead, a subtle reminder to Jay of our relationship status.

I gestured to the couch. 'Do you want to sit?'

'No, I won't keep you. And I'm sorry about before. I didn't realise you guys were back together, but ... he's right, not my business. I hope you're happy.'

'Thanks. So, is it good news or bad news about Henry?

'Good. He wants to meet your mother. I showed him her picture and he cried—he said she's almost exactly half him and half Alice.'

'Was he angry at Alice?'

'I wouldn't say angry exactly ... just sad that she didn't give them the chance, that she didn't trust him with the truth. But at the same time, he said he can't be too sad because if she had, his life would be very different now. And he likes the life he's lived; he loves Shirley and the family they've made together.'

Pregnancy had made me hugely emotional and I found myself tearing up at Jay's words.

'Henry had more questions than I could answer, but I showed him your mother's YouTube channel and he enjoyed her videos. Shirley, Sally and Kate were already huge fans, so they all want to meet her too, but we thought it would be best if we don't overwhelm Marie and start with a smaller meeting.'

I nodded, overwhelmed myself. 'That sounds good.'

'I've got tomorrow off; are you guys free?'

'Yes, I'm sure that will be fine. Mum has her segment on TV early, but we can meet you after that.'

'It's settled then. I'll confirm with Henry and text you.' Jay nodded and shoved his hands in his pockets. 'See you tomorrow, Ged.'

It was only as I shut the door behind him that I realised he hadn't called me Geraldine.

'Is he gone?' Christos emerged from the kitchen and his relief was clear in his voice.

'Yes.'

'Good. Let's eat.'

'Just let me call Mum first.'

She was a combo of ecstatic and nervous. 'What should I wear?' I told her I didn't think Henry would care about her outfit. She'd have talked all night, but I was aware of Christos waiting impatiently, so I made my excuses and disconnected.

We ate on the couch in front of the TV and although I'd been starving earlier, I merely picked at my food—unable to think about anything but tomorrow. If I was honest, I wasn't sure whether I was more anxious about meeting Henry or seeing Jay again. Christos ate until his plate was so empty it was almost clean again, then put it on the coffee table and grabbed his laptop. 'You're gonna love some of these places,' he told me as a real estate website appeared on the screen.

'Can't wait.' I leaned in closer and tried to feign enthusiasm.

A few months ago, scrolling through real-estate-dot-com for possible properties had been one of my favourite pastimes, but now that buying one was actually a reality I couldn't seem to summon much excitement. There was so much else in going on in my head that choosing an actual house felt overwhelming.

'I'm not going to tell you which is my favourite,' Christos said as he clicked on the first place—a three-bedroom renovated cottage in Footscray. Perfect location and surprisingly affordable, considering all the hard work inside had already been done. With polished floorboards and high ceilings, it was exactly the kind of home I'd dreamed about.

'The bathroom is massive.'

'I know, and there's a good-sized backyard as well. It needs a bit of work to make it kid friendly, but we'll be able to put in some grass and bring it up to scratch before Alice is walking. The rooms are big too, which means we can put bunk beds in the spare room for when my kids come to stay.'

It sounded like he'd already made up his mind, but I couldn't imagine Isidore being excited about sharing a room with her two younger siblings, even if it was only every other weekend.

'Let's see the other ones,' I said.

He showed me a couple more places in Footscray and one only just out of our price range in Brunswick. 'But it might be possible if we tighten the purse strings and stop eating out so much. Do you want to go see it? It's open for inspection tomorrow.'

Tomorrow? Quite aside from the fact I'd be busy with Mum and Henry, that seemed so soon. We'd been together almost a year before we broke up and Christos hadn't once mentioned buying a house together and now it was all he seemed to care about. Everything was moving too fast; we hadn't even spoken to the bank yet. I felt as if I'd been put in a box and the walls were closing in around me.

I found myself struggling to breathe. I put my plate on the coffee table and tried to focus on not hyperventilating.

'Are you okay?' Christos tossed the laptop aside and put his hands on my arms. I didn't mean to, but I flinched at his touch.

'I just ...' I held out my hand indicating I needed a moment.

Finally I managed to control my breathing and Christos picked up my glass of water and handed it to me. 'Did you have a Braxton Hicks?'

I took a sip. 'I think I had a panic attack.'

He chuckled nervously as if he wasn't sure what to make of that. 'Have you had enough?' he asked, gesturing to my still half-full plate. I nodded. 'Well, I'll go load the dishwasher and then bring you some dessert. I know you always have room for chocolate cake from the little bakery around the corner.'

He was right, I did, but not tonight. He was doing everything right, but it wasn't enough. Nothing about us being together felt right anymore and no amount of chocolate cake would change that.

'Let's not rush into buying just yet' was what I meant to say, but 'I don't want to buy a house with you' blurted from my mouth instead.

I was unsure who was more surprised by my confession—me or him.

'What?' He recoiled slightly.

I swallowed, my stomach rolling despite the fact I'd barely eaten anything. 'I'm sorry. I can't do this. Six months ago, I wanted to spend the rest of my life with you and I couldn't imagine my love ever fading, but it has.'

I now knew with absolute certainty that getting back together with Christos had been a mistake. By staying with him, I'd be doing exactly what I suspected Mum was doing—choosing the easy option, the one my head told me was right, but was not the most satisfactory one.

'What are you saying?' he asked, his voice shaky.

I felt like the lowest of low, but I couldn't lead him on any longer. 'Things have changed. I know we're having a baby together, but I'm not going to live a lie, not even for my daughter.'

'It's Jay, isn't it? You want to be with him. We were great together, we were happy—until you met him.'

'We were happy until *you* broke us.'

He opened his mouth presumably to object, but I rode over the top of him. 'I know you did it for all the right reasons and I respect your love for your kids, but you still didn't treat *me* right. I thought I was prepared to move past that knowing you'll be a wonderful father to Alice, but that would be a mistake. Having a baby together is not reason enough for me to be with you.'

I *did* have feelings for Jay. I was madly attracted to him, but also suspected there were even more dangerous feelings bubbling beneath the chemistry. I wasn't stupid enough to think they were reciprocated or would ever go anywhere, but it wouldn't be fair to either myself or Christos if I ignored them. I would rather be by myself than in a half-happy relationship.

I wanted my daughter to know that it was okay to be alone.

He shook his head, disbelief and sadness rolled into one on his face as he clutched at my hand and held it close to his chest. 'We don't need to rush into buying a house, but I love you and I know deep down you love me too. Maybe things are just moving too fast.'

'No.' I pulled away, trying to blink back tears that came because I was hurting him. No matter he'd broken my heart first, I'd never wanted to do the same to him, but I couldn't pretend. 'It's not that. I just don't *feel* it here anymore. You're a good man but I'm never going to feel the way I once did.'

I reassured him that I'd respect his rights regarding our baby, that I valued him and never meant to hurt him. I even said I'd still love his help to organise the nursery. But then I let him know, as gently as I could, that it was time for him to go.

'There's nothing I can do to change your mind?'

'No,' I whispered. 'I'm sorry.'

Christos sighed sadly as he let go of my hands. 'I'll go pack my things.'

I sat on the couch, tears rolling down my cheeks. When he returned, a suitcase in each hand, he put them down on the floor. I stood and walked into his arms and he held me tightly for a few long moments.

'Call me any time if you need anything,' he said when we eventually broke apart.

I promised him I would and then he left.

'It's just you and me again, Coco.'

I felt sombre but also knew I'd made the right decision.

36

I picked Mum up outside the television studio and we drove out of the city and towards Geelong where Henry and his wife still lived.

'How are you feeling?' I asked as we got closer to our destination; both of us had been uncharacteristically quiet on the journey.

'Sick.' She placed one hand on her stomach and used the other to press the button and lower her window. Salty air wafted into the car and the coastline out the window was breathtaking.

'That's understandable.' My own stomach was tying itself in knots, but I wasn't sure whether that was down to the prospect of seeing Jay again or meeting my long-lost grandfather for the first time. 'But Henry's excited to see you.'

'I know. It's just … I'm not sure how to act. What if we have nothing to say to each other?'

'Just be yourself, and if all else fails ask questions. Remember Henry is probably just as nervous.'

'Thank you, darling.' She patted my knee as we drove past the Welcome to Geelong sign.

As it was late Saturday morning and the town was bustling, I had to park a fair distance from the beachfront cafe where Jay had told us to meet, but the fresh air and quick stroll probably did us good.

My heart rate accelerated and Alice danced around inside me as if she too was a little shook up as we slowed at the entrance of the cafe's outdoor area.

Mum clutched my arm. 'Can you see them?'

The place was crowded, almost every table full, some people still having breakfast, others ordering lunch, but there was no sign of Jay or Henry. 'Maybe they're inside,' I said, ushering Mum forward.

'Or maybe they decided not to come.'

'No. Jay would have messaged me.'

'Table for two?' asked a waitress as we entered.

'Actually, we're meeting two gentlemen,' I told her.

'Ooh, double date?' The woman's eyes glistened. I didn't have the heart to explain she couldn't be further from the truth.

'Geraldine?' A voice I'd recognise anywhere called and I turned to see Jay and Henry approaching from behind. 'Sorry we're late. Parking was impossible.'

My mouth went dry at the sight of him, but I didn't need to worry about speaking because, in the middle of the crowded restaurant, Mum and Henry's eyes met for the first time.

'Hello, Marie,' the old man said. The skin around his eyes crinkled as he offered his hand. 'It's lovely to meet you.'

Mum pressed her lips together and I knew she was close to tears as she took his hand in both of hers. 'You too,' she sniffed, and then lost it.

Henry whipped a white handkerchief out of his shirt pocket and handed it to her. 'It's clean, I promise.'

'Thank you.' Mum dabbed at her eyes.

'Oh dear.' The waitress's eyes widened as she looked between the four of us. 'How about that table over in the corner?'

'That would be good,' said Jay and I at the same time.

He gestured for Mum and me to go first as the waitress started in that direction. I took hold of my mother's arm and led her to her seat, only to look up and see Jay holding out Henry's for him. He waited until the three of us were seated before he sat himself.

The waitress said she'd give us a few moments and retreated.

'I'm so sorry,' Mum gushed. 'I promised myself I wasn't going to do that, but this is all just …'

'A little overwhelming?' Henry finished. 'Don't apologise. I'm a little choked up myself.'

'Oh.' Mum blinked. 'I'm sorry … and I've used your hanky.'

'You can have mine, if need be, Granddad.' And Jay surprised me by drawing a navy blue one out of his pocket.

'Thanks,' Henry chuckled, then silence fell between us.

I looked at Jay for direction and found his gaze already trained on me. My stomach did a little flip and I racked my mind for something to say to break the ice between the four of us. It would have been much easier if Jay and I *were* related by blood.

Thankfully, the waitress chose that moment to return. 'Can I get you lovely people some drinks to start?'

We glanced at each other.

'Is it too early to share a bottle of wine?' Henry asked. 'Or even some bubbles? It's not every day I meet my daughter.'

Mum beamed. 'That sounds lovely.

'I can't,' I said. 'I'm pregnant, but you guys go ahead.'

Henry chuckled. 'That's right. Jay mentioned that and now I see you it's quite obvious. Congratulations.'

'Thank you.' I couldn't help but wonder what else Jay had said about me.

'Do you do mocktails?' Jay asked the waitress, then looked to me. 'Maybe we can get you one of them?'

'We do a great virgin strawberry or mango daiquiri.'

That sounded amazing. 'I'll have mango, please.'

Mum and Henry decided on a glass of bubbles each, but Jay merely ordered a coffee, then the waitress went through the lunch specials. Although I was normally in a permanent state of starvation these days, I wasn't sure I could stomach much right now, but I ordered a bowl of gnocchi anyway.

'Thank you for driving all this way to see us,' Henry said when the waitress retreated again.

'It's not that far,' I said. 'You've lived here a long time, haven't you?'

'Yes. I met Shirley just after I moved here and we were married not long after. We love it.'

'I can see why,' I said, glancing out the window at the ocean and the people walking along the pier.

'And what about you?' Henry looked to my mother. 'Jay says you live in Melbourne?'

She nodded. 'Yes, Port Melbourne. I've also lived there all my married life.'

Henry smiled again. 'And you have two kids?'

'Yes. Geraldine and William. Will's married to Sophie and has a son and a daughter with another baby due not long before Geraldine's. I love being a granny.'

'Being a grandparent is one of life's greatest joys,' Henry agreed. 'Can I see some photos?'

Mum dug her brag album out of her handbag and Henry gushed accordingly over pictures of Charlotte and Oliver, before asking her if she had any hobbies.

Mum launched into her life loves—cooking and crafting, with the odd bit of gardening thrown in, and it turned out she and Henry didn't just have their Elvis obsession in common. He confessed to doing the lion's share of the cooking in his house and said he enjoyed pottering about in the garden also. I thought about how much more of a modern man he sounded than my father, and couldn't imagine him walking over Gralice or wanting her to act like his little wife if they'd been married. He was clearly a kind and interesting man and my heart ached for what could have been for my grandmother, if only she'd given him the chance.

While they laughed about their love of the King, gushing about their memorabilia collections, Jay and I sat quietly and listened. Occasionally our eyes met and each and every time my stomach tightened.

The food arrived and Jay made sure his grandfather had the salt and tartar sauce he desired before starting on his own veggie burger with the lot—whatever that was when you were a vegan. I picked at my gnocchi, which was really very good, but the truth was my hunger raged for other things.

'And how is your mother?' Henry asked mine.

I looked to Mum nervously. When she appeared unable to reply, I stepped in. 'I'm not sure if Jay told you but Alice has gastric cancer— she's in the final stage and …' I swallowed, willing myself not to cry. 'She hasn't got long left.'

'Oh my goodness.' Henry's face fell and he put down his knife and fork. 'I'm so sorry to hear that.'

At the same time, I felt Jay's leg press against mine under the table. I wasn't sure whether it was an accident or if he was trying to offer comfort, but I didn't have time to dwell on this before Mum said, 'Aren't you angry at her? She lied to you all these years, she lied to both of us. We're sitting here pretending this is a normal conversation, but this is wrong—I shouldn't be meeting my father for the first time when I'm fifty-five years old.'

'Mum, calm down.' I put my hand on her forearm as I noticed other patrons turning to look at us.

'You're right,' Henry said, 'this isn't ideal. We've both missed out on so much. I can't be happy about what Alice did, but I do know that in her heart she thought she was doing the right thing, and I respect her for following her dreams, for all she's achieved. Besides, I believe one is happier if they look to the future rather than dwell on the past. That's always been my life motto. Saying that, I am sad to hear about Alice's cancer—it's a ghastly disease and I only pray they find a cure quickly.'

'Me too,' I said, even though I knew it wouldn't be soon enough for Gralice.

'Yes, well.' My mother picked up her glass and downed half of it.

'Actually,' I said, drawing an envelope out of my handbag, 'Alice asked me to give you this.' I handed him the letter I'd gone to collect early that morning.

Henry looked surprised, but he thanked me like the gentleman he was and slipped the envelope into his shirt pocket.

Mum glared at me and downed the rest of her drink. I looked across to see a puzzled smile on Jay's face.

'Can I get you a top up?' Henry gestured to Mum's glass. 'As you said, we've got lots of catching up to do.'

Mum nodded and finally smiled again. 'Thank you, that would be lovely.'

Our waitress brought another glass for Mum and Henry and, the unpleasantness over, the conversation continued to flow easily. The lunch plates were cleared away and when we were offered the dessert and coffee menu, Henry suggested ice-cream and a stroll along the pier instead.

'That's if you don't have to be getting back to Melbourne yet.'

'No, not at all,' I said, far too eager to prolong my time with Jay. Who knew when I'd see him again after today.

It was a beautiful sunny afternoon—perfect for a walk. After buying ice-creams at a nearby vendor, the four of us started along the pier, Mum and Henry in front, Jay and I following behind. It wasn't long before the distance grew between them and us and I felt compelled to make conversation.

'Well, this is going better than I imagined. Henry is a delight.'

'He's a good bloke,' Jay agreed, before licking his raspberry vegan ice-cream.

I forced myself to look away as I remembered that tongue licking other things and a shiver flew over my skin.

'You cold?' he asked, noticing.

I pointed at my ice-cream—'Brain freeze'—and he chuckled.

As we continued our free hands swung along beside us and occasionally brushed against each other. After about the fourth time, Jay shoved his hand in his pocket and cleared his throat.

'How's your grandmother's biography going?'

'It's coming along—not quite as fast as I'd like, but I'm almost halfway through a very rough first draft.'

'That's awesome. I look forward to reading it one day.'

I laughed, despite the little glow inside me. 'And I look forward to your educated critique.'

'So,' he said after a moment, 'are you and Christos going to stay in Carlton after the baby is born or are you going to look for somewhere a little bigger?'

'I do need a bigger place, but if I go anywhere it won't be with Christos.'

Jay's steps faltered, and he looked at me, clearly confused.

'We ... Christos and I broke up again last night.'

'Really?' He looked incredulous. 'Why?'

'Because ...' I stared right into his eyes and somehow found the courage to confess, 'I'm in love with someone else.'

It didn't take a genius to know who I was talking about. In my fantasy this was where Jay would grab my face in his hands, kiss me senseless and declare he loved me too.

Instead, his cheeks turned red and he glanced at the big black watch on his wrist. 'God, is that the time?' He called ahead, 'Henry, it's getting late. These guys need to head back to Melbourne.'

Normally I'd have been mad at him—or any man—for daring to speak for me, but in this instance I was grateful. Now we'd both made our positions clear, it would be too painful to continue our walk on the pretence everything was okay. I wasn't angry at him. I couldn't force him to love me any more than I could force myself to love Christos.

'Do we?' Mum asked, surprise in her voice.

'Yes,' I said, catching up to them. 'I've just remembered something I've got on this evening. Sorry.'

'Never mind,' Henry said. 'It's been wonderful talking to you and I'm sure there'll be plenty of other times, now we've connected. Shirley would love to meet you, if that wouldn't make you feel too uncomfortable.'

Mum beamed. 'No, that would be lovely.'

'Splendid. And I'd love to meet the rest of your family if possible. Perhaps I'll organise a barbecue.'

'That sounds great,' I said, tugging at Mum's arm, 'but we really do have to go.'

If we stood here any longer making small talk about future catch-ups, I was liable to burst into tears and I didn't want to do that until I was safely in the confines of my apartment with no one to bear witness but Coco.

Part of me wished I hadn't said anything to Jay—I'd put him in an impossible position and probably ruined any chance of us staying friends—but another part of me was proud for speaking out.

It was better to know where we both stood, even if the truth hurt like hell.

I finally managed to drag Mum away from her new-found father and she chatted all the way back to Melbourne. When I dropped her off at her place she said, 'Would you like to stay for an early dinner? Dad's at bowling and won't be back for ages.'

'No, thanks.'

'Oh, that's right, you've got something on. Big date with Christos?'

I shook my head. 'Actually, Mum, Christos and I have broken up.'

She blinked. 'Really? Did he decide to go back to his wife *again*?'

'No. It was my decision this time. I realised he wasn't The One and it wasn't fair to me *or* him to pretend he was.'

'I see.' She didn't ask me what big thing I had on tonight instead but was quiet a long moment. Eventually, she patted my hand. 'Well, good for you, darling. And thank you so much for today.'

With that, she kissed me on the cheek and climbed out of the car.

37

Although Jay and I technically hadn't broken up, I had all the symptoms of a shattered heart when I returned to my apartment late Saturday afternoon and I treated them accordingly. I ordered in pizza, scoffed the lot and then walked Coco to the supermarket around the corner, bought a mammoth tub of cookies and cream ice-cream and sat on the couch eating it while watching one of my favourite movies of all time—*Bridget Jones's Diary*. I know, I know, not exactly empowering, but the mood I was in, I liked feeling as if I wasn't the only woman in the world who didn't have her shit together, who fell in love with the wrong men and had parental woes to boot.

The only difference between Bridget and me was that she got a romantic happy ending.

As it was the weekend, I could have continued my festival of self-pity when I woke up the next morning, but instead I told myself it was time to embrace an alternative ending. I didn't have time to sit around in my PJs all day. Besides, keeping busy would be much better than feeling sorry for myself, so I got out of bed and into the shower where I started making a mental list of everything I needed to do over the coming months.

Number one—ensure myself and my apartment were as ready for my baby's arrival as we could be.

Number two—finish writing Gralice's biography so that she could read and approve it. This was a mammoth task and I wasn't sure I could do it in such a short time, but I was going to give it my best shot.

Number three—somehow get Mum to forgive her before it was too late.

My grandmother's cancer put everything into perspective and she had to be my priority. I hadn't seen her for a couple of days and knew she'd be eager to hear about Mum's meeting with Henry, so I decided to focus on number two first. As soon as I was dressed, I packed up my laptop and headed over to Phil and Craig's.

They were happy to see me as usual, both greeting me with hugs and ushering me into the living room where Gralice was sitting up in her recliner.

'Hello, darling girl,' she said as I kissed her cheek. It felt cool, and I couldn't help noticing the bluish, almost dusky colour of her skin.

Dumping my things, I perched on the arm of the recliner and took her hand. 'How are you feeling today?'

'Never mind about me,' she said, pausing between words to take a breath. 'I want to hear all about yesterday. Did the meeting ... go well?'

Phil and Craig sat on the sofa, also looking expectantly at me. 'Yes. Sorry I meant to call you, but I was shattered by the time we got home.'

'It's fine,' Gralice said as she reached for her glass of water. 'You need to take care of yourself.'

I passed it to her, speaking as she took a sip through the straw. 'Mum and Henry got on like a house on fire. He's a very special man and I can see why you loved him.'

My grandparents offered me a bittersweet smile. I knew they were happy for Mum, but also how hard hearing this must be, especially for Phil who had been her dad in all the ways that mattered all these years. My heart broke for them and I couldn't help wishing that they hadn't decided to tell the truth after all these years. What good had it done?

Sure, Mum's meeting with Henry had gone well and it looked as if she'd found another family, but at what cost? It hadn't made her face her own truth, but it had caused a hell of a lot of hurt. Her anger might be masking her pain right now, but I knew deep down Mum cared about Gralice and Phil and she'd be devastated if it was too late by the time she came around.

Not to mention the fact that if they hadn't said anything I might not have seen Jay again and might still be living in blissful denial.

'Do you think they're going to see each other again?' At Gralice's question I realised I'd been staring off into space.

'Yes.' I didn't want to lie but felt torn between telling the truth and protecting my grandparents' feelings. 'Henry mentioned something about a family barbecue.'

'That's good,' Gralice said. 'I'm glad he's not taking any anger towards me out on Sappho.'

'I don't think Henry's angry at you either,' I told her. 'He seemed a very sensible, level-headed man. He asked after you and I gave him your letter. I wouldn't be surprised if you get a reply, but he was very kind in the way he spoke about you.'

'I see.' Gralice rubbed her lips together and I wasn't sure if my words had made her feel better or worse.

'Are you sticking around for a little while, Ged?' Phil asked. 'Can we get you something to eat or drink?'

Bless my grandfathers—they were always trying to feed and water me. 'I've only just had breakfast so I'm fine for a while, but I was planning on dumping myself on you for the day. I want to run a few things by Gralice about the biography. If you're up to it,' I added.

'Well, I was planning on running a marathon and going sky-diving,' she said, 'but I suppose I can do that instead.'

I grinned, glad that despite her rapidly ailing health, she still had her sarcastic tongue and sense of humour.

'Well,' Craig said, 'if you two are going to be working hard, we might pop out for a bit of fresh air.'

'We'll be back in an hour or so,' Phil promised as they left.

'Those poor blokes feel as if they have to sit with me 24/7,' Gralice said as the door closed behind them. 'I hate being such a damn burden.'

'You're *not* a burden and Phil and Craig definitely don't see you as one.'

'You're a sweetheart, Ged, but those two wonderful men aren't spring chickens either and having to look after me is taking its toll. Not to mention their heartbreak over Sappho. I think maybe it's time for me to hire a nurse—do you think you could help me with that?'

I blinked. 'But ... what about ...?'

If she was getting bad enough to think she needed a nurse, wouldn't that mean the time had come to do what she'd so adamantly told me she was going to do all those months ago?

Gralice smiled at me. 'I thought you'd have guessed I gave up that plan a while ago now.'

'You did?' I could barely breathe as I said this.

She nodded. 'I'm not ready to say goodbye just yet, and maybe it's finally time to surrender some of the control I've been trying to hold on to all my life. Besides, I can't go until you've finished the book in case you write something ridiculous about me.'

Although she'd attempted humour, I couldn't. 'But what about all the suffering ... all the pain?'

'Well, I'm not stupid enough to think it'll be a walk in the park, but I'm choosing to focus instead on what I will have.' She paused a moment and glanced at my bump. 'More time with all of you. So, will you help me find a nurse?'

I was so choked up, so overwhelmed with selfish happiness and relief, that it took me a few long moments before I could form any words.

'What about if I move in here instead?' I finally offered. 'Then I'd be here in the evenings and at weekends to help Phil and Craig.'

I couldn't bear the thought of some stranger taking care of her, doing the role that Mum, Will and I should be shouldering. I felt angry at Mum that she hadn't been here to support Phil and Craig, and while I couldn't force her to step up, I could certainly do so myself.

'No,' she said forcefully. 'You've got your own life. Christos has only just moved in—you need time together to get ready for the baby.'

'Actually, Gralice, Christos and I are no more. I ended it Friday night.'

'Really?' She looked confused but also slightly relieved.

'Yes. I realised my heart wasn't in it. The truth is, I'm in love with someone else.'

'Jay?'

'Yes,' I whispered, sadness engulfing me. I had barely spoken about him with Gralice at all, except to fill her in on the fact we weren't biologically related, but she'd always been able to read me like a book.

'Have you told him?'

'Ah-huh. I blurted it out yesterday and he made it clear he doesn't feel the same way.'

'Oh darling, come here.' She opened her arms and I fell into them, careful not to squash her in the process. I felt like a little girl and couldn't stop a flood of tears, however stupid I felt for crying them. Maybe it would have been some consolation if my baby was Jay's—at least I'd always have a little part of him.

'I feel like such an idiot,' I admitted after a while. 'I knew from the start Jay would never love me back and I still fell for him. I thought I could keep sex separate from emotion, but, turns out I'm not that strong.'

'You're not an idiot. Love doesn't make you weak,' Gralice said. 'And I know it hurts now but you were brave to tell him. At least you won't spend the rest of your life wondering what might have been, wondering if things could have been different.'

I knew she wasn't simply talking about me and my heart ached for her.

All these wonderful, amazing things she'd done in her life—for herself and for other women—and yet she still had regrets. I couldn't let her dwell on them.

'I reckon no matter what choices we make in our lives, we'll never know for sure if they are the right ones, but I want you to know, I'm glad of the choices you made. I'm glad you chose to have Mum and I'm so ridiculously proud of everything you've done. If you hadn't fought for better rights for women, I could be in a pretty precarious position right now. But because you did, being single and pregnant isn't a disaster. My daughter and I have a positive future ahead. I might have liked a certain man in our lives, but I don't *need* him. Women of my generation owe our independence to women like you.'

'Oh, Ged, stop with your gushing.' But there were tears in Gralice's eyes.

I hugged her tightly. 'So, what do you say? Shall Coco and I move in?'

'*Absolutely not*,' she replied. 'I'm already struggling to wash myself and am this close to needing assistance going to the bathroom. I might be relinquishing some control, but I want to maintain some dignity in my final days, and that means not wanting you or Phil or Craig or anyone else related to me to help with such things. You can spend as much time as you like here, but please, let me at least have this.'

'Okay,' I agreed reluctantly. The last thing I wanted was to do anything that would make Gralice feel worse. 'I'll help find a nurse.'

'Thank you. And just so you know, a spunky male one would be quite fine with me if need be.'

I snorted and promised to see what I could do. 'Now, are you up for a little bit of a chat about the book?'

'Yes.' She nodded as I hauled myself up and went across to grab my laptop. 'I read the latest pages you gave me and made a couple of tweaks, but it's coming along well.'

I beamed, happy she approved. 'Thanks, but there's something that's been playing on my mind since you told me about Henry. And now that it's all out in the open, I've been contemplating the segment about you becoming a single mum. I was wondering, do you want me to stick with the story we always had or …'

'Do I want you to tell the truth?' Gralice sighed. 'Let your mother make that decision, if she will. I don't want anything to be printed that she wouldn't be comfortable with, but I also don't want to leave a lie. I want people to know that I wasn't perfect as a mother or a woman, that I had to make choices and that I'll die not knowing whether or not they were the right ones, but that I did my best at the time. I want my final message to be that women should reach for the stars and embrace their independence, but that they should also follow their hearts. If I've realised one thing—perhaps too late—it's that life isn't black and white. It's a million shades of grey and there isn't one truth that fits everyone.'

'That's beautiful,' I whispered, madly scribbling it all down in my notebook. I hoped Mum would agree to let the truth be told, because the love stuff would be gold for the book—it added a whole other dimension to Gralice's life and story. 'Oh my God!'

'What is it?'

My hand rushed to my stomach. 'The baby—Alice is kicking!' I'd felt her before but never anything as strong as this.

'Let me feel.'

I stepped close to Gralice's recliner to give her access to my belly and held my breath as my little girl wriggled beneath her touch.

'That there,' she said, 'is what life is all about.' And the smile that appeared on her face was something I'd remember forever.

The sound of the front door opening jolted us from our moment and I looked up, expecting to see Phil or Craig, but my mother appeared instead. I felt Gralice's hand still on my stomach.

'Is the baby moving?' Mum asked, dropping her handbag to the floor and rushing over.

'Ah-huh,' I said, not sure what to make of her arrival.

She pushed her hand against my stomach—mere centimetres from Gralice's—and squealed as my baby slammed her foot (or maybe hand, who could tell?) into my uterus. 'I felt her!'

Gralice looked as confused as I was by Mum's appearance. And even more confused when Mum addressed her. 'Did you feel it too?'

All she could do was nod as my mother let out a happy sigh. 'Looks like we've got another generation of strong-minded women right there. Where are my dads?'

'Out for a walk,' I said.

'Well, don't just stand there, put the kettle on. What I'm about to say definitely requires a cup of tea.'

I hesitated a moment, unsure about leaving Gralice alone with Mum, but she gave me a little nod, telling me she'd be fine. I kept one ear cocked towards the living room as I headed into the kitchen and set about making tea, but didn't hear anything mind-boggling. Mum was telling Gralice about some little hats she was going to knit for her new grandbabies as if nothing out of the ordinary was going on at all.

Finally, the kettle whistled and I piled the tea things onto a tray and returned to the living room. As I was handing a cup to my mother, I noticed her wedding ring was absent again.

'What happened to your ring?' I asked as I sat on the sofa beside her.

She glanced down at her finger and gave us both a sheepish smile. 'Oh, that. Well, Tony and I have made the mutual decision to separate.'

'What? When?' I said; Gralice appeared too stunned to speak.

'Last night. We had a wonderful long talk about Henry and my new-found family, but all the while I was thinking about the two of you.' She looked to me. 'I'm super proud of you for making the decision to leave Christos when it didn't feel right, and I couldn't help thinking about what you said, Mum, about living my truth. You're right ... I love Tony, but I'm not in love with him. He's been a good husband and we've had a wonderful marriage in many ways, but there's always been something lacking. It would be wrong of me to go on pretending that we have something we don't, and stupid when it could mean the both of us missing out on something magical. Your father is a good man, Geraldine, and he deserves the love of a woman who can give him her all.'

'How's Dad taking this?' I know she'd said 'mutual' but I couldn't imagine him being overjoyed at the prospect of having to take care of himself again.

'He's better this time around. We both want what's best for each other and,' she grinned, 'thanks to you, he's feeling a lot better placed to live alone. He even made dinner for us last night.'

'Wow. Wonders never cease. So, where's Dad now?'

'He's gone to talk to Will and Sophie—we thought it might be better him breaking the news to them.'

'Good idea.' I was glad I wasn't a fly on the wall for that conversation. 'Does this mean you're going to get back together with Rosa?'

'I'm going to talk to her,' she said, a wistful look in her eyes. 'I'm going to apologise for messing her around, but she may not want to listen. And I need to work on finding out who I truly am before I rush into anything else anyway. That is going to be my focus for the foreseeable future—that and my family.'

'But what about your followers? What about the book?' Even as I said these words I was willing myself to shut my mouth—neither of those things mattered in the big picture.

'I've written a statement to post on Instagram and Facebook and I'll probably do a vlog after I've spoken to Holly. I wanted to speak to you first. I'm going to pay back the advance and tell her I'm sorry, but I can't write the book. I'll probably lose my segment on TV too, but that's okay. Getting up that early in the morning had knobs on anyway.'

I laughed.

'I've enjoyed vlogging though,' she said, 'and so although I'll probably have to start from the ground up, I'm going to keep sharing my cooking and craft and my life, but this time I'll be completely honest, the whole truth and nothing but the truth. If people don't like that, they don't have to read it.'

I had a feeling lots of people were going to read it and I was going to be the first person to subscribe. I was probably never going to be the kind of mother she was—making wholesome school lunches and volunteering for the P&C—and that was okay. It didn't make either of us any less.

'I'm so proud of you for coming to this decision,' I said, giving her a hug. 'I know it can't have been easy.'

'If there's one thing I've learned over the last few months it's that nothing worth anything comes easily.'

When we pulled apart, I realised that my grandmother had been quiet throughout this exchange and I looked over to see her crying. 'Oh, Gralice.'

I tried to get up but my bump unbalanced me and Mum beat me to it.

She snatched up a box of tissues from the coffee table and took them to her mother, then perched on the edge of the recliner and pulled Gralice into her arms.

'I'm sorry, sweetheart,' Gralice sobbed. 'I'm so sorry.'

'Don't cry, Mum. It's okay. It's all okay. I love you.'

And then of course I was blubbering too—damn pregnancy hormones—because although Mum hadn't actually said she'd forgiven Gralice, I knew she'd decided to let go and move on.

And that was enough.

38

As I trekked into the newspaper on my last day before clocking off for maternity leave, I felt like the love child of the Grinch and Ebenezer Scrooge. Everyone was Christmas crazy—decorations were strung across the ceiling, Darren even had Christmas carols playing in his office and random people on the tram had been wishing others Happy Holidays—but it was hard to get on board with all the festive fun when Gralice was knocking on death's door.

She'd lasted longer than her doctor had initially predicted, but it was touch and go whether she was going to live to see my father dress as Santa and scare the crap out of my niece and nephew. Despite the fact Mum and Dad had consciously uncoupled, they'd decided to spend Christmas together so that Will and I didn't have to split ourselves between the two of them. A good thing considering Sophie had just had the baby—another little boy—and three kids under school age was enough to handle without more family drama.

We were still planning a big lunch and the usual afternoon game of cricket in Phil and Craig's backyard, but festering beneath the organisation was the knowledge that if Gralice was gone no one would feel like any of it.

'We have to keep positive for the kids,' Mum had told me a few days ago after I'd thrown a dummy spit when she'd asked me what colour scheme I thought best for the table. I simply couldn't summon any enthusiasm for such trivial things. 'And for Gralice,' she'd added. 'We want her last days to be cheerful. She might still be here for Christmas and in that case, we should make it the best one ever.'

I wasn't sure how it could be when she could barely eat or move, but Mum needed to do all this or she'd fall apart.

'Ged! Woohoo! Last day.' Libby danced up to me as I approached my desk. 'How are you feeling?'

'Huge,' I snapped, slumping into my swivel chair.

She laughed, but I didn't find it very funny. At almost thirty-six weeks pregnant, I looked like I'd already finished off my own and everyone else's Christmas dinner and every tiny thing took monumental effort. I only wore slip-on shoes because putting anything else on was now almost impossible. My apartment was a pigsty because I couldn't reach the floor when I dropped something and I seemed to have become the clumsiest person on the planet. I was constantly hungry but in the past few days nausea had also returned.

I was well and truly fed up and ready to meet my daughter, but I still had a whole month to go!

'Yes, well.' Libby eyed my stomach as if she might accidentally get pregnant if she got too close, and backed away. 'I'll see you at your farewell morning tea.'

I groaned as I switched on my computer and let my head fall on my desk, which only succeeded in making my already sore head worse. The last thing I wanted was for everyone to make a fuss over me. I simply wanted to get on with my work, although there probably wouldn't be much for me to do anyway, as Darren wouldn't give me anything that I couldn't finish within the day. Perhaps I should have called in sick.

Sick. Thirty-six weeks pregnant. Was there really much difference between the two?

With that thought I dug into my handbag for a packet of Panadol and downed two with a few gulps from my water bottle. I really didn't like popping pills while pregnant, but I was nursing the mother of all headaches and didn't see how I was going to get through the day without it.

As predicted, Darren left me pretty much alone, so I spent the next couple of hours tidying my desk and emailing my contacts to tell them I'd be on leave for the next six months. I was almost finished and unsure what I was going to do with the rest of the day, when Libby summoned me to the staffroom.

Feigning enthusiasm, I forced a smile as I followed to find all my colleagues surrounding the table that held a massive cake in the shape of a stork, carrying a pink bundle in its beak. Even though it was cheesy and I hadn't wanted a fuss, I felt tears prickle my eyes— the littlest things set me off these days.

'Someone pass her the tissues,' Darren said with an uncomfortable chuckle.

Libby did the honours and then Darren cleared his throat and said a few words about my work ethic, my eye for a good story, and how much I'd be missed over the next few months. I reciprocated by saying how much I'd enjoyed working with him and everyone else and promising to bring the baby in for show and tell in the new year.

Then, finally, it was time for cake. No matter the fact eating it made me feel a little ill, I couldn't decline my own farewell cake, so I shovelled forkfuls into my mouth while accepting unsolicited advice from colleagues who had children.

'Definitely have the epidural!'

'And don't have a video camera there. I know everyone puts everything up online these days, but some things should be private.'

'Like your vagina.'

'Not that it's ever the same again after giving birth.'

They all nodded glumly as if mourning the death of their sex lives. Lucky for me, mine was already DOA, but that didn't mean I wanted to sit here all day and listen to their tales of woe. Why did anyone think pregnant women *wanted* to hear their horrific birth stories? I made a silent vow never to burden anyone with mine unless they begged me.

'I guess I'd better be getting back to work,' I said after swallowing the last morsel of cake. 'Thanks for all your advice.'

The girls reluctantly dispersed and I heaved myself out of my seat and took my dirty plate over to the sink. Christos had been lingering on the edge of the conversation, but he stepped up now.

'You okay?'

'What kind of question is that? I'm thirty-six weeks pregnant, my grandmother is dying *and* I've just had to listen to Fiona telling me about her baby getting stuck in her vagina.'

He grimaced. 'Sorry. But ... physically, how are you feeling? I hope you don't take this the wrong way, but you're a little pale and puffy.'

'I'm *pregnant*, Christos—I'm supposed to be fat!'

'Okay.' He held up his hands. 'I get it. Sorry. I'm just looking out for you and our baby.'

'No. *I'm* sorry.'

I knew he meant well. He'd been a good support over the past few weeks, putting aside our tumultuous romantic history and focusing on our future as co-parents instead.

'Have you had your iron levels checked lately? Carly needed an infusion when she was pregnant with Lexia and it gave her such an energy boost. Maybe you should go see the doctor?'

Although he trying to be helpful, it irritated me every time he compared me or my pregnancy to Carly or one of hers. Then again, perhaps that was unkind, considering I was constantly mentally comparing him to Jay.

'I'm sure I'm just stressed. I've got my obstetrician appointment on Monday morning, but I'll be fine after a weekend of rest.'

'Okay. Well, let me know if you need a lift home from work—I'm happy to drive you.'

'Thanks, but I'll be okay. I'm going to go see Darren and ask if I can leave now. That way the trams will be quiet, and I'm just sitting at my desk twiddling my thumbs anyway. I'd rather be with Gralice.'

'Good idea. How's she doing?'

I took a second so as not to get emotional. 'As expected. She sleeps a lot and sometimes when she's awake she gets confused about where she is or what time of day it is.'

He reached out and squeezed my arm. 'Must be heartbreaking to watch.'

'It is.' And I hadn't even told him the half of it—nothing about the fact she could no long control her own bladder and bowel movements or that her hands and feet already felt like they belonged to a corpse. 'I don't want to lose her, but she has no quality of life anymore.' I placed a hand on my stomach. 'I suspect she's trying to hold on until the baby is born but I don't think she can go on like this much longer.'

'Well, give her my love and let me know if there's anything I can do.'

'Thanks.' I swallowed and went to talk to Darren. 'I think I'm going to head home if that's okay with you. I've done everything I can here and I really want to be with my grandmother.'

Darren nodded—he'd been very supportive of me taking extra time to spend with Gralice as well as for my own doctor's appointments. 'Of course.'

'Well, I guess this is it.' I was so damn hormonal I felt teary at the fact that when I came back to work in six months' time, Darren would be gone. 'Thanks for being such a great boss. I've learned so much from you and it will definitely not be the same around here without you. But I wish you the best in your retirement and your next stage of life. Keep in touch, hey?'

My cheeks coloured. Why on earth had I said that last bit? It wasn't like we'd ever been more than colleagues, but I would miss him. He'd been an unofficial mentor these last few years and as male bosses in media went, he was one of the fairest and best.

'Thanks, Ged, I will.' He smiled warmly at me and sighed. 'I wasn't going to say anything because … well… I wasn't sure I should, but I want you to know you were my first choice for replacing me, and I wasn't the only one who believed you'd do a fabulous job. If I could've stayed for a little longer, until you came back from maternity leave, the position would be yours, but the missus would divorce me if I did. And, after almost forty years, I'm actually still kind of fond of her and am finally looking forward to spending some quality time together.'

His sweet words about his wife, Linda, almost set me off again, and that was even before I registered that deep down he believed I was the best person for the job.

'Thank you,' I managed with a tiny shrug and a grateful smile. 'Sometimes the timing just doesn't work out but I know the lift-out will be in good hands with Libby.'

I meant it too. It had been announced just a week ago that she had pipped Tom and the outside applicants at the post for the reins of the weekend lift-out and, once I'd gotten over the initial disappointment that a miracle hadn't occurred appointing *me* as editor, I had to concede that I was glad the role had gone to another well-deserving woman.

'I do believe it will be,' he said. 'Now, go be with your grandmother and have yourself a baby.'

'How's she doing?' I asked Kent, Gralice's nurse, when I arrived at Phil and Craig's house half an hour later.

'She's still hanging in there. I've just given her a bit of a freshen up.' Which accounted for the large stainless-steel bowl of water he was carrying. 'Go in and say hi, I'll just get rid of this stuff.'

I stepped into the living room where Gralice was lying in bed—she hadn't been out of it and into the recliner for two days now. Mum was sitting on one side of her and Phil and Craig on the other. Neither the massive bunch of roses by the open window nor the fresh air coming through it quite overrode the scent of illness that now permanently lingered in the air.

'Hello, darling,' Mum said, getting up as I came into the room. 'You're earlier than I thought.'

I flopped into the seat she'd vacated and scooped up Gralice's cool, papery hand. 'I'm officially on mat leave.'

She attempted a smile but even that was difficult these days. 'Did they … give you … a send-off?'

'Yep—there was a pink stork cake and terrifying birth stories. I've decided I'm not going to have a baby after all.'

She tried to laugh but started to cough instead.

We all rushed to offer her water and I couldn't help noticing how dry and flaky her lips were now. I dug my lip balm out of my bag and rubbed some over them. 'So, what are we going to do this afternoon?' I asked, glancing between everyone.

'Well, I've got some Christmas presents to wrap,' Mum said, pushing to a stand.

'And I'm going to go in to the shop and help a little,' Craig announced. I knew he was leaving because I'd arrived and didn't want to overwhelm Gralice with too many people at once. 'It's crazy busy this time of year and they could do with a hand.'

'My schedule's all free,' Phil said.

'And mine,' managed Gralice, her eyes still sparkling a little.

'Awesome. What do you say to a *Sex and the City* marathon?' I'd brought round the box set Gralice had given me for my thirtieth birthday and we were almost finished Season 4.

Phil laughed. 'Since when has your grandmother ever said no to that?'

After kissing Gralice goodbye, Craig left and Mum went off to continue her gift-wrapping. She'd moved in a couple of months ago and Gralice had only allowed it because she didn't have anywhere else to go. I spent most of my waking hours here as well, and Will, Sophie and the kids were frequent visitors in the evenings and at weekends. I'd seen more of my family in the last month than I had altogether in the last few years, but despite the fact Gralice now had Kent taking care of her, none of us wanted to stay away too long.

'Did someone say *Sex and the City*?' he said, coming back into the room. 'Now that's a plan I can get behind.'

'You like *Sex and the City*?' I asked, wondering if he was just putting it on for Gralice's benefit.

'Sure.' He came around the bed and proceeded to take my grandmother's temperature. 'A guy can learn a lot about life and love from those ladies.'

I laughed. 'In that case—pull up a pew.'

Over the past few weeks Kent had become like one of the family. As well as being the nice eye-candy Gralice had requested, he treated her like a person rather than a dying woman, and was kind, funny *and* sensitive. It was a miracle he was straight, but his accounts of his Tinder dates (with women) often had us in stitches and proved this point. Both Mum and Gralice had made less-than-subtle remarks about the two of us hooking up, but I just didn't feel that kind of spark for Kent. Not even a minuscule percentage of the spark I'd felt for Jay.

Sorrow caused my heart to cramp—no matter how hard I tried, he still kept creeping into my mind whenever I let down my guard. And when he landed in my head it was always hard to evict him. I wasn't proud to admit that I'd fallen down the rabbit hole of searching for him online more than once but, perhaps because of his job, he didn't have a social media presence, so all I found was Libby's article.

Thank God I couldn't drink or who knows how many drunken texts I'd have sent.

'You okay, Ged?' Kent's question pulled me out of my funk.

'Yeah, fine.' I grabbed the remote and pressed play, once again working hard to banish Jay from my mind. I refused to let him hog so much headspace right now when I wanted to be making the most of the precious time I had left with Gralice.

39

We were keeping twenty-four hour bedside vigil now. Gralice's doctor had warned us it was a matter of days before we would have to say our final goodbye.

She was pretty much permanently asleep, drifting it seemed in and out of consciousness, less and less responsive to our touch or our voices. We kept *Sex and the City* on quietly in the background, but she hadn't managed to stay awake through a full episode since Friday afternoon. Although the weather was heating up outside, Gralice seemed to be constantly cold and we had to use blankets to keep her warm while we gently rubbed her hands and feet to aid her circulation.

I spent most of my time in the recliner (as my grandmother was now permanently in bed) dozing and eating everything Mum made despite the fact most of it now made me feel ill.

'You can't spend another night in that chair,' Mum said just after dinner. 'Why don't you take my bed tonight?'

'Or better still,' Kent added, 'go home and get some proper rest. You need your sleep too, Marie, and I'll be here all night.'

'So will I,' Will said. 'Sophie's mum has come over to help with the kids for a bit.'

In some ways the lure of my own bed was tempting, but what if in my few hours' reprieve Gralice chose to slip away? I couldn't bear the thought of not being here when she took her final breath.

As if reading my mind, Kent said in a low voice, 'I don't think we're quite there yet, and you shouldn't forget you're very heavily pregnant. Your sleep is important and I know your grandmother would agree with me.'

Only after they'd promised to call the second there was any significant change did I relent. I needed a change of clothes, and my appointment at ten o'clock tomorrow morning was closer to my place than it was to Phil and Craig's.

Dad drove me and Coco home. I fed her a late dinner, had a much-needed shower, took another couple of painkillers to hopefully ease my headache, then fell into bed. And damn my own mattress and sheets felt good. Once during the night I woke with slight abdominal pain and I wondered if I was going into labour, but the pain faded so I didn't worry too much and ended up catching more Zs than I had in weeks.

I woke to Coco standing on the bed beside me, her terrible breath washing over me as she panted excitedly, her leash hanging between her teeth. She hadn't been totally neglected in the last few weeks—she always came with me to Phil and Craig's and there was always someone there to take her for a walk, but I hadn't taken her myself for quite some time.

My heart thudded at thought of my grandmother. What if I'd slept through a phone call?

I sat up quickly, ignoring the dizziness that rushed to my head, and snatched my mobile off my bedside table. There were no missed calls on my screen but I called Mum just in case.

'Morning, sweetheart. How did you sleep?'

'Fine. How's Gralice?'

'Still the same, honey. Would you like me to come to your appointment with you this morning?'

'It's okay. I'll be fine and I'll be over straight after. Tell Gralice I love her.'

'I will.'

As I hung up, I looked at Coco, her head cocked to one side, the lead still in her mouth. The last thing I felt like was moving, but there were still a couple of hours until my appointment and perhaps a little fresh air would do me good—I glanced down at my swollen feet—not to mention the exercise.

'Okay, girl. You twisted my arm. Walkies it is.'

As Coco scoffed down her breakfast, I forced myself to eat a slice of Vegemite on toast, then popped two painkillers before we set off to the park. I thought of going further afield to eliminate the risk of running into Jay but quite aside from the fact I didn't have the energy, I couldn't live my life around him. Carlton Gardens had a fabulous playground and I would want to take my daughter there.

It was already busy by the time we arrived—lots of young families and the usual joggers, all in festive spirits. Most of the kids were dressed in Christmas T-shirts and two joggers I passed were even wearing Santa hats (if not much else). I 'Merry Christmas'd everyone while inwardly thinking the twenty-fifth of December could take a hike. Trying to keep my cool when it was already getting warm, for once I didn't mind Coco stopping every five seconds to sniff something.

As she nosed around a tree, I took a moment to catch my breath. I was seriously unfit but that was another thing to worry about when I was no longer harbouring another person inside me.

'I think it's time to go home,' I told Coco as she tugged at the leash and we took off again.

We'd barely walked two feet when a sudden dizziness overcame me and a sharp pain stabbed in my belly. *Please don't let me go into labour here.* Clutching my stomach, I staggered towards a park bench, letting go of the leash in my panic. By the time I reached it, my feet were growing numb with pins and needles and the headache I'd been nursing for days appeared to have exploded. Barely able to function with the pain, I dug into my pocket for my phone, only to realise I didn't have it.

'Shit!' Tears rushed to my eyes. What the hell was I going to do?

As if sensing something wasn't quite right, Coco laid her head on my knee and whined. The pain in my head so strong now I could barely concentrate. I looked around for someone I could cast as my good Samaritan, but there was not a soul in sight. I appeared to have taken respite in the one unpopulated part of the park.

Just when I was about to start yelling for help, a jogger appeared in the distance and relief swamped my body. As the figure grew closer, Coco lifted her head and her tail began to wag. Although my vision was a little blurry, I managed to make out the reason for her excitement.

'Geraldine? Are you okay?'

Just my luck. Of all the people. Of all the days.

I opened my mouth to offer Jay some snarky answer to his clearly stupid question but before I could answer, everything went black.

40

I opened my eyes to find myself in a hospital bed, Mum and Dad sitting on either side of me. I felt as if I'd been hit by a truck.

'Oh, Geraldine, thank God,' my mother exclaimed, leaning close and clutching my hand to her chest.

At the relief in her voice, I glanced down at my stomach to see it was much flatter than I remembered. My hands quickly followed my gaze and I gasped in pain and panic as a squidginess greeted them.

'My baby! Where's my baby? Is she okay?!'

'It's alright, love,' Dad said, patting my shoulder. 'Your little girl is fine.'

'She was born by caesarean yesterday afternoon and she's gorgeous.' Mum's smile was wide. 'It's you we've been worried about.'

The breath rushed through my lungs and out my mouth, but the relief was short-lived. I tried to sit up as I looked around the room, but it hurt too damn much. 'Where is she then?'

'Alice is with the nurses. I'll go get them now you're awake.'

'Here, have some water,' Dad said as Mum left the room. He reached for a remote and the bed inclined a little, pushing me upwards. Although parched, I barely drank anything before bombarding him with questions.

'What day is it?'

'Tuesday, sweetheart.'

My mind scrambled to put itself together and make sense of what this meant. The last thing I remembered was Monday morning at the park. I recalled feeling unwell, but I couldn't remember getting home.

'What happened?'

'You had a seizure due to a condition called eclampsia. You were rushed to hospital in an ambulance.'

'Eclampsia? But …' I knew about this condition of course, but wasn't pre-eclampsia supposed to come first? Suddenly my drastic weight gain, dizziness, headaches and returned nausea made sense. How had I been so stupid, so distracted, so as not to see the signs?

'Apparently, it's quite serious,' Dad continued, 'and you're both lucky to have pulled through. The baby spent the night in the special care nursery but she's doing well. Her blood sugar was a little low and she can't maintain her temperature yet, but the doctor said she's going to be just fine.'

Again, relief overcame me and I started to cry. Dad offered me a tissue and took my other hand in his. 'There, there, sweetheart, it's going to be okay.'

My heart stilled at his words, which reminded me that not *everything* was going to be okay. Nothing was going to be okay ever again. 'Gralice?' I blurted. 'Is she still …?'

He nodded. 'She was delighted to hear the news of Alice's birth and she actually managed to say to tell you congratulations.'

I sniffed. 'So, how did I get here?'

'Well, apparently a friend of yours came to your rescue. You and Coco were in the park and he stumbled upon you just as the seizure began.' Dad frowned. 'I shudder to think what could have happened if he wasn't there.'

Goosebumps erupted on my skin as a memory flashed into my mind: I'd been panicking on the park bench when Jay had appeared in the distance. Looked like I owed him my and my baby's life. 'Hang on ... where's Coco now? Is she with Phil and Craig?'

Dad shook his head. 'Your friend Jay is looking after her. Lovely bloke—said he'd keep her as long as you need.'

At that moment, Mum reappeared, bringing with her a nurse and Christos, who was wheeling a see-through hospital bassinet with a tiny white cocoon in it.

'Hey, Ged.' His voice full of emotion and a proud smile on his face, he lifted the bundle from the bassinet and sat down beside me. 'Our little girl is gorgeous.'

I stared at her—utterly speechless and mesmerised by her perfection. She wore a white beanie on her head, her eyes were closed, her nose and mouth like a painting, and one tiny hand was poking out the top of the swaddling. Her skin was milky, but her cheeks had a lovely tinge of red, just like a porcelain doll, only even more perfect.

'Let me just do your obs and then you can hold her,' said the nurse.

Dad stepped back so she could do so and I barely noticed as my blood pressure and temperature were taken. I couldn't drag my eyes off my girl.

'Are you ready to hold her?' Christos asked when the nurse was done.

I nodded, then she inclined the bed even more and helped me into a sitting position.

'Here you are.' Christos laid our daughter in my arms and for a few moments I forgot to breathe. I'd never held anything so precious and I was terrified I might do something wrong and break her. The nurse stepped back a little as Mum got her camera out and snapped a few photos.

Slowly, I began to relax. Still keeping her firmly against me, I extracted one hand and ran a finger over the soft skin of her cheek. 'Does she have any hair?'

Christos nodded. 'A fair bit.'

'What colour is it?'

'You can take her hat off and see for yourself,' said the nurse with a smile. 'She's warm enough for now.'

My hand shaking, I peeled back the little white hat and gazed down at her thick black hair. Guess there was no question of who her father was now.

'She looks almost exactly like Isidore did as a baby,' Christos said. 'By the way, the kids are super excited about their new sister and can't wait to meet her.'

I grinned at him, then turned my attention back to our daughter. More confident now, I unwrapped her slightly to continue my examination. 'Oh my goodness, look,' I gushed at the sight of her perfectly tiny toes.

Christos, Mum and Dad chuckled and I'm not sure whether it was their noise or my disturbance, but Alice stretched out her little arms and blinked open her eyes. She took one look at me and started to wail. Immediately my breasts tingled.

I panicked, glancing from Christos to the nurse. 'Is she okay?'

The nurse gave me a smile. 'She's fine. She's just hungry. Do you think you're feeling well enough to try and feed her?'

I nodded, both nervous and excited by the prospect.

Mum, Dad and Christos made themselves scarce while the nurse—who I discovered was called Susan—patiently showed me how to hold Alice against my chest. My arms were a little shaky and I also felt a little woozy, which Susan assured me was normal in my condition. Apparently, I was on medication to get my blood pressure and protein levels back to normal but that would take a while.

Once again, I held my breath as Susan took my breast in one hand and Alice's little head in another and, after a little manoeuvring, Alice latched on to my nipple. It was the weirdest sensation in the world, and it wasn't the wonderful experience I'd been fantasising about whenever I'd thought of breastfeeding. Alice remained attached for a grand total of five seconds, before tearing her head away and screaming again. For a little person she sure as hell made a lot of noise.

Susan didn't appear fazed and immediately tried to put us back together. This time Alice lasted only two seconds, which made me want to cry along with her. I felt like such a failure. Not only had I needed a caesarean, I hadn't even been awake during the birth, and now this.

'Am I doing something wrong?'

'No, darling,' Susan assured me. 'Even after the most complication-free delivery, it can sometimes take a while to establish breastfeeding. We'll keep trying, but don't lose heart—Alice is getting everything she needs in the meantime.'

'But isn't breastmilk best?'

'Of course, which is why we'll get you expressing ASAP. But formula is also wonderful these days, and you stressing over how your baby is feeding won't be good for anyone. You've been through a lot. Why don't I go get a bottle and you can feed her and then, if you're feeling up to it, you can express.'

'Okay. If you're sure.' I was exhausted and just wanted Alice to stop crying.

Susan nodded, swiftly plucking my baby from my arms. She went to the door and called Christos back into the room. He took a screaming Alice as the nurse went off to fetch the bottle.

'I'm not sure I'm going to be any good at this,' I said, watching as he expertly rocked her.

He smiled down at me. 'You'll be fantastic. The fact you're already worrying about doing the best by her proves that, but you need to take care of you and get better, so you can properly take care of her.'

There was a knock on the door and Mum poked her head back around. 'Can we come in?'

'Yes.' I sniffed and wiped my eyes with the back of my hand.

'How'd the feeding go?'

'Terrible,' I said and burst into tears again.

'There there, sweetheart.' Mum stroked my hair softly as she spoke. 'It took me weeks to conquer the whole breastfeeding thing with Will. Give it time.'

Susan returned with the bottle and before I knew it Alice had been placed back in my arms and the bottle into my hand. Instinctively, I brushed it against her lips and she latched on and began suckling away as if her life depended on it. *Thank God*. A rush of gratitude hit me and once again tears welled. I hoped the hospital had a big supply of tissues.

Everyone was silent as Alice suckled, all of us watching her in awe. Her eyes were closed and she was so beautiful, so perfect, that I reckoned I could watch her forever and never get bored.

'She doesn't seem to be actually drinking much,' I said after a while. The bottle still looked quite full.

'Newborns take a long time to drink,' Susan explained, 'and she's had a bit of an ordeal. She's doing well, considering.'

I nodded and returned my attention to my daughter who suddenly opened her eyes and looked right into mine. I swear my heart turned over in my chest.

'Hello, little one,' I whispered. 'I'm your mummy and I'm so happy to meet you. Mummy loves you so very much.'

There was a knock on the door and I looked up to see my obstetrician enter.

'Morning, Ged,' Dr Eberlen said, with her usual full-faced smile. 'You gave us quite a shock there yesterday, so I'm very pleased to see you sitting up. Isn't your daughter divine?'

'I think so,' I replied, unable to stop the smile spreading on my face.

'When she's finished, I need to take a quick look at your caesarean site and also check a few things.' She looked to my parents. 'I know you've all been anxious, but now Ged's awake we might need a few moments' privacy.'

'Of course,' Mum and Dad said in unison, then Mum added, 'I should be getting back to ...' She didn't finish the sentence but I knew she was thinking of Gralice. 'We'll be back later this evening, that's if you think you'll be up for visitors? Or maybe we should wait until tomorrow morning? I know Will, Sophie and the kids are desperate to come see you as well.'

'And my three,' Christos added. 'Not sure I can keep them away much longer.'

Visitors? I had nothing against visitors in theory, but I just wanted to get out of hospital so I could go see my grandmother—I couldn't miss the chance to say goodbye.

'Do you think I'll be able to go home tonight?'

Dr Eberlen's eyes widened. 'I'm afraid you won't be going home for quite a few days, Ged. We need to make sure Alice is gaining weight and also get you healthy again before we can discharge you both.'

'What? But I've read of women getting out of hospital hours after giving birth!'

'That's when delivery is straightforward, and even then we prefer them to have established good feeding before we send them off to fend for themselves. You're very sick—I don't want to scare you, but you could have died, and we're not completely out of the woods yet.'

While this made sense and I felt stupid for thinking otherwise, my circumstances were extenuating.

'But what about Gralice?' I clutched her namesake a little too tightly and suddenly struggled to breathe.

How could I live with the knowledge that my two Alices had been in the world at the same time and yet were unable to meet? It was a miracle my grandmother had lasted this long—she'd held out for this—but I knew even a few more days would be pushing it.

The hospital suddenly felt like a prison and this felt like both the happiest and worst day of my life.

Alice stopped suckling and I looked down to see that she'd fallen asleep.

'Do you think your kids could wait until tomorrow?' I asked Christos. 'I'm knackered.'

Although he looked disappointed, he nodded. 'Of course.'

'Thanks. And Mum, do you mind telling Will and Soph tomorrow too? I'm sure I'll be feeling much better after a good night's sleep.' I thought no such thing, but I wanted to give them hope.

'Okay, sweetheart.' Mum leaned over and kissed me on the forehead, then did the same to Alice. 'We'll let you rest and see you tomorrow but message me if you need anything.'

'I will.' I swallowed hard to stop from crying again. 'And can you tell Gralice I love her?'

Mum nodded and we both lost the battle with tears. 'How about I call you when we get home? I'll hold the phone for her and you can tell her yourself.'

Mum and Dad left and Christos lifted Alice from my arms and placed her back in the bassinet. 'I'll let the doctor do her stuff and then I'll be back.'

'You don't have to hang around,' I said. 'We're fine and I really need to rest.' I'd never felt so tired in my life and I just wanted to be alone with my baby.

'Okay. No worries.' He pulled out his mobile and took a few more shots of Alice. 'I'll be back tomorrow. And remember, call me if you need anything.'

He kissed our little girl goodbye and then, with one last smile for me, left.

'I'm going to take Alice back to the nursery for a bit,' Susan said, 'So Dr Eberlen can examine you.'

'Can't she stay with me?' I was already unnerved by the thought of parting with her.

Susan offered me a sympathetic smile. 'We still need to keep an eye on her temperature and sugar levels, but I'll bring her back as soon as she wakes for her next feed. In the meantime, you get as much rest as you can.'

Following the examination, another nurse came in to change the dressing on my scar and then I was left alone. I stared at the ceiling and once again struggled to control my tears. The books had told me that tears and heightened emotions in the first few days post-birth were normal, but nothing else felt like it was.

I wished Alice could stay with me, I wished I could see Gralice one last time, I wished dogs were allowed in hospitals, and I wished things had turned out differently with Jay. At the thought of him,

I remembered what Dad had said about him looking after Coco, which only made me love him more.

Noticing my phone on the bedside table, I reached across for it and opened a new message. What did I have to lose?

Hey Jay, thanks so much for saving me yesterday and thanks for looking after Coco. It means the world. Give her a hug for me and in case you haven't heard, I delivered a beautiful baby girl. Her name is Alice Sappho and I'm besotted with her. Chat soon. Love Ged.

I held my breath as I pushed send, wondering if he would respond. Before too long, a message popped up on my screen.

Congratulations. I can't wait to meet her.

With a sigh, I placed the phone back on the table and closed my eyes. I couldn't help wishing for more, but at the same time I was thankful for this much.

I woke a while later to a commotion outside my door and guessed it might be an orderly bringing me dinner. I didn't feel like eating but would force food into my mouth for Alice's sake—Susan had told me how important it was for me to eat and drink enough to help my milk production.

To my utmost delight, it wasn't food, but a new nurse wheeling in Alice's bassinet. I was immediately awake and anxious to hold her. The nurse introduced herself as Karen and helped me incline my bed.

'Are you ready to try feeding Alice again?'

I nodded, despite my heart fluttering nervously at the thought.

'Okay.' Karen plucked my little girl from the bassinet. She was grizzling, but thankfully not fully screaming. I'd already opened the top of my gown in anticipation, but I held my breath as Karen helped me position Alice. I braced myself for the pull back and the screams, but miraculously, they didn't come. Alice lifted her tiny arm and placed her tiny hand on my bare breast, let out what sounded like a contented sigh and suckled away.

By the time she'd finished, I was feeling victorious and so when Karen suggested she help me with a shower, I leapt at the opportunity. I hadn't realised just how icky I was feeling until she mentioned it.

Showering with a painful cut across my abdomen wasn't the easiest of tasks, but I felt so much better once I was in fresh pyjamas. Karen was just settling me back into the bed when there was a knock at the door.

'Expecting anyone?' she asked.

I shook my head. My guess was that Christos couldn't keep away from Alice and, as I glanced down into the bassinet at our peacefully sleeping baby, I couldn't blame him.

But when the door peeled open, it was Granddad Phil and Granddad Craig who stepped into the room—Phil holding a mammoth rainbow-coloured teddy bear and Craig a bunch of bright gerberas so big he was barely visible behind them.

'Oh my goodness,' I shrieked. 'Come and meet your new great-granddaughter.'

They kissed me and gushed accordingly over Alice.

'Do you want to hold her?' I asked, looking to Karen for confirmation this was okay.

She nodded, but Phil and Craig exchanged a look. 'Actually, do you think you have room for one more visitor?'

I frowned, but before I could reply, there was noise at the door and I looked over to see Mum and Will pushing Gralice in a wheelchair.

'Oh my God!' I gasped as my eyes poured out my joy. Forgetting my scar, I flung back my covers, but the pain stopped me in my tracks.

'Take care,' Karen said, reaching out a steadying hand.

'Ged.' Gralice managed only one word, her face was so gaunt and her eyes sunken, but I saw the love in her heart as she looked at me.

Will pushed her wheelchair as close to both the bed and bassinet as he could get and I reached out my hand, clasping her frail one. 'Alice, meet Alice.'

And then the most wonderful thing in the world happened. Karen lifted my baby from her bassinet and placed her in the crook of my grandmother's arm; she was too weak to hold Alice on her own, but my mother and Karen supported her.

A smile grew on Gralice's face as she gazed down at her great-granddaughter and my heart felt so full I was sure it would burst. Craig and Will took photos and I knew those pictures would be my most treasured possessions always.

I didn't even try to rein in my tears when, fifteen minutes later, Mum and Will wheeled Gralice out of my hospital room, with Craig and Phil following behind.

I knew I would never see her again.

41

The following day, I woke up to the fright of my life. The room was only dimly lit and there was a man sitting next to my bed. It took all of five seconds for me to identify him as Jay but that didn't calm my heart any.

'Merry Christmas, Sleeping Beauty.'

Thinking I must still be asleep, and this a dream, I rubbed my eyes and felt around for the little remote thingy that would help me sit up.

'Here.' He found it first and handed it to me. As he did, our fingers brushed against each other and my heart skipped a beat.

'What are you doing here?' I blurted, cringing inwardly at just how shocking I must look.

He lifted a bottle of Moët with a silver ribbon wrapped around it. 'I promised you a bottle of bubbles when you popped and I'm a man of my word. Congratulations.'

'Wow, thank you. If it wasn't ...' I glanced around me for a clock but came up blank. 'What time is it?'

'Just after six.'

'If it wasn't so early and I wasn't breastfeeding, I'd guzzle the lot of that right here right now. How long have you been here?'

He shrugged. 'About half an hour—I snuck in when the nurses weren't looking. I'd have come yesterday but there was something I couldn't get out of at work. It was a late one, or rather an early one, but I came as soon as I could. I must say you're looking a lot better than you did a couple of days ago.'

It was hardly a compliment, considering the last time he'd seen me I'd been carrying litres of extra fluid and convulsing, but I couldn't deny the buzz inside me.

'Do you want to see a picture of my daughter?' I offered him my phone, which already contained a zillion shots of Alice.

'She's beautiful,' Jay said as he gazed down at the screen and then slowly looked back to me, 'just like her mother.'

Despite the fact my body still bore stitches and my breasts were tingling as if about to leak milk, everything inside me quivered, but I knew I shouldn't read anything into it. 'Thank you for rescuing me the other day. I don't know what would have happened to me and Alice if you hadn't come along.'

'I'm sure some other person would have stopped.'

'Well, I'm glad it was you. And I'll forever be in your debt.'

'No, you won't. I'm glad I was there too.' He rubbed his lips together a moment. 'Although I've never been so scared as I was when I watched the paramedics hurry you off in the ambulance, lights and sirens blaring, so don't ever torture me like that again, okay?'

I wasn't sure whether to laugh or cry. His words sounded so heartfelt, as if he really cared about me, but I knew it was probably new mum hormones messing with my sensibilities. 'I'll try not to,' I promised.

'Good.' His deep voice sent shivers down my spine and suddenly the air in the room felt stifling. Our gazes met, and I dared to wonder if the thoughts whirling through his head were even slightly in alignment with mine.

The door opened and we both startled, turning to see a nurse—Susan from yesterday—walking into the room wheeling a crying Alice in her bassinet.

'Good morning,' she sang softly. 'Oh.' She blinked and looked from me to Jay. 'I see you've already got a visitor.'

'Hello.' He nodded at her.

'Hi, Susan,' I said. 'This is my friend, Jay. He's here to meet Alice.'

'Lovely to meet you,' Susan said as she lifted my little girl from the bassinet, 'but I think Alice has one thing on her mind right now and I'm afraid it isn't socialising.'

She passed her to me. It was already instinctual to shift my gown and I smiled as my little girl snuggled into me, latched on and made that little mewl of satisfaction.

'Well,' Jay cleared his throat. 'I guess I'll be going. It was great to—'

'No,' I interrupted. 'Stay.' I wasn't ready to say goodbye just yet, even though I had a feeling that I would see him again. 'You're not scared of a little bare female flesh, are you?'

He raised his eyebrows. 'Who me? Never.'

'Well then,' I said, 'make yourself useful and pour me a glass of water—breastfeeding is thirsty work.'

He chuckled and did as he was told.

'You two seem to have the hang of things now,' Susan said, 'so I'll leave you in peace a little while. Buzz me if you need me.'

'Thank you.' I smiled as Susan left the room and refocused my attentions on Alice, to see that Jay was also staring down at her.

'I'm sorry,' he whispered.

'What have you got to be sorry for?'

He gave me a look of disbelief. 'For the way I reacted when you told me you were pregnant. I was a complete and utter jerk.'

'No arguments here, but,' I smiled at him and stretched out my free hand to squeeze his, 'I accept your apology.'

'Thank you.'

We sat in silence a few moments, our hands linked. It was a perfect, peaceful, beautiful moment and my heart filled with love for these two people.

Whether it was the fact I was feeling invincible after having a baby and surviving the ordeal that had brought us to the hospital or something else entirely, I suddenly found the courage to ask Jay what had been weighing on my mind for months. 'Why are you so scared?'

He frowned. 'Of what?'

'Of getting close to anyone—of having kids and making connections. And don't give me any bullshit about the carbon footprint.'

'The carbon footprint isn't bullshit.'

I cocked my head to one side and glared at him. 'You know what I mean.'

He sighed and his shoulders dropped. 'Okay. You're right. I am scared.' There was a pause, but I didn't rush to fill it. Eventually he admitted, 'My dad was a monster. What if I am too?'

I could tell it was his deepest, darkest fear.

'You're not like your dad. You do good every day, fighting crime, fighting monsters. But even if I didn't know that, I'd know that you aren't anything like your father. A monster wouldn't take care of me the way you did when you thought I was sick.' His lips quirked a little at that, but I went on. 'A monster wouldn't treat my dog like a real lady. A monster wouldn't walk little old ladies' dogs either.

A monster wouldn't go on a cruise they didn't want to go on because they loved their grandparents. And, I saw the way you were with Henry—I saw the love in your eyes for him. A monster wouldn't be capable of that.'

'You know how I told you my wife cheated on me?'

I nodded.

'Well, when I found them, I saw red. I've never felt such anger and it terrified me. I wanted to hurt not only my friend, but also my wife—I wanted to hit her. I swear I could have killed them both.'

'So, what did you do?'

'I walked out of the room and punched my fist into a brick wall. I broke all my knuckles and my hand has never been the same again, but it's a constant reminder of what I'm capable of.'

I looked down at his hand and smoothed my fingers over the slightly misshapen knuckles.

'A monster would have hit her,' I said. 'A monster would have killed them, but you didn't.'

He looked at me with such intensity, as if he wanted to believe me but couldn't quite bring himself to do so, and then Alice murmured, reminding us of her presence.

Jay turned his gaze on her. 'You two really are the most beautiful girls in the world,' he said. 'And I'm really glad I met you, Ged Johnston.'

A lump formed in my throat. 'I'm really glad I met you too.'

We stared at each other a few long moments, then Jay dropped my hand and dug into his backpack. 'I almost forgot. I bought a little gift for Alice as well. What do you think?'

He held up a tiny blue jumpsuit, with none other than a picture of Elvis on the front and a caption: 'Shake, Rattle and Roll.'

It was the best present ever. 'I absolutely love it. Thank you.'

Epilogue

'Cute dog, cute baby,' said a stranger with a smile as I pushed Alice's pram along the path in Carlton Gardens.

'Thanks.' I smiled as the stranger walked on and paused to look down at my little girl, all rosy-cheeked and sucking on the edge of the soft yellow blanket Christos had given her. Already she knew her mind and squealed whenever we tried to take it off her.

I'd been a mother for five months and Gralice had been gone exactly the same amount of time—she died at Phil and Craig's place, with them, Mum and Will by her side, a few hours after visiting me and Alice in hospital. It might not have been the way she'd wanted to go but she was surrounded by loved ones, she'd seen my little girl, and apparently she'd looked peaceful when she shut her eyes for the final time.

Adjusting to motherhood and life without my grandmother took some time, although I wasn't sure I'd ever be completely accustomed to either. Don't get me wrong, little Alice was the undisputed light of my life, the best decision I ever made, but some days I still had to pinch myself when I woke up and heard her gurgling in her cot. In the same way, I often went to call Gralice and was gobsmacked when I remembered she can't answer.

I finished the first draft of her biography in the early months of Alice's life and polished it up. A few friends commented how amazing I was to have written a book while taking care of a baby, but I couldn't deny I'd had a lot of support. Alice is still living full-time with me, but Christos is a major player in her life, often coming over on his days off to take her out for long walks so I could work. In a wonderful way, finishing my grandmother's biography helped me not only feel close to her still, but also gave me an outlet from the monotony of changing nappies hour after hour.

Mum and I were closer than we'd ever been. She's been travelling and blogging her way around Brazil with Rosa (yeah, they got back together) but in the early months with Alice, she was a major practical and emotional support and we've spoken almost daily while she's been away. She'll be back in a couple of weeks because I'm returning to work at the end of June and she's going to look after Alice two days a week. She'll go to daycare two days, and Dad is going to have her for the fifth.

He's been incredible in the past few months as well—people who haven't seen him in a while wouldn't recognise him if they passed him in the street. With Jay's encouragement, he joined a gym, lost a lot of the middle-age spread he'd been carrying, and learned to cook himself very healthy meals. He's happier than I've ever known him and confessed to me last week that he'd just started seeing one of the women who used to play bowls with him and Mum.

Libby called me yesterday to discuss my return to work. Weirdly, I wasn't as excited as I thought I'd be. It's not that I wasn't looking forward to the actual job, it was the prospect of leaving Alice day in, day out that filled me with dread. She just seem so little, yet at the same time something exciting happened with her almost every day. Nothing made me happier than when I did something inadvertently that made her laugh. The thought of maybe missing her milestones and not being around to make her laugh as much actually made me feel physically ill.

I honestly never thought I'd be one of those women who contemplated giving up work to stay home with their baby. I'm not—not that there'd be anything wrong with that—but I just wanted a little more time. Maybe if I hadn't had the outlet of writing Gralice's biography, I *would* be itching to go back to work, but I didn't miss the paper nearly as much as I'd imagined I would.

Not having kids herself, I didn't think Libby would understand, but when I confessed how I was feeling, she was surprisingly supportive. We had a long chat about the need to make the working environment more friendly for working mothers and not only did she suggest that maybe I could work a bit from home, together we're going to rally for getting on-site childcare facilities.

'Which is something your great-grandmother would very much approve of,' I said as Alice started to grizzle. I leaned down, plucked her out of the pram and held her up in the air before bringing her down again and kissing her on her sweet little nose.

She squealed in delight.

'Ged!' I startled at the sound of my name and turned to see Jay jogging towards me.

I wasn't expecting him—we'd only said goodbye to each other about ten minutes ago—but I was always happy to see him. If you'd told me when I'd first met him on the cruise we'd have become such good friends, I'd probably have laughed, but he'd also been a wonderful support since Alice was born. I loved the stimulating and sometimes heated conversations we had about practically everything, and the way he'd been monumental in helping our two families—the Frenches and the Johnstons—come together. There'd already been a number of family get-togethers that even Phil and Craig had been invited to. I really couldn't have dreamed of Mum meeting her biological family going any better, but at the same time, I couldn't help the occasional twinge of disappointment that things hadn't become romantic between Jay and me.

Every nerve ending in my body still tingled whenever he was near, yet I tried not to focus on what I didn't have, but rather the wonderful things I did. Having Jay in my life as a friend was definitely better than not having him at all.

'I thought you were off to work,' I said as he stopped in front of us. He'd no doubt run all the way from his house and he hadn't even worked up a sweat.

He smiled at Alice and brushed his thumb affectionately over her cheek. 'As I was leaving, I heard your phone ringing and realised you must have dropped it down the side of my couch.'

I looked at his outstretched palm to see my mobile resting in it. This is how different my life was now—I hadn't even noticed it was missing. 'Thanks,' I said, remembering that I'd taken it out of my bag to take a photo of Alice while he and I were having a coffee.

'I usually wouldn't answer your phone ...' He looked a little sheepish. 'But it rang again as I was heading out, and once more on my way. I thought it might be important and maybe I could take a message, so ...' Sheepish turned to full-blown grin. 'It was Holly Pearson. She said she's finished reading *My Grandmother's Way* and she wants you to call her back ASAP.'

My heart slammed to a halt. 'Holly called?'

He nodded and I gulped, my body suddenly awash with nerves. I'd only sent it to her a couple of days ago. 'What if she's calling to tell me how shite it is?'

Jay shook his head. 'She won't be. I've read it, remember.'

I most certainly did. He'd turned up at my apartment the day after I'd given it to him wearing a T-shirt that declared 'This is what a feminist looks like', and then proceeded to tell me he'd pulled an all-nighter to finish it and it was one of the most moving books he'd ever read.

'Well,' Jay urged, 'don't just stand there. Call her back. Or I will.'

I blinked, laughed nervously, glanced down at my phone and thrust Alice at Jay. He took her happily. My heart stammering, I stepped a few feet away as I pressed Holly's name on my screen.

She answered in less than two rings. 'Ged,' she exclaimed. 'You are a freaking genius! Best biography I've read in over a decade. Your writing ... it's ... it almost reads like fiction. It's so evocative, yet at the same time this is a powerful must-read for all Australians—women *and* men. It's a positive and timely reminder of how far we've come but also how far we've still got to go.'

'Wow,' was all I managed to say, stunned at her high praise.

She laughed. 'Oh, I've got much more to say about *My Grandmother's Way* and I'd love you to come in to the office to talk to the team about it.'

'Oh my God.' My knees wobbled. Tears rushed to my eyes. 'Really?'

'Yes. I know it's not usually the kind of book I publish, but I'm desperate to publish this one. I couldn't sleep guilt-free at night if I didn't tell you I think there'll be other publishers who'll want it just as badly as I do, so it would probably be remiss of you not to submit it elsewhere, but I'm thankful we at Bourne have a head start on putting together an offer.'

I couldn't believe my ears. Was she serious? Was this for real?

'Geraldine,' she said, 'are you still there?'

'Yep. Sorry. I'm just ...' My knees wobbled. Tears rushed to my eyes. I just wished Gralice were here to experience this with me.

'Say no more. I've got to go anyway, but I wanted to give you the heads up before I had my assistant email to set up a meeting. You have a good day and we'll talk soon.'

Before I could even say goodbye, she'd gone.

Jay and Alice were both looking at me as I turned back to face them.

'Well?' he asked. 'What did she say?'

And so I told him, my voice shaking because I was almost unable to believe what had just happened.

'I'm not surprised in the slightest. But congratulations.'

'Hold the congratulations.' I held up my hand, trying to stop myself from bursting into tears. 'It's not a done deal yet.'

'Only a matter of time,' he said, 'only a matter of time. We're both super proud of you, aren't we, Alice?'

In response my daughter cocked her head to one side and made a gurgling noise. We both laughed, then Jay leaned forward and, taking me completely by surprise, kissed me on the lips.

At first I thought it was just a congratulatory peck, but as Jay's mouth lingered on mine, his free hand reached up to my head, his fingers slid through my hair and his tongue nudged open my lips. He stole the breath from my lungs as he kissed me like I'd been dreaming of being kissed for the past five months.

He tasted like all my favourite foods rolled into one fantasy dish and I never wanted to stop eating, but the little person witnessing this passionate frenzy jolted me from the moment and back to the real world.

'What was that?' I asked as I pulled back and all but snatched my daughter from Jay's arms.

He smiled down at me with the expression that once infuriated me, then comforted me, and now infuriated me all over again. 'It was a kiss. And a hell of a good one if you ask me.'

Well, that was undebatable, but also not the point.

'You can't just go around kissing people!' My heart was still racing from the experience. 'Especially not when you know how they feel about you. It's not fair.'

As I blinked back tears, he lifted his hands and cupped my face. 'Would it be okay to kiss you if I told you I feel exactly the same about you as you do about me?'

His hands felt so good on my skin, his mouth once again inches from mine and his breath warm and sweet.

'What?' I whispered, deciding that this whole day must be a dream, that I must indeed still be asleep.

'I was going to ask you out and declare my feelings over a fancy romantic dinner, but … I couldn't wait to kiss you another moment longer.'

'What are you saying? What do you want?'

'You,' he said, his voice low as his thumb stroked over my cheek. 'I thought that was obvious. I love you and I want us to be together, to be partners, lovers, a family, the whole nine yards.'

I shook my head, trying to rid it of confusion or maybe wake myself up. 'But what about Mars?'

He chuckled. 'I dropped out of the program months ago.'

'What?' I couldn't have been more surprised if he'd slapped me. 'Why?'

'Because earth got a whole lot more interesting.'

And, before I could reply, before I could tell him I loved him too, he kissed me again and I wasn't sure what I was happier about—his lips on mine, the possibility of a publishing deal, or the promise of everything that was to come.

Whatever, this day was a very good day indeed.

Dear lovely readers

Here we are again. It brings me so much joy that you picked up *Just One Wish* to add to your to-be-read pile—if yours is anywhere as crazy full as mine, I really appreciate you choosing to read this book and I'd love to share with you a little bit about what inspired the story and also the writing process.

A few years ago, at Perth Festival Writers Week, I was lucky enough to sit in on a session with the talented author Lauren Groff, who was in Australia promoting her book *Fates and Furies*. She told a story about how she'd always been adamantly against the institution of marriage and didn't ever want to enter into it. But then she met this wonderful guy and after they'd been going out for a while, he proposed. Her instinct was to refuse but she looked into his eyes and knew that if she rejected his proposal, she'd lose the best person in the world, and so she said yes. Yet, her story got me wondering, what if, because of her values and principles, she had rejected him? Would there come a time in her life when she regretted that decision? It was these questions that sparked the first seed of Alice Abbott.

At the same festival, I also listened to Helen Ellis, author of the fun and fabulous book *American Housewife*. In a way, Helen sparked the character of Alice's daughter, Sappho, although my character is nothing like the author. Sappho is the complete opposite of her mother, Alice—she chose to marry young and stay at home rather than go out to work, but has recently become famous online as a voice for 'new domesticity'.

New domesticity is something I stumbled across online and also read an intriguing book about, *Homeward Bound* by Emily Matchar. It's about how and why many young modern women are choosing to embrace the domestic tasks (such as bread-baking, jam-making, flower-arranging, etc) that their mothers and grandmothers wanted to be rid of.

With these two strong, opposing characters in my mind, I started to think about what it would be like to grow up torn between them and that's when my main character, Ged, was born. She's living in a time when we are told women can have it all, and I wanted to explore this notion. Does she want it all? Does she place more value on her professional or personal life? Can you really have love, a happy family *and* a thriving career?

Through the three women in *Just One Wish* I wanted to explore my own feelings about what it means to be a woman in today's world and I also wanted to touch on feminism and what it means to different people. Feminism is something we hear a lot about lately— some people embrace it, others fear it and, again, I wanted to work out exactly how I felt about it and I guess that was my mission in writing this book!

We are lucky in that we are living in exciting times for women—we have so many more options than we ever had in the past, but sometimes this can also be confusing and stressful and leave us wondering 'what if?' And 'what ifs' are always good fodder for fiction.

In essence, *Just One Wish* is about being true to yourself, whatever your truth may be. I had a wonderful time getting to know Ged, Sappho and Alice who are all at different stages in their lives and so, whatever stage you're at, I hope you enjoyed reading about these three different women as well.

Acknowledgements

Writing a book is hard—I won't lie about that—but writing the acknowledgements is sometimes almost as difficult because I'm so terrified of missing someone vital. As a reader I love the acknowledgments page in a book and often flick forward to read it first because I love to read who helped the author with their research or simply supported them in other ways to get the book done. It's often said that writing a book is a solitary experience, but I haven't found that at all. Sure, sitting down at the computer and getting the words down is something you generally do alone, but so much about publishing a book is collaborative and that's why, without further ado, I want to thank the following people who make up my support crew.

My name might be on the front of the book, but there are a number of people at HarperCollins Australia who should also get credit: James Kellow and Sue Brockhoff who lead such a fabulous team; Annabel Blay who makes sure I cross my t's and dot my i's (okay, she does a lot more than that); Adam Van Rooijen and Natika Palka who work so tirelessly to spread the word about my books; Johanna Baker who is behind the scenes keeping everyone on track, and invisibly ensuring the team runs as smoothly as it does; the sales managers across Australia and New Zealand who take my book into stores and get booksellers excited. And thanks also to the rest of the awesome team who do so many other things that most people don't even realise need to happen. Next time you pick up a book off the shelf, remember it's not just the name on the front of the book who got it there!

Thanks to the amazing Dianne Blacklock, the editor for *Just One Wish*. Your insight and wisdom have made this book so much better than I could ever have done on my own and you have taught me so much. You've also probably saved a few trees by helping me get rid of all those extraneous words. And thank you to Sarah JH Fletcher, for her eagle-eyed proofreading.

Big thanks to my agent, Helen Breitwieser, who believed in this book from the moment I told her my vague concept and got even more excited than me about some aspects.

Thank you to my family (to Craig, Hamish, Lachlan and Archie) who put up with so much having a wife and mum who is a writer. Not only do I work full time, but my work lives with us and in my head 24/7 (yes, there are even voices talking to me while I sleep). Thank you not only for your support but for the sacrifices you make when I'm on deadline. And to Hamish—thank you especially for taking an interest in my stories and how they work. I love that you are interested in pursuing a creative career and it's so special to be able to talk about creativity and ideas with you. Man, you were a cute baby, but I'm loving this new stage of life where we can share our interests and passions so much more.

Along this writing journey I've met many readers, some who have even become friends. I want to particularly mention and thank Brooke Testa who I now talk books with on a regular basis and who also kindly read this book in first draft format to give me some much-needed feedback. You don't know how much I appreciate you taking the time to do so when I know your to-be-read pile is even more ridiculous than mine!

To my author friends who have become close friends and who help me brainstorm, celebrate and commiserate when necessary. When I decided I wanted to be a writer, I hoped to get published and have books on shelves, but I never imagined the other wonderful things this career would bring me. There are too many of you to mention, but a special shout out to Writer's Camp (you know who you are) and The Secret Life of Authors, and, for this particular book, Fiona Lowe who helped with a few technique queries and Anthea Hodgson, who put up with me doing copyedits while on our 'research' trip to New Orleans. Not only did she take photos of me editing in weird and wonderful spots (including on the floor of a massage parlour while we waited for back massages), but she also helped me make a few critical editing decisions. Much better than tossing a coin! And to Beck Nicholas, who is always at the end of an email or Vox, whether I need brainstorming help or general life wisdom, but who is also happy to play a game I call 'Finish this sentence' when I have no idea how to do so. For this reason, at least three or four sentences in each book are probably hers.

To the folks in my online book club, you've made this writing/reading life even greater. I love reading your posts about books you are reading, chatting about life and discussing our monthly reads. Thank you for helping me create such a wonderful community—I hope we read many more books together in the years to come. (For anyone who'd like to join us, simply search 'Rachael Johns' Online Book Club' on Facebook.)

And finally, but definitely not least, thank you to all the bloggers, journalists, librarians and bookshop people who have helped spread the word about my books. Nothing is more important than word-of-mouth in the book world, so I thank you from the bottom of my heart.

Turn over for a sneak peek.

The Patterson Girls

by

Rachael
Johns

Out now

Chapter One

'Dad.' The word slipped from Lucinda Mannolini's lips on a whisper as she emerged from gate 21 at Adelaide Airport and spotted her father. Her heart squeezed. His standard uniform of black work trousers and checked shirt seemed to hang from his lanky body. In the last six months, he appeared to have gone a little whiter on top. He still stood tall though, his glasses perched on his nose and his arms folded across his chest as he waited amidst a sea of people desperate to claim their loved ones so the holiday season could kick off. Overhead, announcements were being made about delayed flights and missing passengers, but Brian Patterson looked lost in his own little world.

Thrusting her shoulders back and pushing her chin high to give an air of confidence she didn't feel, Lucinda slipped into the stream of passengers, approaching a couple so lost in their passionate reunion that they either didn't care or hadn't noticed they were holding up the traffic. Once upon a time she and Joe had been like that whenever he returned from his two weeks on the goldfields, but lately, not so much. Pushing that thought away, she stepped around them as Dad rushed forward, his arms wide open for her. Her leather handbag slapped against her back as she flung herself into them and dropped her head against his strong, broad shoulders.

'Dad,' she said again as tears welled in her eyes.

'Lucinda,' he whispered back. 'My Lucinda.' His voice held raw emotion, making her feel safe and loved and needed all at once. Still holding her, he shuffled them out of the throng of people rushing past. There wasn't room for her and him *and* the tongue-locked lovers.

'How are you, sweetheart?'

His heartfelt question almost unravelled her. He was the one who had been six months without his soulmate. Although she'd been as long without her mother, living away in Perth she'd sometimes forgotten that her mum wasn't still in their South Australian home town, making beds, cooking meals and greeting guests at the Meadow Brook Motel. Living away she could still pretend that Mum was alive, but being back home for Christmas would put an end to that illusion pretty damn quick.

'I'm good,' she lied, forcing a smile. She didn't know whether to mention Mum. 'How are you?' she asked instead.

'Fine, fine,' he waved away the question as he led her towards the baggage carousel. She guessed he wasn't speaking the whole truth either but neither pressed the other for this wasn't the place for a conversation that would quite likely end in messy, messy tears—hers not entirely related to the loss of her mother.

She wasn't sure her problem was the kind one discussed with one's father. Her sisters maybe, although she doubted any of them would understand.

Madeleine might appreciate her desire to have a child but would no doubt tell her to stop being so emotional about it. She'd say science could fix almost anything these days and suggest she book herself an appointment with a fertility clinic. All very well to say, but you had to have been trying to conceive for a year before a specialist would give you the time of day and she'd only gone off the pill eight months ago. Charlie would ask if she'd tried alternative therapy and suggest she and Joe go on a yoga holiday to get in touch with their inner fertility, or worse, visit some kind of sex therapist—as if that was the problem. And Abigail—the youngest—would get her drunk to try and take her mind off it all.

The Patterson girls were as different as the four seasons. Once upon a time, before careers and in her case a husband had scattered them, they'd been close—the way Lucinda thought sisters were supposed to be—but time and distance had drawn them apart and she missed the companionship they used to share.

'Lucinda?' Dad's voice echoed around her head and she blinked. The crowds had thinned around them.

'Sorry, Dad. What did you say?'

He frowned and then shook his head. 'Abigail's plane lands in half an hour but she'll no doubt be a while getting through customs. Charlie's next, then Madeleine. We'll probably have an hour or so to wait then before Madeleine's flight, but I thought we could grab some lunch.'

'Sounds great.' Lucinda injected chirpiness into her voice and linked her arm through her father's as she looked for her suitcase.

'Dammit.' Abigail Patterson cursed and tapped her Manolo Blahnik heel against the grubby floor of the airport as she eyed the hundreds of suitcases that were doing the rounds of the carousel while weary travellers waited ready to pounce. None of them held her violin, which she'd rashly decided to leave in London. *What a stupid mistake.*

For one, she never travelled without her instrument, and doing so would likely raise suspicion amongst her dad and older sisters.

And for two, how the hell would she get through the week ahead without being able to sneak off to her room and play some Pachelbel or Vivaldi? It would be hard enough trying not to let slip her recent failure, but the first Christmas at home without Mum was going to be plain and simple hell.

However, still raw from being kicked out of the orchestra, she had barely been able to look at her beloved violin while packing for this trip two days ago. She'd shoved it under the bed and decided that a little time apart would do them good. It would give her the chance to work out what to do with herself when she returned to London. What *did* one do with oneself when the dream you'd been working towards your whole life went up like a puff of smoke?

"Scuse me, coming through.'

A short, stocky woman with a face as red as her carrot-coloured hair barged past and launched herself at a massive purple polka-dotted suitcase. Abigail glared as the woman tried to wrestle her suitcase off the carousel and then felt a spark of jealous irritation when a tall, well-built blond God of a man slipped past her to assist, lifting the case as if it were no heavier than a box of movie popcorn. He smiled at the redhead as he deposited the case on a trolley and the woman started blathering her thanks. Maybe Abigail should feign difficulty with her case and he could help *her*? She glanced around the carousel again but saw no sign of it. Anyway, it wasn't much bigger than an overnighter. If there was one thing Abigail was good at—besides playing the violin—it was packing lightly but still managing to look a million dollars.

Maybe that's what she could do ... start some kind of boutique travel consultancy. She would specialise in helping women like her sister Madeleine, who always took practically her whole wardrobe on holiday, to pack smarter. Not that Madeleine ever had holidays. This trip home was a necessary exception.

'I swear my stuff is always the last,' said a dreamy voice beside her.

Thoughts of the fashion-travel-consultant business fading, Abigail turned to smile at the owner of the voice. She met his gaze and her tummy fluttered at the way he looked her up and down, obviously admiring her long legs in their tiny yellow shorts and sexy heels. Perhaps there was a God after all.

'Well, this might be your lucky day, 'cause my belongings have a habit of being last as well.' The guy smiled as her fingers inched up to her hair and she flicked her straight blonde locks over her shoulders, flirting without being fully conscious of it.

'Pity there's not a bar this side of customs,' he said. 'I'd buy you a drink.'

She swallowed, warmth flooding her at the idea of sitting down for a cocktail with this guy. He could be just the kind of tonic she needed. 'Yes, pity indeed.'

'Were you on the flight all the way from London?'

She nodded. 'You?'

'Yep.' He ran a hand through his lovely thick hair. He looked like a surfer, which would account for his lovely body. 'I always tell myself that next time I'll stop over for a night somewhere, break up the journey, but I never do.'

Why-oh-why couldn't she have been seated next to him instead of the two teenagers she'd been dumped next to? Apparently their parents had been up front in first class, drinking proper champagne and not supervising their sons, who kept pestering the flight attendant for soft drinks and talking loudly about the games they were playing while the rest of the passengers were trying to sleep.

'You do this trip often then?'

'Often enough.' He hit her with that melt-your-insides smile again. 'I work in London but the fam are still in Oz. I'd be written out of the olds' will if I didn't come home for Christmas. What about you?'

'Pretty much the same.' She wasn't about to go into the details with a stranger—that one of her 'olds' had recently passed away and she technically didn't have a job anymore.

'That's my bag.' He turned away and bent over the carousel, scooping up a large navy-blue backpack just before it went in through the little hole and did another round. The action gave Abigail a rather nice view of his taut behind and she felt her tummy do that flutter thing again. She'd been so focused on her career the last few months (make that years) that she hadn't had much time for men. There'd been that brief fling with the orchestra's assistant manager, but after discovering he was married—he hadn't mentioned it of course, but she should have done her research because everyone, she later found out, knew he was—she'd been avoiding the opposite sex. She had her violin, the true love of her life, and she didn't want anything to get in the way of her career.

Unfortunately it had turned out that she didn't need anyone else to stuff it up. She'd done a perfectly good job of that on her own. She sighed as the guy turned back towards her and hit her once again with his killer smile.

'I don't suppose you want to get a drink anyway?' he said, tilting his head to one side like an adorable puppy. 'I could wait for you to get your bag and then we could ...' His voice drifted off as he nodded towards the customs line and the exit that led into the rest of the airport.

Her imagination skipped forward to what he'd want to do once they'd finished their drinks. She'd never had a one-night stand before but right now the idea of a few hours in the arms of a handsome stranger was more appealing than facing her family, who would no doubt take one look at her and know something was up.

'I'd love to, but my dad and sisters will be waiting out there.'

'Damn.' He didn't hide his disappointment and it echoed her own.

She was about to suggest they exchange numbers and maybe catch up when they were both back in London, but she spotted her case out of the corner of her eye and instinctively lunged past him. 'Sorry. That's mine.'

He didn't help her like he had the middle-aged woman and when she turned back she could already see that the moment—the opportunity—was over. He was moving on, ready to get on with his own family Christmas and forget they'd ever met. She didn't even know his name.

'Well, nice meeting you. Have a good Christmas.' He heaved his backpack a little further up his shoulder, smiled and then turned away.

'Bye.' Abigail watched a moment as he headed towards customs and joined the other passengers in the line. How different her holiday could have been if she'd been able to say yes to that drink with whatever his name was. It would be something hot and masculine like Jack or Adam, of that she was certain. One drink would have led to another, which likely would have led to some red-hot fun. How she longed for some red-hot fun.

But there was no point standing here and wishing things were different. The fact was, she wasn't home for a holiday fling. She was here to help Dad get through his first Christmas without Mum. Her chest tightened at the thought, the emotion rising up into her throat, making crying in the customs line a very real possibility. It certainly put her orchestra woes into perspective.

Nothing had ever been as bad as losing Mum.

Charlotte Patterson smiled with a mixture of relief and anticipation as she waited to exit the plane. She'd almost missed this flight, which was becoming a nasty habit and would have made her the brunt of her sisters' jokes. Again. It hadn't been her fault, though. She'd been all packed and ready to go when the little old lady in the house next door had come knocking, sobbing her heart out because she'd locked her keys inside. Of course Charlie hadn't been able to leave Mrs Gianetti until she'd called the locksmith and made sure he was on his way. As a result she'd almost been late to the airport.

It had been touch and go, but thankfully her taxi driver had been a pro at negotiating Melbourne's morning traffic and she'd arrived in the nick of time. The flight had been uneventful and now she couldn't wait to disembark and see everyone. They hadn't had a family Christmas since Madeleine had moved to America five years ago and although Mum wouldn't be there, going home to be together for this first Christmas without her felt like the right thing to do.

They'd sit around the table where she used to help them with their homework and they'd share a few wines and special memories. They'd uphold Mum's Christmas traditions—attend the local church service on Christmas Eve, maybe help Dad make breakfast for the motel guests on Christmas morning and then open their presents sitting around the tree that was decorated solely with the primitive handmade ornaments she and her sisters had made in primary school. Mum had loved them and sworn she'd never ever throw them out. Charlie swallowed the lump in her throat and blinked back the water in her eyes at the thought of going back to Meadow Brook, back to their home and the motel, without Mum there to welcome them.

The line of people started shuffling forward. For a moment Charlie froze, unable to tell her legs to move as her excitement made way for fear and dread. Fear of going home and having Christmas with a gaping hole where Mum should be. Dread that her sisters' dismissive glances would turn her into the crumbling mess she was whenever they were around. She wished they'd come to Melbourne, visit her in Brunswick where she helped manage a very busy café and ran hula-hooping classes in the evening. She might not have university letters behind her name but that didn't make what she did any less important. Her sisters might think her an airy-fairy hippy but she was happy with who she was. Most of the time, at least.

'Ahem.' A man cleared his throat behind her. 'Are you waiting for anything in particular?'

'Oh. Sorry.' Startled from her reverie, she shot forward and forced a smile back to her face. She wanted this to be a good Christmas, a cathartic experience, a chance for her family to share their grief, which would hopefully assist them in their recovery and maybe, just maybe, bring them closer together again.

Striding forward, her bag swinging over her shoulder, she appeared at the top of the ramp and glanced around the faces of people waiting in the arrivals hall.

'Over here!'

Charlie turned at the sound of a familiar voice—Abigail's—and most of the dread and fear dissipated. Her heart soared as she saw her little sister waving wildly with one hand, her other arm wrapped tightly around their father. Dear Dad, he looked weary even from this distance and Charlie swore that however bad she felt these next few days, she'd remember that he probably felt worse. Lucinda was on Dad's other side; she was also waving but not as enthusiastically as Abigail. Her golden blonde hair was pulled back into a high ponytail whereas Abigail's perfectly straight tresses hung free, almost down to her bum. Charlie's eyes once again prickled with unshed tears as she rushed towards her family and threw her arms around them.

'So good to see you.' Lucinda squeezed her arm and pressed a kiss against the side of her face.

'Hello, my darling,' Dad said, his voice a little shaky. 'Good flight?'

Abigail didn't give Charlie the chance to answer. 'I love that bag,' she gushed. 'Did you make it yourself?'

Bless Abigail, thought Charlie. Despite their differences, she always made an effort.

'No.' Charlie pulled out of the embrace and shook her head. 'I bought it at the St Kilda markets last weekend.' A brief pause to swallow the lump that was back in her throat. 'Oh my gosh, it's so good to see you all.'

They all grinned back at her and then Lucinda gestured to a trolley beside them. 'Dad and I have put my stuff in the car but we thought we could collect yours, dump them and then go get some lunch before Madeleine arrives.'

'Sounds good to me.' Charlie glanced at the trolley, frowned and then looked to Abigail. 'Where's your violin?'

She swore she saw a look of discomfort flash across Abigail's face, but if it were there she covered it over quickly with a smile and a shrug. 'I decided to take a real holiday. Besides, I know how much you guys *love* listening to me practise.'

Lucinda snorted and wrapped her arm around Abigail, drawing her close. 'We *do*, we really do love it, don't we, Charles?'

'Oh yeah … Why else do you think I agreed to come spend a week with you lot?' Charlie retorted, secretly not believing a word Abigail said and vowing to get to the bottom of whatever was going on with her. The truth was they all loved listening to Abigail play. From the moment she'd started music lessons at all of five years old, she'd been amazing.

'Girls, girls, girls.' Dad feigned a stern tone but his chuckle gave the game away. He loved seeing his daughters together, liked it when they bantered in the way they used to do when they lived together all those years ago. And Charlie liked seeing him smile, even if it didn't quite reach his eyes.

'Sorry Dad,' they said in unison, grinning at him.

Lucinda took hold of the trolley and Abigail and Charlie linked arms with Dad as they followed the hordes towards the baggage carousel. For the first time in her life, Charlie's patchwork holdall was already doing the rounds of the carousel when they arrived. Thankful they wouldn't have to wait, she scooped it up and dumped it next to Abigail's little suitcase on the trolley.

'Dad, give me your keys.' Lucinda held out her hand. 'I'll take all this to the van while you guys go and find a table.'

Charlie couldn't hide her smirk. Although the grey shadows beneath Lucinda's eyes indicated she might not have been sleeping the best lately, she was still in top organisational form. She knew her other sisters sometimes found Lucinda's bossiness stifling and annoying but it comforted Charlie. For as long as she could remember, Lucinda had been like a second mum. Four years older than Charlie and seven years Abigail's senior, she'd often made sure her younger sisters were fed and dressed when their parents were too busy with motel guests. Madeleine was the oldest but had always had her head stuck in a book, far too busy studying to bother with tiresome little sisters. It wasn't surprising that Lucinda had chosen primary school teaching as a career and been the first (and only) one of them to get married. Charlie guessed it wouldn't be long before she and Joe had children of their own to fuss over.

'There's a table over there.'

At Abigail's words, Charlie realised she'd walked from the carousels to the café without even noticing. 'Yes, that looks fine,' she said, following Abigail and Dad to the table.

Abigail slumped into a seat and picked up the menu. 'I'm having pancakes. The food on the plane was crap. What do you want, Dad?'

'Just a coffee, love.'

'What about you, Charlie?' Abigail asked.

'Give me a chance to look at the menu,' Charlie replied, not looking at Abigail but instead to her father, who looked like he'd aged more than six months. The loss of his wife and looking after the motel by himself had obviously taken its toll and Charlie felt a stab of guilt for not being more available. Living in Melbourne, she was the closest in proximity but she may as well have been in Baltimore like Madeleine or London like Abigail for all the good it did. She reached out and took his hand across the table. 'How are you, Dad?'

He squeezed back and nodded. 'I'm as good as can be expected, but seeing you three and knowing Madeleine will be here soon helps. I've missed my girls.'

'Oh, Dad.' Abigail dropped the menu back on the table and threw her arms around him.

The three of them sat there, chairs close together, holding each other tightly, not daring to say any more for fear of shedding unsightly tears in public. That was how Lucinda found them when she returned ten minutes later.

'Have you ordered yet?' she asked.

At the sound of her voice, Abigail and Charlie pulled back from their father and looked up at their older sister.

Charlie shook her head. 'We were waiting for you.'

Lucinda smiled. 'Thanks. What do you all want? My shout.'

'Oh no, we can pay for ourselves,' Charlie protested.

'Speak for yourself.' Abigail shot Charlie a glare and then smiled sweetly at Lucinda. 'I'll have pancakes with extra ice-cream please.'

Lucinda rolled her eyes. 'What kind of lunch is that?'

'You're not my mother,' Abigail snapped.

Dad flinched as if someone had come along and slapped him on the back.

Charlie saw Lucinda swallow. 'I never said I was. Fine, have whatever you like. Dad? Charlie? What do you want?'

'Just a coffee,' Dad said.

'I'll have the sweet potato quiche, with salad.' Charlie pushed back her chair to stand. 'But I'll come with you to order.' She let out a deep breath as she and Lucinda weaved their way through the few tables to the front of the café. 'How's Joe?' she asked as they waited to place their order. 'It's a pity he couldn't come with you.'

Lucinda smiled tightly. 'Everyone has to take their turn working Christmas on the mine.'

Which didn't answer Charlie's question but she decided to let it lie. Lucinda likely didn't want to dwell on the fact she was going to spend her first Christmas without her husband since they'd been married.

'I suppose so,' she said and then glanced ahead at the specials blackboard.

Madeleine Patterson grunted as she retrieved her heavy suitcase from the carousel, yanked out the handle and then started towards customs. *Hello, Adelaide.*

If she had to choose a holiday destination, Adelaide was one of the last places on earth she'd have considered. Meadow Brook—the town she'd grown up in—was the *very* last. Despite the fact that her family owned the local motel, there was nothing holiday-like about the place. Sure, thousands of grey nomads passed through on their journey along the Eyre Highway to or from Western Australia, but why some of them stayed more than a night had always been a mystery to her.

As far as Madeleine was concerned, the most attractive thing about Meadow Brook was its name, which she'd always thought far too pretty for the dry, rugged terrain of the northern Eyre Peninsula, in which the primary industry was agriculture, followed closely by mining and supposedly (although it continued to flummox her) tourism.

No, if she'd chosen to take a holiday her destination would be a resort where she could relax on the beach or a city where she could shop till she dropped, somewhere like Paris or New York, or—if she did come back to Australia—then Sydney or Melbourne. A place where her childhood friends weren't all married with babies, making her wonder if she'd sacrificed too much in order to climb the career ladder.

She sighed. This vacation wasn't about her, it was about Dad.

It had been Lucinda's idea to get them all together for Christmas, and although Madeleine's first instinct had been to say she couldn't get away from work, the guilt and grief had gotten to her. Despite the agony of that long-haul flight and her initial reluctance to come, she now found herself impatient to get through customs and see everyone. The location wouldn't matter, it would be good just to be together at this time of the year. To celebrate Mum and help Dad through this first Christmas alone.

She sniffed and dug into her bag for a tissue, unable to imagine Meadow Brook without her mother. She blew her nose, wiped her eyes and then continued on.

The line through customs moved surprisingly fast and when she got to the front of the queue she slapped her immigration form down on the counter and answered the routine questions, hoping nothing would hold her up. After the officer waved her through, Madeleine all but ran towards the doors that would see her into the arrivals hall.

It felt better than she could possibly have imagined when she spotted the faces of her family in the crowd and even better falling into their arms. There weren't a lot of words exchanged at first but their embraces said more than enough. She wasn't usually one for too much hugging, but this felt right. This coming together, this Christmas, was always going to be difficult but it was something they all needed in order to move on.

'Finally, all my girls together again,' Dad said, as he let go of her and took a step back to survey his daughters. Madeleine smiled sadly, thinking that there was one key girl missing, but she pushed that thought aside. She didn't need to make a scene in the airport.

She didn't consider herself an emotional person but maybe she was more jet lagged than she thought, because standing here among her three sisters, next to her dad, she felt an overwhelming love for all of them.

'Right, where's the van?' she asked, tapping her suitcase. 'I'm in dire need of a shower and a drink.'

'Lead the way, Dad.' Abigail linked her arm through Madeleine's as Lucinda took the handle of her case and started to walk towards the exit.

'What on earth have you got in here?' Lucinda asked. 'How long are you planning to stay?'

Everyone laughed but Madeleine shot her a warning glare. Just because Lucinda dressed like a Perth housewife, didn't mean Madeleine couldn't take pride in her appearance. It wasn't like she could buy anything she forgot on the main street of Meadow Brook, so she'd come prepared for all occasions.

Ignoring her sister, Madeleine addressed Dad as they walked out into the bright and stiflingly hot South Australian afternoon. 'Thanks for coming to collect us. We could have hired a car.'

'Nonsense.' Dad shook his head. 'I've been counting down the days. Besides, I wouldn't want any of you driving after travelling so far.'

Charlie laughed. 'Melbourne's only an hour's flight away.'

Madeleine yawned. 'How's the motel? Lots of bookings?'

Dad shrugged as they came to the ticket payment machine. He dug his wallet out of his pocket. 'It's all right. Not as many guests as we usually have at this time of the year.' He slid the ticket into the machine and then fumbled around looking for change.

'Here, I'll get this.' Lucinda whipped her purse out of her handbag and fed a twenty dollar note into the machine, which in turn spat her out some coins. She took the returned ticket and handed it to their father.

Dad and Lucinda led the way to where the old Meadow Brook Motel people mover stood tall in the sea of vehicles around it. An ageing Toyota Tarago in faded yellow with the motel's logo and name (also faded) plastered across the sides, it looked a sorry sight. Madeleine thought it was about time Dad upgraded, but now wasn't the time to start discussing such things.

Lucinda rearranged the luggage that was already in the back and then heaved Madeleine's suitcase on top.

'Careful of Abigail's violin,' Madeleine warned.

'She didn't bring it,' Lucinda replied, closing the boot with a thunk.

'What?' Madeleine peered in through the open door at Abigail, who was settling herself on the back seat. 'Why? Are you sick or something?'

Abigail glowered. 'What's the big deal? Did you bring a host of pregnant women so you could deliver their babies while you were on holiday?'

Madeleine raised her eyebrows. It wasn't like Abigail to be so snarky. Charlie and Lucinda laughed as they climbed into the car, leaving the passenger seat beside their father for Madeleine. At least she hadn't had to remind them of her travel sickness. 'Sorry for asking,' she muttered under her breath.

No one said anything more. Seatbelts were clicked into place. Dad started the ignition and then drove out of the airport, heading west as they began the three-and-a-half journey to Meadow Brook.

talk about it

Let's talk about books.

Join the conversation:

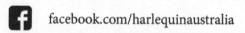 facebook.com/harlequinaustralia

 @harlequinaus

 @harlequinaus

harpercollins.com.au/hq

If you love reading and want to know about our
authors and titles, then let's talk about it.